Enthusiastic acclaim for **WILLIAM DIETRICH** and

THE DAKOTA CIPHER

"William Dietrich is a born stylist, moving characters around on an historical chessboard with the assured hand of a master novelist firing on all cylinders. Ethan Gage is a wiry, battle-scarred hero, with great decency, who rings absolutely true. And *The Dakota Cipher* is a supple, elegant thriller that carries the reader triumphantly from one exciting climax to the next."

STEVE BERRY, *New York Times* bestselling author of *The Venetian Betrayal*

"Fast, fun, and full of surprises ... The tale twists and turns like a spitted serpent, but Dietrich shows his sure hand as a storyteller, leavening a tale rich in intrigue and impressive historic detail with abundant wit and humor."

Publishers Weekly (*Starred Review*)

"[A] ripping yarn ... Lovely Indian maidens, double-crossing rascals, and a brief cameo by Thomas Jefferson feature in Gage's witty derring-do."

Seattle Times

"Gage has many of the same moves as the late George MacDonald Fraser's irresistible anti-hero, Sir Harry Flashman."

Sacramento Bee

"If there weren't already an Indiana Jones, Dietrich's Ethan Gage could certainly fit the bill. ... Dietrich does an excellent job of creating the historical settings of the novels, and the real-life characters Ethan meets along the way ... feel just right ... A spirited installment of what promises to be a long-running series."

Booklist

By William Dietrich

Fiction
THE DAKOTA CIPHER
THE ROSETTA KEY
NAPOLEON'S PYRAMIDS
THE SCOURGE OF GOD
HADRIAN'S WALL
DARK WINTER
GETTING BACK
ICE REICH

Coming Soon in Hardcover
THE BARBARY PIRATES

Nonfiction
ON PUGET SOUND
NATURAL GRACE
NORTHWEST PASSAGE
THE FINAL FOREST

WILLIAM DIETRICH

THE DAKOTA CIPHER

AN ETHAN GAGE ADVENTURE

HARPER

An Imprint of HarperCollinsPublishers

This book was originally published in hardcover and trade paperback April 2009 by Harper.

HARPER

An Imprint of HarperCollins*Publishers*
10 East 53rd Street
New York, New York 10022-5299

Copyright © 2009 by William Dietrich
Excerpt from *The Barbary Pirates* copyright © 2010 by William Dietrich
ISBN 978-0-06-156808-4

First Harper paperback printing: February 2010
First Harper special trade paperback printing: April 2009
First Harper hardcover printing: April 2009

HarperCollins ® and Harper ® are registered trademarks of Harper-Collins Publishers.

Printed in the United States of America

Visit Harper paperbacks on the World Wide Web at
www.harpercollins.com

10 9 8 7 6 5 4 3 2 1

To my son-in-law, Sebastian

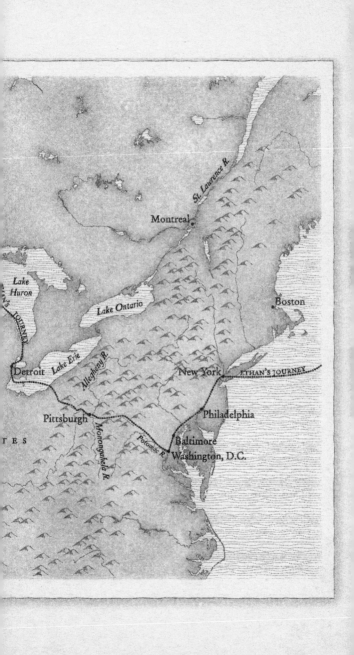

THE
DAKOTA
CIPHER

CHAPTER 1

I suppose it's not precisely true that it was solely I who consolidated Napoleon's power and changed the course of world history. I *did* contribute to his idea of crossing the Alps and outflanking the Austrians, and then had to help save the day at the Battle of Marengo—but frankly, my role was somewhat accidental. Yet what of that? Enlarging one's part does make a good tale for the ladies, and while I, Ethan Gage, am a paragon of candor when it suits my purposes, I do have a tendency toward exaggeration when it comes to matters of the bed.

It *is* true that my timely service in northern Italy got me back in Bonaparte's good graces, that my affable charm made me instrumental in forging the Treaty of Mortefontaine with American diplomats, and that my raffish reputation won me a place at the glittery château gathering to celebrate that Convention. There I managed to get embroiled in the new diversion of roulette, was sidetracked into a tumultuous tryst with Napoleon's married sister, and still squeezed in enough time to almost be killed by fireworks. I may inflate my history to women, but no man can fault me for not keeping busy.

Unfortunately, my incautious boasting also persuaded a half-mad Norwegian to enlist me in a dubious and mystical quest a continent away from comfort—proof again that vanity is peril and modesty the wiser course. Better to keep one's mouth shut and be suspected of being a fool than open and confirm it.

Ah, but the breasts of Pauline Bonaparte were lifted like white pillows by her bewitching gown, her brother's wine cellar had my head swimming, and when powerful men are urging you to share your exploits, it's difficult not to admit you've had a role directing history. Especially when you've taken your audience for a hundred francs at the gaming table! Pretending to be important or clever makes one's victim feel better about losing. So on I prattled, the eavesdropping Norseman with a beard the color of flame eyeing me with ever-greater interest, and my own eye on flirtatious Pauline, knowing she was about as faithful to husband General Charles Leclerc as an alley cat during a full moon. The minx had the beauty of Venus and the discrimination of a sailor in a grog shop. No wonder she winked at me.

The date was September 30, 1800—or, by the French Revolutionary calendar, the eighth day of Vendémiaire in the Year IX. Napoleon had declared the revolution over, himself as its culmination, and we all hoped he'd soon throw out the annoying ten-day-a-week calendar, since rumor had it that he was attempting to cut a deal with the Pope to bring back Catholic priests. No one missed Sabbath services, but we all were nostalgic for lazy Sundays. Bonaparte was still feeling his way, however. He'd only seized power some ten months before (thanks in part to the mystical Book of Thoth I'd found in a lost city), and barely won Marengo by a whisker. Settling France's hash with America—my nation had won some impressive duels with French warships and played havoc with French shipping—was another step toward consolidating rule. Our feuding countries were, after all, the world's only two republics, though Napoleon's autocratic style was straining that definition in France. And a treaty! It was no accident that the French elite had been turned out at Mortefontaine for this celebration. No warrior was better at publicizing his peacemaking than Bonaparte.

Mortefontaine is a lovely château some thirty-five kilometers north of Paris. Far enough, in other words, for France's new leaders to party in style well out of sight of the mob that had put them there. The mansion had been purchased by Bonaparte's brother Joseph, and none of those assembled dared suggest it was a tad ostentatious for the inheritors of the Revolution. Napoleon, just thirty-one, was the most astute observer of human nature I ever met, and he'd wasted little time giving France back some of the royalist trappings it had missed since chopping off the head of King Louis and guillotining the nation's lace makers. It was permissible to be rich again! Ambitious! Elegant! Velvet, which had been forbidden during the Terror, was not just permitted but in style. Wigs might be a relic of the last century, but gold military braid was de rigueur in this one. The lovely grounds were swarming with newly powerful men, newly seductive women, and enough silk and brocade to get the haberdasheries of Paris humming, albeit on more classical, Republican lines. Lafayette and La Rochefoucauld had invited every prominent American in Paris, even me. Our total assembly numbered two hundred, all of us heady with American triumph and French wine.

Bonaparte had insisted that his festival organizer, Jean-Etienne Despeaux, achieve perfection in record time. Accordingly, that famed marshal of merriment hired the architect Cellerier to revamp the theater, recruited a troupe from the Comédie Française to play a ribald sketch on transatlantic relations, and prepared the fireworks display with which I was about to become all too familiar.

Three great tables were set out in the Orangerie, in three adjoining rooms. The first was the Room of the Union, the head wall hung with a scroll of the Atlantic, with Philadelphia on one side and Le Havre on the other, the intervening sea topped by an airborne half-naked woman who represented peace by holding an olive branch in her fingers. Why the doxies in these European paintings always have their clothes slipping off I don't know, but I must say it's a custom my own more staid America could emulate. Next to the mural were enough foliage, flowers, and folderol to start a forest fire.

The next two rooms had busts of my late mentor Benjamin Franklin and the recently deceased George Washington, respectively. Outside in the park was an obelisk with allegorical figures representing France and America, and the whole affair was frocked with tricolor bunting. Rose petals floated in pools and fountains, rented peacocks strutted on lawns, and artillery banged salutes. It seemed to me that Despeaux had earned his money, and that I, finally, was among friends.

At Joseph Bonaparte's request, I'd brought along the longrifle I'd helped forge in Jerusalem. A nasty thief named Najac had knocked the piece about, but I'd disposed of him by pushing a ramrod through his heart and later paid twenty francs to restore the stock's finish. Now I gave a demonstration of the gun's accuracy. I broke a teacup at one hundred paces and struck a cavalry breastplate five times running at twice that distance, a perforation that impressed officers resigned to the stray aim of muskets. While more than one soldier remarked on the tedious time the rifle took to load, they also said it explained the feared accuracy of our frontiersmen in the North American wars. "A hunting piece," one colonel judged, not inaccurately. "Light to carry, wickedly accurate. But look at the narrow neck! A conscript would break this beauty like a piece of china."

"Or learn to take care of it." Yet I knew he was right, this was not practical for massed armies.

Rifles clog with powder residue after half a dozen shots, while cruder muskets can be banged away by idiots—and are. A longrifle is a sniper's gun. So I fired again, this time drilling a gold louis at fifty paces. Pretty ladies applauded and fanned themselves, uniformed men sighted down the barrel, and hunting dogs yelped and ran in furious circles.

Napoleon arrived in the September glow of late afternoon, his open carriage drawn by six white horses, gold-helmeted cavalry clopping in escort, and cannon thumping in salute. A hundred paces back, his wife followed in an ivory-colored coach that gleamed like a pearl. They pulled up with a flourish, steeds snorting and pissing on pea gravel as liveried footmen swung doors open and grenadiers snapped to attention. Bonaparte stepped out in the uniform of his personal guard, a blue tunic with red and white collar, and a sword and scabbard with filigree of wrestling warriors and reclining goddesses. Far from haughty, he was gracious: the fame of the victor at the Pyramids and Marengo spoke for itself! You don't rise to first consul without some measure of charm, and Napoleon could seduce grizzled sergeants, ladies of the salon, conniving politicians, and men of science in turn—or, if need be, all at once. His calculated sociability was on display this evening. He deferred to Lafayette, who'd helped my own country win independence, and toured the American peace commissioners through the gardens like a country squire. Finally, when the clocks chimed six, Charles Maurice de Talleyrand-Périgord, the minister of foreign affairs, called us to hear the text of the treaty read.

Josephine had popped out of her coach too, and it was all I could do not to scowl. Power became her, I must admit: Though never quite beautiful (her nose a little too sharp, her teeth a little too discolored), she was more charismatic than ever. She sported a string of pearls that had reportedly cost a quarter million francs, coaxing state finance ministers to cook the books so the strand would escape Bonaparte's scrutiny. Yet no one else begrudged her the jewels. While her husband's moods could be mercurial, she was consistently well-mannered in gatherings like this, her smile earnest as if the well-being of every guest were her personal concern. Thanks to my help, she'd staved off divorce after cheating on Napoleon and in a few years would find herself empress. But the ungrateful wench had betrayed me and my Egyptian love Astiza, sending us into Temple Prison as payment, and it was because I hadn't forgiven her that the risk of rutting with Bonaparte's sister Pauline was somehow more tempting. I wanted to tup a Bonaparte as I'd been tupped. I'd been made a fool of (not the first time), and Josephine's inevitable presence as first lady, beaming as if she'd won the Revolution's lottery, was to me a small cloud on an otherwise brilliant day. Widowed by the Terror, she'd bet on the young Corsican and improbably found herself in the Tuileries Palace.

If Josephine brought back pained memories of Astiza's parting, I was flattered that the American commissioners who'd sought my counsel were generous enough to offer public thanks. Oliver Ellsworth had worked on my nation's Constitution and served as chief justice of the Supreme Court before taking on this diplomatic task. The two Bills were almost equally renowned: William Richardson Davie, a hero of the Revolutionary War, and William Vans Murray, a Maryland congressman who was now ambassador to the Netherlands. All three had risked the diplomatic snubbing earlier envoys had received in hopes of salvaging John Adams's sagging presidency. I, their adviser, was younger and rawer and a frustrated treasure hunter, gambler, sharpshooter, and adventurer who had somehow wound up on both the French and the British sides in the recent fighting in Egypt and the Holy Land. But I'd also served briefly as an assistant to the late, great Franklin, had a growing reputation as an "electrician" myself, and—most importantly— had Bonaparte's ear when he was inclined to listen. We were both rogues (Napoleon was simply better at it than me), and he trusted me as a fellow opportunist. Honorable men are hard to control, but those of us with self-interested common sense are more predictable. So after Marengo I was enlisted as go-between, shuttling from Talleyrand to the impatient Americans, and here we were, making peace.

"What I like about you, Gage, is that you focus on what is practical, not what is consistent," Bonaparte whispered at one point.

"And what I like about you, First Consul, is that you're as happy to use an enemy as to destroy him," I cheerfully replied. "You tried to have me executed, what, three or four times? And here we are, partners in peace." *It's splendid how things work out,* the English captain Sir Sidney Smith had told me.

"Not partners. I am the sculptor, you are the tool. But I care about my tools."

This was hardly flattering, but part of the man's charm was his blunt, sometimes clumsy honesty. He'd tell women their dresses were too bright or their waists too thick, because he liked his females slim, demure, and dressed in white, apparently as part of some fantasy of virginal beauty. He got away with it because his power was an aphrodisiac. I, meanwhile, was learning to be a diplomat. "And I appreciate your toolbox, Paris."

I can be obsequious when I'm in the mood, and Napoleon's chambers at the Tuileries were littered with grand plans to make his city the most beautiful in the world. The theater was flourishing from new government subsidies, the tax and civil codes were being overhauled, the economy was recovering, and the Austrians were beaten. Even the whores dressed better! The man was a brilliant rascal, and gambling salons were so crowded with newcomers that I'd been able to supplement my modest salary with winnings from drunks and fools. Things were going so well that I should have crawled into a hole and braced for the worst, but optimism is like wine. It makes us take chances.

So here I was at the French château of the first consul's brother, semirespectable to my American brethren, and with a certain cachet as a savant who had charged a chain to electrocute attaching soldiers at 1799's siege of Acre in the Holy Land. The fact that I'd done this for the British side, not the French, seemed to bother no one, since I was presumed to have no real loyalties or convictions in the first place. Rumors that I had slain a prostitute (absolutely untrue) and burned a sorcerer (accurate, but he had it coming) simply added to my allure. Between that, my longrifle, and my tomahawk, I was accorded the distinction of being a potentially dangerous man, and there is nothing more likely to raise a flush on the neck of a lady.

I sat smugly through the interminable speeches (my name was actually mentioned, twice) and ate energetically at the state dinner since the food was better than what I could normally afford. I pretended to modesty as I shared adventures that left me with a reputation as somewhat diabolical, or at least oddly durable. Many leading Americans were Freemasons, and theories of Knights Templar and ancient mysteries intrigued them.

"There may be more to those old gods and ancient ways than we modern men of science have allowed," I said grandly as if I knew what I was talking about. "There are still secrets worth recovering, gentlemen. Mysteries yet veiled." Then we joined in toasts to martyrs for liberty and finally stood from the ceremony. My vanity satisfied, I looked forward to a night of gaming, dancing, and sexual conquest.

The music began and I wandered, gaping like the American I was, at the splendor of French architecture. Mortefontaine made the fancy houses I'd seen in my homeland seem like stables, and Joseph was sparing no expense—now that his brood had access to the French treasury—at making it even better.

"Grand, but not entirely different from our new

home for our president," a voice murmured at my side.

I turned. It was Davie, amiable after those champagne toasts. He was handsome, with thick hair, long muttonchops, and a strong, cleft chin. Being in his midforties, he was a good ten years older than me.

"Really? If they produce *this* in that swamp between Virginia and Maryland, my nation has come a long way indeed."

"The president's house is actually based on a government building in Ireland—used to be a Masonic temple, I understand—and yes, quite grand for a new nation."

"They use a Masonic lodge for the president? And what an extraordinary idea, building a new capital in the middle of nowhere!"

"It was the fact that it was nowhere—and near Washington's home—that made political agreement possible. The government is moving into a place that has more stumps than statues, but our capital of Washington, or Columbia, is expected to grow into itself. Our nation has doubled in population since Lexington and Concord, and victory against the Indians has opened the Ohio country."

"The French say that they rut like rabbits and we Americans breed like them."

"You are a confirmed expatriate, Mr. Gage?"

"More a confirmed admirer of the civilization that produced this château, Mr. Davie. I do not always like the French—I even found myself fighting them, at Acre—but I like their capital, their food, their wines, their women, and, at this scale, their houses." I picked up a new novelty from one of the tables, chocolate that had been cleverly hardened into little squares instead of taken as liquid in a cup. Some ingenious Italian had solidified the delicacy and the French made it fashionable. Knowing how quickly fortunes can turn, I pocketed a fistful of them.

Good thing, for they were about to save my life.

CHAPTER 2

"You would not consider returning home, then?" Davie asked me.

"Frankly, I'd planned to, but then I became embroiled in Napoleon's recent Italian campaign and these negotiations. The opportunity has not arisen, and perhaps I can do more for my country here in France." I'd been seduced by the place, as Franklin and Jefferson had been.

"Indeed. And yet you're a Franklin man, are you not? Our new expert on the science of electricity?"

"I've done some experiments." Including the harnessing of lightning in a lost city and turning myself into a friction battery to ignite my arch-enemy, but I didn't add that. Rumors floated, and they served my reputation well enough.

"The reason I ask is that our delegation has encountered a gentleman from Norway who has a particular curiosity about your expertise. He thinks you may be able to enlighten each other. Would you care to meet him?"

"Norway?" I had a vague mental picture of snow, dank forest, and a medieval economy. I knew people lived up there, but it was hard to understand why.

"Governed by Denmark, but increasingly interested in its own independence after our American example. His extraordinary name is Magnus Bloodhammer—it's of Viking origin, apparently—and his looks fit his moniker. He's an eccentric, like you."

"I prefer to think of myself as individualistic."

"I would say you both are . . . open-minded. If we find him, I'll introduce you."

A modicum of fame requires you to meet people, so I shrugged. But I was in no hurry to make conversation about electricity with a Norwegian (to tell the truth, I always worried about betraying my own considerable ignorance), so I had us stop at the first amusement we came to, a new gambling device called a roulette, or "little wheel." Paulette was playing there.

The French have taken an English device and improved upon it, adding two colors, more numbers, and a patterned board that offers intriguing betting possibilities. You can wager on anything, from a single number to half the wheel, and play the odds accordingly. It's been eagerly seized on by a nation enthralled with risk, fate, and destiny since the Terror. I don't play roulette as much as cards, as there is little skill, but I like the convivial crowding at the tables, men smelling of smoke and cologne,

ladies leaning provocatively to give a glimpse of dé-
colletage, and croupiers raking chips as adroitly as
fencers. Napoleon frowns on both the wheel and
the new female exhibitionism, but he's smart enough
not to prohibit either.

I talked Davie into placing a small bet or two,
which he promptly lost. Competitive enough to bet
again, and then again, he lost still more. Some men
are not born to gamble. I repaid his losses from my
own modest winnings, earned by conservative wagers on column and row. Pauline, excitedly leaning
across from me, bet more recklessly. She lost money
I'm sure she'd been given by her famous brother,
but then did win a single number at odds of 35 to 1
and clapped her hands, squeezing her breasts together most enchantingly. She was the loveliest of
Napoleon's siblings, sought after by portraitists and
sculptors. There were reports she was posing in
the nude.

"Madame, it seems your skill matches your
beauty," I congratulated.

She laughed. "I have my brother's luck!" She
wasn't particularly bright, but she was loyal, the
kind who'd stick to Bonaparte long after craftier
friends and siblings had deserted him.

"We Americans could learn from a Venus such
as you."

"But, Monsieur Gage," she returned, her eyelids
flashing like a semaphore, "I am told you are a man
of much experience already."

I gave a slight bow.

"You served with my brother in Egypt in the
company of savants," she went on. "Yet found

yourself opposed to him at Acre, embroiled with him at 18 Brumaire when he took power, and allied yet again at Marengo. You seem a master of all positions."

The girl did make herself clear. "Like a dance, it's all in the partner."

Davie, no doubt seeing banter with the first consul's married sister as a diplomatic disaster in the making, cleared his throat. "I don't seem to share the luck of you and the lady, Mr. Gage."

"Ah, but you really do," I said generously—and honestly. "I'll tell you the secret of gambling, Davie. You lose eventually as certainly as we all die eventually. The game is about hope, and the mathematics about defeat and death. The trick is to beat the arithmetic for a moment, take your winnings, and run. Very few can do that, because optimism trumps sense. Which is why you should own the wheel, not play it."

"Yet you have a reputation as a gambling winner, sir."

"Of battles, not the war. I am not a rich man."

"But an honest one, it seems. So why do you play?"

"I can improve my odds by taking advantage of the less practiced. More important is the game itself, as Bonaparte himself told me. The play's the thing."

"You are a philosopher!"

"All of us ponder the mystery of life. Those of us with no answers deal at cards."

Davie smiled. "So perhaps we should adjourn to a table and let us supplement your income by playing *pharaon*. I suspect you can handle your rustic countrymen. I see Bloodhammer over there, and there's considerable curiosity about these experiments of yours. Moreover, I understand you've experience in the fur trade?"

"In my youth. I daresay I've seen some of the world. A cruel, fascinating, rather unreliable planet, I've concluded. So, yes, let's have some claret and you can ask me what you'd like. Perhaps the lady would care to join us?"

"After my luck turns here, Monsieur Gage." She winked. "I do not have your discipline to retreat when I am ahead."

I sat with the men, conversing impatiently until Pauline—I was thinking of her as a pretty Paulette by now—could drift over. Ellsworth wanted to hear about the Egyptian monuments that were already inspiring Napoleon's plans for Paris. Vans Murray was curious about the Holy Land. Davie beckoned to the odd bear of a man lurking in the shadows, the Norwegian he'd referred to earlier, and bade him sit. This Magnus was tall like me, but thicker, with a fisherman's rough, reddened face. He had an eye patch like a pirate's—his other eye was icy blue—and a thick nose, high forehead, and bushy beard: most unfashionable in 1800. There was that wild glint of the dreamer to him that was quite disturbing.

"Gage, this is the gentleman I told you about. Magnus, Ethan Gage."

Bloodhammer looked like a Viking, all right, as ill fit in a gray suit as a buffalo in a bonnet. He gripped the table as if to overthrow it.

"Unusual to meet a man from the north, sir," I said, a little wary. "What brings you to France?"

"Studies," the Norwegian replied in a rumbling bass. "I'm investigating mysteries from the past in hope of influencing my nation's future. I've heard of you, Mr. Gage, and your own remarkable scholarship."

"Curiosity at best. I'm very much the amateur savant." Yes, I can be modest when women aren't around. "I suspect the ancients knew something of electricity's strange power, and we've forgotten what we once knew. Bonaparte almost had me shot in the garden outside the Tuileries, but decided to retain me on the chance I might be useful."

"And my brother spared a beautiful Egyptian woman at the same time, I heard," Pauline murmured. She'd come up behind us, smelling of violets.

"Yes, my former companion Astiza, who decided to return to Egypt to continue her studies when Napoleon talked of sending me as an emissary to America. Parting was sweet sorrow, as they say." In truth I longed for her, yet also felt unshackled from her intensity. I was lonely and empty, but free.

"But you're not in America," Ellsworth said. "You're here with us."

"Well, President Adams was sending you three here. It seemed best to wait in Paris to lend a hand. I *do* have a weakness for gaming, and the little wheel is rather mesmerizing, don't you think?"

"Have your studies helped your gambling, Mr. Gage?" Bloodhammer's voice had a slight aggression to it, as if he were testing me. Instinct told me he was trouble.

"Mathematics has helped, thanks to the advice of the French savants I traveled with. But as I was explaining to Davie, true understanding of the odds only persuades that one must eventually lose."

"Indeed. Do you know what the thirty-six numbers of a roulette wheel add up to, sir?"

"Haven't thought about it, really."

The Norwegian looked at us intently, as if revealing a dark secret. "Six hundred and sixty-six. Or 666, the Number of the Beast, from Revelations." He waited portentously for a reaction, but we all just blinked.

"Oh, dear," I finally said. "But you're not the first to suggest gambling is the devil's tool. I don't entirely disagree."

"As a Freemason, you know numbers and symbols have meaning."

"I'm not much of a Mason, I'm afraid."

"And perhaps entire nations have meaning, as well." He looked at my companions with disquieting intensity. "Is it coincidence, my American friends, that nearly half of your revolution's generals and signers of your Constitution were Masons? That so many French revolutionaries were members as well? That Bavaria's secret Illuminati were founded in 1776, the same year as your Declaration of Independence? That the first boundary marker of the American capital city was laid in a Masonic ceremony, as well as the cornerstones for your capitol building and president's house? That's why

I find your two nations so fascinating. There is a secret thread behind your revolutions."

I looked at the others. None seemed to concur. "I frankly don't know," I said. "Napoleon's not a Mason. You're one yourself, Bloodhammer?"

"I'm an investigator, like you, interested in my own nation's independence. The Scandinavian kingdoms united in 1363, a curious time in our region's history. Norway has been in Denmark's shadow since. As a patriot, I hope for independence. You and I have things to teach each other, I suspect."

"Do we, now?" This Viking seemed rather forward. "What do you have to teach me?"

"More about your nation's beginnings, perhaps. And something even more intriguing and powerful. Something of incalculable value."

I waited.

"But what I wish to share is not for all ears."

"The usual caveat." People have a habit of talking grand, but what they really want is to milk me for what I know. It's become a game.

"So I ask for a word with you in private, Gage, later this evening."

"Well." I glanced at Pauline. If I wanted a private word, it was with her. "When I complete my other engagements, then of course!" I grinned at the girl and she returned the volley.

"But first the American must tell us his adventures!" she prompted.

"Yes, I'm curious how you found yourself in Italy," Ellsworth added.

So I played up my deeds in the season just past,

more anxious to explore Napoleon's randy sister than my nation's beginnings. "France this spring was beset by enemies on all sides, you'll recall," I began with a storyteller's flair. "Napoleon had to win a European peace before he had the strength to negotiate an American one. Despite his skepticism of my loyalties and motives, I was called to the Tuileries to answer some questions about America. I wound up making a casual remark about Switzerland." I smiled at Pauline. "Without exaggerating too much, I think I played a critical role in the French victory that followed."

She fanned herself, the crowd and candles making all of us too warm. A little moisture glistened in the vale between her enchanting orbs. "I think it grand you could aid Napoleon as Lafayette helped Washington," she cooed.

I laughed. "I'm no Lafayette! But I did have to kill a double agent . . ."

CHAPTER 3

The Tuileries Palace, neglected after the construction of Versailles and then damaged by Paris mobs during the Revolution, still smelled of wallpaper paste and enamel when I was summoned to visit Napoleon the previous spring.

Since my stay of execution and unexpected employment by Bonaparte in November of 1799, I'd conferred with his ministers about the slow negotiations with America. But beyond offering ignorant opinions—I was badly out of date with events in my own homeland—I really hadn't done much for my French stipend besides renew acquaintances and read months-old American newspapers. Apparently, Jefferson's Republicans were gaining on Adams's Federalists, as if I cared. I gambled, flirted, and recovered from the injuries of my latest adventures. So I could hardly complain when I was finally ordered, in March of 1800, to report to the first consul. It was time to earn my keep.

Napoleon's secretary, Bourrienne, greeted me at eight in the morning and led me down the corridors I remembered from my duel with Silano the autumn before. Now they were bright and refurbished, floors gleaming and windows repaired and bright. As we neared Bonaparte's chambers I saw a line of busts carefully selected to show his historical sensibility. There was a marble Alexander (his boyhood hero) and stalwarts like Cicero and Scipio. When the cavalryman Lasalle was asked by his captors how old his youthful commander was during Napoleon's first Italian campaign, he had wittily replied, "As old as Scipio when he defeated Hannibal!" Also frozen in marble was the late George Washington to show Napoleon's love of democracy, Caesar to suggest his command of government, and Brutus for his act of stabbing Caesar. Bonaparte covered all his bets.

"He begins his day in the bath and will receive you there," Bourrienne said. The novel idea of bathing every day was a new fad among French revolutionaries. "He can spend two hours in the tub reading correspondence."

"I don't remember him as so fastidious."

"He has a rigorous regimen of cleanliness and exercise. He keeps telling me he fears growing plump, though I can't imagine why. His energy leaves him meatless, and us exhausted. He's still lean as a boy. It's odd for a man in his prime to have a picture of himself heavier and more torpid in the future."

Odd unless you've lain in the sarcophagus of the Great Pyramid as Napoleon did, and possibly saw visions of your own coming life. But I didn't say that, and instead pointed at one of the busts. "Who's this bearded fellow, then?"

"Hannibal. Bonaparte calls him the greatest tactician, and worst strategist, of all time. He won almost every battle and lost the war."

"Yes," I said, nodding as if we shared the military assessment. "Hannibal and his elephants! Now that must have been something."

"I've seen one of the animals at the menagerie the savants have founded at the Jardin des Plantes," Bourrienne replied. "God has an imagination."

"Franklin told me they've found bones of ancient elephants in America."

"Your famous mentor! We should have his bust here too! I will make a note of it." And with that I was ushered into the bathroom, the door clicking shut to hold the heat. There was such a fog of steam that I could barely see Napoleon, or anything else.

"Gage, is that you? Come forward, man, don't be shy. We've all been in camp."

I groped forward. "You seem to like your bath hot, General."

"Four years ago I could barely afford my uniform. Now I can have all the water I want!" He laughed, and splashed at a servant waiting with a towel in the murk, spattering the poor man with suds. "It wilts some of my correspondence, but most is moldy in thought and soggy in prose anyway." As I came up to the tub I saw him in a convivial mood, dark hair plastered, gray eyes bright, the fine hands he was so vain of shuffling missives from across Europe. The brass basin had a relief of mermaids and dolphins.

"You seem more relaxed than when we last met, when you seized power," I remarked. He'd been quite anxious to shoot me.

"A pose, Gage, a pose. The Directory has left me at war with half of Europe! Italy, which I conquered just four years ago, is being taken back by the Austrians. In Germany, our troops have fallen back to the Rhine. In Egypt, General Desaix would have surrendered to Sidney Smith in January except an idiot English admiral wouldn't accept the terms, giving our General Kléber the chance to beat them again at Heliopolis. Still, without a navy, how long can my poor colleagues hold out? And how can I deal with the Austrians? They're pushing Massena back toward Genoa. I have to win or expire, Gage. Conquest has made me what I am, and conquest alone can sustain me."

"Surely you don't want my military advice."

He stood in the tub, water pouring off as a servant wrapped him. "I want to know how I can settle with the Americans. I'm wasting ships fighting your country when our two nations should be deep friends. Don't think the British don't want you back! Mark my words; you'll have to fight them again one day! France is your greatest bulwark. And lack of a proper navy is my curse. I can't waste frigates clashing with your republic." Servants ushered him to a dressing room. "Tell me how to deal with your Anglophile president, Gage. The man distrusts us French and flirts with the perfidious English. President Adams would move to London if he could!" Adams had been a reluctant diplomat in France who found Paris effete and untidy. He'd spent his days cranky and homesick.

I waited awkwardly as Napoleon began to be dressed. Hair was combed, nails filed, and unguents rubbed into his shoulders. The general had come a long way.

"John Adams?" I opined. "He's a prickly sort, to tell the truth. My understanding is that it's become a test of national pride. Adams's Federalists, who favor a stronger central government, are using the conflict with France as an excuse to build a bigger navy and levy larger taxes. Jefferson's Republicans say we've picked the wrong enemy, that Britain is the real threat. He and Burr are vying to take the next election. If you offer Adams a way out, I think he'll take it."

"I have agreed to new peace commissioners. You are to work with them and Talleyrand, Gage, and make everyone see reason. I need trade and money from America, not gunfire." He looked down. "By God, will you finish with those buttons!" Then, dressed at last, off he rushed to the next room where a map of Europe, stuck with little pins, was spread like a carpet on the floor. "Look at the ring my enemies have me in!"

I peered. Little of it made sense to me.

"If I march to relieve Massena in Genoa," Napoleon complained, "the Riviera becomes a narrow Thermopylae where Melas and his Austrians can block me. Yet Italy is the key to outflanking Vienna!" He threw himself down on the map as if it were a familiar bed. "I'm outnumbered, my veterans trapped in Egypt, raw conscripts my only recruits. All revolutionary enthusiasm has been lost, thanks to incompetence by the Directory. Yet I need victory, Gage! Victory restores spirit, and only victory will restore me!"

He looked restored enough, but I tried to think of something encouraging. "I know the siege of Acre went badly, but I'm sure you can do better."

"Don't talk to me of Acre! You and that damned Smith only won because you captured my siege artillery! If I ever find out who told the British about my flotilla, I'll hang him from Notre Dame!"

Since it was I who told the British—I'd been a little peeved after Napoleon's riffraff had dangled me above a snake pit and then tried to include me in a massacre—I decided to change the subject. "It's too bad you don't have any elephants," I tried.

"Elephants?" He looked annoyed. "Are you once more employed to waste my time?" Clearly, the memory of Acre and my ignorance at the pyramids still rankled.

"Like Hannibal, out in the corridor. If you could cross the Alps with elephants, that would get their attention, wouldn't it?"

"Elephants!" He finally laughed. "What nonsense you spout! Like that silly medallion you carried around in Egypt!"

"But Hannibal used them to invade Italy, did he not?"

"He did indeed." He thought, and shook his head. But then he crawled and peered about on the map. "Elephants? From the mouths of imbeciles. I *would* come down into their rear. And while I lack pachyderms, I have cannons." He looked at me as if I'd said something interesting. "Crossing the Alps! That would make my reputation, wouldn't it? The new Hannibal?"

"Except you'll win instead of lose, I'm sure of it." I hadn't dreamed he'd take me seriously.

He nodded. "But where? The accessible passes are too near Melas and his Austrians. He'd bottle me up just as he would on the Riviera."

I looked, pretending I knew something about Switzerland. I saw a name I recognized and a chill went through me, since I'd heard it bandied about in Egypt and Israel. Do certain names echo through our lives? "What about the Saint Bernard Pass?" This was farther north, away from the little pins. French mathematicians had told me about Saint Bernard of Clairvaux, who'd seen God in width, height and depth.

"Saint Bernard! No army would attempt that! It's twenty-five-hundred meters high, or more than eight thousand feet! No wider than a towpath! Really, Gage, you're no logistician. You can't move armies like a goat." He shook his head, peering. "Although if we *did* come down from there we could strike their rear in Milan and capture their supplies." He was thinking aloud. "We wouldn't have to bring everything, we'd take it from the Austrians. General Melas would never dream we'd dare it! It would be insane! Audacious!" He looked up at me. "Just the kind of thing an adventurer like you would suggest, I suppose."

I'm the world's most reluctant adventurer, but I smiled encouragingly. The way to deal with superiors is to give them a harebrained idea that suits your purposes and let them conclude it's their own. If I could pack Napoleon off to Italy again, I'd be able to relax in Paris unmolested.

"Saint Bernard!" he went on. "What general could do it? Only one . . ." He rose to his knees. "Gage, perhaps boldness is our salvation. I'm going to take the world by surprise by crossing the Alps like a modern Hannibal. It's a ridiculous idea you've had, so ridiculous that it makes a perverse kind of sense. You are an idiot savant!"

"Thank you. I think."

"Yes, I'm going to try it and you, American, are going to share the glory by scouting the pass for us!"

"Me?" I was appalled. "But I know nothing of mountains. Or Italians. Or elephants. You just said I'm to help with the American negotiations."

"Gage, as always, you are too modest! The advantage is that you've proved your pluck on both sides, so no one will be certain who you're sleeping with now! It will take months to get the new American commissioners here. Haven't you wanted to see Italy?"

"Not really." I thought of it as poor, hot, and superstitious.

"Your help with the American negotiations can wait until their delegation arrives. Gage, thanks to your elephants, you are going to once more share my fame!"

CHAPTER **4**

Some fame. The Alps in spring, I learned, are cold, windy, and wet, with snow the color of snot. The Saint Bernard of Switzerland was not even the Saint Bernard of Clairvaux: there are too many saints in the world, apparently, including two Bernards within a few hundred miles of each other. And no one believed I was hiking to the pass out of idle American curiosity, carrying my Pennsylvania longrifle like a walking stick. Everyone assumed I was exactly what I kept denying, an early scout for Bonaparte, since the first consul was visiting the encampments near Geneva and taking the unprecedented step of actually explaining to the common soldiers what it was he wanted them to do—to emulate the Carthaginians who'd stormed Rome. I was so obviously an agent that I found myself bargaining with the monks at the summit hospice to supply Napoleon's troops with food. Indeed, the first consul ran up a bill of forty thousand francs from wine, cheese, and bread sold from trestle tables the enterprising friars put out in the snow. What the holy men didn't grasp is that Napoleon always bought on credit, and was a master of evading bills at the same time he was extorting tribute from provinces he'd overrun. "Let war pay for war," his ministers said.

The painter David gave us a portrait of Bonaparte at the crest on a rearing charger, and it's as inspiring a piece of nonsense as I've ever seen. The truth is that Napoleon ascended the Alps on a sure-footed mule and slid down the far side on his own ass, he and his officers whooping with delight. Most of his sixty thousand soldiers walked, or rather trudged, up steadily worsening roads until, for the last seven miles, they were on a trail of ice and mud, potential avalanches poised above and yawning gorges below. Each hour they'd rest for a five-minute "pipe," or smoke, which was one of the two pleasures of army life—the other being to curse the stupidity of their superiors. Then on again! It was a hard, dangerous ascent that had them sweating in the cold. The soldiers slept at the summit, two to a blanket, great heaps of them huddled together like wolves, and by morning half had fevers and raw throats. Ice cut shoes to pieces, lungs gasped at thin air, and gaiters couldn't keep cold mud out of socks. Extremities went numb.

Yet they were proud. It was one of the boldest maneuvers of its age, made more so when the French snuck by a stubborn Austrian fort on the far side of the pass by muffling the hooves of their animals with straw. They hauled their artillery muzzles across the Alps in hollowed-out pine trees. Sixty thousand men crossed that pass, and every powder keg, cannon ball, and box of biscuit was packed or pulled by men with tumplines to their foreheads.

They sang revolutionary tunes. I handed out cups of wine in encouragement as they passed the summit. A friar kept tally.

Once over the pass, Bonaparte was everywhere, as usual. He studied the mountain fortress of Bard from concealing bushes, ordered different placement of his siege guns, and got it to capitulate in two days. We entered Milan on June 2. In a masterstroke he'd occupied the Austrian rear and made the French surrender of Genoa suddenly irrelevant. (The siege had been so horrific that Massena's hair had turned white.) The Austrians had driven their enemy out one side of Italy, only to have Napoleon's army show up on the other! Of course there was nothing to prevent General Melas from doing what Napoleon had done. He could have marched the opposite way across a different Alpine pass, left the French stranded in Italy, captured Lyon without a shot, and probably forced Bonaparte's abdication. Except that the Austrian was forty years older and didn't think in such sweeping terms. He was a superb tactician who saw a few leagues at a time. Napoleon could see the world.

Unless, that is, Napoleon was distracted. While Josephine's infidelities had made him come close to divorcing her, he set no such moral bounds on himself. Milan featured the famed diva Giuseppina Grassini, who conquered the French general first by song and then with her smoldering eyes, swollen lips, and bountiful bosom. Bonaparte spent six long days in Milan, too much of it in bed, and that was time enough for Melas to wheel his troops from the Italian coast and concentrate toward the French. Somewhere between Genoa and Milan, the great showdown would take place. It happened at Marengo.

My plan was to be well away. I'd seen plenty of war in the east, had played my part as scout for Hannibal, and was more than ready to scuttle back to Paris. There was no diva in Milan for me, and no other amusement, either. The Italians had been looted by rival armies too many times, and the best women had too many generals to choose from.

Then Bonaparte found a way to harness my talents. A spy had come, a swarthy imp of a man named Renato, oily as a neapolitan salad, who told us Melas and the Austrians were running. The French had merely to march forward to scoop up the reward for their alpine crossing! The spy carried Austrian documents in his boot heel as proof, and displayed a con man's confidence. But as a rogue myself, I was suspicious. Renato was a little *too* ingratiating, and kept glancing at me like a rival. In fact, he looked almost as if he knew me.

"You don't believe my spy, Gage?" Napoleon asked after the agent had gone.

"He has a rascal's manner." I should know.

"Surely I pay better than the Austrians. I must, at his price."

That was another thing that annoyed me: Renato

undoubtedly made more money than I did. "He may be too slippery to be properly bought."

"He's a spy, not a priest! You Americans are squeamish about such things, but agents are as necessary as artillery. Don't think I don't have my own reservations, about everyone." He gave me a hard stare. "I remain outnumbered two to one, my army is living on captured supplies, and I'm fearfully short of cannons. One loss and my rivals will have my throat. I know very well I have no true friends. Thank God Desaix has arrived from Egypt!"

Louis-Antoine Desaix, his favorite general, had landed in Toulon the same day we'd left Paris and been given a division here in Italy. Loyal, modest, shy of women, and extremely able, he was happiest sleeping under a cannon. He had Napoleon's talent without his ambition, the perfect subordinate.

"Perhaps I could carry word of your predicament to ministers in Paris?" The last thing I wanted was to be caught on the losing side.

"On the contrary, Gage, since you're so suspicious I want you to spy on our spy. Renato suggested a rendezvous to pass on the latest from the Austrians and mentioned your reputation for daring. Take the road to Pavia and the Po, trail Renato, make the rendezvous, and report back. I know you like the perfume of gunsmoke as much as I do."

Perfume of gunsmoke? "But I'm a savant, not a spy, First Consul. And I don't speak German or Italian."

"We both know you're an amateur savant at best, a dabbler and a dilettante. But when you look, you actually see. Humor me, Gage. Take a ride toward Genoa, confirm what we've been told, and *then* I'll send you back to Paris."

"Maybe we should just believe Renato after all."

"Take your rifle, too."

CHAPTER 5

So off I went, on a confiscated Italian horse (that's a fancy word for "stolen" that invaders use) and nervous as a virgin that I might stumble into the Austrian army. When you read about campaigns it's all arrows and rectangles on a map, as choreographed as a ballet. In reality, war is a half-blind, sprawling affair, great masses of men halfheartedly groping for each other across yawning countryside while looting anything that can be carried. It's all too easy for the observer to become disoriented. Gunshots echo alarmingly: fired accidentally, or from boredom, or sudden quarrel. Frightened, homesick eighteen-year-olds poke about with thirteen-pound muskets topped by wicked, two-foot bayonets. Passed-over colonels dream of suicidal charges that might restore their reputation. Sergeants stiffen a line in hopes for a sleeve of braid. It's no place for a sensible man.

Within an hour after setting out on June 9, I

heard the ominous thunder of combat. Lieutenant General Jean Lannes had crashed into the Austrian advance force at the villages of Casteggio and Montebello, and by day's end I was riding past long columns of Austrian prisoners, white uniforms spattered with blood and powder, expressions weary and sour. French wounded called insults to the prisoners plodding by. Wrecked wagons, dead horses and cows, and burning barns added to my disquiet. Gangs of pressed peasants were commandeered to tip heaps of battlefield dead into mass graves, while survivors matter-of-factly cleaned the muskets they called "clarinets" with beef marrow and whitened crossbelts with pipe clay. Some soldiers hoped filth might make them less tempting a target, but others thought fastidiousness brought luck. They used a slit piece of wood called a patience to hold their buttons out from their uniform cloth, shining them with mutton fat until they gleamed.

"Bones were cracking in my division like a shower of hail falling on a skylight," Lannes reported to Napoleon. The battle had produced four thousand casualties between the two sides—a mere dress rehearsal—and it was through this carnage that I reluctantly passed to skulk in the wake of the retreating Austrians into that netherworld between two armies.

What Napoleon didn't realize is that, look as I might, I couldn't really see. The Po Valley is flat, its fields bordered by tall poplar and cypress, and rain that June came down in buckets. Every rivulet was swollen, the landscape as different from Egypt and Syria as sponge from sandpaper. I could have plodded by the Golden Horde of Genghis Khan and not spotted it, should they happen to take this muddy lane instead of that one, down a cut and behind a hedge. So I wandered, asking directions of Italian refugees in sign language, sleeping in hayricks, and squinting for the missing sun. If Renato was lying, I was unlikely to catch him at it.

Instead, he told me himself.

At an abandoned farmhouse near Tortona I spied a red sash draped on a loose shutter, the agreed signal that our spy was waiting with information. Families had scurried out of the path of the armies like mice darting between the hooves of cattle, and rummaging soldiers had torn off the home's door, eaten the barn's animals, and burned the furniture. What was left, walls and a tile roof, offered shelter from another spring downpour. I was nervous, but the Austrians seemed to be falling back. The enemy had reportedly destroyed the bridge leading to lightly defended Alessandria, and more Austrians were running southwest toward Acqui. Accordingly, Bonaparte had split his forces, with Lapoype's division racing north and Desaix's division south. In the confusion, we spies were surely safe. I tied my horse, checked the load on my longrifle, and warily entered the dark home.

"Renato?" I almost tripped. He was seated on the stone floor, muddy boots outstretched and bottles at his side. I heard the click of his pistol hammer. "It's Gage, from Napoleon."

"You'll forgive my caution." A softer tap as the hammer was eased back to rest near the pan. As my eyes adjusted I saw the muzzle lower, but he didn't put his pistol away. He was watchful as a cat.

"My orders are to meet you."

"How convenient for us both. And your reward, American?"

Why not the truth? "I go back to Paris."

He saluted me with his pistol muzzle and laughed. "Better than this cold farmhouse, no? You have the loyalty of a mosquito. Some blood, and you're off."

I seated myself across from him, rifle by my side, only slightly reassured by our candor. "I'm no warrior. I've been riding around in the rain for four days, no good to anyone."

"Then you need this." He tossed me a bottle sitting next to him. "I found the trap to the cellar's sparkling wine, just the thing for a party. To a fellow spy! And of course I *could* believe you really *are* a mosquito, irritating and aimless. On the other hand, I've heard you have a reputation for pluck and persistence as well. No, don't deny it, Ethan Gage! So perhaps you're here to fetch my latest missive. Or perhaps to spy on *me*."

"Why would I spy on you?"

"Because the French don't trust me! Yes, we men of intrigue see things clearly." He nodded to himself. "I don't blame you for trying to get back to France. Can you imagine being a soldier in regimental line, shoulder to shoulder with a rank of similar idiots just fifty paces distant, everyone blazing away?" He shuddered. "It's amazing what armies get conscripts to do. If the morons survive, it will be the highlight of their lives."

I took a drink, thinking. His bottle was two-thirds empty, the champagne loosening his tongue. "People better than me say they believe in something, Renato."

He drank again too, and wiped his mouth. "Believe in Bonaparte? Or that old ass, Melas? What are they fighting about, really? Ask any of those soldiers to explain a war of a hundred years ago and they'll go blank. Yet they'll march to their death for this one. They're all fools, every one. Fools universal, except for me."

"You serve the French, too, don't you?"

"Alas." He winked. "The cabbages pay better than the vain Corsican."

"Napoleon would find that hard to believe, at your price."

"I'm a double agent, my naïve friend. If you are really that naïve." He belched, and drank again. "While I report, I spy, and then cross the lines to report and spy again. Why not keep everyone informed? Now Bonaparte is going to get a surprise."

"What do you mean?" I took a more vigorous swallow and lightly reinserted the cork, eyeing the pistol he kept in his lap.

"The Austrians are not running. They're concentrating. Napoleon has split his forces to catch an army massing against him."

"But you told him the opposite!"

He shrugged. "If he wanted the truth, he should have paid more than Melas."

"Men will die!"

"You think they won't die otherwise? Bonaparte believed what he wanted to believe. He remembers the clumsy Austrians of four years ago and gives Melas no credit. That old man is a fox, let me tell you. Fox enough to outbid Bonaparte for me. So I tell the French what they want, and the Austrians what I've told the French. Now the little despot will get his comeuppance."

He massaged the butt of his pistol, making me feel safe as a goose at Christmas. Why was he telling me this? I rocked my bottle, considering.

"Yes, American, Napoleon is about to get his nose bloodied. When he loses, I'll sell him still more advice—he'll be desperate enough to pay double— and then I'll go back and sell what I sold him to the Austrians for triple. This is how to make money in our business."

"Our business?"

"Bringing people together." He laughed.

"You're very candid."

He shrugged. "Just half-drunk. And confident of your discretion."

"Because I'm a spy, too?"

Now he looked at me seriously. "Of course not! You're a man like me, American, able to see the value in what you've been told. You'd betray me in an instant just as I've betrayed Bonaparte, and count your thirty pieces of silver as I swing from a tree. No, no, don't deny it . . . I'd do the same if our positions were reversed. This is the way of the world." Lazily he raised his pistol. "So you'll go to your grave with a secret! Ah, don't touch your rifle!" He smiled. "You must realize by now that I was sent to find *you*, not Bonaparte. My true employers remember your crimes."

"True employers?"

He pulled the hammer back. "Do you think the Rite forgets?" He aimed for my heart.

So I shot him with my cork.

He was a little *too* confiding and *too* confident, see. I'd seen reptiles like him before, so I got up some pressure in my bottle of bubbly and popped the cork just as he pulled to fire. The bottle gushed, cork and spray flying in his face, and it was enough of a surprise that the pistol jerked as I rolled. The ball whined past and thudded into the wall behind, raising a little puff of dust. He heaved up, pulling out a second pistol, but I beat him with a sidearm throw of my tomahawk. There was a crack as it struck between chin and teeth, enamel flying, and then I brought up my rifle. We fired at the same time, but it's even harder to aim with a hatchet in your face. He missed, and I didn't.

The bullet slammed him backward and he jerked as he died. I reloaded as I watched, ready to club him, then yanked my tomahawk out of his face and cleaned its steel on his coat. His split lips were fixed in a snarl. It was a nasty business, but after the events of the past two years the extermination of his kind of vermin didn't bother me overmuch.

The Rite? Now I understood my own apprehension. I dragged him through his own blood to the doorway for better light and ripped open his coat and shirt. Burned into his chest was a small tattoo of a pyramid wrapped with a snake. Apophis, the snake god! I shivered. Was this spy in the same confederacy as my old nemesis Silano, another branch of the perfidious Egyptian Rite that had pursued me in Egypt? And now, thanks to this serpent, Napoleon was dividing his forces as the Austrians were massing. Even if I hurried back to Napoleon this instant, it would be too late to pull in Desaix and Lapoype. The French center would be overwhelmed.

Damn Renato!

No, there'd be no quick exit to Paris. I'm not exactly steadfast, but I'm no traitor either, even if it wasn't my country. The only thing to do was to gallop after Desaix, who I faintly knew from Egypt, and get him hurrying back to the battle about to erupt in his rear. It would be a near-run thing, but if I rushed there might just be time enough!

I glanced down at the lifeless body. As I said, don't boast. And me? Not only was I occasionally useful, I might be developing integrity as well. By the saints, how had Napoleon guessed I might be worth betting on?

The spy stared upward with the surprised gaze of the dead, his body in a widening pool of gore. I buttoned his bloody shirt to hide his mark and wearily mounted my horse to go off and save the battle. And did I see the flicker of someone else, sinking back into a hedgerow, from the corner of my eye?

CHAPTER 6

The whole world knows what happened next. It dawned bright, the air scrubbed by recent rain, and by afternoon we had a high, hot Italian sun, the kind of weather that allows cavalry to actually charge, cannons to actually deploy, and dry muskets to actually fire. If you want to kill each other, there's nothing like a sunny day.

As Renato had predicted, the Austrians attacked in force at Marengo, long lines of white pushing through fields and cow pens in irresistible numbers. They took terrible casualties as they plunged across the moatlike Fantanone River, but they were drilled to obedience and didn't falter. There were a hundred heroic charges on each side, men dying for a vineyard or goat paddock, the battlefield a fog, and by the time Napoleon realized he'd stumbled into the full Austrian army and was desperately outnumbered, his troops were in reluctant, bloody retreat. Bonaparte had twenty-two thousand men and forty guns against thirty thousand men and one hundred cannons, and the Austrians sprayed grapeshot at every French rally. Hannibal had allowed himself to be outwitted, and Napoleon's career as leader of France was about to end before it had properly begun.

I arrived by midday with the bad news that Renato had been a double agent, and the better news that Desaix was coming. Then I watched the battle, its discipline filling me with appalled wonder. I'd seen war in Egypt and the Holy Land, but nothing like this drilled European slugging. Regimental formations marched shoulder to shoulder like automatons, stopped, and blasted each other in ferocious, unflinching determination. How gloriously gaudy they looked, infantry shakos topped with plumes, flags a beacon in gun smoke! The front rank kneeled, the second fired over their head, and the third passed up freshly loaded muskets, soldiers leaning into opposing volleys as if weathering sleet. Men coughed, yelped, went down, and new ones stepped smartly up like puppets. Dead and wounded sprawled everywhere, the green grass stained with red, but the living gave ground only grudgingly. Entire companies disintegrated rather than yield. Why did they endure? The individual soldier had little idea how his sacrifice was affecting the whole, but was acutely aware how his courage helped the small universe of friends and comrades. Men fought for their standing among men. The ranks would actually ripple as the bullets tore into them, sagging, and then stiffen until a charge with bayonet would push them back another fifty yards.

Back and back the French fell, Napoleon finally committing his Consular Guard in hopes of a final, decisive blow. His elite folded under withering musket and cannon fire like paper curled by heat, pride and power ground down in a few hot minutes. An Austrian cavalry charge scooped up four hundred prisoners.

The battle was lost.

And then I saved the day.

I got no official credit in the campaign histories, of course; I was an agent of no official standing. I was simply one of the "couriers" sent to fetch Desaix. But I got to the little general a full eight hours before any messengers Napoleon sent, and Desaix finally came in time. He reined up near Napoleon late afternoon, his division filing into line, and listened patiently to his commander's glum recitation of the day's reverses.

"The battle is certainly lost," the divisional commander agreed. "But there is still time to win another." And then Desaix counterattacked.

After eight hours of brutal fighting, the Austrians thought victory was theirs. The aged Melas, badly bruised after being thrown from his horse two times, had left the mopping-up to his subordinates and retired from the field. Napoleon's columns were wrecked, and his exhausted opponents assumed they'd sleep in San Guiliano.

But Desaix's fresh division hit them like a shock, an Austrian ammunition wagon blew up, and then General François Etienne de Kellermann saw an opening and led four hundred French dragoons into the side of the enemy. It was a brilliant charge of the kind they put into paintings, a rumble like an earthquake, green clods flying from the pounding hooves, sabers bright, plumes waving above the dragoons' towering bearskin hats—an equine avalanche that took the Austrians when they were weariest. The enemy, victorious one minute, were in headlong retreat the next, hundreds captured by the hurtling horsemen. I hadn't seen anything so astounding since Napoleon's own timely arrival at Mount Tabor in the Holy Land, converting a certain Turkish victory into a Turkish rout with a cannon shot.

Bonaparte was less surprised. "The fate of a battle is a single moment," he remarked.

Brave little Desaix was shot dead at Marengo at the moment of his greatest triumph, and there has been as much romantic nonsense over this tragedy as Napoleon's crossing of the Alps. "Why am I not allowed to weep?" the conqueror was later recorded as saying, suggesting a tenderness I never saw him display toward any man, or any woman, either. Napoleon weep? To him, life was war and people were soldiers to be used. He was sad, yes—Desaix was as valuable as a good horse—but hardly morose about one more corpse in a square mile of carnage. The truth is that the bullet entered through Desaix's back, either from Austrian fire as he swung around to exhort his men or, just as likely, from an errant bullet from his own side. The number of men accidentally killed or wounded by their excited, confused, and frightened comrades is one of the dirty secrets of war.

We'd learn later that General Kleber, whom I'd

soldiered with on the beaches of Alexandria and the battlefield of Mount Tabor—and who Napoleon had left in command in Egypt—was assassinated by a Muslim fanatic at almost the same moment Desaix fell. So go the people who have been chapters in our lives. Generals are spent like coins.

By day's end there were twelve thousand Austrian and French dead or wounded, dead and dying horses, shattered caissons, and dismounted artillery. The Austrians had lost another six thousand prisoners and forty cannon.

"I have just put the crown on your head," Kellermann remarked, an impolitic truth he wouldn't be forgiven for. Let honor be bestowed; don't grasp for it.

I made no such boast, but could have. At 4:00 p.m. at Marengo, Napoleon's rule was finished; by 7:00 p.m. it had been confirmed. Instead, wisely keeping my mouth shut for once, I wangled my way onto Bonaparte's swift carriage back to Paris after the Austrians agreed to armistice.

On our journey Napoleon confided that his ambition had merely been whetted. "Yes, I have done enough, it's true," he told me. "In less than two years I have won Cairo, Paris, and Milan, but for all that, were I to die tomorrow I should not at the end of ten centuries occupy half a page of general history!"

Who else counted their history pages a thousand years hence?

Back in Paris, I was put to work helping negotiations with the newly arrived American commissioners. The confidence I'd won from Bonaparte eased the way for the Franco-American treaty. And so I concluded my tale of derring-do at Mortefontaine where we'd gathered to celebrate peace. We toasted, Pauline Bonaparte's eyes sparkling at my tale, and even grim Magnus Bloodhammer looking at me with grudging respect.

I downed another glass and smiled modestly. It's good to be the hero.

"Monsieur Gage," Pauline invited, "would you like to see my brother's cellar?"

CHAPTER 7

One of the promises of our new nineteenth century is the practical simplicity of women's clothing. In the old days, getting past the skirts, corsets, and garters of a noblewoman was as complicated as reefing a barkentine in a gale. A man might be so wearied by ribbons, stays, laces, and layers that by the time he got to squeezable flesh he'd forgotten what all the effort was for. The new revolutionary fashions, I'm happy to report, are less complicated, and getting at Pauline, nestled between two wine kegs, was not much more complicated than lowering the gallant at top and hoisting the mainsail at bottom, noting she had dispensed with chemise and bunching what little there was at her waist while she sang like a choir. Lord, the girl had enthusiasm! Her breasts were even better than what portraiture has recorded, and her thighs nimble as scissors. We bucked and plunged like a Sicilian stagecoach, Pauline as hot as a Franklin stove, and I could happily have had her in a few more cellar nooks and crannies, sampling the vintages this way and that, if rough hands had not suddenly seized me and jerked me back like a cork popping out of a bottle.

The indignity!

It's hard to fight back with your trousers about your ankles, and I was too surprised in any event to react. Damnation! Had General Leclerc come back from his cantonment after all? I could try to explain we were merely dusting the bottles, but I didn't think he'd believe me, given that both Pauline and I were both more exposed than a Maine lighthouse in a howling nor'easter.

"He assaulted me!" she shrieked, which was no more likely to be believed, given her amorous reputation.

"You shouldn't thrust yourself in where you do not belong," one of my assailants said with an accent I couldn't place, just before a clout to the head blurred my vision and buckled my knees. My manhood was wilting and my longrifle and tomahawk had been checked with my greatcoat in the anteroom upstairs. I have an all too fervent imagination of what various enemies might do to me and woozily tried to cross my legs.

"I know what this looks like . . . ," I began.

A gag went into my mouth.

Instead of having my throat or something even more valuable cut, they seemed determined to truss me like a sausage. Ropes were thrown around me as they pummeled and kicked, and in my daze I had the wit to do only one thing: fetch a handful of the chocolates I'd filched from my waistcoat pocket and slip them into my shirtsleeve just as my wrists were being bound. Having been tied before, I'd spent time giving the problem some thought.

I dimly saw Pauline was allowed to flee, pulling up and pushing down her filmy garment. One does not tie up Napoleon's sister! Then, my own pants hauled up as well, I was dragged down a dark corridor to a cellar door that led to the gardens beyond. Given the situation, I didn't expect her to call for my rescue.

So I tried to reason my way out. Unfortunately, my gag reduced my logic to muffled mumphs and growls.

"Save your breath, American. You don't even understand what you're involved in."

Hadn't I been in the first consul's sister? Or was this about something else entirely? I'd assumed I was being manhandled by the vengeful minions of Pauline's husband or brothers, but perhaps some other retribution was going on. I tried to review who else might want me dead. Had someone really seen me leave that ruined Italian farmhouse, and was Renato just the first attempt at Egyptian Rite retribution, given that I'd incinerated Count Alessandro Silano? Had the Apophis snake cult from Egypt somehow trailed me to Paris? The British might be annoyed that I was once more with the French, like a shuttlecock in the wind. Then there were a few young ladies less than satisfied with the circumstances of our parting, a gambling victim or two, the occasional creditor, the entire Austrian army, the English sailors from HMS *Dangerous* whose pay I had taken in cards, the angry Muslims from the Temple Mount in Jerusalem. . . .

For someone as likeable as me, I'd acquired an astonishing list of potential enemies. I suppose it doesn't much matter *who* kills you, given that you will be dead anyway. Still, one likes to know.

I was dragged down a garden path like a log, thrown in a small, saucer-shaped coracle about as seaworthy as a leaf, and towed by rowboat across the château lake. I half expected to be weighted and tossed in the water, but, no, they beached our craft on the island where the fireworks were to ignite and bundled me past the shrubbery to where the combustibles were mounted. As near as I could tell, Despeaux had stockpiled enough incendiaries to light the Second Coming.

"You always want to be at the center of things. Now you will end that way, too," my assailants said. I was lashed to a stake in the middle of the display of rockets and mortars as if I, too, were a rocket set to shoot skyward. I realized that at the climax of the celebration of the Convention of Mortefontaine I would go up in flames like a roman candle. If anyone could identify my remains, they'd conclude poking around fireworks was just the thing the bold, foolish electrician Ethan Gage would try.

"When the gag burns through you can scream, because by that time it will be impossible to hear you over the explosions," a captor said, not altogether helpfully. "Each shout will suck burning air into your lungs." And then they lit a slow fuse and departed without so much as an *adieu*, their oars quietly dipping as they made for shore.

I was doomed, unless my chocolate melted.

Having been tied before, upon return to Paris I'd made some study of the matter. It seems that the knack of getting out of knots is to have some slack, and that expanding the chest and bulging the muscles is a trick escape artists use to get them started on their bonds. In the case of my wrists, the chocolate in my sleeves had made their circumference bigger. Now, as the hard candy turned liquid, I squeezed my wrists together and the confection squirted out, loosening my ropes. Thank goodness for culinary invention! Being able to twist and move my hands, however, was not the same thing as being free. I saw with growing panic that the crowd from the party had come outside the château to watch the fireworks, their gaiety backlit by the glowing windows. Flirtatious laughter floated across the water and paper lanterns were set afloat on the lake. I could smell the burning fuse.

Sweating, unable to call out, I worked my wrists raw, thumbs pulling at strands, the mess of chocolate both lubricating the ropes and making them sticky. Finally, a key cord came loose.

Then there was a flash at the corner of my vision, and a sizzle. The pyrotechnics were about to ignite!

Thrashing my lower arms, I got the last bonds off my aching hands, freeing my arms to my elbows. By reaching up I managed to snag my gag and haul it to one side. "Help!"

The bloody orchestra, however, had broken into

a rousing version of "Yankee Doodle," as cacophonous as a flight of geese. The crowd whooped as the fuse flamed toward the arsenal, its spark bright as a tiger's eye.

So I clawed at the ropes holding my torso to the pole. My upper arms were still tied to my chest, but I had enough freedom below my elbows to get one end of the bond free and begin to awkwardly fling it to unwind myself, moaning at my own slowness. There was a whistle of powder and the first cluster of skyrockets soared up, smoke blinding anyone to my presence on the island. They exploded in a galaxy of stars, bright bits raining down. Some of the mortars coughed and burped, shells soaring. It was getting damnably hot damnably fast, and I was sweating. On and on the loose rope flew, growing longer and beginning to burn, even as the vile choir of exploding fireworks increased. If the climax was reached and the ground display turned the island into a fountain of flame, I was cooked, and dead.

"Help!" I called again.

Now they were playing the "Marseillaise"!

Finally I unwound myself free of the pole, went to run, and fell. My feet were still bound! Something was still strapped to my back! I didn't have time for this! Skyrockets were screaming up in every direction, hot sparks were raining on my hair and clothes, and I was dazed and half-blinded by the excruciating light. I began hopping toward the water, clawing at the bonds at my chest.

Then the island seemed to erupt.

To the shrieking delight of the crowd, the ground

display went off like a sun's corona. Huge sheets of sparks shot up in pulsing arcs, the air a hell of sulfur, smoke, and stinging ash. The cords around my ankles caught fire, and if I hadn't still had my boots on (Pauline and I had been in a hurry) I would have been badly burned. On I hopped like a panicked rabbit, until I spied the saucer-shaped coracle I'd been towed out in. I collapsed on it, my momentum pushing it into the lake and dragging my own feet into the water. The flames extinguished with a hiss. Now I had my arms mostly free, but some rope still around my chest and biceps. My hair was smoking, and I threw water on that and got the now-burnt-through ropes off my feet. Finally I kneeled, barely balancing in the wobbly craft, and hand-paddled toward the crowd, Hades in tumult behind me.

"Look, what's that! Something's coming from the island!"

The damned idiots began to applaud, drowning my complaints once again. They thought I was part of the show! And just when I finally got near enough to shout about brigands and kidnappers, my hair nearly ignited again!

Or, rather, a molten fountain my torturers had cruelly stuck to my back, held by cords still around my chest, went off with a whoosh. The wooden tail was tucked in the back waist of my trousers, and apparently its fuse had ignited as I was fleeing the island. Now it—I—was a flaming torch. I reached behind and yanked the missile out of my bonds before it could finish roasting me and desperately held the spouting tube away from me by its hot nose, sparks shooting great, pulsing gouts of flame out the tail. The exhaust illuminated my figure, and actually giving me slight propulsion as I drifted toward the onlookers. Now everyone was cheering.

"It's Gage! What a character! Look, he's holding up a torch to celebrate our convention!"

"They say he's a sorcerer! Lucifer means 'light-giver,' you know!"

"Did he plan the entire show?"

"He's a genius!"

"Or a prima donna!"

Not knowing what else to do, I held my rocket upside down as flames spewed skyward and tried to muster singed dignity, my smile gritted against the pain of the burns. There! Were hooded onlookers melting into the trees? The final sparks were cascading past my figure to hiss into the water as I grounded and finally stepped ashore, like Columbus.

"Bravo! What a scene stealer!"

I bowed, more than a little shaken. I was half-blind, coughing from the acrid fumes, and wincing from my burns and abrasions. My watering eyes cut rivulets down my blackened cheeks.

The American commissioners pushed their way to the front of the throng. "By heavens, Gage, what the devil are you trying to symbolize?" Ellsworth asked.

I dazedly tried to think fast. "Liberty, I think."

"That was quite the performance," Davie said. "You might have been hurt."

"He's a plucky daredevil," said Vans Murray. "It's an addiction, is it not?"

Then Bonaparte was there, too. "I might have known," he said. "I'm grateful you are not in politics, Monsieur Gage, or your instinct would be to upstage me."

"I'm afraid that would be impossible, First Consul."

He looked skeptically from me to the island. "You were planning this stunt all along?"

"It was a last-minute inspiration, I assure you."

"Well." He looked at the others. "Holding that torch aloft was a nice touch. This will be an evening for us all to remember. The friendship of France and the United States! Gage, you obviously have flair. It will stand you in good stead as you carry my messages to your president."

"America?" I glanced around for Pauline's husband, Egyptian snake worshippers, Muslim fanatics, or British agents. Perhaps it *was* time to go home.

An arm went around my shoulder. "And now you have new friends to keep you safe!" said Magnus Bloodhammer, squeezing me like a bear. He smiled at Napoleon. "Gage and I have been looking for each other, and now *I* will go to America, too!"

CHAPTER 8

Magnus pushed me into shadows at the edge of the crowd, his embrace rough and his breath smelling of alcohol. "You should not have crept off with that Bonaparte wench," the Norwegian lectured quietly. "You would have been safer with me!"

"I had no idea her husband's men were lurking around. Nor that he was so possessive. My God, her reputation . . ."

"Those were not Leclerc's men, you fool. Those were Danes."

"Danes?" Why did they care whom I was rogering?

"Or they were the church, or worse. It's too late for you now, Gage, you've been seen with me. They know how crucial you are to our cause. Your life is in terrible danger."

"*Who* knows? *What* cause?" I swear I draw lunatics like bees to honey.

"Were they going to burn you on the island?"

"Yes. If it hadn't been for this newfangled solid chocolate . . ."

"They're trying to warn me off. And make a statement. Don't think they didn't mean for us to mark the similarities to the medieval stake of the Inquisition. Your incineration was to be a signal to the rest of us. Which only convinces me the map is real. I tell you Gage, your nation needs me as much as I need it."

"*What* map?"

"How many are there? Are they well-armed?"

"Frankly, I didn't get a good look. I was rather busy . . ."

"Who can we trust? The odds appear long. Do you have any allies at all?"

"Bloodhammer . . ."

"Call me Magnus."

"Magnus, can you take your arm from my shoulder, please? We're barely acquainted."

Reluctantly, the big man did so, and I got some breathing room. "Thank you. Now, I don't know any Danes, the church has been thrown out of France by the revolution, and I know nothing of any map. We're here to celebrate a Franco-American peace treaty, if you'll recall, and I try to be a friend to everyone, when I can. Including Pauline Bonaparte. Perhaps my assailants made some mistake. They gagged me, so I couldn't explain who I really was."

"Your new enemies don't make mistakes."

"But I don't have any new enemies!" I glanced about. "Do I?"

"I'm afraid my enemies are now yours, because

of your fame and expertise. You are an electrician, are you not? An investigator of the past? A protégé of the great Franklin?"

"More of an assistant, at best." It was beginning to occur to me that while boasting of my exploits might win me alliance with fine ladies, it also seemed to draw the attention of the worst kind of men. Someday I'm going to be more careful. "I'm a wastrel, actually. Hardly worth caring about."

"Gage, I'm on a quest, and there's only one man in the world with the curious combination of talents I need to help me succeed. That man is *you*, and everything you've said tonight only confirms it. No, don't protest! Has not Bonaparte himself put his trust in you? Destiny is at work. What I am after is important, not only to Norway but to your own young nation. You are a patriot, sir, are you not?"

"Well, I like to think so. God rest George Washington. Not that I ever met the man."

He leaned close, his whisper masked by the noise of the milling, inebriated crowd. "What if I were to tell you that Columbus was not the first to reach your shores?"

"The Indians were there, I suppose . . ."

"My own ancestors reached North America centuries before those Italian and Spanish interlopers, Ethan Gage. Norse voyagers were the real discoverers of your continent."

"Really? But if they did, they didn't stick, did they? It doesn't count."

"It does!" he roared, and people looked at us. He dragged me back even farther, to the shadow under an oak, and seized my shoulders in the dark underneath. "The Norse came, and drew a map, and left behind an artifact so powerful, so earthshaking, that whoever finds it will control the future! I'm talking about the fate of your own United States, Ethan Gage!"

I was suspicious. "What do you care about the United States?"

"Because the rightful return of this artifact to my own nation will be a rallying point for its independence at the same time it saves your own from foreign domination. We have a chance to change world history!"

Well, I'd heard this kind of talk before, and what did I have to show for it? I'd run around Egypt and Jerusalem on the hinge of history and ended up bruised, singed, and heartbroken. "I'm not much for affecting history, I'm afraid. It's hard, dirty work, quite tiring, with very little recompense, I've found."

"And we'll discover something worth more than an emperor's crown." He looked at me with the crafty expertise of a mule salesman.

That stopped me, shameless mercenary that I am. "Worth more? As in money?"

"You're a gambler, Ethan Gage. Wouldn't you like to be rich?"

This Bloodhammer, who had the gleam of a Pizarro eyeing a roomful of Inca gold, was suddenly more interesting. I coughed to clear my throat. "My primary interest is the advancement of knowledge. I am a man of science, after all. Yet if there is reward to be had, I'm not opposed to compensation. As my mentor Franklin said, "Rather go to bed without dinner than to rise in debt."

"You didn't have dinner?"

"I'm chronically in debt. Just what is this treasure, Magnus?"

"I can only confide in a place less public than this." He surveyed the assembly, now drifting back inside and preparing to go home, the way Bonaparte took in a battlefield. "Soon they will scatter, and we will be at risk again from the foul brigands who accosted you. Our first challenge is to make it out of Mortefontaine alive."

▫   ▫   ▫

When you're watchful, every stranger seems to be watching. What had seemed an hour before to be an assembly of friends now looked ominous and menacing. With so many soldiers about, my assailants could most easily have infiltrated by being invited guests—but if so, which ones were they? I hadn't gotten a proper view in the dark. Gaiety still reigned, inebriation was almost universal, laughter and wit were loud, and the only person who looked out of place was the one proposing to be my companion, Magnus Bloodhammer. Wouldn't Danes be blond? I looked at every light-haired male with suspicion, but none even noticed my scrutiny.

Perhaps they were lurking by the gate. My hired coach wouldn't be hard to spot and follow, once I climbed in, and in the dark forest between the château and Paris I'd be easy prey. I could ask Bonaparte for escort, but then I'd have to explain about Magnus, treasure, and his married sister. Better to steal off discreetly. I was considering how when a small hand pulled my arm.

"Come," Pauline whispered. "There's time for another round in a boudoir upstairs!"

By Cupid's arrow, the randy girl didn't discourage easily, did she? I'm dragged off, half-cooked, have to boat myself back to the party with my hair on fire, and she behaves like all we've had is a lover's recess. I couldn't imagine what a full night with the minx would be like. Actually, I *could* imagine, and it was intimidating.

"I'm afraid I have to leave." Then inspiration struck. "Say, could I share your carriage? I'm trying to avoid those men who interrupted us."

Her eyes sparkled. "Such delightful temptation! But if you were seen by my brother or his officers, word could get back to my husband." She cast her eyes down, as if demure. "I do have my reputation."

Indeed she did. "I could disguise myself as a footman. Do you have one my size I could trade clothes with? It would be a great favor to have him draw those rascals off. He could have my coat as payment."

Now she looked impish. "And how might you repay *me*, monsieur?"

I bowed. "By discussing the customs of a Cairo harem I once visited." No need to tell her it had been more discouraging than a cold tub in an unheated woodshed.

"I do adore geography."

"There are all kinds of places we could explore," I encouraged. "Say, I have a friend . . ."

"Monsieur!" Her eyes widened. "Ménage à trois?"

"Who would be happy to ride outside beside the coachman."

I swear, the girl looked disappointed that there would be no threesome. But I didn't have time to gauge her full reaction, instead quickly ushering her through the crowd so she could send a message to the stables where the servants loitered. Two of her men were to trade places with Magnus and me. While the lads were fetched, I retrieved my rifle and tomahawk to secrete in her coach. Then I sought out Jean-Etienne Despeaux, the organizer of the festivities, and asked if there were any leftover fireworks from the display.

"You didn't get a close enough look on that island, Monsieur Gage?" he asked with raised brows.

"It was such a powerful experience I'd like to do some experimentation. Might electricity be harnessed to augment such a magnificent spectacle?"

"Do you ever rest, American?"

"It's surprising how difficult that is to do."

He did have some pyrotechnics remaining—it hadn't been clear just how much of the arsenal would fit in the middle of the pond—and I carefully packed as many explosives as I could in a small trunk liberated from the château. I sprinkled loose powder on top and fastened a spare rifle flint on the lid against the lock so that when the box opened, there would be a spark. Then I made something of a show of carrying it through the dispersing crowd, looking secretive and important, and lashing it to the back of the carriage I'd ridden to reach Morte-fontaine. Once this pantomime was acted out, I disappeared to change clothes with Pauline's servants, inspecting the laundry of the lower class for fleas.

"You can keep my coat as payment for this favor," I told a strapping lad.

"And you mine, conjurer," he said cheerfully. "And now I get to play the Yankee, with sprawling stride, loose elbows, and gaping curiosity." He pretended to imitate me in an annoying manner as he marched out in the dark to my carriage, cloak and hat masking his features. I daresay my posture and walk is more elegant than *that*.

At the same time Magnus and I made our way to Pauline's coach where it waited in line. He had a leather cylinder strapped on his back like a quiver, but I took it to be a case for his promised map. He'd also bundled an old cape and slouch hat under one arm. He went to climb inside but I blocked him. "Up on top, Bloodhammer, where the servants ride. Unless you'd rather hang off the back."

"Your disguise is no different than mine, Gage," he hissed. "Why do you get to be inside and I have to be outside?"

"Because I'm the servant with the service our hostess requires."

"Are you mad? Hasn't she caused you trouble enough?"

"Actually, no. We didn't sample the vintage as much as I'd hoped."

He was frustrated, but much more arguing and we'd draw attention to ourselves. "Caution, American," he muttered. "We're not out of danger yet."

"Which is precisely why you need to climb to the top of our conveyance. Keep a lookout, will you?"

Pauline departed the château and minced quickly across the gravel, her woolen cloak flaring behind as she held its throat shut against her flimsy gown. I sunk low in the coach as she boarded. "To Paris!" she ordered, rapping the ceiling, and we moved out with a jerk and smart pace, on a journey that wouldn't be completed until well after the sun rose. My own carriage had already departed, and I hoped that the Danes, if that's what they were, had taken the bait and followed it and its tempting trunk.

I figured they'd howl when they realized I'd switched places with a footman, but do the servant no harm. In frustration they'd have a look at my things. And then . . .

"You've had quite the brilliant evening, Monsieur Gage," Pauline murmured once I risked sitting higher.

"More dramatic than I intended."

"Who were those horrid men in the cellar? I should have my brother arrest them and shoot them for their rude timing. I was not really finished, you know."

"I'm not sure of their identity. Maybe they were jealous of your beauty."

She sniffed. "I shouldn't blame them. I'm sitting for portraits."

"You must favor me with one."

She smiled. "I'm sure you can't afford it, but it's sweet of you to ask. And so bravely escaped! Did you thrash the rascals?"

"They ran."

She looked up at the brocaded ceiling. "Is your friend along, as you asked?"

"He's playing watchman next to the coachman at this very moment."

"How gallant. Then you and I can continue our discussions of antiquity." She hoisted a bottle. "I liberated this from Joseph when I fled his cellar."

"You have foresight as well as beauty."

"It's a long way to Paris. Is that where we're going?"

"Actually, Madame, it would suit my purposes better to set course for Le Havre." I'd been thinking ahead. While I hated to leave the comforts of Paris, it would be the first place any enemies would look for me. How long before Leclerc learned I was dallying with his wife? "I have pressing business in America."

"Then we must make the most of your time here." She rapped the coach roof again. "Henri! The coast road!"

"Yes, madame."

She turned back to me. "We'll take you to a public coach, but only when we are far enough away from Mortefontaine that you're safe. Meanwhile, I have glasses in the compartment there. Let us toast."

"To survival?"

"Monsieur Gage, I always survive. To reunion!"

As we clinked glasses I heard the echo of an explosion through the estate's forests and looked out the window. There was a glow, two rockets arcing through the air. My assailants apparently *had* followed my carriage. And ransacked my things.

I sat back inside. "Brigands."

She shook her head. "My brother will put an end to them, I assure you."

"I think I already have."

"Ethan!" Bloodhammer called from above. "Did you see that? What the devil?"

"A parting for our friends, Magnus. Do stay alert!"

"I'm cold up here!"

"Pity!"

Pauline opened her cloak and I snuggled inside, sharing its volume.

"We must get you out of those dreadful clothes, Monsieur Gage. A man of your fame and station should not be mistaken for a commoner."

"And I could warm my lady more efficiently without the encumbrance of that flimsy gown," I suggested. "There's a science to combustion."

"I love science as much as geography." She pulled up her gown to show the delightful thatch between her thighs, nicely trimmed to a Cupid's heart.

And somewhere we took the fork to Le Havre, though I swear I didn't hear anyone remark on it, given all the moaning.

CHAPTER 9

A North Atlantic crossing in autumn is like a long-winded opera without a private box seat or a female companion to cuddle. You can endure it, but it's tedious, cramped, and noisy, and there isn't enough to do. I was sick the first three days, and then merely damp, cold, and bored the ten awful weeks it took us to beat into a succession of gales before making New York. Green water polished the decks, the planking writhed and groaned, and leaks sustained a tributary on the torture rack called my berth. When I popped my head topside one morning and saw the mast tops obscured by snow flurries, ice on the ratlines, I was so desperate for distraction that I volunteered to help the cook pick mold off the last of the vegetables.

"Took a look at the sea, did you, Monsieur Gage?"

"Yes. It looks exactly as it looked yesterday."

"*Oui*. This is why I am content to stay by my brick oven."

Bloodhammer was in his element, circuiting the deck with his beard flapping like a sail and the gleam of a Viking berserker ready to stave in a few civilized heads. His slouch hat was pulled down against the weather and his cloak wrapped him like an Indian blanket. He was as impatient to get to America as I was, but he saw beauty in the great mountainous swells I never quite shared, though there were some days—sunlight glowing through their crests like emerald fire, great arcing rainbows on the black horizon—when I admitted the ocean had an odd charm, like the desert. Great seabirds sometimes hung over us without moving a wing, riding the wind, and once a seaman cried out and we saw the great gray back of some leviathan slide by our hull, its misty exhalation smelling of fish and the deep.

"My ancestors believed the world was encircled by endless ocean, and in that sea lives a serpent so great that it encircled all, its head reaching to its tail," Magnus said. "When it constricted, it could cause the sea to rise in a deluge."

"If the ocean was endless, how could it be encircled?" I'm becoming something of an amateur theologian, given all the gods and goddesses trampling through my life, and I take amusement in picking at the logical inconsistencies.

"The world was made from the bones and teeth of a frost giant, and the lakes by his blood."

So it went. In the long dark hours we were confined below, Magnus talked, and with talk so strange I felt I'd slipped the moorings of our modern century. He crammed the hours with names like Thor,

Asgard, Loki, Boverk, Jarl, Sneg, Feima, and Snor. I couldn't make heads or tails out of much of it, but I've a weakness for stories of the fabled past and he told them well, with a bass rumble and saga rhythm that seemed to match the pitch and yaw of the ship. The past always seems simpler than the complicated present, and Magnus was one of those dreamy men half-stranded there, a troll with the heart of a boy. His cyclopean blue eye would catch fire, he'd lean forward with urgency, and his hands would dance like swords.

Our captain had taken to calling our big shipmate Odin, and when I finally asked him why, the officer looked at me in surprise.

"From his guise, of course. Surely you recognize the king of the gods."

"King of the gods?"

"Odin the one-eyed, the Norse equivalent of Zeus, wandered the world disguised by his broad hat and flapping cape to add to his knowledge, the one thing he had an unquenchable thirst for. You were not aware of the resemblance?"

"I just thought he had no taste for smart clothing."

"Your friend is very odd, monsieur. But odd in a significant way."

So I listened to my replica of Odin tell his myths. The forest people of the north had feisty and lusty gods, it seems, carousing with dead heroes in a great hall called Valhalla when they weren't making mischief for mortals below. Each day the Vikings would spend a jolly good time hacking each other to pieces, and then come dinnertime they'd all be resurrected for another drunken feast. Magnus summoned a time of sky gods and rainbow bridges, and the great Norse tree Yggdrasil, which held the nine worlds, an eagle at its top and the dragon Nidhogg gnawing below. It reminded me of the serpent Apophis in Egyptian legend. One of this tree's roots was moored near a place called Hel, ruled over by a ghastly goddess of the same name who'd been banished there by Odin. Her hall of the dead, beyond the sheer rock Drop to Destruction, was named Eljudnir, and she lorded over corpses who hadn't become battlefield heroes with a plate called Hunger and a knife called Famine.

Halfway up Yggdrasil's trunk was Midgard, our human world, to which the gods sometimes descend and leave mischief and artifacts. Up near the top there was Asgard, a kind of Norse heaven.

"Hel?" I asked. "You mean like the Christian hell? The Vikings believed in the Bible?"

"No, it is the Christians who believe in the old myths. The new faith borrows many ideas from the old. Did you know that one-eyed Odin, who gave half his sight to drink from the well of wisdom, had himself hung from Yggdrasil like Christ on the cross, to learn still more? He called out in agony and took a spear thrust in the side."

"Half his sight? You mean he wore an eye patch like you?"

"Or just a hideous empty socket." He flicked his patch so I could glimpse his own ghastly scar, and then grinned. It was a crater I could stick my thumb into.

"And what happened to *your* eye?"

"I traded it for knowledge, too. I lost it when I was caught in the secret archives of Copenhagen, researching the history of my nation and old Knights Templar lore. A sword tip got past my guard and I had to fight my way out with a face full of blood. Fortunately the pain focused me when I leaped into the slushy harbor and swam deep to avoid their gunshots. You'd have done the same, of course, but perhaps with more skill at arms to avoid being wounded. You don't seem to bear many scars."

That's because I would have surrendered to the first stern librarian, but no need to be absolutely candid. I decided to change the subject. "Asserting that the Christians took some of their best ideas from the pagans was the same kind of blasphemous claim a woman named Astiza used to make about the Egyptians. Contradicting this nonsense is like trying to stamp out a grass fire. You can't believe hell is a *Norwegian* idea, Magnus. Especially since it's supposed to be hot."

"Some hells are cold, like our Nilfheim. And no, it's a universal idea—like so many stories in the Bible—echoed across time and culture. That's why the biblical stories strike us as true. The Bible has the Flood, and the Norse have Ginunngigap, the periodic rising of the sea that swallows the world. The Bible has the Apocalypse, and the Norse have Ragnarok, the final war between gods and giants. Newer religions pass on the old. It's no heresy to recognize the deep origins of religious belief, Ethan. By understanding the roots, we begin to comprehend the truth."

"How do you know all this? Are you some kind of Druid priest?"

"I'm a patriot and a utopian, and as such an agent of the past because it was there, long in the past, that we lost the keys to a bright future."

"But now there's science. Fifteen years ago, the French astronomer Comte de Corli proposed that fragments of a passing comet struck Earth and that is the cause of some of the disasters and miracles the Bible relates."

"Is that any likelier than Yggdrasil and Asgard? Your science is just the myth of our times, supplying a beginning. Aye, we've forgotten as much as we've learned, almost as though we've had a blow to the head that obliterated vital memory. Then the Knights Templar began to rediscover the truth. I'm on that path, and you've appeared to help me."

"Appeared, or dragooned by you and your mad Danes?"

"Our being here, on this pitching ship, was foreordained."

"By whom?"

"That's the mystery, isn't it?"

◻   ◻   ◻

All nonsense, of course, but I suppose it was just as well the voyage gave him time to jabber and me to rest. By the time we'd parted company with Pauline on the coast highway in France I was wrung out as a dishcloth, had a cramp in one leg, and was thoroughly unsettled by a visit from a squadron of

French dragoons sent to look for me after the ambush of my carriage. They caught up with us just a few miles on our detour toward Brittany. I was frantically pulling on my boots, hoping to outrun what I assumed was General Leclerc's vengeance, when a lieutenant saluted me through the coach door as if I wore epaulettes. He handed me an envelope. "Compliments of the First Consul, sir. You slipped away before orders could be issued." He carefully kept his eye off Pauline.

"Orders?" Was it back to Temple Prison as an unrepentant fornicator of the consul's sister? Or simply a quick firing squad in the woods?

No, it was a directive, in Napoleon's quick hand, ordering me to wait on the coast for final instructions before departing for America.

"You're not here to arrest me?" I sounded incriminating, but I'm not used to such luck.

"Our orders are to see you to a public coach and escort Pauline Bonaparte back to Paris," the man said, his face a careful mask. "We are to ensure that everyone is on their correct path."

"So gallant is your concern, Lieutenant," said Pauline, who at least had the decency to redden.

"The concern is your brother's."

Once again Napoleon was demonstrating his command of the situation. I was to be hurried off to America, and Pauline back to her home. Frankly, it *was* time to get distance from the girl. Nor, once I was spent, did I feel entirely moral about my performance. Conquering a Bonaparte was not as satisfying a revenge for my rough treatment as I'd imagined. Once again I wondered if I'd learned anything from my tumultuous adventures; if I was, in fact, impregnable to sense and good fiber. "He is a governor that governs his passions, and he a servant that serves them," old Ben had lectured. Bonaparte thought too much about the future, I of the moment, and Bloodhammer of the past.

So Magnus and I, tired and reprieved, climbed down from the stage and gave fumbled salutes to the dragoons. My new companion was tipsy from having warmed himself with a bottle of aquavit he'd smuggled from Mortefontaine with more sly initiative than I'd have given him credit for. We waved Pauline off to Paris, caught a public stage at first light, and eventually arrived at the coast like two vagabonds. With my rifle and tomahawk and Magnus's map case our only luggage, we were about as inconspicuous as a gypsy circus—but seaports draw odd men, so no one questioned us too closely when we showed enough francs. The Breton rebel Georges Cadoudal was rumored to have returned to France from England to conspire against Napoleon, and we could have been anything from Bourbon sympathizers to the secret police. Accordingly, we were left alone.

We found a brig for New York that was waiting for a break in the weather and the British blockade. The foul season was the ideal time to slip out.

In Le Havre, my decision to take a break from France was reinforced when I received further instructions and one hundred silver American dollars, minted in Mexico, from the French foreign minister, Talleyrand himself. He informed me that the American commissioners were writing to my government to alert them of my coming. He added that France itself had a particular interest in my mission. Talleyrand wrote:

> *It is in the utmost confidence and secrecy that I must inform you that agreement has been reached with Spain to return to France her rightful possession of Louisiana, a territory four times the size of my nation that, as you know, was lost in the Seven Years' War. Announcement of this accord will probably be made early next year. The government of France has the keenest interest about conditions in Louisiana, and expects that your investigations with the Norwegian Magnus Bloodhammer may lead you to that territory. I must also advise that rumors of an amatory nature make it advisable for you to be at some distance from Paris, out of the sight of Pauline Bonaparte's husband and brothers, for a while.*

It's about as easy to keep a secret about a tryst in France as it is a sea profit in Boston, and no doubt my absence with Pauline rivaled my fireworks performance as theater gossip. Best to set sail.

> *As a confederate of the First Consul, I hope you will be able to (1) ascertain if the Norwegian's theories are at all true, (2) inform us and your own country of Britain's designs on the northwest frontier, and (3) explore the possibility of new alliances between the Indian tribes of that region and France, so as to secure the sovereignty of both French holdings and the border integrity of your*

own United States. Our two nations, I trust, will always live in harmony along the boundary of the Mississippi River. In return, I enclose a preliminary payment for expenses, and a letter and seal to gain you the assistance of any French representatives you may encounter in your travels. Make no mistake: France's enemy, England, is the enemy of your young nation as well. Treat all British representatives with the utmost caution and suspicion, and work toward the rebuilding of the natural alliance between our two republics.

—TALLEYRAND

Louisiana back to France? I dimly remembered, from my reading of aged American newspapers, about Spanish threats of closing New Orleans to American shipping down the Mississippi, choking off the west's only access to the sea. If Napoleon had somehow bamboozled the Spanish into giving New Orleans back, the United States and France might find themselves in commercial partnership, with me neatly in the middle. Surely there was money to be made!

All I had to do was stay friends with all sides.

CHAPTER 10

So we put to sea, and if the ship had once stopped heaving up and down so distractingly I might have had the presence of mind to leverage my secret knowledge into a fortune. Instead, I had to listen to the fairy tales of Magnus, who like all fanatics seemed to live as much in his imaginary world as the real one. He displayed that unwavering conviction that always accompanies meager evidence, because to admit *anything* might be untrue would be to undermine his entire edifice of belief. He was entertaining, but eventually I had to interrupt his yarns about drunken gods and sly elves.

"Enough, Magnus!" I cried. "I've been assaulted in a wine cellar, nearly incinerated by fireworks, forced to flee to America in weather that could sink a continent, and am allied to a lunatic who babbles about a mysterious map. What is going on?"

He looked about. "What lunatic?"

"You!"

"Me! The man who saved you at Mortefontaine?"

"Magnus, you said those were your enemies, not mine. I have nothing against Denmark. I could barely find Norway on a globe. I don't care what the numbers of a roulette wheel add up to, or coincidences in 1776, and I'm not entirely certain what we're supposed to do when we reach the United States."

"Uncertain? You, the famous Freemason?"

"I'm not a famous Freemason. My late friend Talma took me to a lodge meeting or two."

"Do you deny the significance of October 13, 1307?"

"The significance of what?"

"Come, Ethan, don't be coy. Let's agree that the events of that black Friday the Thirteenth were momentous for world history."

Now I remembered. That was the night the French king Philip the Fair had arrested hundreds of Knights Templar, two centuries after the order's founding in Jerusalem during the Crusades. My old jailer, Boniface, had told stories about it. Grand Master Jacques de Molay, unrepentant at the end, had gone to the stake in 1314, vowing correctly that both Philip and the pope behind him would follow him to the grave within a year. Philip had allegedly tried to plunder an organization both mysteriously rich and annoyingly independent, and found frustratingly little to steal.

"The Templars were crushed. Musty history."

"Not to true Masons, Ethan. While some Templars died or recanted their order, others fled to places like Scotland, Ireland, Scandinavia . . . and perhaps America."

"America hadn't even been discovered then."

"There are Viking legends of exploration, and rumors of just such a Templar escape. Legends tied up with stories about Thor and Odin. And then, eight months ago, in a secret crypt below the floor of a Cistercian abby on the island of Gotland, exploring monks found a map and the legend became truth. *That* is what is going on."

"This map you claim to have."

"The Cistercian order was founded by Saint Bernard of Clairvaux, you may recall, nephew of André de Montbard, one of the Templar founders."

Now I felt a chill. I'd found the tomb of Montbard—or some Christian knight, anyway—in a subterranean chamber beneath a lost city in the Holy Land, and with it the Book of Thoth. Despite my best efforts, the villain Silano had used the book to help usher Napoleon Bonaparte to power. Now Napoleon called the Tuileries home, and I was on a ship to America. My lost love, Astiza, who had returned to the sun of Egypt, would agree with Bloodhammer that it was all foreordained. For a world in which everything is supposedly predestined, life seems awfully complicated.

"You know what I'm talking about," Magnus went on, watching me. "Saint Bernard was a mystic who saw holiness in geometry and inspired the greatest of the Gothic cathedrals. His monasteries became some of the most prosperous and powerful in Europe, rising hand-in-hand with the secular power of the Templars. Was it coincidence that some of the persecuted knights fled to Gotland where the Cistercian order was particularly strong? The monks succeeded in winning Norse pagans over by blending some of the old beliefs with the new, or rather in recognizing a continuity of religious belief as old as time. Not so much one true God as that *every* god was, in its own way, a manifestation of the One. And not just God, but the Goddess."

Damnation. Pagans pop up on me like pimples on a youth. And if you get involved with one or two of them, as I have, the others seem to seek you out.

"You're saying Saint Bernard and the Cistercians weren't Christians?"

"I'm saying Christianity allows more freedom of thought than many denominations will admit, and that Bernard recognized that devotion can take many forms. Of course they were Christian! But both the knights and the monks recognized the many paths the holy have walked, and the many manifestations of their power. It's rumored the knights brought some secret back from Jerusalem. That's why I wanted to meet you at Mortefontaine, to learn if it is true."

It was gone, so why not tell him? "*Was* true. It was a book."

I could hear his sharp intake of breath even over the roar of the sea. "*Was* a book?"

"It burned, Magnus. Lost forever, I'm afraid. I could hardly even read it."

"This is a monstrous tragedy!"

"Not really. The scroll caused nothing but trouble."

"But you believe me, then? If the Templars found and hid a sacred book, why not an important map? Correct?"

"I suppose. The book was in a crypt, too."

"Aha!"

I sighed. "What led to the discovery of your map?"

"Snow and thaw. It was a bad winter, water penetrated the foundations, and cracks developed in the masonry of the chapel floor. A bright young monk realized there was a cavity under what had been assumed to be a solid foundation, and when it was excavated for repair they found the tombs. Curiously, the entrance had been sealed so no one could spot it. In one sarcophagus of a monastery leader, dated 1363, a parchment map was encased."

"I don't suppose it was in a golden cylinder?"

"Gold?" He looked surprised. "Now that would have gotten our attention. No, a leather tube, sealed quite effectively with wax. Why do you ask?"

"My own book was encased in gold. Splendid piece, carved with figures and symbols."

"By the steed of Odin! Do you still have it? It could be of incalculable value in understanding the past!"

I felt sheepish. "Actually I gave it away to a metallurgist, probably to be melted down. I'd cost him his home, see. There was this woman, Miriam . . ."

He groaned. "Your brain is in your breeches!"

"No, no, it wasn't like that. I was going to marry

her, but she was engaged, and her brother was laughing at me . . ." It sounded puzzling even to me. "Anyway, it's gone too."

Magnus shook his head. "And to think you have a reputation as a savant. Are you an expert in anything beyond the female form?"

"Don't act superior to me! Don't *you* like women?"

"Aye, I like *them*, but they don't like *me*. Look at me! I'm no dandy."

"You have a certain, umm, mutilated, bearlike charm. You just haven't found the right one."

Instantly, he was gloomy. "I did, once."

"Well, there you go then."

"And if she *does* like you, and then you lose her . . . well, there's nothing more painful than that, is there?"

It was the kind of confession that makes you realize someone has the potential to be a friend. "It hurts, doesn't it?" Yes, I'd been in love, too, and with far better women than Pauline Bonaparte. "You've had your heart broken?"

"Not in the way you think. I lost my wife to illness."

"Oh. I'm sorry, Magnus."

"It's not so bad, I think, never to know joy, never to see paradise. But to have it, to see it, and *then* lose it. . . . After Signe's death I dedicated myself to learning the truth of legends I'd first heard as a boy. I've searched libraries and archives, sailed to mines and hiked to dolmens, lost an eye and offered my soul. While Signe has gone on, I remain in our earthly purgatory, trying to get back in."

"Get back in what?"

"Paradise."

"You mean another woman?"

"No!" He looked offended.

"What, then?"

"Suppose it didn't have to hurt?"

"What do you mean?"

"Imagine there was a place, a way, where bad things didn't happen? Or where bad things could be reversed, corrected?"

"What, heaven? Valhalla? Not in the world I've seen, Magnus, and believe me, I've looked."

"Suppose there was a better world we've lost? A real place, in a real time, not a legend."

"These myths you talk about aren't real, man. They're stories."

"Stories like Templars escaping to America, more than a century before Columbus. Stories about secret books, and underground tombs in lost cities."

He had a point. The planet seemed fuller of inexplicable oddities than I'd ever imagined. I had, after all, scooped treasure beneath the pyramid, found a secret chamber beneath the Temple Mount, swum in a secret well to a Templar's grave, and gotten help in the middle of a dire fight from a long-dead mummy. Who's to say what's impossible? "Let's see your map, then."

So he pulled it out of that tube he carried. I noticed the map case was longer than the scroll, and wondered what was at its hidden end.

"There are stories of other maps. The Earl of Orkney, Prince Henry Saint Clair, is said to have taken thirteen ships west at the end of the fourteenth century, nearly one hundred years before Columbus, and come back with a map showing Nova Scotia and perhaps New England. But this one is earlier, and better."

The chart was on some kind of skin parchment, not paper, with the coastline of Europe clearly visible and what appeared to be Iceland and Greenland at the top. There was a crude compass rose, which meant an origin no earlier than medieval times, and Latin inscription. But what drew the eye, of course, was the map's left-hand side. It appeared to show the northeast coast of an unbounded land mass with a large, almost circular bay. From this, squiggly lines, like rivers, led south into a blank interior. In the middle of nowhere was a curious symbol, like a squat, fat *T*. Near it was a little peak.

"What's this mountain here?"

"That's not a mountain. It's a Valknot, the knot of the slain."

I peered closer. The mountain was actually a cluster of overlapping triangles that intersected like a knot, as Magnus had said. It created an odd illusion, like an abstraction of a mountain range. "I've never seen anything like it."

"It's also called Odin's triangle," Bloodhammer explained. "It connects the battlefield dead to Valhalla, like a power lifting them up."

"So why is it on this map?"

"Why indeed?" Now his eye was bright.

Near the symbols were what appeared to be rivers leading away in the four cardinal directions, as if the symbol were near a central spring.

"That tomb had not been opened since 1363,"

Magnus said. "The crypt itself had apparently been closed at least since 1400—well before Columbus and the other explorers sailed. And yet what does that bite in the continent look like to you, my skeptical friend?"

There was no denying it. "Hudson Bay. But the 1300s . . ."

"Were two centuries and better *after* Vikings were rumored to have reached a mysterious Vinland to the west," Bloodhammer said. "And two and a half centuries *before* Henry Hudson found the bay that bears his name, and where he was marooned to die by his own mutinous crew." He stabbed the parchment. "Norsemen were in the middle of North America a century and a half before Columbus sailed. How about *that*, eh?"

"But what the devil has this to do with Knights Templar?"

"Here we have speculation. The Templars are crushed, politically, beginning in 1307. Some flee to Gotland. This map is generated half a century later. We know that famine racked Europe in the 1320s, and that the Black Plague came next, reaching Norway about 1349. The church was continuing its persecutions, fearing the disease to be God's judgment. Suppose descendants of the knights, sheltered by the Cistercians, who do not see eye-to-eye with Rome, decided to seek refuge in a New World first discovered by pagan Viking explorers a few centuries before? They would escape persecution, famine, and disease. In 1354, there is a record of one Paul Knutson setting out to check the colonies of Greenland, which had fallen silent. Suppose our medieval Norsemen went even farther, into this vast bay? And then inland? We know Hudson's crew was trapped by ice for the winter, prompting their mutiny the next spring. What if Norsemen, more comfortable with winter, decided to strike south on the frozen rivers instead of waiting for the thaw? Or perhaps they did wait for spring, and ascended the rivers you see once they were free of ice. The rivers on my map correspond closely to the rivers today's Hudson's Bay Company uses to access the Canadian interior for furs. Might they have penetrated to the center of North America? Might they have seen sights and made claims hundreds of years before any European?"

"But why?" I pondered the map. "Even if these Templars, or monks, or whatever they were, decided to go to the New World, why would they go north to a place like Hudson's Bay? Why not the eastern coast of the United States? There's a line for it right there." I pointed. "No Viking is going to paddle or march to the middle of America."

"Not Viking. Medieval Norse who are descendants of the Knights Templar, or Templars themselves."

"Medieval Norse, then. It still makes no sense. What did they expect to find?"

"Not just find. Hide."

"Hide? What?"

"What they had to flee the church and the authorities to secrete away. One of the mysteries the

Templars had uncovered in their untiring research into the old faiths. One of the grails itself."

"The grail?" I swallowed. Given my past adventures, I didn't have good association with that word. I'd babbled it myself once to get out of being tortured and bitten by snakes, but that was just expediency.

"Here!" He pointed, indicating the mysterious *T* symbol near Odin's triangle. It looked a little like a fat Templar cross, but with the upright piece at the top missing. Bloodhammer's gaze was fierce again. "Mjolnir. Thor's hammer!"

□   □   □

U nderstand that at this point, any normal savant would have thrown up his hands and walked away, or at least walked as far as you can on a pitching ship. Thor's hammer? I knew little of Norse mythology, but I'd heard of Thor, and of a weapon he carried, a hammer. It was fearsome, shot lightning, and came back to the god's hand when he threw it. The trouble was, it's all a myth. Thor's hammer? Probably kept in a cubby with Neptune's trident, Jason's fleece, and the club of Hercules.

But I felt sympathy for Magnus because once I'd been in his exact position, explaining a story every bit as crazy as this one to my old confederates in Jerusalem and trying not to sound like a madman. So I sat where I was and asked the obvious:

"Thor's *what*?"

Magnus looked triumphant. "The hammer of the gods! It really existed!"

"Thor really existed? A Norse god?"

He nodded excitedly. "Not God as we understand him. Not the Creator, or the Great Architect, as the Masons would say. Rather a superior being, a first ancestor, of a company of heroes we can never hope to emulate. They preceded our own race, in a golden age long lost. Thor taught things that humankind has since forgotten. And he put some of his power, some of this thought, into his hammer!"

"You realize that you should be restrained."

"I know it sounds fantastic! How do you think we of the Forn Sior felt when we realized there might be artifacts of the hero's age left on this earth? But the Templars took seriously the notion that ancient beings instructed primitive men."

"Wait. Forn Sior?"

" 'Old Custom.' That's what we call ourselves."

"What *who* calls themselves?"

"Those of us who are keepers of the past, who believe the old stories are as valid as the new, and that truth is a blending of all threads. We're a secret fraternity, my friend, who seek out those like you who might help us. I was in despair when Signe died, suicidal, when they appeared to recruit me. They gave me hope. Mankind has learned much, Ethan: we live in a strange new modern age, the nineteenth century! And who knows what wonders are to come! But we've forgotten as much as we've learned. There are powers in the forest, spirits in the stones, and magic secrets that have been forgotten for three thousand years. But the Templars began relearning them! They started in Jerusalem and searched the entire world!"

"Secrets like my book?"

"Yes, like your book. Written by whom, exactly? Or should I say what?"

"Some kind of Egyptian being called Thoth. He looked like a bird in some representations. A baboon in others."

"Or a tree, a unicorn, a dragon, or an angel. Don't you see, Ethan? It's all the same, these mysterious forebears, the origin of our kind, and they've left clues about their history for us to rediscover."

"A Frenchman named Jomard told me the Great Pyramid incorporated fundamental truths, and that everything since has been a long forgetting."

"Yes! Exactly! Like your Book of Thoth or Mjolnir, Thor's hammer. Eight hundred years after our conversion to Christianity its symbol still adorns many a necklace, because it's perceived as a good-luck piece in my country!"

"Let me get this straight. You think there really was a Thor. With a magic hammer. Which Knights Templar found. And which was taken to America centuries before Columbus?"

He nodded happily. "Isn't it exciting?"

It's because I'm so tolerant and easygoing, I suppose, that I draw theorists of this sort. I made a resolution then and there to become stern and crabby, but it's entirely contrary to my character. Besides, I half believed him.

"So there was more than one Thoth?"

"Probably. Or he was well-traveled, flying through the air to different places on Earth and leaving a different legend with each ancient people. He gave us gifts to start our civilizations, and we remember it dimly as myth."

"But where was this hammer after Thor disappeared?"

"Ah. That we don't know. There are legends of men in white tunics and red crosses going to mines far to the north, where in summer the sun never sets and in winter it never rises. However they did it, we of Forn Sior think the Templars found the hammer and stored it with the other amazing artifacts they were collecting, while using them to increase their power. That's what the king of France and his ally, the pope, were hoping to seize! But the Templars hid their treasure, smuggled it to distant isles like Gotland, and when the church at last followed them there—when they were betrayed by doubting Cistercian monks, perhaps—they fled farther. To America!"

"Suppose for a moment I concede they could have sailed that far. Why would they go so far inland?"

"To hide the hammer, of course, in the remotest place they could find. A lost place. A mystical place. A *central* place. Perhaps they were going to found their own colony around it, and create a utopia based on Templar and Cistercian principles in the one place where no one would ever find them to persecute them."

"Except the Indians."

"Well, yes. We must assume the effort failed,

since no one has heard of any such colony. And attacks by Red Indians could indeed have been the cause."

"So *you* want to go there? I mean here?" I pointed to the hammer symbol on the map.

"Yes, to look for the hammer. Do you realize the symbolic power it would have, regardless of whether it really spits lightning? It would reawaken Norse culture and pride. It would be our flag, our liberty tree. It would be the symbol for revolution against the Danes, and Forn Sior would lead the way to a new society!"

"Which is why Danes are trying to kill us?"

"Yes." He nodded encouragingly. "If we succeed, we tear their little empire apart! It's flattering they're after us."

"You keep saying 'we,' Magnus. But I never signed on for all this. Certainly not to look for a mythical hammer in the middle of Indian country a thousand miles from any proper post, in hopes I can free a frozen backwater in Europe I've never been to!" My voice was rising at the absurdity of it.

But his smile was impregnable. "Of course you'll help. The hammer will be the greatest treasure on Earth, and if anyone understands its electrical and lightning powers, it will be you, Ethan Gage, heir to Franklin, the electrician of the age."

"No. No, no, no, no."

"It will make you rich. It will make you famous. And it will make you a hero to your own country."

"Why would it make me a hero to *my* country?"

"Because no one needs the hammer found more

than your own leaders, Ethan Gage. No one is depending on you more."

"What would the leaders of the United States know about this Thor's hammer? It's absurd."

"Not absurd. Awaited."

"What?"

"Ethan. Don't you know your own nation was founded, created, and guided by the descendants of the Knights Templar?"

CHAPTER 11

The island of Manhattan, logged clear of trees by British desperate for firewood when confined during the American Revolution a generation before, was in winter a muddy, brushy, dreary place of second-growth wood lots, overgrazed dairy farms, fallow vegetable gardens, and leaden ponds. At its southern end, however, was my nation's second-biggest city after Philadelphia, a commercial Gomorrah with fewer manners and more ambition than its rival. The number of merchants had quadrupled in just the past ten years, and its sixty thousand people were packed into a warren of tight streets, squeezed churches, and practical counting houses, their architects expressing a better eye for cost than art. Cobbled streets were combed by wagon wheels into lines of slush and manure, while poorer mud lanes were lined by two-story townhouses crammed with cobblers, wheelwrights, glassblowers, butchers, fishmongers, chandlers, coppersmiths, carpenters, clothiers, saddlers, bakers, green grocers, furriers, bookmakers, brewers, gunsmiths, jewelers, weavers, watchmakers, teahouses, and taverns. Like all cities New York stank: of manure, wood smoke, human sewage, sawdust, beer, and the reek of tanneries and slaughterhouses that clustered around a polluted pond called the Collect.

It was a city of newcomers and strivers—not just the Dutch and English but New Englanders riding its commercial wave, French émigrés escaping the revolution at home, thick and industrious Germans and Swedes, entrepreneurial Jews, Spanish grandees, Negroes both slave and free, and occasionally an Indian chief, Chinaman, or Hawaiian Kanaka who gaped and were gaped at in the crowded markets. Some five thousand refugees from the slave revolts in Haiti had recently debarked, including "mestizo ladies with complexions of the palest marble, jet black hair, and the eyes of the gazelle," in the words of one journal. Indeed, there were women aristocratic, wives buxom, maids slim, servants dusky, whores powdered, actresses late-rising, and Dutch girls scrubbing stoops, their energetic bottoms oscillating with a charm that made me happy to be back home.

Magnus was an unfashionable oddity himself, with burgeoning whiskers, a mane of rusty hair, a black eye patch, and hands like hams. I enjoyed notoriety, too, from reports that I was connected to the newly risen Bonaparte. My mission was the new capital of Washington, but a flurry of invitations persuaded me to pause and take rest.

Since it was winter, the mercantile frenzy of New

York was largely confined indoors, businessmen laying ambitious plans next to warming fires while the wind whistled down the Hudson, freezing fast New York's garbage until it could be used to extend landfills in the spring. Ice floes scudded by the village of Brooklyn, and bare yardarms made crosses of snow.

The city's primary talk was politics. After a bitter election campaign between Adams's Federalists and the upstart Republicans, the two candidates of the latter, Thomas Jefferson and Aaron Burr, had tied in the number of electoral votes, or so the rumor went. The ballots that were cast December 3 would not be officially counted until February 11 of the New Year, but the results were about as secret as Admiral Nelson's dalliance with Lady Hamilton, half a world away. The presidency would be decided in the House of Representatives, as the framers of the constitution had anticipated, and everyone had an opinion of how the vote might go. While Jefferson was widely acknowledged as the intellectual leader of his party, speculation was that the defeated Federalists in Congress might deny the office to the sage of Monticello and give it instead to the more ferociously ambitious and recklessly high-living Burr, a New Yorker who'd gone back on his promise to be content with second place. The jockeying was, all agreed, unseemly, ruthless, naked, and irresistible.

"The titan Washington is gone, and lesser men are scrambling for power!" a barkeep at Fraunces Tavern declared. "The age of heroes is over, the present is corrupt, and the future promises disaster!"

"Things are normal then," I toasted. "To democracy!"

Every candidate had been tarred. Jefferson was accused of shirking military duty during the revolution and of being a Jacobin and atheist. Incumbent John Adams was portrayed as incompetent, power-mad, and a secret ally of the perfidious British. Burr was a tin-pot Napoleon. In other words, it was little different than the sniping and backstabbing one heard in the salons of Paris, and I discounted all of it, given what lies have been told about even earnest and likable types like me. There were tales of a Federalist plot to assassinate Jefferson, arm the slaves, or seize the arsenals. Some feared civil war! Yet none of the Americans thought the undignified tumult warranted a king. The ones I drank with were as proud of democracy's chaos as gulls playing the winds of a tempest.

"Our congressmen will have our say, by God!" the barflies declared. "They are rogues every one, but they are *our* rogues."

"Speaking as an expert on roguery, America has an above-average set," I seconded.

I found myself a minor Republican celebrity. Jefferson liked the French, and my peacemaking in Paris had made me the "hero of Mortefontaine." The naval war with France had sent insurance rates on a vessel as high as 40 percent of the value of ship and cargo, and word of permanent peace had been received with celebration. Somehow the tale of my fireworks escape had preceded me across the Atlantic, and I was agreeably toasted as having held aloft the "torch of liberty." Someone even suggested it would make a model for a good statue, though of course nothing ever came of that idea.

I was determined to enjoy my moment of renown, since reputations turn soon enough. Being a celebrity, however, buys you little more than supper, often with dull company who expect the famed to provide the entertainment. I found my supply of silver dollars dwindling and had to take to the gaming tables to staunch the leak.

My modest fame *did* provide the chance for liaisons with American merchant daughters curious to know how diplomacy was waged in storied France, lessons I was happy to take to their bed. I taught them to cry *"Mon dieu!"* at full gallop, the hypnotic bounce of their breasts providing ample testimony to the healthy diet of meat and cream in the New World. French girls, while prettier, tend toward the bony.

Magnus was disinclined to join me. "I told you, I had a love and lost her. I don't want to dishonor her memory or suffer the pain of lost love again." The man was a monk, and just as tiresome.

"This isn't love, it's exercise."

"Signe's memory is enough for me."

"You'll dry up!"

"*You* exercise, with all the risks that go with it, and I'll explore the map shops." Magnus, impatient to be going despite the inclement season, prowled New York in his cloak and broad slouch hat, looking for Freemason symbolism, Viking relics, and Indian legends. The amount of nonsense he received was directly proportional to the amount he was willing to spend for ale on those he interviewed.

I left him to it, scouting instead the holy ground the whores occupied adjacent to Saint Paul's Chapel. But when I'd come in at three hours after midnight I'd catch Magnus reading the tomes he'd collected from the fourteen bookstores on Maiden Lane and Pearl Street, lips moving to the nonnative English like a bull practicing Thucydides. He collected piles of speculative literature on the biblical origins of Indians, Masonic conspiracies, and odd pamphlets like William Cobbet's contention that the new century started in 1800, not 1801, a theory that had set off impressive brawls near the Battery.

"I admire your fidelity, I really do," I told him. "I resolve to copy you, eventually. But there's more to life than a mission, Magnus."

"And more to life than the moment." He put down a book on the lost tribes of Israel. "Ethan, I know you have a reputation as a Franklin man and a savant, but I must say you haven't shown why. You've been skeptical, tardy, procrastinating, and shallow ever since I met you, and I don't quite understand why you're famous at all. You don't take our quest entirely seriously."

I pointed skyward. "There's just not much thunder and lightning in winter for us electricians. And my international diplomacy with the new president has to wait until they pick one. Why not enjoy a respite?"

"Because we could be preparing for the test. Life is for accomplishment. If your nation was still in thrall to another, you'd understand that."

"I'm not so sure. The accomplishers I've met

seem as likely to leave behind a heap of bodies, crackpot ideas, and financial ruin. Look at the French Revolution. Every time they accomplish something they're dissatisfied with it and want to accomplish the opposite. My philosophy is to wait until the world makes up its mind."

"Then let's wait in Washington, not this commercial Babylon of gossip and greed. The longer we linger in New York, the more chance our enemies have to catch up to us."

"I took care of our enemies in Mortefontaine, and Denmark is an ocean away! Relax, Magnus, we're in America. And the farther west we go, the safer we'll be."

Still, his criticism of my procrastination rankled, and once more I vowed to reform myself. "Waste not life," Franklin had counseled. "In the grave will be sleeping enough." So I seduced a widow with hips and hair to hang onto like a frisky mare, shattered rum bottles in target practice with my longrifle, tried to teach French to dullard merchants' sons at the Redhook Inn in return for their buying the rounds of drink, and worked with a Yankee mechanic on a turntable mechanism for a New World version of roulette. "Own the wheel, don't play it," I advised him.

I also tried the New York lottery, making a chain necklace of my losing tickets.

This recess from reality was interrupted one day by a visit from an old employer, the maniacally ambitious Johann Jakob Astor. This German immigrant, who began as a musical instrument salesman but turned to furs, had earned far more in commerce than I'd ever even tossed away in treasure hunting. (A telling lesson, should I ever become industrious.) Astor had the drive of a dozen men, a wife who combined her blood ties to old Dutch families with a keen eye for fur, a fine new brick house on Dock Street, and the inability to enjoy anything but his ledger totals, given that he coupled his love of money with the parsimony of a preacher. When he found me at a tavern, I was the one who had to pay for the wine.

"Gage, I didn't think a gamesman like you would live to see thirty, yet here you are as diplomat and envoy," he greeted. "It makes one wonder if biblical miracles could indeed be true."

"I hear you're doing well too, John," I said, feeling as usual somewhat defensive about my lack of progress. His coat was finest wool, his waistcoat was brocaded green silk, and the knob on his cane looked to be gold.

"Rumor has it that you're planning to venture west again," Astor said. He never wasted much time in pleasantries or reminiscence.

"After consultation with the new president, when he's chosen. I'm bearing messages of goodwill from Bonaparte and hoping to play a role in improved ties between the United States and France."

"Tell me the truth, Gage—is your giant Norwegian lured by the fur business? Yes, I've heard of him, assembling maps and asking questions about distances and compass bearings. He's a moody sort, and people wonder what the one-eye is up to."

"He's a patriot who hopes to free Norway from the Danes. I took pity on him in Paris and offered to give him introductions in Washington. Mad as a mule milker, but with a good strong back. As for me, I've done some scouting for Bonaparte in the past, and the first consul asked me to take a peek at Louisiana. Great things are stirring that I can't talk about."

"Are they now?" His eyes were bright as a watch fob. "Bonaparte and Louisiana? Now that would be a turn, to have the French back in the North American game."

"Napoleon's curious, that's all."

"Of course he is." Astor inspected me over the rim of his cup. "I always liked your spirit, Ethan, if not your work ethic. So if you want a job after this sojourn of yours, keep count of the fur animals you see and come back to extend our enterprise. The future is in the west, Ethan—to the Columbia and beyond, all the way to China. This is the nineteenth century! Trade is global now!"

"Isn't the globe far away? The other side of it, I mean."

"A ship can take fur to China, return with tea and spices, and double your money in a year. But the fur, Ethan, the fur! That's the key."

Well, that was the one thing we were likely to actually find where we were going: not mythical hammers, but small, rank, fuzzy, and rather valuable beasts. I'd count what I could, but my recollection was that the critters were rather furtive, for good reason.

I asked about the current state of the fur trade, dominated by Montreal's North West Company.

"Four nations are vying for empire: Britain,

France, Spain, and the United States. The English have the very best furs in Canada, blast them, and the Illinois country is being trapped out. The real fortunes are going to be made west of the Mississippi. The United States must confine the British to Canada or they'll take it all! Between the North West Company and the Hudson's Bay Company, they dominate. But Louisiana! That's the real question. Who will control America to the Pacific? Which is why I looked you up, Ethan, even though I'm a busy man, very busy indeed. You're in danger, you know."

"If you mean Bloodhammer's enemies . . ."

"I don't know who they are or what they want, but rumors are rife that bad sorts have their eye on you. Millions of square miles are at stake, and a man who has worked for the British, the French, and the Americans in turn is in a position to make a difference—and have foes. You're quite the momentary celebrity, Ethan Gage, but lie low, lie low. New York can be a dangerous, brutal city."

"Anyone who meets me knows I mean no harm."

"Anyone you meet could *do* you harm. That's a fact. I understand you have a rifle?"

"Made by a craftsman in Jerusalem."

"Keep it as close as a frontiersman, Ethan. Keep it as ready as a Minute Man."

CHAPTER 12

Not knowing how to explain the Norwegian and his odd theories, I took him to dinners and balls as an example of an oversized Scandinavian idealist come to see democracy in action.

"So you're a man of liberty yourself, Mr., er, Bloodhammer?"

"The Danes are our British," he would growl.

"And you hope to emulate our republic?"

"I want to be the Norwegian Washington."

When I confided Astor's warning he took to wearing his map case like an arrow quiver everywhere we went, and with his eye patch, his cloak, and a new cane topped with an ivory unicorn's head, its horn a steel protuberance, he was inconspicuous as a rooster in a henhouse. "We should go west *now*," he insisted.

"We can't in the dead of winter."

In February word finally came that a president

had indeed been chosen. "Ethan, shouldn't we be journeying on to Washington?" Magnus pressed.

"Exploration needs money," I said as I dealt another hand of faro, which I was playing along with piquet, basset and whist. "Talleyrand's silver dollars are already half-gone." Like so many men, I consistently ignored the good advice I gave others, particularly about gambling. But my real reason for stalling was that we'd recently been given hospitality, thanks to my minor fame, in the home of one Angus Philbrick. He had a young German serving girl with braids that bounced on her breasts like drumsticks, and I suspected she'd be a fine bed-warmer if I had just a day or two more to practice diplomacy. The fact that I knew no German, or she English, seemed an advantage.

It's true that Magnus and I had been experiencing a curious run of bad luck I blamed on coincidence. There was a sausage cart that somehow got away from its donkey and almost ran us down. Then a fire in a hotel that led to Philbrick's offer of temporary shelter. We'd slipped on a midnight sheet of ice from a carelessly spilled bucket, our downhill skid arrested only by the horn of Bloodhammer's cane, which sent up a shower of sparks. Hooded figures coming up to presumably assist us took one look at the potential weapon in the fist of my hulking, one-eyed companion and disappeared.

"I think we've been followed," Magnus concluded.

"Across the ocean? You're daft, man."

That night, however, when I arranged for

Gwendolyn to come to my room and tidy up when the others were abed, our Manhattan sojourn came to an abrupt end. She arrived as promised, and performed as hoped, and I had drifted off when something—the click of the door and the scrape of heavy furniture, perhaps—startled me awake. Gwendolyn's place beside me was cooling, and there was an odd smell to the air. I slipped on my nightshirt, went to the door, but couldn't pull it inward: it felt like the latch on the other side was tied to a dresser or chest jammed against the outer wall. I sniffed. Sulfur? I looked more closely. Smoke was drifting from under my bed.

The window was stuck fast, too, and my long-rifle and tomahawk were gone!

Gwendolyn clearly had not finished as sleepy as I had, and had actually been quite busy, the cunning trollop. With no time to think, I picked up a heavy crockery washbasin, swung it to smash the glass and sash of my locked window, and dove headfirst toward the backyard. I managed to roll as I came down, cartwheeling into cold snow, and came up bearing the durable basin as a shield.

"Ethan!"

I looked toward the kitchen door and there was Magnus Bloodhammer, twirling his cane overhead and looking straight at me as if to attack. Was *he* my enemy? I crouched, holding out the basin as meager protection and then it exploded in my hands—but not from his cane, which went whickering overhead. I dimly realized a shot had come from somewhere, and then there was a surprised grunt and I turned to see a black-clad assailant pitch backward into the necessary house, a pistol dropped, and the point of Bloodhammer's walking stick stuck fast between the bastard's neck and shoulder. As he crashed down into the outhouse, I saw the flare of another fuse.

"What in Hades?"

There were twin roars. Behind me my bedroom erupted in a gout of flame, glass, and brick, making me crouch even more, and then poor Philbrick's necessary house blew up in thunderous counterpoint, sending skyward a fountain of slivers, my would-be assassin's body parts, and sewage. I tucked into a ball between the two blasts. Debris, much of it odoriferous, rained down to pock-mark the snow and spatter me with offal. Feathers from my destroyed mattress drifted down like flakes, sticking to my nightshirt and hair in each spot I was splattered with shit. I realized that my enemies had intended to be thorough. If the bedroom bomb could not be set, I was to have met my maker when I mounted the outhouse throne.

Though half-deaf, I could hear dogs barking and bells ringing.

Before I could do something more productive about my situation—like run—Magnus appeared again, waving my longrifle. I cringed, but he didn't shoot me.

"I charged her with a poker and she dropped this after she missed her shot and hit your basin," he explained. "You've used up three lives in thirty seconds! Plus my perfectly good cane!"

"I thought I'd performed with her better than *that*," I said with numb wonder, shaking at my near-escape. I tottered toward him, my bare feet freezing and my body covered with feathers, and he began laughing. My assassins may not have killed me, but they had certainly finished off my dignity.

"You look like a drowned chicken!" my companion said. "You need more care than a three-legged dog!"

"I wonder if the lovely Gwendolyn was really speaking German. Maybe it was Danish." I brushed at the feathers.

"Too late to ask her. She ran to some horsemen and galloped away."

A flabbergasted Philbrick was looking out at us from the gaping new hole in the side of his house.

"Maybe it's time to get on to Washington, after all," I said.

CHAPTER 13

Our hurried departure was in late February, shortly after Jefferson's election in the House on the thirty-sixth ballot—a contest so drawn out and nefarious that it resulted in proposals to amend the Constitution. Burr would be vice president after all, and both men would be inaugurated on March 4. I kept notes because Napoleon would press me for details. He was as curious about our democracy as he was skeptical.

"Magnus, do you really think Danish assassins trailed us here?" I asked, looking warily back as our hastily hired stagecoach rolled out of New York before Philbrick recovered wit enough to bring suit. "It's not like we've found anything to prove your claims. Why bother? And why me instead of you?"

"They could be church agents," he said, ticking the possibilities off on his fingers, "believing you a pagan blasphemer by association. If it's the Danes, they assume you're my guide and easier to finish off than a true warrior like me. The British, of course, will suspect you as an agent of the French. The American Federalists think you a Republican, while the Republicans are whispering that I bought too many maps from the disgraced Tory book-seller Gaine. French royalists no doubt believe you a Bonapartist, while French revolutionary veterans might want to seek some measure of revenge for your defense of Acre against their comrades. The Spanish probably want to delay your announce-ment about the change in ownership of Louisiana, and all the powers fear I'll prove Norway has first claim to the continent. Who *cares* who's after us? The sooner we get protection from your young government, the better."

The trip south over the rock, rut, and root of American highways was travel's typical misery. We shared our coach squeezed shoulder to shoulder with six other male passengers smelling of tobacco, onions, and wet wool, and at the end of winter the road was a wreck. Puddles were the size of small lakes and brooks had swollen into rivers. At the Delaware, we ferried.

The landscape was a somber brown quilt of win-ter farms and woodlots. At least twice a day we passengers would be commanded to shoulder the wheel to get us unstuck, and our privy was what-ever brush we were near when need struck our driver. We'd shamble out, stiff and cold, to piss in line like a chorus. The inns were squalid, all the men having to share beds and all the beds sharing rooms. Magnus and I squeezed onto a tick mat-tress no wider than a trestle table, with four other beds in our dormitory besides. The crammed bodies provided the sole heat. My bedmate snored, as did half the company, but did not turn overmuch, and he was always solicitous enough to ask if I had enough room. (There was no point to stating the obvious: "No.") Exhaustion brought me blessed unconsciousness each midnight, and then the innkeeper would rouse us for breakfast in darkness at six. Philadelphia is supposed to be a two-day journey from New York, but it took us three.

"Do you really want to be Norway's Washington?" I asked my companion once to break the tedium. "It sounds like the kind of ambition Napoleon boasts of."

"That was just flattery for you Americans."

"So what *is* your modest goal, Magnus?"

He smiled. "Immodest. To be much *more* than Washington."

Eccentrics always aim high. "More how?"

"With what we seek. To reform the world, good men have to have the power to control it."

"How do you know you're good?" This is a more complicated question than many people admit, in my opinion, since results don't always match intentions.

"Forn Sior enlists the righteous and grooms the good. We try to be knights ourselves in ethics and purpose. We're inspired by the best of the past."

"Not tilting at windmills, I hope."

"People call quests quixotic as if to ridicule them, but to me it's a compliment. Purpose, perseverance, purity. Believe me, it will be worth the hardship to get there."

In Philadelphia I was regarded as somewhat the prodigal son, having many years before unwisely deflowered one Annabelle Gaswick and fled to an apprenticeship in Paris with Benjamin Franklin, who offered refuge, thanks to his Masonic connections with my father. I'd managed to spend my meager inheritance in six months of gambling, but now I'd returned with a measure of notoriety: a hero of sorts, bridge between nations!

"We thought you a rascal, but you have some of your sire's character after all."

"None of his sense," I admitted.

"Yet you know men like Bonaparte and Smith and Nelson."

"Franklin's mentorship allowed me to travel in high circles."

"Ah, Franklin. Now *there* was a man!"

We were stalled two days in Delaware by late snow, and then reached Baltimore a wearying five days after leaving Philadelphia.

"We're close, are we not?" Bloodhammer finally asked crankily. "This is a big country you've invented here."

"You've seen but the smallest fraction. Are you beginning to wonder if your Norsemen could have marched as far as your map claims?"

"Not marched, but rowed, paddled. Sailed."

The road to the new city of Washington was little more than a track. Gone were the neat farms of Pennsylvania, and the woods between Chesapeake Bay's principal city and the new seat of government were as raw as Kentucky. Our way would open to a clearing of stumps and corn, with shack cabin and ragged children, and then close up again into a tunnel of trees. Some homesteads were attended by two or three slaves, and while Magnus had seen Negroes in Paris and New York, he was fascinated by their ubiquity and misery here. They made up, I knew, more than a fifth of my nation.

"They're black as coal!" he'd exclaim. "And the rags . . . how can they work outside dressed like that?"

"How can an ox work without an overcoat?" said one of our coachmates, a Virginia planter with a whiskey-reddened nose and gnawed pipe he never actually lit. "The Negro is different than you and I, sir, with smaller brain and broader shoulders. They're as fit for the field as a mule. You might as well worry about the birds of the air!"

"Birds can fly where they wish."

The planter laughed. "You have wit, sir! You have wit! And our darkies are as content as a good milker, following the path to the barn each night. They are certainly more content than they look, I assure you. They have longings, but only for the belly, music, and the bed. It's a favor we've done, bringing them here. Saved their souls, we have."

"Yet they don't seem grateful." Magnus, I'd observed, had a sly way of getting to the heart of an issue, and his eye would take on Odin's gleam.

"God has made the order of things plain, sir," the planter said, looking flustered. "The Indian has done nothing with America, and the black man nothing with Africa. The Negro harnessed and the Indian confined—both for their own good!"

I was too much the Pennsylvanian, exposed to

Quaker beliefs, to accept this nonsense. "How can Americans claim to be free when some of us are in fetters?"

"As I told you, sir, they are not us." He looked annoyed. "You have contracted liberal ideas in France, but stay with us here in the South and you'll see what I mean. Washington knew. So does our new president. All things, and all men, in their place." Then he turned his head to end the conversation, looking out the coach window at the endless trees. I could hear branches clawing at the top of our vehicle as we creaked on, the driver halting occasionally to chop the worst away.

I began to fear we were lost when we finally hailed a passing black freeman with a box of carpenter tools, and asked him where America's capital was.

"Why, you's in it!" he replied. "You passed the boundary stone half a mile back."

I looked out. There were two farms, a pile of cleared slash smoking from a desultory fire, and a split-rail fence that seemed to contain nothing.

The Negro pointed. "That way to the Big House!"

We came to the crest of a low hill and saw the awkward infancy of Washington. Four months after its occupation by the three hundred and fifty clerks of the federal government, my nation's capital was a cross between swampy wilderness and ludicrous grandeur. Mud avenues broad enough for a Roman legion cut diagonally across farm, forest, and marsh, extending grandly from nothing to nothing. Beyond, the broad Potomac glinted. There were thousands of stumps, still bright yellow, and three hundred brick and wooden houses thrown like dice on a plan a hundred times bigger than required. I'd heard the district for this city was ten miles square, but why? A decade after the start of construction, all of Washington had just three thousand inhabitants.

The houses, poking up from muddy yards paved with sawdust, led like crumbs toward a neighboring village called Georgetown, far away on the Potomac. There was a small port there, and more homes across the river on the Virginia side. The four official buildings in Washington were preposterously imposing and oddly isolated from each other. These, I was to learn, were the President's House, Congress, the Treasury, and the War Department. Most of the legislators lived in a cluster of rooming houses and hotels between the capitol building and the president's house along a road called Pennsylvania Avenue, still not entirely cleared of stumps. I suppose Washington will grow into itself—institutions have a way of evolving to serve their employees instead of the other way around, and any intelligent clerk will hire yet more clerks, to make himself a foreman—but still, it seemed laughably grandiose. The only good news was that the place was so empty it would be hard for assassins to sneak up on us.

"It's as stupefying as Versailles, but in completely the opposite way," I murmured. "There's nothing here."

"No," Magnus insisted, leaning excitedly out the coach window. "Look at the angles those avenues cut. This is sacred Masonic architecture, Ethan!"

CHAPTER 14

Sacred Masonic architecture, it turned out, was a street pattern that appeared—if studied on a map—to make Pythagorean triangles, stars, and pentagrams of the type I'd seen in Masonic lodges and documents. Given that the geometry could really only be grasped on paper and that the "avenues" were little more than tracks, I failed to see any mystical significance.

"Magnus, this architecture of yours is no different than the stars and patterns I saw in Egypt and the Holy Land."

"Exactly! Look, there's the new Capitol, its cornerstone laid in a Masonic ceremony, facing a mall like a new Versailles. And at an angle to them, connected by an avenue to make a right triangle, the President's House! See how the streets echo the Masonic symbols of square, compass, and rule? And did not the colonies themselves total the mystical number 13?"

"But there're sixteen states now."

"They rose as one when there were thirteen. Surely it is no coincidence, Ethan, that the cornerstone of the executive mansion was laid by high-ranking Freemasons, led by Washington himself, on October 13, 1792?"

"Coincidence of what? No, let me calculate . . . ah, the four hundred and eighty-third anniversary of Black Friday, you're going to tell me, when the Templars were crushed. But isn't it more likely that it was three hundred years and a day after the landing of Columbus?"

"But why add that day?"

I shrugged. "Maybe it rained."

"You're being naïve! Or intentionally obtuse. Why the thirteenth instead of the twelfth? Because thirteen has always been sacred. It is the number of lunar months in a year, the number of attendees at the Last Supper, the number of days after our savior's birth that the magi appeared before the baby Jesus, and the age at which the Jews considered a child to become an adult. It is the number of Norse gods when Loki invaded their banquet and slew Balder with a shaft of poisoned mistletoe. The Egyptians believed there were thirteen steps between life and death, just as the English put thirteen steps to the gallows. Thirteen is a Fibonacci sequence number. In the Tarot, the thirteenth card in the Major Arcana is Death. And thirteen because now the Templars' Freemason descendents are building a new nation on the continent the Templars saw as their refuge and repository. Half your revolutionary generals were Masons! Your own mentor Franklin, who helped draft your Declaration of Independence and Constitution, was a Freemason! All this is coincidence? No, Ethan. Your new nation's destiny is to stretch west, my friend: west to discover the sacred relics that Norse Templars left for them, as the foundation to a better world!"

"You believe this because of a street plan for a capital that hasn't even been built yet?"

"I believe it because destiny brought you and me together, here in the utopian wilderness, to follow my sacred map to the end. Fate is our ally."

"Utopian wilderness? You're quite mad, Bloodhammer."

He grinned. "So was Columbus. So was Washington when he challenged the world's biggest empire. So was your Franklin, flying his kite in a lightning storm. Only the mad get things done."

◻   ◻   ◻

Despite a rusticity that would have made a French aristocrat laugh, flags to celebrate the inauguration were everywhere. Patriotic bunting hung from roofs, and visiting carriages were jammed hub-to-hub under hastily erected plank sheds. Several cannon sat poised for celebration, and militia drilled. Magnus and I sent word we wished to meet with Jefferson and that I bore tidings from France, but any audience had to wait until he took office. So on the morning of March 4 we awakened at Blodgett's Hotel to a breakfast of biscuits, honey, cold ham, and tea, dressed as formally as we were able, and hurried to the Capitol. Adams had already sourly crept out of town at four that morning, unable to bear the sight of the political enemy who'd defeated him.

Only the Senate side of the Capitol was finished. A planned lobby and squat dome was still a gaping hole in the middle, and the Representatives' chamber lacked a roof. Magnus and I found seats in a Senate gallery jammed with a thousand spectators like a Greek theater, the place smelling of paint and plaster. The construction was so hastily done that there were already stains on the ceiling from roof leaks, and wallpaper was starting to peel in the corners. Two fireplaces threw smoky heat, unnecessary given the throng.

No matter, the chatter was excited and proud. A hotly contested election like that of 1800 was something new in the world, as different from Napoleon's coup d'état as a feather from a rock. Vice President–elect Aaron Burr, restlessly ambitious but restrained this day, took the oath of office first. I was curious to see him because he'd been compared to Napoleon. He was dark like the Corsican, and handsome, too—both conquered the ladies. Given his reputation for ambition I expected him to try to steal the stage from Jefferson, but in fact he was a model of frustrated restraint, greeting the chief justice and then taking a seat behind the podium to scan the crowd with sharp eyes, as if trolling for additional votes. His expectant pose communicated that Jefferson's triumph was but a momentary setback in his own inevitable rise to the presidency.

And then with a thump of cannon and a swirl of fife and drum, Jefferson arrived from his boarding house, walking like a common man because there were still too many stumps for a grand procession of coaches. He entered in a plain dark suit, without the powdered hair and ceremonial sword of Washington and Adams, and without cape, scepter, or courtiers. He was tall, red-haired, handsome in a ruddy, country way—and taken aback by the crowd. After a quick glance to the galleries he shyly focused on the papers he held in his fists, licking his lips.

"He doesn't like to give speeches," one of Adams's outgoing cabinet ministers whispered to a lady friend.

"Good. I don't like to sit through them," she whispered back.

My first reaction was disappointment. Jefferson was almost as much a hero in France as my mentor Franklin, but I was used to the command and bluster of Napoleon. The sage of Monticello was unexpectedly diffident before an audience, with a scholar's bent posture and a voice soft and high as a woman's. I could see his sheen of sweat, the windows checkering the inauguration with light and shadow. Chief Justice John Marshall gestured and the new president began to read, his voice firm but quiet.

"Why doesn't he speak up?" Bloodhammer asked, and the Norwegian's baritone carried so well that everyone briefly looked at us instead of the new president. Jefferson, thankfully, seemed not to notice and plowed on while we strained to listen.

We relied on the reprints in newspapers to clarify what we did hear, and yet the Virginian's famed intelligence shone through. After a bitter and nasty election, he assured that "we are all republicans, we are all federalists," and called for a "wise and frugal government" directed not by ministers but by the American people. The federal government should be small, and civilians masters of the military. Napoleon would laugh at such sentiments and I began to realize just how extraordinary, how revolutionary, this quietly confident man really was.

The blood of the American Revolution, he said, had been shed for freedom of religion, freedom of the press, and the right to fair trial, and these were "the creed of our political faith." Jefferson made it sound so extraordinary that I found myself blushing over my long stay in France. Well, I was home now! No guillotines here!

So was the entire idea of my country planted by shadowy Templars and secretive Freemasons? Was the extraordinary idealism of my nation an accident of geography, or did it really have something to do with dim Norse history? I knew Jefferson was no Freemason, and not even a Christian in the traditional sense: he was a freethinking deist elected because a majority of his countrymen didn't go to church either, despite my nation's Puritan origins. It seemed obvious in 1801 that religion was dying before science and rationality, and would be entirely gone by 1901. So how could there be a whiff of ancient secrets and musty gods in this bright new American world? Or was America simply a place where every man, even Magnus Bloodhammer, could read his own desires onto what was still mostly an empty map?

Jefferson finished, the rattle of polite, somewhat puzzled applause died—"What did he say?" people whispered—and then Marshall administered the oath of office. The new president walked quietly back to Conrad and McMunn's, where he waited like every other boarder for a chair for dinner. He would not follow Adams into the President's House for another two weeks, because he wanted modifications done.

¤   ¤   ¤

As was my custom, I lived—while we waited for an official audience—on my modest fame, my skill at cards, and my affability, making friends by telling stories of an Egypt and Jerusalem my listeners couldn't hope to see. I also kept an eye out for menacing strangers and an ear ready for rumor. Oddly, the threat seemed to have disappeared: there were no narrow escapes, no skulking strangers. Magnus busied himself by studying his texts of Indian legends and making lists of supplies for our expedition west and, not as trusting as me, put up makeshift bars across our hotel door and windows.

"Maybe we frightened the villains off," I theorized.

"Or maybe they wait where we're going."

While my colleague studied, I cultivated an air of importance, trading on my connections to Bonaparte and Talleyrand. More than one Washington

damsel hinted that she was available if I was interested in permanent disciplined domesticity but I
was not, trying out the whores who served Congress instead. One adventuress, Susannah by name,
said she'd made it to Washington one week after
the clerks and two weeks before the first lawmak-
ers, and it was the best relocation she'd ever made.
"They seems able to get a dollar from the government whenever they need," she explained, "and the
most of them don't take more than half the hour to
finish off."

Businessmen, meanwhile, tried to reform me.

"Now then, Gage, we aren't getting any younger,
are we?" a banker named Zebulon Henry put it to
me one day.

"Aging does annoy me."

"We all have to think about the future, do we
not?"

"I worry about it all the time."

"That's why investments that compound are just
the thing for a man like you."

"Investments that what?"

"Compound! As your investment grows, you
earn money not just on your original sum, but its
growth as well. In twenty or thirty years it can
work financial miracles."

"Twenty or thirty years?" It was an abyss of
time nearly inconceivable.

"Suppose you were to take a job with a firm like
mine. Ledger clerk to begin, but possibility for a
man of your ambition and talent. And let's say you
invest ten percent of earnings as I advise, and don't
touch it until, ah, age sixty. Here, lean in and we'll

do the arithmetic. You could purchase some property, take on some debt, let your wife supplement with mending or washing until the children are old enough to contribute . . ."

"I do *not* have a wife."

"Details, details." He was scribbling. "I say, Gage, even a man with as tardy a start as you—what *have* you been doing with your life?—could have a respectable estate by, say . . ." he pondered a moment. "1835."

"Imagine that."

"It requires punctuality and consistency, of course. No raiding the nest egg. A smart marriage, work six days a week, business contacts on the Sabbath, hard study in the evenings—we could develop a plan that makes sense even for someone as improvident as you. The magic of compounding interest, sir. The magic of compounding interest."

"But this involves work, does it not?"

"Damn hard work. Damn hard! But there's joy in a job well done!"

I smiled as if in agreement. "Just as soon as I see the president."

"The president! Remarkable man! Remarkable. But by rumor not all that financially prudent himself. Spends beyond his means, what? Word has it he's ordering bric-a-brac for Monticello out of excitement with his new executive salary while retaining no real financial understanding. The man, like most Virginians, is chronically in debt! Chronically, sir!"

"I hope he doesn't want a loan from me."

"Mention my advice, Gage. Tell him how I've

helped *you*. I could straighten Jefferson out, I'm sure of it. Discipline! That's the only secret."

"If our talk turns to money, I will."

He beamed. "See how men in high places help each other?"

I knew Zebulon Henry meant well, of course . . . but to live your brief life for compound interest seemed wrong somehow. I'm a man cursed with the compulsion to toss the dice, to bet all on the main chance, to listen to dreamers. I believe in luck and opportunity. Why else was I allied with Bloodhammer? Why else did I orbit Napoleon?

Magnus did say this hammer, if it existed, might be worth money, or power, or *something*. So treasure hunting was an investment of another kind, was it not? It's not that I'm lazy, just easily bored. I like novelty. I'm curious to see what is over the next hill. So I resolved to let my lunatic have his say, nod encouragingly—and put it all in Jefferson's hands.

CHAPTER 15

The President's House, smart enough on the outside with its limestone sheen and classical decorations, was still just half-finished without and half-occupied within. The pile was a grand two-story affair, ostentatious for a democracy, with a little republican rawness provided by a plank walkway that reached the posh porch and pillars by crossing a yard of mud and sawdust like a drawbridge. The house had two rows of ten grand windows each on the north side where we entered—hellish to heat, I'd bet—and the lower row was capped by fancy narrow pediments like eyebrows. The paneled door itself was unexpectedly human-sized, not some bronze gate, and when we pulled a cord to ring its bell the modest oak was opened not by a servant but by a secretary, in plain suit. He was a shy, strapping, strong-chinned young man with prominent nose and small, thin-lipped mouth who looked out at the pillars as if surprised at his own surroundings. His hair was neatly clipped in the Roman fashion I now favored myself, and his feet were shod in moccasins.

"Howdee-do," he said in the patois of the frontier, pulling us in. "I'm Meriwether Lewis. Only arrived a few days ago from Fort Detroit and still exploring. You can make an echo in this pile. Come, come: President Jefferson is expecting you."

The entrance hall had eighteen-foot ceilings but was barren of furniture or paintings. Like the Capitol, it still smelled of paint. Directly ahead was a paneled door leading into a rather elegant but empty oval room, its windows framing a view of the Potomac. Lewis led us to the right, past stairs that I assumed led up to the president's private quarters, and into a smaller salon with a couch and side table. "I'll tell him you've arrived." The secretary stepped through another door with the stride of a hunter, his experience as a frontier soldier obvious.

Magnus looked about. "Your president isn't much for furniture, is he?"

"Jefferson's only just moved in, and Adams lived here only a few months. It's a challenge to decide what fits a republic. He's been a widower for nearly twenty years."

"He must rattle around in here like a pebble in a powder horn."

Then we heard a bird call.

A door to Jefferson's office opened and we were beckoned again. This room, in the southwest corner, was more inhabited. The mahogany floor was bare of any carpet but a long table covered with green baize occupied the room's middle, and fires burned at either end. Three of the walls were occupied by bookshelves, maps, writing tables, cabinets, and globes; the fourth was windows. One shelf bore an elephant tusk of extraordinary width, curled at its end in a peculiar manner. Others displayed arrowheads, polished stones, animal skulls, Indian clubs, and beadwork. On tables by the windows on the south side were terra-cotta pots, spring shoots just poking through the black dirt. There were also bell jars, boxes of planting soil, and, in one corner, a bird cage. Its inhabitant sang again.

"The most beautiful sound in nature," Jefferson said, rising from a chair at the table and putting a book aside. "The mockingbird inspires me while I work."

Close up, Jefferson was more commanding than he'd seemed at the inauguration: tall, with a planter's fitness, his striking red hair matching his ruddy complexion. The speech I'd heard was one of the few Jefferson would ever give; with his high voice he preferred to communicate by letter. But his eyes had a bright intelligence more arresting than any I'd seen. Napoleon had the gaze of an eagle, Nelson a hawk, Djezzar a cobra, aging Franklin a sleepy owl. Jefferson's eyes danced with curiosity, as if everything he encountered was the most interesting specimen he'd ever seen. Including us.

"I'd not expected the president's office to be a naturalist's laboratory," I said.

"My habit at Monticello is to bring the outdoors in. Nothing makes me more content than tending my geraniums. I am a student of architecture, but nature's architecture has the most pleasing proportions of all." He smiled. "So you are the hero of Mortefontaine!"

I gave a slight bow. "No hero, Mr. President. Merely a servant of my country. May I introduce my companion from Norway, Magnus Bloodhammer?"

Jefferson shook our hands. "You look like your Viking forebears, Magnus. Not entirely inappropriate for your mission, perhaps?" The American commissioners in Paris had written him of our coming, and we'd sent a note ahead ourselves explaining our quest for evidence of early Norse explorers.

"I'd be honored to emulate my ancestors," my companion said.

"Not with a war ax, I hope!" Our host had a sense of mischief. "But I admire your spirit of inquiry; it would do Franklin proud. And you, Gage, of Acre *and* Marengo? Most men are content to ride with just one side. How do you keep it all straight?"

"I have odd luck. And my fame, I'm afraid, pales beside the writer of the Declaration of Independence. Few documents have so inspired men."

"Compliments all around," the president acknowledged with a nod. "Well. My gift is words and yours action, which is why I'm delighted you've come. We've much to talk about. I'm anxious to hear your impressions of France, where I, too, served—just after our revolution and before theirs. Extraordinary events since then, of course."

"Bonaparte is a meteor. But then you've done well, too."

"This house is a start, but Adams and his

architects had no sense. A privy outdoors? The man hung his laundry there too. Most undignified for a chief executive. I wouldn't move in until they installed a water closet. There are a hundred improvements needed to make this a proper place to receive dignitaries, but first I must pry out of Congress more than the $5,000 they've allotted. They have no concept of modern expenses." He looked about. "Still, there is elegance here, a balance between national pride and republican sensibility."

"The place needs furniture," Magnus said with his usual bluntness.

"It will fill up, Mr. Bloodhammer, just as our capital and country will. But enough about housekeeping! Come, good dinner makes better conversation!"

He ushered us into an adjoining dining room for our midafternoon repast, Lewis coming too. As soup was served by Negro servants, I began mentally rehearsing the carefully edited description of the Great Pyramid I typically shared, certain Jefferson would be curious about Napoleon's mystic experience in that edifice. Then a word about Jerusalem, an observation on French military success, some comments about my experience with electricity, an assessment of Bonaparte's government, something learned about one of Jefferson's wines . . .

The president sipped his soup, set down his spoon, and took me by surprise. "Gage, what do you know about mastodons?"

I'm afraid I looked blank. "Mastodon?" I cleared my throat. "Is that near Macedonia?"

"Elephants, Ethan, elephants," Magnus prompted.

"The American name is mammoth, while European scientists have suggested mastodon," Jefferson said. "It's the name scientists have given to the bones of prehistoric elephants that have been found in Russia and North America. Nearly an entire skeleton has been obtained from the Hudson Valley, and many bones from the Ohio. They dwarf the modern kind. Perhaps you noticed my tusk?"·

"Ah. Franklin mentioned this once. Woolly elephants in America. You know, Hannibal used elephants." I was trying to hide my ignorance.

"Just one mastodon would fill this room to the ceiling. They must have been extraordinary creatures, majestic and magnificent, with tusks like a curved banister."

"I suppose so. I encountered a lion once in the Holy Land . . ."

"A mere kitten," Jefferson said. "I have the claws of a prehistoric lion of truly terrifying stature. For some curious reason, the animals of the past were bigger than those now. As for mastodons, no live specimen has been encountered, but then our cold, heavily wooded landscape is not the landscape for elephants, is it?"

"Certainly not." I took a sip of wine. "Excellent vintage. Is this Beaujolais?" I knew Jefferson was something of an obsessive when it came to the grape, and felt safer with a subject I had some practice in.

"But in the west, beyond the Mississippi, the landscape reportedly opens up. Isn't that so, Lewis?"

"That's the word from the French fur trappers

I interviewed," the young officer said. "Go far enough west, and there are no trees at all."

"Like a cold Africa, in other words," the president went on. "Home only to Indians with their primitive bows, the arrows of which must just bounce off mastodon hide. There are rumors, Gage, that the great beasts might still survive in the west. Is it possible that where civilization has not penetrated, the giant beasts of the past might still exist? What a discovery to actually find one, and even to capture it and bring it back!"

"Capture a woolly elephant?" I was not prepared for this.

"Or at least sketch one." He pushed his bowl aside. "Let's talk business." Our congenial host had revealed a new briskness. "You might expect me to be cautious about your proposal to look for Norse ancestry, but in fact I'm intrigued by it. Here is an opportunity for all of us. I can help you two look for whatever artifact you're after, and you can look for my elephants, plus any other natural wonders you might encounter. Magnus," Jefferson said, turning to my companion, "you've come to America to look for signs of Norse exploration, correct?"

"Aye. I believe my people came here in medieval times to found a utopian community and might possibly have left things of value," my companion said with the enthusiasm one gives to a newly discovered soul mate. Having braced for skepticism, he was looking at Jefferson with delight. "Ethan, who is an expert in ancient mysteries, has agreed to help me. This would mean a great deal to the pride of my people and perhaps inspire them to seek our own independence from Denmark. From the cradle of liberty I can carry liberty, perhaps."

"The ideals of America may infect the world and bring fear to tyrants everywhere, from the czars of the steppes to the pasha of Tripoli."

"I have a group, Forn Sior, dedicated to this goal. You've heard of it?"

"'Old Custom'? It really exists?" The president seemed to know more about Bloodhammer's group and mission than I did. "Why am I surprised? Look at Ethan here, always embroiled in the thick of things. I want you to see the elephant, Gage. I want you to prove it exists."

I cleared my throat. "You support, then, the idea of our going west?" I'd rather hoped he'd prohibit the entire idea and send me back to Paris.

"What wonders must lie between the Mississippi and the Pacific!" Jefferson had the dreamy tone of one who'd never been beyond the Blue Ridge, did his exploring in atlases, and would be pressed to camp in his own yard. If I sound a little cynical, well, I'd been hard-used the past three years. "All kind of strange creatures could be out there, rivaling the menagerie already found. There are also rumors of odd volcanoes far up the Missouri. There has been speculation about vast mountains of salt. Not to mention more conventional prizes, such as waterways to cross the continent and furs to supply our commerce. We've found the mouth of the Columbia, gentlemen; now we must find its beginning! Geographers speculate it is but a short portage from the source of the Missouri to the source of the Columbia."

I didn't like the prospect of volcanoes any more than room-sized mammoths. "So you want Magnus and me to find the headwaters?" I tried to confirm.

"Actually, I hope to send young Lewis here on an expedition to answer what lies between the oceans. Captain Lewis is my protégé, a lad—well, you're twenty-six now, aren't you?—who grew up about ten miles from Monticello and for the last six years has served with the First Infantry Regiment, attaining the rank of captain. I have every confidence in him. But I must persuade Congress to finance an expedition. Plus, there's a little matter of boundaries and empires. The Spanish stand in our way."

Here I could earn my dinner. "Actually, sir, it is the French."

Jefferson beamed. "Then that rumor is true as well! This is an auspicious start to my presidency."

"According to Foreign Minister Talleyrand, a secret agreement was signed the day after the Convention of Mortefontaine conveying the Louisiana Territory back to France," I confirmed. "The French asked me to inform you. That gives Napoleon Bonaparte an empire in America as big as our own United States, but he's not at all decided what to do with it. I'm to report back to Paris the condition of Louisiana."

"And report to me," Jefferson said. "We're as keen as Napoleon. You're the bridge between nations, Ethan Gage. You can serve Bonaparte and me at the same time. Are he and I at all alike?"

"In curiosity," I assured. "The first consul envisions a friendly boundary along the line of the

Mississippi and ready American access to the sea via New Orleans."

"I'm glad to hear of friendship. We've come near war with the Spanish. And yet I see the west beyond the Mississippi as the natural territory of the United States, not the European powers. If Russia can stretch to the Pacific, so can we. A single nation, Ethan, from Atlantic to Pacific!"

First mastodons, now this. "What would the United States do with all that land?"

Jefferson glanced out the west-facing windows. "Hard to imagine, I admit. I've calculated that just filling up the frontier between the Appalachians and the Mississippi will take a thousand years. Yet our population *is* growing. We have more than five million now, a third of Britain and a fifth of France, and we're gaining on those nations. That's what you must impress upon Napoleon, Gage. Mere demographics suggest American hegemony. Do not tempt him with thoughts of American empire!"

"The French remain obsessed with the British. Talleyrand asked me to scout out their designs and inquire about alliances with the Indians."

"So everyone is plotting, with Louisiana as the prize. Tell me, what kind of man *is* Bonaparte?"

I considered. "Brilliant. Forceful. Ambitious, to be sure. He sees life as a struggle and himself at war with the world. But he's also idealistic, practical, sometimes sentimental, and tied to his family, and he has a wry view of human nature. He's obsessed with his place in history. He's as hard and multifaceted as a cut diamond, Mr. President. He believes in logic and reason, and can be talked to."

"But a tough negotiator?"

"Oh, yes. And that rarest of men: he knows what he wants."

"Which is?"

"Glory. And power for its own sake."

"The old tyrant dream. What I want is human happiness, which I believe comes from independence and self-reliance. Right, Lewis?"

The frontier officer smiled. "So you have told me."

"Happiness comes from the land," Jefferson lectured. "The independent yeoman farmer is the happiest of all men—and the need for land justifies our need for expansion. For democracy to work, Gage, men must be farmers. If Greece and Rome taught us anything, it is that. Once we cluster in cities we become slaves to a few, and the American experiment is finished. Land, land—that's the key, isn't it Lewis? Land!"

"There's no shortage of that in the west," the secretary said. "Of course, it's occupied by Indians."

"And now we have a Norwegian, Magnus Bloodhammer, who wants to explore it. Indians, bears, wolves—none of that daunts you, does it, Magnus? What is so fascinating that you take such risk?"

"That America's social experiment in fact started with Norwegians," my companion said. "My ancestors sought refuge here first."

"You really think Vikings preceded us all on this continent?"

"Not just Vikings, but Norsemen. There's evidence they came here in the fourteenth century, nearly one hundred fifty years before Columbus."

"What evidence?"

Magnus shoved his china aside and took out his map from his cylinder. Once more I wondered what was in the compartment that must be at the cylinder's end. "You'll see the significance immediately," he said, unrolling the chart. "This was found in a knight's tomb in a medieval church, meaning it was drawn about 1360. Is this coastline mere coincidence?"

Jefferson stood, peering. "By the soul of Mercator, it looks like Hudson Bay."

Lewis came around the table to look and nodded. "Remarkable, if true."

"Of course it's true," Magnus assured.

My mind was caught on the president's comment of Indians, bears, and wolves. Yet instead of the mockery I'd half expected, the other three had formed a little triumvirate. "I'm surprised you're not more surprised," I said.

"At what?" Lewis asked.

I gestured to the map. "At what may be one of the most startling historical finds of all time. The Norse before Columbus? You believe it?"

Jefferson and Lewis looked at each other. "There have been rumors," Lewis said.

"Rumors of what? Tigers as well as elephants?"

"Of blue-eyed Indians, Mr. Gage," Jefferson said. "Pierre Gaultier de La Verendrye reported them when he explored the lower Missouri River in 1733. He came across a tribe called the Mandans, who live in communities reminiscent of northern European habitation in medieval times. A dry moat, stockade, and wooden houses. They farm instead of roam. And some of them are surprisingly fair in coloring, with their leaders sporting beards. Never heard of an Indian with a beard."

"There's also an old legend that a Prince Madoc of Wales set out from Britain to the west in 1170 with ten ships, never to return," Lewis explained. "The names Mandan and Madoc are enough alike to make one wonder if the legend could somehow be true."

"Wait. The *Welsh* got to the middle of America?"

Jefferson shrugged. "It's a possibility. The Mississippi and Missouri, or the Saint Lawrence and the Great Lakes, or the Nelson and Red rivers from Hudson's Bay—all could lead wanderers to the general area of the Mandan, the center of our continent."

"I've seen fair-eyed Indians myself at Kaskaskia, in the Illinois country," Lewis said. "General George Rogers Clark has reported the same. Where did they come from?"

"Mr. President, I believe past men of power in your country wouldn't have been entirely surprised at my information either," Magnus interrupted. "Many, like Washington or Franklin, are or were Freemasons—true?"

"Yes. But not me, Bloodhammer."

"Still, if these leaders were your friends, you know of Masonic ties to the persecuted Knights Templar," he insisted.

I groaned inwardly. We were about to lose any credibility.

"Is it possible Templars fled to America?" Magnus went on. "And created a utopian idea that is being recreated, even here in your new capital? These are very grand buildings and avenues for a new nation. And your streets make intriguing patterns to anyone familiar with the sacred geometry of the east."

"Simply modern planning." The president looked guarded.

"No. The United States was created for a purpose, I'm certain of it. A secret purpose. I think it was to recreate a golden age long lost, an age of gods and magic."

"But why would you think that?"

"This city, for one. When it was founded, when cornerstones were laid, its size. And because of that." He pointed to the hammer symbol on his map.

"What is that, Magnus?"

"It's a symbol for the hammer of the god Thor."

"You think you'll find Thor in America?"

"No, just his legacy."

I expected Jefferson to have us packed off to a madhouse, but his bright eyes flashed with more understanding than I was comfortable with. "His legacy? How interesting. Well, I'm a scholar of the past myself, with quite the library. I've read of your Forn Sior, and more besides. We don't know just *what* lies beyond, do we, or who walked there? Pale Indians. Prehistoric beasts. Rumors of violent weather unknown in Europe. Medicine men warning of baleful spirits. I am not certain of any of it, gentlemen. But I am curious. I'm curious."

Magnus said nothing. I, meanwhile, was realizing why I was reluctant to leave New York. Baleful spirits?

"The Welsh are one possibility," Jefferson said. "That you two have given us another just strengthens the possibility that Verendrye was not exaggerating. What if a lost colony of Welshmen, or Norsemen, interbred with the native population and persists as a tribe living in walled towns somewhere up the Missouri? Alternately, there are theories that some of the lost tribes of Israel might have somehow made their way to America and provided the ancestry of the American Indian. And tales that the Carthaginians defeated by Rome might have fled across the Atlantic to escape the sack of their city."

"Yes!" said Magnus. He nodded at me.

"Plato wrote of a lost Atlantis, and the astronomer Corli has contemplated its location. Indians say tobacco grows where the hairs of a burning god fell from the sky. Is the bloodline of King David or Hannibal roaming the western desert? All these groups might have forgotten their origins. But if it could be proven, the stakes are significant."

"How so?" I asked.

"European empires in the New World are based in part on claims of first arrival," Lewis explained. "If it turns out the first arrivals from Europe were other groups entirely, it undermines the legitimacy of British, French, and Spanish claims to land ownership."

"Which could improve the chances of United States' claim or purchase," Jefferson said. "Our expanding population gives us the possibility of ownership by occupation, but that can lead to wars we don't want. A sale is preferable, from a party whose past claim is in historical doubt. If the Norse came first, it could shake world politics. The important thing is that we learn the truth, and ideally learn it before the French, Spanish, or British do. That, gentlemen, is why you can count on my support for your scouting expedition—but only if you confide to me. I trust your first loyalty is to your home country, Ethan?"

"Of course." Actually, it was to self-preservation, but that seemed down the list of everyone else's priorities.

"What you learn will, I hope, provide information that Captain Lewis will expand on, if I can persuade Congress to send a more ambitious quest."

"How ambitious?"

Jefferson shrugged. "Perhaps twenty to forty men and several tons of supplies."

"Impressive. And how many men will accompany my expedition?"

"Why, just one, I believe. Magnus Bloodhammer."

The Norwegian beamed.

"One?"

"I want you two to go swiftly and silently, scouts before an army."

"What supplies, then?"

"I'm prepared to furnish one hundred dollars and a letter of introduction to the newly acquired American forts at Detroit and Michilimackinac, asking for escort. I suggest you travel as far west as you can on the Great Lakes before starting overland. With luck, you can finish your exploration within the season and report back, and we can refine our strategy for both Lewis's expedition and dealing with Napoleon. If you survive."

I took a big swallow of wine. "I was hoping for more help."

"I've just started in office and Adams left a mess. It's the best America can do. Fortunately, Gage, you're a patriot!"

"Meaning anything valuable you find is properly the property of the United States," Lewis added.

"Not if it's not on American soil," Magnus countered. "And the Norse went farther than any American yet has. Which means it is Norwegian soil . . . *gentlemen*." It was amazing how much force he packed into that last word.

Jefferson smiled. Magnus had taken the bait. "Then you *do* think you'll find something valuable, even priceless, that is tangible *proof* of Norse exploration?"

"Yes, and such artifacts by right are mine and my country's. And Ethan's. Am I not correct, Gage?"

"Rusty trifles only," I hastily assured. "Old spearheads. A rivet here, a stud there." No need to talk about magical hammers that might be worth a king's ransom.

"I want to back an explorer, not a treasure hunter, Gage."

I pretended mild indignation. "It seems to me we've earned your trust. I've secretly carried word of the French-Spanish treaty on Louisiana. Magnus here has shared a map of incalculable value.

We've confided in you, Mr. President, and only ask that you return our confidence."

"Well said. We're all partners here, gentlemen, in one of the greatest adventures in history. So I leave you to it. Your only competitors are the British in Canada, the French and Spanish in Louisiana, howling wilderness, gigantic animals, and hostile Indian tribes. Nothing more than what you've faced a dozen times before, eh?"

"Actually, I think we might need two hundred dollars."

"Come back alive, with useful information, and I'll pay *three* hundred. But a hundred to start. I know a sharpshooter like you will want to live off the land!"

It was dark when we left, my head full of woolly elephants, lurking Indians, baleful spirits, mountains of salt, and the usual dubious state of my finances. Well, I was in it now. "You found a fellow visionary, Magnus," I said as we stood outside looking at the candles in the President's House. "I expected more skepticism."

"Jefferson wants to use us, Ethan, just like Bonaparte uses us. As we use them! So we'll see their Louisiana and let them fight over it if they wish." There was a tone of hard realism in his voice, very different from my usual Norwegian dreamer. "As for you and me, if we find Thor's hammer we'll have a chance to change the entire world!" His eyes were dark and gleaming in the twilight.

"Change the world? I thought we just wanted to profit from it."

"Restore it. There's more at stake here than you think."

"Restore what?"

He patted his map case. "The human heart."

And I wondered again just who my new companion really was.

CHAPTER 16

For our journey west, Magnus chose a musket that could be used as a fowling piece and a huge double-bladed ax that he strapped to his back like a Norse marauder. "Jefferson gave me the idea!" He spent happy hours shining it with file, oil, and cloth. "With this and that little tomahawk of yours, we'll have no problem making a fire."

"Make a fire? That ax is big enough to heat hell, deforest half the Ohio Valley, or serve as a dining table."

"If I ever shaved it would make a good mirror, too." He held it up for inspection. "I wish I had a broadsword." He was as excited as I was dubious.

Our route was northwestward up the Potomac and across the Appalachians on the road first carved out by the British general Braddock before his disastrous defeat during the French and Indian War. Then we'd go down to Pittsburgh at the confluence of the Monongahela and Allegheny rivers, take the Ohio River to the Great Trail established by the Indians to Lake Erie, and board a boat to Fort Detroit, five hundred miles from Washington. From there, Lakes Huron and Superior would provide a water route of another five hundred miles to the edge of the blank wilderness on Bloodhammer's map.

The first artifact of civilization that disappeared as we rode up the Potomac was paint. As we ascended the mountains, farmhouses faded to weathered wood; milled lumber gave way to squared logs. Our road followed an undulating scar of vegetable plots, trampled pasture, and wounded hillsides of stumps and slash. No firmer than porridge, it curved and coiled tighter than a barrister's argument and was worn to a trench by traffic that never paused to repair it. Always we smelled smoke, hardscrabble farmers trying to burn back the forest to make room for corn. And then, deep in the mountains, finally there were no farms at all. Winter-barren brown ridges, the tops still frosty most mornings, ran like multiple walls into haze. Hawks orbited by day, and wolves howled in the dark. When the wind blew, the brown carpet of last winter's leaves rustled like tattered pages. It sounded like the forest was whispering.

We slept outdoors when the weather was fair, hardening ourselves to our new lives as frontiersmen and avoiding the stiff fees and biting fleas of Appalachian accommodation. We'd make a bed of boughs, have a simple dinner of ham, cornbread, and creek water, and listen to the night sounds. Through the lattice of slowly budding trees, we had a spangled canopy of a million dazzling stars. Magnus and I talked sometimes of the ancient belief that each was an ancestor, gone to reside in the sky for all eternity.

"Maybe one is Signe," he said, wistful.

"How long were you married?"

"Just one year." He paused before going on. "The only time I've truly been happy. I loved her as a youth, but my family had filled my head with tales of gods and mysteries, so I sailed north to where the Templars might have been, so far north that the sun never set and the air barely warmed. I found mines so deep they might have been driven by dwarves, but no relics. By the time I came back she was married to someone else, and then I lost my eye, and pretty much put happiness aside. Bliss is reserved for the few."

"At least you had someone to haunt you." I thought of Astiza.

"Then I inherited my ancestral farm, her husband drowned, and against all expectations she and her family accepted me for a second match. I thought myself mutilated, hideous, but she was Beauty to my Beast. When she told me she was with my child I was in a daze of happiness. I severed my connections with Forn Sior and dedicated myself to domesticity. Have you ever known contentment, Ethan?"

"Now and again, for an hour or two. I don't know if it is men's lot to be content for very long. Franklin said, 'Who is rich? He who is content. Who is that? Nobody.'"

"Your mentor was wrong on that one. By his

definition I was rich, fabulously so. What need had I of Norway or Templars when I had Signe? And then . . ."

"She died?"

"I killed her."

He was haunted, I saw, and not just by dwarves and elves. His expression was suddenly withered as a garden in winter. I was stunned, not knowing what to say.

"She died trying to give birth to my baby."

I swallowed. "Magnus, that could happen to anyone."

"The neighbors had already made fun and called me Odin. But in my torrent of grief I saw destiny's hand and realized I wasn't done. I think the knights of old were seeking a grail that could mean the worst things could be undone, and that I'm doomed to search the world as the old god did, on a quest for my own kind of bitter knowledge. I'm on a search in my wife's memory, Ethan. That's why I can't share your sport with women."

"Oh." Once again I felt shallow—but more easily healed, too. You can't lose what you don't risk, including your heart. "Surely she wouldn't begrudge a remarriage. She did it herself."

"No, I gave up my quest and killed her by my selfishness in doing so. Now I must complete it, out here in the American west, as penance."

"Penance! And you bring the innocent *me* along?"

"You need purpose, too. I could see it at Mortefontaine, where all you had were food, drink, cards, and women. I've saved you, though you'll never appreciate it."

"But we've come to the edge of nothing," I said with exasperation, gesturing at the brown hollow below us, mist pooled like a puddle.

"No. This is the edge of Eden." His breath was a cloud in the chill.

I felt sour about my recruitment. "I always pictured Eden warmer." I pulled my blanket over my head, shivering despite myself at the sorrow of his tale. The eager boy suddenly seemed a thousand years old, and the empty woods watchful.

"Have you ever wondered where Eden was, Ethan?"

"Not really." I realized my partner was quite mad.

"I mean it had to be somewhere. What if it could be rediscovered?"

"If I remember the scriptures, Bloodhammer, the door to that particular inn slammed shut," I grumbled. "Eve, the apple, and all that."

"But what if it could be reopened?"

"With a key?"

"Thor's hammer."

I rolled over to go to sleep. "Then stay away from apple pie."

By the next morning Magnus was cheerful again, as if our conversation had been a weird, bad dream. He made no mention of poor Signe, chattering instead about the open brownness of our forests that was apparently different from Norwegian woods. He was a madman who couldn't remember his own fantasies. But just as we saddled our horses he called out, "Here!" and impishly threw me something.

I looked. It was an apple, kept over from the harvest before and bought in Washington's market.

"Encouragement." His grin was wry.

"Then I'm taking a bite." It was still firm enough to crunch, and I chewed. "I don't feel any wiser."

"We just haven't found the right tree yet."

So off we rode. When I finished I threw the core into the spring woods, from where it might sprout.

◻   ◻   ◻

When it rained we took shelter in crude public inns, the lodging invariably close, smoky, pungent, and loud. Men spat, swore, farted, and grumbled as they shared beds for warmth. Come dawn, all of us picked bugs off each other like monkeys and then paid exorbitant prices for a breakfast of salt pork, corn mush, and watered whiskey, the standard diet of frontier America. I didn't find a clean cup or a pretty hostess between Georgetown and Pittsburgh.

Out of moody boredom, Magnus got in the habit of splitting hostel firewood with his heavy-bladed ax, earning us enough each time to buy a sixpence loaf of bread. I sometimes kept him company, watching the ripple of his great muscles with the same wary awe one watches a bull, calling out advice he usually ignored. I'd help stack the result, but declined to do the chopping.

"For the hero of Acre and Marengo, you seem to have an aversion to a fighting man's exercise," he'd finally tease good-naturedly.

"And for a man expecting to control the world,

you seem all too willing to do a peasant's work for pennies. Hedging your bets, Magnus?"

After nine days of hard travel it was a relief to come down out of the steep, cold mountains, the country taking on a fuzz of spring green. Pittsburgh was a triangular city of three hundred houses and fifteen hundred souls, its apex pointing down the Ohio formed by the junction of the Allegheny and Monongahela. The old British fort at the point was long gone, its brick pillaged for new construction and its earthen ramparts washed out by floods. The rest of the town was thriving under a pall of coal smoke, bustling with boatyards, lumber mills, and factories for rope, nails, glass, and iron. Its smell of hen coops and stables carried a good two miles, and the streets had as many pigs as people. Getting to a riverboat down the Ohio required a steep climb down the city's bluffs and across boards laid on the mudflats to deep water.

A flatboat took us and our horses down the Ohio twenty miles to a landing at the Great Trail, now a crude road running north. What used to be dangerous Indian country just a decade before had become, thanks to the victory at Fallen Timbers, an immigrant highway. War, disease, and the collapse of the game population had reduced tribes like the Delaware and Wyandot to penury, and the dirty, emaciated survivors we saw bore little resemblance to the proud warriors I recalled from my trapping days. Were the Indians already finished, as doomed as the mastodon?

Magnus studied them with interest. "The descendants of Israel," he murmured.

"I've been to Palestine, and I hardly think so."

"The lost tribes, Jefferson speculated."

"Magnus, they're a dying race. Look at them! I'm sorry, but it's true."

"If it's true, then we're about to lose more than we ever dreamed. These people know things we've forgotten, Ethan."

"Like what?"

"The past. How to truly live. And how the world is alive with things we cannot see. Scholars say they know the spirit world. Thor could have walked with their manitou: perhaps they were similar spiritual beings! Franklin was inspired by the Iroquois government to help craft your Constitution. Johnson complimented their oratory."

"And yet at our last inn they were described as thieving, drunken, lazy scalp hunters. Pioneers hate Indians, Magnus. That whiskey trader had a tobacco pouch made from a warrior's scrotum. Our word for their women, 'squaw,' means cunt. Europeans have been fighting them for three hundred years."

"Fear has made us blind, but that doesn't mean the Indian can't see."

New settler trails branched off in all directions, forests were being toppled, and so many plumes of smoke rose that the entire Ohio Territory seemed a steaming stew. The meanest European peasant could come, girdle trees, plant his corn in the spaces between, set loose his pigs, and call himself a farmer. Their cabins were no bigger than a French bedroom, their yards mud, their children feral, and their wives so hard-used that their beauty was shot by twenty. But a man was free! He had land, black and loamy. Ohio seemed to be writhing with transformation as we rode, its skin twitching with change. I wondered if Jefferson's prediction that this west would take a thousand years to fill had been too pessimistic. There were already fifty thousand people in the territory, and when we stopped at a tavern or bought a night in a farmer's barn, all the talk was of statehood.

"This dirt makes New England look like a rock pile!"

While the Ohio Territory was pockmarked with new clearings, it retained vast tracts of virgin forest where the world remained primeval. Oak, beech, hickory, chestnut, and elm, budding now with spring green, reared up to one hundred and fifty feet in height. Tree trunks were so thick that Magnus and I couldn't encompass them with linked arms. Limbs were fat enough to dance on, and bark so wrinkled that you could lose a silver dollar in the corrugations of an oak. The arcing lattice of branches met neighbors like the peak of a cathedral, and above that great flocks of birds would sometimes fly, so thick and endless that they blocked out the sun, their cries a raspy cawing. The trees seemed not just older than us but older than the Indians, older than woolly elephants. They made me think of Jefferson's baleful spirits.

"You could build a grand house out of a single tree," Magnus marveled.

"I've seen families camp in hollow ones while they work on their cabin," I agreed. "These trees are as old as your Norse explorers, Magnus."

"From the time of Yggdrasil, perhaps. These are the kinds of trees the gods knew. Maybe that's why the Templars came here, Ethan. They recognized this land *was* the old paradise, where men could live with nature."

I was less certain. I knew my race, and couldn't imagine any white men coming to America and not doing what these settlers were doing right now, converting these forest patriarchs to corn. It's what civilization does.

"Why do you think the trees here grow so big?" Magnus asked.

"Electricity, perhaps."

"Electricity?"

"The French scientist Bertholon constructed what he called an electrovegetoma machine in 1783 to collect lightning's energy and transfer it to plants in the field, and said it radically enhanced their growth. While we know lightning can damage trees, could electrical storms also make them grow? Perhaps the atmosphere of the Ohio country is different than that of Europe."

At last we ferried the Sandusky and, at its outlet to Lake Erie, a clearing finally gave a view.

"It's not a lake, it's a sea!"

"Three hundred miles long, and there are bigger ones than this, Magnus. The farther west we go, the bigger everything gets."

"And you ask why the Norse went that way? Mine were a people fit for big things."

He made a point of cupping his hand to drink, confirming this vastness wasn't salt. We could see the lake bottom to forty feet. As planned, we sold our horses and took passage on a schooner called *Gullwing* for Detroit, since the land route from here led into the nearly impassable Black Swamp that divided the Northwest Territory from Ohio. We sailed across Lake Erie, breasted the current of the Detroit River, and came at last to the famed fort. There I found us an easier way west—by flirting with a woman.

I have a knack for agreeable company.

CHAPTER 17

Detroit was one hundred years old when I arrived, but had been under the American flag for only the past five. What had first been a French post and then a British one—finally surrendered under the terms that ended the American Revolution almost two decades before—now sat atop a twenty-foot-high bluff along the short, broad Detroit River connecting Lakes Erie and Saint Clair. The establishment consisted of approximately a thousand people and three hundred houses behind a twelve-foot log stockade. Canada was on the opposite shore, the Union Jack flapping there as a reminder of former rule.

Despite the political division, trade across the river was ample. Detroit's economy was governed by furs and farming, with Norman-style French farmsteads spread up and down the American and Canadian sides for twenty miles.

"It's a mongrel town," described Jack Woodcock, our schooner's skipper. "You've got the Frenchies, who have been there nearly as long as the Indians and do all the real work. The Scots, who run the fur trade. The American garrison, made up mostly of frontier misfits who can't find a job anywhere else. Then there's the Christian Indians, the tribes who come to trade, the black servants and freemen, and across the river the British waiting to take it all back again."

"Surely there's new pride in being a part of the United States."

"The French like us even less than the British. They're hiving for Saint Louis. Town's lost half its population."

The land and waterscape was flat, the sky vast, and the April sun bright. The most curious sight was the scattering of windmills, their arms turning lazily against the scudding white clouds of spring.

"The land's such a pancake there ain't no rapids for water power," our captain explained. "We's like a bunch of damn Dutchmen."

Near the walls were clusters of domed bark wigwams and crude lean-tos used by the deposed Indians who clung near the post. Our craft tied to a long wooden dock at the base of the bluff, gulls wheeling and crows hopping in hunt of spilled corn or grain. Sloops, canoes, flatboats, and barges were tied along the pier's length, and the boards rang and rumbled from stomping boots and rolling kegs. The language was a babble of English, French, and Algonquin.

"We're not even halfway to the symbol of the hammer," Magnus said with wonder, consulting the charts he'd bought in New York City.

"If we can continue by water it will be faster and easier," I said. "We'll show Jefferson's letter of support to the commander here and ask for military transport to Grand Portage. We have, after all, the backing of the American government."

There was a dirt ramp leading from the dock to the stockade gate, split logs bridging puddles. A steady stream of inhabitants moved up and down like a train of ants, not just transporting goods to and from ships and canoes but dipping water. The wells had been spoiled by the town's privies, said Woodcock.

Three-quarters of the inhabitants looked to be either French or Indian. The former had long dark hair and skin burned almost as brown as the tribes. They wore shirts, sashes, and buckskin leggings, with scarves at their neck, and they were crowned with headbands or bright caps of scarlet. Clad in moccasins, they had a jaunty gaiety that reminded me, however remotely, of Paris. The Indians, in contrast, stood or sat wrapped in blankets and watched the frantic industry of the whites with passive, resigned curiosity. They were refugees in their own country.

"The drunk and diseased fetch up here," the captain said. "Be careful of the squaw pox."

"Not much of a temptation," I said, eyeing the squat and squalid ones.

"Wait till you been out here for six months."

Inside the stockade was crowded with white-washed log houses and dominated at its center by a large stone Catholic church. "Headquarters is that way," Woodcock said, pointing. "Me, I'm stoppin' at the tavern." He disappeared into a cabin rather more populated than the others.

The western headquarters of the United States Army, governing three hundred unruly soldiers, was a sturdy command building of squared logs and multipaned windows of wavy glass, its official purpose marked by a flagstaff with stars and stripes. There was no guard, so we walked unannounced into a small anteroom, where a grizzled sergeant sat hunched over a ledger book. We inquired about Samuel Stone, the man Lewis had told us was the commanding officer.

"The colonel's out at the graveyard again," said the sergeant, mumbling through a bristle of gray whisker while he held a quill pen like a dart, as if uncertain where to point it. He had none of Meriwether Lewis's military bearing and squinted at a ledger sheet as if looking at the alphabet for the first time. Finally he scratched through a name.

"Has there been an illness?"

"Nah, another shootin'. The garrison don't have nobody to fight so they fights each other. The colonel, he banned dueling, but every time he tries to punish someone for it, half of them is already dead, and the other half usually cut up or wounded. Besides, he's a fighter too. Keeps the blood up, he says."

"Good God. How many have died this way?"

"Half a dozen. Hell, we lose lots more to drownin',

ague, consumption, Injuns, squaw pox, and bad water. Better to die for honor than the bloody flux, eh?"

"We're on a mission from President Jefferson," I said, adopting a tone I hoped expressed gravity and my own importance. "Will the colonel return soon?"

"I suppose. Unless he don't."

"What does that mean?"

"The colonel, he keeps his own schedule."

"We have a letter from the president requesting we be granted military transportation. Has no advance correspondence reached you?"

"You mean letters? About you?" He shook his head. "Where you goin'?"

"To the head of the Great Lakes."

"Head of the lakes? Grand Portage?"

"Yes."

"That's redcoat country, man." He looked at Magnus. "Your friend here looks to be a Scot. Ask him. They're the ones who run the North West Company. You a redcoat? They run all the freight canoes, too."

"Magnus is Norwegian, and we want passage on an American ship. Surely there are brigs that go to Michilimackinac."

"Canoes, mostly. No American ships." He looked at us as if we were daft. "Ain't you seen the river? Ain't no navy. Besides, we's army."

This was getting us nowhere. "I suppose we'd better speak to the colonel."

He shrugged. "Won't change things." He looked around, seemingly surprised there was no colonel, and no chairs, either. "You can wait on the porch if you like if he ever comes to wait for. Or, try again tomorrow." He shifted in his seat, raised a thigh, and broke wind with a pop like a signal gun. "Sorry. Reveille."

We stepped back outside, surveying the bowed logs, mossy roofs, and muddy lanes that were Detroit. "If that's what's defending us, I don't blame our boat captain for making for the tavern," Magnus said. "Let's join him and try again in an hour or two, when the grave's filled. This Stone may move like one."

So off we strode, Magnus pointing out the magnificence and stink of drying fur pelts and I commenting on the paucity of white women. There were a few pretty Indian ones, but they had the mix of native and European clothing that marked them as brides of the French. Younger ones looked to be Métis, or half-breed.

We'd almost reached the tavern when a voice cried, "Look out!"

A man bulled us against the logs of a candle shop while a black cannon ball, a four-pounder by the look of it, shot from the intersecting lane and went hurtling where we'd been standing a moment before. It disappeared between houses and there was a crash and the sound of toppled wood.

"Sorry for my rudeness," our savior said, "but you were about to walk into a bowl-lane without looking. Broken ankles are chronic in Detroit, and the town is at odds about it. There's talk of an ordinance."

"I didn't hear a cannon."

"The ball wasn't fired, it was rolled. Bowls are a mania, and the debate to ban them has exercised more gums and produced less result than your American Congress. The young men throw whenever the streets are halfway dry or frozen. Keeps them occupied, Colonel Stone says."

"The players give no warning?" Magnus asked.

"We learn to watch and hop soon enough." He looked at me with new interest. "Say! Aren't you the hero of Acre?"

I blinked, puzzled to be recognized. "Hardly a hero . . ."

"Yes, Ethan Gage! What splendid coincidence! My employers were just speaking of you! Rumor had it that you were headed this way and tongues are wagging, as you might imagine. Who can guess what your next mission might be! And now here you are! No, don't deny it, I was told to look for a pretty longrifle and a hulking companion!"

"This is Magnus Bloodhammer, son of Norway. And who are you?"

"Ah! I forgot my manners in all the excitement!" A cheer went up and another cannon ball went bouncing by. "Nicholas Fitch, aide to Lord Cecil Somerset, a partner in the North West Company. He's staying at the Duff House in Sandwich across the river, with his cousin Aurora. He's most anxious to meet you. Damn curious about the scrape at Acre. Something of a student of ancient fortification, he is. He's an acquaintance of Sidney Smith, who you served with."

"We're trying to meet with Colonel Stone about transport up the lakes."

"Oh, I don't think you'll see Stone again today. Tends to go hunting after a burial. Says it clears the mind to kill something else. And the traffic north is all British anyway. Please, be our guests—we're having a party. Quite the gathering for these parts: traders, farmers, chiefs! And Lord Somerset is going north. Perhaps we could help each other!" He smiled.

Well, one of my missions was to sniff out British intentions in the west. There's no better place than a social gathering, where tongues are loosened by drink. "If you don't mind men rough from a little traveling, then certainly."

"We have a bath, too!" He winked. "You'll want to be clean for Aurora!"

CHAPTER **18**

Alexander Duff's house on the Canadian shore was a three-story, whitewashed trading house that transplanted British propriety to the wilderness in order to impress French voyageurs, visiting Indian chiefs, and Scottish investors. There were grand windows and a pediment porch, and inside ostentation was achieved with massive mahogany tables, brocaded chairs, silk curtains, pewter candelabra, fine china, lead crystal, and heavy silver with ivory handles. The bric-a-brac was a claim to imperialism much more effective than planting a flag.

Magnus and I were welcomed by Alexander Duff himself, told that our fortuitous arrival indeed coincided with a gathering of notables that evening, and were shown to an adjacent bathhouse to make ourselves presentable. By dusk we were as scoured, mended, and straightened as possible. I clipped my hair to republican fashion, while Magnus trimmed the wilder boundaries of his beard to mere prophet dimensions. Our boots were so worn by our travels that Duff gave us freshly beaded moccasins that were wonderfully soft and quiet. "The only things for canoes," he said.

Then we were primed with scotch, lubricated with brandy, and had our appetite whetted with port. This was just as well, given the shock of the guests who arrived. I'd no hash with the English and Scottish fur captains, German Jews, and French canoe captains who first crowded in, leaving their native brides on the back porch as custom demanded. They were dressed to the frontier nines, showing up in calf-high beaded moccasins, embroidered sashes, silk vests, feathered caps, and that jaunty self-confidence earned by wresting money from the frontier.

Rather, it was the trio who arrived when the main room was already hot and close with pressed bodies and raised laughter. There was a draft as the door opened, merriment faltered, and men backed to make a space as if these new dignitaries were either renowned or contagious. In this case—by my lights as an American—they were both.

One was a lean, hawk-nosed, long-haired white man of sixty dressed in Indian buckskin leggings tied below the knee, savage breechclout, and a long French jacket of faded blue cloth. He wore a bright officer's gorget at his chest, like a silver crescent moon, and a hunting knife in a beaded sheath at his waist. He was a good three days unshaven, his gaze made fiercer by a sliver of bone in his nose and silver earrings the shape of arrow-heads. His yellowy eyes, small under heavy brows, had a raptor's stare.

The other two were Indians, both tall and of imposing bearing. One was the white man's age but shaved bald except for a scalp lock, and dressed in a black European business suit. His pate, high cheekbones, and Roman nose were the color of beaten copper, setting off eyes dark as a rifle ball. His manner conveyed dignity, his posture tall and straight.

The second native, thirty years younger, had black hair to his shoulders in the Shawnee fashion and was dressed entirely in fringed buckskin. If the first chief kept his gaze remote, this one's bright and oddly hazel eyes took us all in with a sweep, as if examining the heart and soul of each man before flickering on. He had a string of three tiny brass moons hanging from his nose, and on his chest was an antique medal of King George, brightly polished. A single feather lay in his hair and he had that electric magnetism more inherited than learned. It was interesting that his inspection finally rested on Magnus. He said something to his companions.

"Tecumseh says that one's different," the white man interpreted.

"A Scandinavian giant is what he is!" said Duff. "We also have an American visitor, Ethan Gage. They wish to visit the west beyond Grand Portage."

"American?" The gray-haired, grizzled white fixed on me and spoke rapidly to his companions in the native tongue. The long-haired Indian said something more, and he translated again. "Tecumseh says Americans go everywhere. And stay."

The company laughed.

"I don't think I've had the pleasure," I said coolly.

"This is Tecumseh, a chief of the Shawnee," Duff introduced. "Born with a comet, so his name means Panther Across the Sky. He thinks your country has enough land and its people should stay where they are."

"Does he now?"

"His grasp of geography and politics is quite remarkable. His companion is the famed Mohawk Joseph Brant, and their translator is frontier captain Simon Girty."

Girty! Everyone waited for my reaction. Here was one of the most famed villains in America, an Indian fighter who had switched sides during the revolution and even bested Daniel Boone. Enemies claimed he delighted in the torture of white captives. He just looked like a feral old man to me, but then his war was a generation in the past. "What's Girty doing here?" I blurted.

"I live here, Mr. Gage," he replied for himself, "as do thousands of other loyalists forced from their rightful homes by an insane rebellion. I'm a refugee farmer."

"Brant fought for the king as well, as you know," Duff said. "He's visiting to speak to Tecumseh. All of us think highly of the young chief."

I couldn't pretend to pleasantries since Girty's infamy had reached across the Atlantic. "You turned on your own people like Benedict Arnold!"

He eyed me in turn like a piece of gristle spat out on a plate. "They turned on *me*. I mustered a company for the Continentals and they denied me a commission because I was raised captive by the Indians. Then they were going to betray the very tribes that helped them! But I don't have to explain about switching sides to Ethan Gage, do I?"

I flushed. It was circumstance, not betrayal, that had left me bouncing between the British and French side in the Holy Land, but it was damn difficult to explain. This was Girty's point, of course. "Mr. Duff," I managed, "I recognize that I'm a guest on foreign soil here in Canada, and a guest in your house. You've the right to invite whoever you please. But I must say that if this trio were to cross the Detroit River there is every possibility they would be hanged, or worse. Simon Girty committed the worst kind of atrocities on American captives."

"That's a damned lie!" Girty said.

"My guests are well aware of their reputation in the United States, Ethan, which is why they are in Canada," Duff said. "But Simon is right, the rumors are untrue. They're simply brave soldiers who fought for another cause. Mr. Girty in fact tried to save captives from Indians, not torture them. He was, and is, a man of honor wronged by the foolishness of your own nation and then slandered by men embarrassed by their wrongs. We share dinner tonight as a fraternity of warriors."

"Like Valhalla," Magnus said. "Where the Viking hero goes to feast."

"Exactly," Duff said, glancing at my companion

as if he might be daft. "I included you, Bloodhammer, because we're curious about your purpose. Lord Somerset wishes to meet you, and Gage has a reputation as a man—usually—fair and broadminded."

His point was obvious and it would do no good to make a scene. I took a long swallow from my cup. "And where *is* Lord Somerset?"

"Here!"

And he did look the lord, descending stairs from the bedrooms above as if stepping to a coronation. Tall, fit, and impeccably dressed in green swallowtail coat and glistening black boots, he was a handsome man in his forties, with a crown of prematurely silvered hair, eyes focused at some point just above our heads, and sensually sculpted nose and lips like those marble generals in Napoleon's hallway. He seemed born to command, and the only ones who matched him for presence were the two Indian chiefs. There was an actor's precision to Somerset's movements, a sheathed rapier swinging theatrically from one hip. Something in his poise, however, made me suspect that unlike many aristocrats, he actually knew how to use the weapon.

"An honor to make your acquaintance, Mr. Gage." Somerset's rank negated the need for him to hold out his hand. "My friend Sir Sidney Smith has spoken quite highly of you, despite your disappearance back into France. You are not just a warrior, but something of a wizard, I understand." He spoke to the others. "Mr. Gage, by reputation at least, is an electrician!"

"What's an electrician?" Girty said suspiciously.

"A Franklin man, interested in lightning, the fire of the gods," Somerset replied grandly. "Explorer, savant, and counselor. I'm flattered, Mr. Duff, by the august company you've assembled. Any one of these men is a hero, but to put them together—well."

Damn it, the man had a title, and even though I'm a solid Yankee democrat, I couldn't help but preen. I'd caught the lightning!

"Nor should we neglect notice of Mr. Gage's companion, the Norwegian adventurer Magnus Bloodhammer, scholar of history and legend. A descendant of noble blood himself, a lost prince so to speak. Am I correct, Mr. Bloodhammer?"

"You flatter me. I'm interested in my country's past. And yes, I trace my ancestry to the old kings before my nation lost its independence."

This was the first I'd heard of that. Magnus was royalty?

"Now you're here in the American wilderness, very far from Norway and its illustrious past," Somerset said. "Or are you? We may find we all have things in common, what?"

Tecumseh spoke again.

"He says the big Norwegian has medicine eyes," Girty translated. "He sees the spirit world."

"Really?" Somerset's appraisal was intent as a jeweler's. "You see ghosts, Magnus?"

"I keep an eye out."

The company laughed again, except for Tecumseh.

Cups were refilled and we began to relax, even

though I half-expected Girty, Brant, or Tecumseh to pull out a tomahawk at any moment and commence howling. The frontier wars during the American Revolution had been brutal and merciless, and memory of their cruelties would linger for generations. What intrigued me this night was that the two older and notorious warriors seemed almost deferential to the younger one, Tecumseh, whom I'd never heard of. And what was an English lord doing in this corner of Canada, opposite the desultory garrison of Detroit? I sidled over to Nicholas Fitch, the aide we'd met across the river. He seemed well into his cups and might say something useful.

"Mr. Fitch, you did not warn of such interesting company," I gently chided.

"Joseph Brant has long buried the hatchet."

"And the younger savage?"

"A war chief who fought you Americans for the Ohio country. Beat you twice, he did, before Fallen Timbers. Hasn't given up, either. Has an idea to outdo Pontiac by uniting every tribe east of the Mississippi. He's an Indian Napoleon, that one."

"And you British support him in this scheme to set the frontier on fire?"

"We British are the only ones who can properly control Indians like Tecumseh, Mr. Gage," said Lord Somerset, coming up to my elbow. Fitch retreated like a well-trained butler. "We can be your nation's closest friend or deadliest enemy, depending on your willingness to set reasonable boundaries on expansion. There's room for all of us on this vast continent—British, Indian, and American—if we keep to our own territories. Tecumseh may threaten war, but only with our help. He could also be the key to a remarkable peace—*if* your new president can rein your immigrants in."

"But not room for the French?" The British, after all, had driven the French out of Canada some thirty-eight years before.

"Ah. There are rumors that France is retaking possession of Louisiana. And now you come, fresh from Napoleon's court, reportedly headed that way. A remarkable coincidence, no?"

"I'm beginning to understand why I was invited to this gathering, Lord Somerset. You're as curious about my mission as I am about an English aristocrat in the wilderness."

"My role is no secret. I have investments and am on my way to Grand Portage to discuss a future alliance with our primary competitors, the Hudson's Bay Company. Again, cooperation might suit better than competition. And I hear you were once in the employ of John Astor's fur company?"

"As a young laborer, nothing more."

"And that he called on you in New York?"

"Good God, are you spying on me?"

"No need to. This is a vast continent geographically, but a small one when it comes to rumor and dispatch, especially for those of us in the fur trade. Fact travels with each dip of the paddle, and rumor seems to fly even faster. Ethan Gage, from Syria to the Great Lakes? How curious. And rumor has it your departure from New York was in haste after a rather spectacular explosion. Not that I credit such tales."

He knew entirely too much. "I like to see new things."

He smiled. "And you will." He turned toward the staircase and the crowd's conversation faltered once more. "My cousin, for example."

CHAPTER 19

And so Aurora Somerset made her entry. Like Cecil, she descended from the upper floor, but while he had stepped down regally, she seemed to float in her floor-length gown, as if riding a cloud down the flaming rainbow bridge Bifrost in Bloodhammer's Asgard. Her presence as a white woman was reason enough for the company's appreciation, but it was her beauty that took us all aback, even the stolid Indians. She was an exquisite portrait come to life, a sculptor's ideal given animation. A cascading torrent of auburn ringlets framed an aristocratic face of high cheekbones and fine chin, her eyes emerald, her nose upturned, her smile a dazzling display of perfect teeth and pouty, rouged lips so sensual as to make a man think of a woman's little purse below. There was a beauty mark on one cheek that called out to be kissed, and whether real or pasted it hardly mattered, did it? A newly fashionable high-waisted dress called attention to the glory of her bosom, an inch of cleavage revealed and the silk wonderfully betraying the bump of her covered nipples. The shimmering pink fabric clung to a classical form, hips swaying as she descended, and the slippers that peeked out at bottom were embroidered with tiny seed pearls. Her crown was a small turban sporting what looked like an ostrich plume, and at her throat was a silver choker with a large emerald to complement her eyes. The very candles seemed to bow to her passage, and her gaze danced across the crowd of men before settling on Lord Somerset and, I was certain, me.

I grinned. I was in love, or at least besotted with lust, the two easily confused in us men. It's shameful to be so shallow, but by Casanova's court, she stirred the juices: the most impressive piece of architecture I'd seen since leaving Mortefontaine and the best painted, too, her lips cherry and cheeks peach. Aurora was as transfixing as a cobra, as frightening as temptation, and as irresistible as Eve's apple.

"That one's more trouble than Pauline Bonaparte," Magnus whispered. He could be as annoyingly corrective as a parson at a wine press.

"But not necessarily more trouble than she's worth."

"Cecil," she trilled, "you did not tell me our company would be so handsome!" She beamed at all of us, and more than one grizzled, wilderness-hardened Scot fur monger blinked and blushed. She eyed Tecumseh as well and licked a lip, but the young chief was alone in regarding her as nothing more than pretty furniture. For just an instant she betrayed annoyed uncertainty, and then her gaze swept on.

I, in contrast, bowed like a courtier. "Lady Somerset. The advertisement of your beauty does not do you justice."

"It's so wonderful to have an excuse to dress up. And you must be the remarkable Ethan Gage." She held out a slim white hand to be brushed with my lips. "Cecil told me you know all kinds of secrets, of electricity and ancient powers."

"Which I reveal only to my confidants." I grinned and Magnus rolled his eyes.

"That sets me a goal, doesn't it?" She spread a fan and veiled herself a moment behind it. "I *so* want to hear of your adventures. I *do* hope we can be friends."

"Your cousin has been suggesting much the same thing. But a man with the reputation of Mr. Simon Girty is going to give any American pause, I'm afraid. I don't want to be perceived as a traitor in the company I keep, Lady Somerset."

"Call me Aurora, please. And friendship does not betray anyone, does it?"

"Some have accused me of having too many friends and too few convictions."

"And I think some cling to conviction because they have no friends." She fluttered her fan.

"Ethan was just telling us what he's doing in the northwest," Cecil Somerset prompted.

"I enjoy travel," I said.

"With giant Norwegians," he amended.

"Another friend, again. I am oddly popular."

Magnus put his hands on my shoulder. "We both are students of Freemasonry. Did you know, Lord Somerset, that many of the American generals your armies fought in the revolution were Masons? Is it possible you are one yourself?"

"I hardly think so." He sniffed. "Rather odd group, I think. There was some scandalous off-shoot in London . . ." He turned to his cousin. "Egyptian Rite?"

"It is reported the secret Egyptian Rite admitted women and that their ceremonies were quite erotic," Aurora said. "Occult and succulently scandalous."

"For a secret you seem to know a lot about it," Magnus said.

"Three can keep a secret if two of them are dead," I put in. "Ben Franklin said that."

Aurora laughed. "How true! And Norwegians don't gossip, Mr. Bloodhammer? What *do* they do up there all winter?" Magnus turned even redder than his normal apple hue.

I knew that my dispatched enemy Silano had been a member of that Egyptian Rite, and it was interesting that this English pair knew of that organization. But then the cult had been salon talk in London and Paris, and it was Magnus who had brought up Freemasonry. Despite my misgivings about Girty, I enjoyed the poised presence of this pair. Their elegant style reminded me of Europe. "You have sauce to travel into the wild, Aurora."

"*Au contraire*, Mr. Gage, I have trunks and trunks of clothes. Cecil complains of it all the time, don't you, cousin?"

"I don't know if I'm moving a woman or a caravan."

"For any proper lady it's necessity. Our comforts introduce civilization. This is why you should come with *us*, Mr. Gage. The scenery is the same no matter how you go, so why not enjoy it with a proper brandy? Have you tried the American corn whiskey?" She shuddered. "Might as well drink turpentine."

"Come with you?" Sharing a boat with the British was contrary to the intentions of my American and French sponsors, but whiling away the journey with Aurora Somerset was tempting. I could learn what the English are up to.

"We're traveling to Grand Portage for the summer rendezvous. Surely that is in the direction you and your Norwegian companion are traveling anyway?"

"We were planning to take American transport," Magnus said.

"Which apparently doesn't exist," I quickly added. "Our reception at Fort Detroit has been less than reassuring."

"I'm not surprised," Somerset said. "Frightful discipline, what? I do hope your young nation can hold onto the northwest." I recognized from his condescension that he hoped just the opposite, but that was not my concern.

"Can you explain the summer rendezvous?"

"Each spring," Cecil said, "the posts in the Canadian interior package the furs they've acquired during the winter from trade and trapping and canoe them south and east to the fort at Grand Portage.

Meanwhile, the North West Company sends freight canoes full of fresh trade goods for the Indians west from Montreal. The two groups rendezvous at the fort, frolic in the grandest party ever, exchange the furs for the trade goods, and reverse their paths before the ice returns. The Montreal party takes the furs back for global distribution, and the voyageurs take the trade goods to the interior posts. We plan to meet the freight canoes at Michilimackinac, near the head of Lake Huron. It's the safest, quickest, easiest way to go west."

Once again, my charm had solved all our problems! Instead of a military escort and the rigors of camping, I'd head northwest in luxury. "But what of your other guests?" While Aurora would be a delightful companion, Girty made me fear for my scalp.

"They're simply here for the evening, Mr. Gage," Cecil assured. "Mr. Girty is a near neighbor of Mr. Duff, and unlike the Americans we try to cultivate friendship and alliance with the Indians. I frankly was surprised at your reaction: the War of Rebellion is old, old, history, and Girty and Brant are old, old warriors. Let the past rest. It's future peace that you and I need to work to guarantee. The continent divided, as I said, each group with its sphere of influence. What could be more harmonious than that?"

Magnus put a hand on my arm. "Ethan, we're on a mission for Jefferson and the French." He looked at Aurora with suspicion.

I shook him off. "Part of which is to maintain peace with the English."

Cecil beamed. "Exactly."

"I don't entirely believe in missions," I went on. "People who are absolutely certain of things seem to do most of the shooting, in my experience, because they collide with people equally certain about the opposite thing. Yet how can we be certain of anything?"

"You are a philosopher, sir, and one after my own heart. If people simply lived for themselves, and tolerated others, like my cousin and I, then friendship would be universal."

I looked at Aurora. "Given my experiences with both sides in the Orient, I can think of no one better than myself to bridge the unfortunate gap between France, England, and America. With the close cooperation of the Somersets, of course."

"Mr. Gage, I want to work in *intimate* partnership," Aurora said.

"Please, call me Ethan."

"Ethan . . ." Magnus nagged. "People who agree with everything end up being used by everyone."

"Or helped." I was more than happy to be used by Aurora Somerset. Let Magnus be a Templar; I was ready to enjoy life. "Here we are all headed in the same direction and after much the same goal. We'll accompany you to Grand Portage, Lord Somerset, and then go our separate ways." I smiled at his cousin. "I want to watch you spread civilization."

"And I want to put you in the middle of things when I do."

CHAPTER 20

I sent Colonel Stone a note announcing we would accompany the Somersets on my mission for Jefferson, just in case someone back in Washington wondered what the devil had become of us. I didn't go to the officer in person because I didn't want to risk him offering alternative transportation, costing me the chance to escort the lovely and enticingly risky Aurora. I persuaded the dubious Magnus that this was the fastest way to get to the supposed hiding place of Thor's hammer, and that it never hurt to have countries like Britain on your side if you were trying to liberate your country from the Danes. "This way, no matter who prevails in the struggle between England and France, you'll be allied with the winner!"

"And an object of revenge for the loser," he grumbled with annoying logic.

We boarded a cutter, *Swallow*, for a trip up Lake Huron to the American post at Mackinac Island.

From there, we'd join the freight canoes taking trade goods to Grand Portage. Then a jaunt into the interior, a quick glance around for blue-eyed Indians, woolly elephants, and electric hammers, and back to civilization with treasure at best, burnished reputation at the least.

It's good to have new friends.

I did have a moment of disquiet when I saw, as I waited for the last trunks and servants to be loaded, that Lord Somerset was holding an intense conversation with Girty, Brant, and Tecumseh on the lawn of Alexander Duff's house and that glances were cast my way. I feared for a moment that the trio meant to join us, but no, they looked hard in our direction and then gestured good-bye to Cecil, as if some decision had been made. I had, after all, the protection of my new president and the first consul of France. With that, the aristocrat strode aboard, nodded as if to reassure me, and we cast off for the north, firing a salute to Detroit on the opposite shore. No canoe full of American officers came out, begging me to come back and become their responsibility.

We passed wooded Ile Aux Cochons, or Hog Island, where feral pigs were still hunted, and anchored that night on Saint Clair, which would be a giant lake in any other country but hardly a puddle in this one. The next morning we rose after sunrise, breakfasted pleasantly on tea, biscuits, and cold cuts left from Duff's party, and were on our way again in a building breeze. This was the way to travel! I stretched out on deck to take in the view as we made our way up the Saint Clair River to Lake

Huron, while Magnus studied his maps of vast blank spaces and Somerset bent to fur trade bookkeeping. Even aristocrats have to work, it seemed.

Aurora and I got on famously. She found my stories about Napoleon's Egyptian campaign and his unsuccessful siege of Acre the height of entertainment, never failing to laugh gaily at my little jokes with that flattery that goes with flirtation. She was, I presumed, understandably smitten by my charm, inflated reputation, and agreeable good looks. I related bright little stories about Sir Sidney Smith and Bonaparte, Franklin and Berthollet, old Jerusalem and ancient Egypt . . . and now I had descriptions of mercantile New York, rustic Washington, and the curious new president to offer as well! The Somersets in turn told me how threatening Bonaparte seemed to England and how they hoped his acquisition of Louisiana would not set off a new North American war. "You and I must work to keep the peace, Ethan," Aurora said.

"I prefer affection to fighting."

"Someday, England and America will be reconciled."

"Reunion can start with us!"

Aurora and I had both met Nelson, I on a warship and she in London, and the lady was brimming with gossip about his rumored infatuation with Emma Hamilton, a one-time adventuress who had married well and was sleeping her way even higher. "She's a beauty with her portraits all over London, and he's the greatest hero of the age," Aurora sighed. "It's magnificent scandal!" There was envy in her voice.

"You'll eclipse her, I'm sure."

Cecil educated us on fur politics in Canada. The Hudson's Bay Company operated from its huge namesake in the north and had the advantage of being able to transport its trade goods to the shore of the bay in cargo ships, meaning shorter river distances to trading posts in the Canadian interior. Magnus nodded at this, since his theory was that his Norsemen had used the same route. The Bay Company's disadvantage was short summers and long winters. The rival North West Company, dominated by Scots who employed French voyageurs in long-distance canoes, operated out of Montreal on an epic, five-thousand-mile water route across the Great Lakes and connecting rivers. Their season was longer, but they were limited to canoes, requiring an immense workforce of two thousand men. And then there was Astor, who had organized trappers on the American side of the border and monopolized the fur trade going to New York via the Mohawk and Hudson rivers.

"Each route has its advantages and problems, and the sensible thing would be to form an alliance," Somerset said. "Cooperation always achieves more than competition, don't you think?"

"Like us on this boat. You sail me to Mackinac, and I'll use my letter of introduction from Jefferson to smooth the way with the American garrison. We have a little league of nations here, with you representing England, Magnus Norway, and me America with ties to France." I looked at Aurora. "Partnership has its pleasures."

I wished the boat had been bigger so the girl and

I could get off by ourselves, but each night she commandeered the captain's private cabin like a pampered princess while we dozen men slept on deck between the trunks, bags, satchels, and shipments that made up the Somerset luggage. There were Fitch, a cook, a butler, a French Canadian maid who slept in Aurora's cabin, and a master-of-arms who looked after the assortment of sporting weaponry and swords that Cecil had brought with him. The English lord greeted each dawn with fencing exercises at which he thrust and slashed while balanced on the bowsprit, the captain keeping a wary eye lest the nobleman cut an important line.

Meanwhile, civilization slipped steadily away.

As we sailed north on the vast freshwater sea that is Lake Huron, the sky seemed to inflate, stretching to ever-emptier horizons. The shoreline, when we could see it, was a flat, unbroken expanse of forest. Not a white village, nor a farm, nor even a lonely cabin broke its endless green face. We once passed an Indian encampment, bark wigwams set on a sandy shore, but spotted only a couple figures, a wisp of smoke, and a single beached canoe. Another time I saw wolves loping on a sand beach and my throat caught at their easy wildness. Eagles soared overhead, otters splashed in the shallows, but the world seemed emptied of people. The planet had turned back to something infinite, pristine, and yet oddly intimidating. Here, Earth didn't care. The custodial God of Europe had been displaced by the lonely wind and the spirits of the Indians. So much space, such yawning possibility, everything unrealized! Even in bright sunlight, the great northern forest seemed cold as the stars. Nothing and no one out here had ever heard of the famed Ethan Gage, hero of the pyramids and Acre. I had shrunk to insignificance.

While the crew of the ship regarded this unbroken forest as so expected and monotonous to be beyond comment, Magnus was transfixed by the ceaseless rank of trees. "This was the world of the gods who were the first men," he said to me as we cruised. "This is what it all was once like, Ethan. Great heroes wandered without leaving a mark."

"It's the world of the Potawatomi and the Ottawa," I replied. "And whatever they are, it's not gods. You've seen a few: poor, diseased, and drunk."

"But they remember more than we do," he insisted. "They're closer to the source. And we've just seen the ones corrupted by our world. Wait until we get to theirs."

CHAPTER 21

Mackinac Island was a green knob between the reflecting blue platters of lake and sky, its American garrison of ninety men guarding the straits that led to Lake Michigan. It represented the edge of the United States. Beyond were only British posts, trappers, and tribes. Our little cutter banged a one-gun salute as we coasted into the island pier, and the fort replied in turn, the bark of its guns flushing great clouds of birds from the forest and then echoing away into emptiness.

The fort was in the shape of a triangle, with three blockhouses and two ramparts for cannon, earth and stone on the water side, and a log stockade facing the land. The high white officers' quarters, with hipped roof and twin chimneys, was the dominant building. Other cabins and sheds marked out a parade ground. The forest was cut back around the fort to make pasture and cropland, giving the outpost light to breathe.

"We British moved the post here after Pontiac's Indians overcame the old French fort of Michilimackinac on the mainland shore," said Lord Somerset, pointing. "It was a masterful attack, the braves pretending at lacrosse, following the ball through the fort gate and then seizing weapons from their waiting women who had hidden them under their trade blankets. The fort fell in minutes. The new post doesn't let the Indians land, though in winter you can walk to Mackinac across the ice. With the boundary settled we've passed this fort to you Americans, while we build a new one on the Saint Mary's River, near the rapids that lead to Lake Superior."

"Ninety Americans to guard all the Northwest Territory?"

"In North America, empire hangs by a thread. That's why our alliance is so valuable, Ethan. We can prevent misunderstandings."

Here the commandant was a mere lieutenant named Henry Porter, who met us on the dock to escort us up the dirt causeway to the fort gate. He was impressed by my letter from Jefferson—"I'd heard there's a new president, and here he is," he marveled, looking at the signature as if written in the statesman's blood—and he positively gaped at Aurora in a moony way I found annoying. The lieutenant seemed less plagued than Colonel Stone with dueling and bowling, and in fact his fort felt empty. "Half the garrison is off-post at any one time fishing, hunting, cutting wood, or trading with the Indians," he said. "We've room aplenty in the officer's quarters while you wait for your freight canoes."

There might be room aplenty, but not enough for Lady Aurora Somerset. She took one look at the spare military cubicles and announced that while her trunks might fit in a closet, she certainly could not. After brisk inspection of every possibility she declared that the top floor of the eastern blockhouse would just barely serve for her privacy and comfort. With inherited authority, she ordered Porter to shove its two six-pounders out of the way, asked for a squad of American infantry to carry in a cornhusk bed with down comforter, declared the ground floor sufficient for her maid, and said she would require a certain number of furs to carpet the rough planking of her new abode to make it habitable.

"But what if we come under attack?" the young lieutenant asked, clearly overawed by the imperiousness of the English nobility.

"My dear lieutenant, none would dare attack a Somerset," Cecil replied.

"And I will take my cousin's squirrel gun and shoot them between the eyes if they do," Aurora added. "I am a crack shot—yes, my cousin has taught me. Besides, the blockhouse is the safest place, is it not? You do care, Lieutenant, for the safety of women?"

"I suppose." He squinted at Jefferson's letter again, as if it might include instructions on handling this demand.

"I will keep a sharp lookout for red savages— and for any of your garrison that dare intrude on my privacy! This is how we do things in England and it would be well to pay attention. It will be instructive for you." She sniffed. "This has a *little* of the smartness of a British post." She touched his cheek and gave a thankful smile. "I *do* appreciate your hospitality, Lieutenant."

With that Porter was in full retreat, Bunker Hill taken, Yorktown avenged, and Britannia triumphant. If she'd asked for his own washbasin, he would have surrendered it in an instant, and Indiana Territory, too.

I, of course, am more experienced when it comes to women. But, alas, no more sensible than poor raw Porter: I am a man, after all, anxious as an insect, and I immediately set to scheming.

"You want to jeopardize our passage north and infuriate Cecil by going after his cousin?" Magnus hissed while I looked hungrily at the blockhouse, just begging to be assaulted. "This is as irresponsible as your dalliance with Pauline Bonaparte!"

"He's not her husband or father. And believe me, Magnus, conquering Aurora might prove as useful to our safe passage as Pauline Bonaparte was in getting us away from Mortefontaine. Women can be resourceful allies when they're not betraying you." I am ever the optimist.

"She's above your station and has two cannon to hold you off."

"Which means I have to be as wily as Pontiac's Indians when they took Michilimackinac."

I didn't think I could follow a lacrosse ball to her boudoir, but I had a Trojan horse of another sort. I took my most prized possession, my longrifle, and enlisted Aurora's maid to place it on the bed of my quarry's blockhouse sleeping quarters, with a note offering it for her protection and amusement and applauding her claim of marksmanship. Meanwhile we dined at the officers' mess. Everyone was curious about Jefferson, so I told them what I thought.

"The man writes like Moses, but can't speechify enough to hold a schoolhouse. He keeps a live bird and dead elephant bones in his office and knows more about wine than the Duke of Burgundy. I think he's a genius, but mad as a hatter, too."

"Like all leaders not born to the post," sniffed Cecil. "The American democrats are admittedly quite clever, but there *is* breeding, is there not?"

"At table he's the most entertaining man I've met since my mentor Franklin," I said. "Insatiably curious. He's fascinated by the west, you can be sure."

"I admire your young country's talent," Aurora said, "given that the highest-born fled to Canada or back to England during the revolution. I've read your Constitution. Who would have thought such genius could be found in common men? It's a remarkable experiment you're defending, Lieutenant Porter. Remarkable." She gave him a smile so dazzling it made me jealous.

He blushed. "Indeed, Miss Somerset. And the bitterest of enemies can become the best of friends, can they not?" Then *he* smiled like a courtier. I swear, the young rascal had recovered his grit!

When she obligingly left for her little fortress so we men could talk over port and pipes—Somerset making a show of lighting a cigar, an innovation out of the Spanish Main—I made an excuse, crept out before Porter or anyone else could maneuver ahead of me, and scampered across the parade ground to her blockhouse. My knock was answered by her maid. I announced I'd loaned out my weapon and wanted to make sure it was handled properly. Smirking, the girl let me in.

"Is this what you're inquiring about, Mr. Gage?" Aurora's voice floated down from above. The muzzle of my longrifle appeared in the trapdoor entrance that led to her chamber above, like a probing serpent. "I *was* surprised to find this tool in my bed, though I'm informed by a note that it may be useful."

"Your comment about shooting savages made me think you might enjoy practicing with a well-made rifle," I said. "We could study this evening."

"Forged in Lancaster, I presume," her disembodied voice said.

"Jerusalem, actually. It's a long story."

"Well, if we are to go shooting together, *do* come up and tell the tale. Aim is improved with understanding, don't you think?"

So up I scrambled, closing the trap and dropping a couple of furs over it to muffle her expected cries of passion. At her invitation I perched myself on a trunk while she smoothed her gown to sit daintily on the edge of her bed, her eyes flashing and her wondrous hair glowing in the candlelight. She was just disheveled enough to look erotic, two buttons carefully undone, escaping strands of hair artfully aglow, her slim boots slipped off her white stockings.

"The gunsmith was a British agent, and the stock was carved by his beautiful sister," I began.

"Was she really?" Aurora tossed her hair.

"Not as beautiful as you, of course."

"Of course." She stretched like a cat, giving a dainty yawn. "But you'd tell this other woman the same thing, wouldn't you? Naughty man. I know your type."

"I'm sincere in the moment."

"Are you?" The rifle was across her lap. "Well, Mr. Gage. Then do come over and show me how your weapon works."

And so I did.

Now the most astonishingly beautiful being in all nature is a woman, and the best become a gate to heaven. I appreciate a sweet girl. But then there are the hotter, more disturbing, more tempestuous types who are a gate to a place of an entirely different sort. That was the ruby fire of Aurora, her auburn hair tumbling to white shoulders, eyes flashing, mouth hungry, breasts pink-tipped and as taut and aroused as I was, skin flushed, all curve and fine waist and wondrous, mesmerizing shank: there was no mountain as glorious as the rise of her hip when she lay beside me, no glen as lush and mysterious as her particular vale. She was a paradise of fire and brimstone, an angel of desire. I was lost in an instant, except I'd already been lost when she came down the stairs at Detroit. The smell of her, the glow of her skin, the beauty mark on her cheek that demanded obeisance: oh yes, I'd thrown the reins away and would go wherever she stampeded. We writhed like minks and gasped like fugitives, and she coaxed sensation out of me I didn't know was there, and suggested things I'd never quite imagined. Yet pant as we might, she never seemed to lose her curiosity about the famous Ethan Gage, her sly questions about my rifle giving way to murmured entreaties as we embraced that I share just *what* exactly it *was* that we were looking for beyond Grand Portage.

"Elephants," I mumbled, and went at her again like a starving man.

My mention of pachyderms only added to my mystery and so when we finally caught our breath I tried to put her off by explaining curious ideas I'd picked up from Napoleon's savants and the new American president. They thought that the world might be older than the Bible, and home to strange creatures now entirely extinct, and that the whole puzzling cornucopia of life, while testimony to the Almighty, also raised questions about just what our Creator was up to, so as a naturalist myself . . .

"You are toying with me!" She was beginning to stiffen, just as I was not.

"Aurora, I'm on a diplomatic mission for President Jefferson. I can't share all the pertinent details with every bedmate . . ."

Then I was rolling from her furious push, landing with a thump on a wolverine pelt on the floor.

"Every bedmate!"

I peeked above the mattress. "That's not what I meant. We just don't know each other well yet."

So she attacked me with a pillow, breasts heaving, and it was such a wondrous sight that if she'd smothered me then and there, I would have died happy. Blazes!

But at length she was spent, flopping on the bed,

her rump graceful as a snow drift, her lips ripe and pouted. "I thought you loved me and would share everything."

"I have shared all I am capable of this evening, believe me."

"Pah."

"I am entirely boring, I know. I go where greater men direct me, a simple savant with some slight knowledge of electricity. To find Venus on the edge of the wilderness is a greater discovery than any elephant."

She rolled onto her back, her gaze lazy, and blessed my compliment with a slight smile. "So you think I'm pretty?"

"I think if you were painted, it would set off such frenzy that there would be a riot. If you were sculpted, it would cause a new religion. I think you are manufactured of moonbeam, and fired by the sun."

"Fancy words, Yankee Doodle."

"But so true they should be chiseled into the stone of Westminster."

She laughed. "What a flatterer you are! But you are a scamp not to trust me. I don't think you can go in my cousin's canoes after all."

This was worrisome, since our only transportation off this island was with the British. "But we will be useful!"

"How?"

I looked at my longrifle, which had found itself onto the plank floor in all our maneuvering. "I can shoot that, too." I gave my most fetching smile. "We'll practice together."

She shook her head. "What an ungrateful rascal you are."

"Not ungrateful, believe me."

Now the look was hard. "All right then, you and your hairy Norwegian can come with us to Grand Portage, but in a separate canoe, and when you look at me across the water, when I'm beneath my parasol, I will not deign to return your glance because I am a great lady of England and you are a directionless adventurer who will not share any confidences."

"I am a victim of your beauty."

She wriggled back to rest herself more upright against the pillows. "You will be punished for your secrecy, at camp, by my indifference. You must attend to me or I will persuade Cecil to leave you behind for the Indians. They eat their enemies, I've heard. But we will have no more intimacy there until you demonstrate your trust by confiding in me. Until you reform, this is the last time you can gaze upon my body."

"Aurora, I believe we are already the deepest of friends."

"So prove it. Again." She parted her thighs. "And again. And then maybe someday I will take pity on you—if it suits me, and if you have earned it."

I gulped and nodded, summoning new enthusiasm.

It's a challenge being a diplomat.

CHAPTER 22

A North West Company freight brigade of six canoes fetched us from Mackinac Island on its way to Lake Superior. Each vessel, improbably made of nothing but birch bark, wood strips, and roots used for twine, was thirty-five feet long, carried sixty 90-pound packs of trade goods, and had a guide at the bow, a steersman at the stern, and eight paddlers as driven as galley slaves. In the segregation of labor that had followed the British conquest of Canada, all the laborers were French Canadian, while four of the canoes each carried either a Scot, an Englishman, or a German Jew as *bourgeois*, or gentleman fur partner or clerk, who rode amidships like a little sultan. The other two would carry the Somersets, Magnus, and me. We could hear the paddlers' song in French as the flotilla neared the island, the lilting melody floating over the blue water in time to the dip of the paddles:

C'est l'aviron qui nous mène
M'en revenant de la jolie Rochelle
J'ai rencontré trois jolies demoiselles.
C'est l'aviron qui nous mène, qui nous mène,
C'est l'aviron qui nous mène en haut.

It is the paddle that brings us
Riding along the road from Rochelle city
I met three girls and all of them were pretty.
It is the paddle that brings us, that brings us,
It is the paddle that brings us up there.

The verses set the time for the stroke. We would journey on a tide of French folk song.

Our course would first pass the new British post of Fort Saint Joseph being constructed at the north end of Lake Huron, and then through the thirty-mile-long Sault Ste. Marie, or the "Saint Mary Jump" of rapids that led to Lake Superior. Then we would hug the northern shore of that inland sea until we reached Grand Portage at its western end.

As promised, Aurora and her cousin took a canoe different from that of Magnus and me, the woman seating herself primly on one of her trunks and holding a parasol as shade. The year had warmed now and the forests had erupted in full leaf and flower, but no public warmth emanated from Aurora, who looked steadfastly away. I tolerated this coolness because the inevitable end would be so sweet, and because it saved me from having to pay court to her whims or explain our tryst to others. I could pretend nothing had happened! I knew she'd reheat quickly enough once she missed my prowess.

Like most men, I have an optimistic appraisal of my own charm.

Cecil, after greeting the other bourgeois, took up position in a second canoe, natty as ever in fawn-colored coat, high marching boots, and beaver-skin top hat. He carried a fowling piece on his lap to plunk at birds, and a petty novel in his pocket to pass the time. He seemed so at home in this wild country that I suspected his fine manners coated a core of experienced steel.

The voyageurs wore buckskin leggings, loose white shirts, bright caps, and, if needed, blanket coats called *capots*. Physically they tended to be short-legged and broad-shouldered, almost like muscular dwarves bred to the canoe. Here was our transport west! The canoe we would ride glided in and the bowman who commanded—wiry, tanned, with impish dark eyes and a jaunty red cap— bounded onto the island's dock to block us before we could board. While the Somersets had been catered to, this captain put hands to his hips and dubiously eyed us like specimens of flotsam.

"*Mon dieu*, an ox and a donkey! And I am supposed to paddle your weight to Grand Portage, I suppose?"

Magnus squinted. "No little man needs to paddle me."

"Little man?" He stood up on his toes, thrusting his nose in my companion's face. "*Little man*? I am Pierre Radisson, a North Man with three winters at the posts and the guide of this master canoe! The Scots pay me a full nineteen English pounds a year! I can stroke twenty hours in a single day without complaining and travel a hundred miles before sleeping! Little man? None know the rapids like the great Pierre! None can portage faster than I, or drink more, or dance more splendidly, or jump higher, or run faster, or more quickly win an Indian bride! Little man?" He crowded into Magnus, the crown of his head at the Norwegian's collarbone. "I can swim, shoot, trap, chop, and fuck better than the likes of a clumsy oaf like you, eat my own weight, and find my way from Montreal to Athabasca with my eyes closed, cyclops giant!"

Bloodhammer was finally forced to take a step back. "I just meant a Norwegian pulls his own oar."

"Ha! Do you see any *oars* on my canoe? You think me master of a dinghy? I think perhaps that a *Norwegian* is an *imbecile*!" He eyed Magnus up and down like a tree he was considering chopping. "But you are big, so perhaps I will let you try my paddle—if you promise not to break it or use it to pick your big horse teeth, or lose it in that thicket of moss that is your face. Do you know any songs?"

"Not French ones."

"Yes, and it sounds from the gravel of your throat that you will sing like a grindstone. *Mon dieu!* It is hopeless." He turned to me. "And you, even skinnier and more useless than him! What do you have to say?"

"That the girls of Rochelle are pretty," I replied in French.

He brightened. "Ah, you speak the civilized tongue? Are you French?"

"American, but I lived in Paris. I worked as an aide to Bonaparte."

"Bonaparte! A brave one, eh? Maybe he will take back Canada. And what do you do now?"

"I'm an electrician."

"A what?"

"He's a sorcerer," Magnus explained, using French as well.

Now Pierre looked intrigued. "Really? What kind of sorcerer?"

"A scientist," I clarified.

"A scientist? What is that?"

"A savant. One who knows the secrets of nature, from study."

"Nature? Bah! All men know savants are as useless as priests. But sorcery—now *that* is a skill not altogether useless in the wilderness. The Indians have sorcerers, because the woods are filled with spirits. Oh yes, the Indians can see the world behind this one, and call the animals, and talk to the trees. Just you wait, sorcerer. You will see the cliffs wink and storm clouds form into a ram's horn. Wind in the cottonwoods will whisper to you, and birds and squirrels will give you advice. And when night falls, perhaps you feel the cold breath of the Wendigo."

"The what?"

"An Indian monster who lives in the forest and devours his victims more thoroughly than the werewolves the gypsies speak of in France." He nodded. "Every Ojibway will tell you they are real.

A sorcerer—that is what we truly need." He looked at me with new respect, even though he clearly had never heard of electricity. "And can you paddle?"

"I'm probably better at singing."

"I don't doubt it. Though I bet you can't sing very well, either."

"I'm good at cards."

"Then you're both lucky you have the mighty Pierre Radisson to look after you! You won't need cards where we are going. But what is that you are carrying?" he asked Magnus, staring at what was strapped to his back.

"My ax and my maps."

"Ax? It looks big enough to sled on. Ax? We could hold it up for a sail, or use it as a roof in camp, or lower it as an anchor. Ax? We could recast it as artillery or start a blacksmith shop. So you might be useful after all, if you don't let it drop through the bottom of my canoe. And you with your longrifle . . . that's a pretty gun. Can you hit anything with it?"

"I have impressed the ladies of Mortefontaine."

He blinked. "Well. Paddle hard enough and I, Pierre will baptize you voyageurs if you satisfy me. That is the greatest honor a man could have, yes? To win recognition from a North Man? This means, if you are so blessed, that you must buy the rest of us a round of shrub from the company kegs. Two full gallons from each of you."

"What's shrub?" Magnus asked.

"You might as well ask what is bread! Rum, sugar, and lemon juice, my donkey friend. Are you ready for such honor?"

I bowed. "We seek only the chance to prove our-selves."

"You will have that. Now. You will sit carefully on the trade bundles and will enter and leave my canoe with the utmost care. You must not tip her. Your foot must be on a rib or strake because you can step through her birch bark and I do not care to drown in Lake Superior. You will stroke to the time of the song, and you will never let my canoe touch a rock or the shore. When we camp we will jump out when she is still floating, unload the bales, and gently lift her ashore. Yes?"

"We will be careful."

"This is for your own safety. These canoes are light for their size, fast, and can be repaired in an hour or two, but they bruise like a woman." He pointed to Aurora. "Treat them like her." Actually, the girl might already have a couple bruises, the way she writhed and wrestled, but I didn't say that. Certain memories you keep to yourself.

And so with a cry and a saluting gun from the American fort, we were off.

A bark canoe might seem like a fragile craft to tackle an inland sea, but these were ingenious prod-ucts of the surrounding forest, fleet and dry. Pitch and bark could repair damage in an afternoon, and they could be portaged on shoulders for miles. Pierre kneeled in the bow, watching for rocks or logs and leading us in song as the paddles dipped in rhythmic cadence, up to forty strokes a minute. At the stern a steersman, Jacques by name, kept us on unerring course. The paddles flashed yellow in the sun, drops flying like diamonds to chase away the ambitious and persistent insects that buzzed out from land to escort us. The air off the lake was cool and fresh, the sun bright and hot on our crowns.

Always we stroked to song, some French, some English.

My canoe is of bark, light as a feather
That is stripped from silvery birch;
And the seams with roots sewn together,
The paddles white made of birch.
I take my canoe, send it chasing
All the rapids and billows acrost;
There so swiftly, see it go racing,
And it never the current has lost . . .

The voyageurs might be smaller than Magnus and me, but the tough little Frenchmen had the inexhaustibility of waterwheels. Within half an hour my breathing was labored, and soon after I began to sweat despite the chill of the lake. On and on we stroked, moving at what I guessed was six miles an hour—double the speed of the fleet Napoleon had taken to Egypt!—and just as I felt I could paddle no longer, Pierre would give a cry and our brigade would finally drift, the men breaking out pipes to smoke. It was the chief pleasure of their day, occurring once every two hours, and it reminded me of the measured pauses of Napoleon's Alpine army. The men would break off a twist tobacco, a ropelike strand preserved in molasses and rum, crumble it in the bowl of the pipe, strike flint to tinder, and then lean back and puff, eyes closed against the sun. The quick drug made them content as babies. Our little fleet floated like dots on this vast water, the liquid so clean and cold that if thirsty we could dip our palms for a sip.

Then another cry and our pipes were tapped clean, embers hissing on the water, paddles were taken up, and with a shout and a chorus we were on again, driving hard to make maximum use of the lengthening days. Aurora stayed prim and regal under her parasol while Cecil read his little books, of which he had a full satchel, flinging each he finished into the water with the unspoken assumption that none of his rough companions were likely to be literate. Occasionally he would spy a duck or other waterfowl, put down his current volume, and blaze away, the bark of his gun echoing against the shore. He never missed, but we never paused to retrieve the game, either. It was only for sport. As the bird floated away he'd reload, rest his piece on his lap, and go back to reading.

We camped at sunset at a cove marked by a tall "lopstick," a pine tree denuded of its lower branches but left with a tuft at the top as a landmark. These, we learned, were pruned on all the canoe routes to mark camping places. We drifted into a pretty point with a pebble beach and high grass under a stand of birch, Pierre jumping from our canoe into knee-deep water to halt its advance and then drawing it gently toward shore. We each in turn sprang stiffly out.

"It's cold!" Magnus complained.

"Ah, you are a scientist too?" Pierre responded. "What an observer you are! Here is the trick: it makes us work all the faster to build our fires."

As the canoe lightened it was drawn closer, never touching the smooth pebbles of the shore, all of us lifting out the freight bales and arranging them in a makeshift barricade covered with an oilcloth. The empty canoes were finally heaved up with a great cry, flipped with a spray of water, hoisted overhead, marched up the strand, and then propped up on one side by paddles to make an instant lean-to. Fires were lit, guns primed, water fetched, and pipes smoked as peas, pork, and biscuit were cooked and served. It was dull fare that I ate like a starving man.

"Yes, eat, eat, sorcerer!" Pierre encouraged. "You, too, giant! Eat to lighten Radisson's canoe, and because you will lose weight on this trip no matter how much you gobble! Yes, the work burns your body! Eat because there is no pork past Grand Portage, which is why the Montreal men are called the Pork Eaters and only those of us who have wintered over are true North Men."

"What do you eat past Grand Portage?" Magnus asked as he chewed.

"Pemmican. Dried game, berries, and sometimes a mush of rice or corn. Any city man would spit it out, but it's nectar to a working man after a day at the paddles. A pound of pemmican is worth eight pounds of bread! Of course, a few months of that and you long for a squaw. Not just for her quim between her legs, mind you, but her ability to find good things to eat in the woods."

"Why are we going so fast?" I asked, sipping water. "I'm so sore that I feel like I've been stretched on the rack."

"Fast? We're like snails on a carpet, so vast is this country. Do you think the sun will linger forever? At Grand Portage she will turn back south, a lover bidding good-bye, and the days will begin to shorten. Always in our mind is the return of the ice! We paddle to beat the ice! We drive hard to give the North Men time to return to their posts in Upper Canada before their watery highways freeze solid. The winter is good for travel, yes, if you have snowshoes, but not for carrying freight."

"But at this rate we'll be there before the rendezvous."

"Don't worry, sorcerer, we'll have wind and storm enough on Superior to keep us penned. That lake is cold as a witch's heart, and she never lets a man cross freely."

CHAPTER 23

Each night on our canoe voyage, Aurora and Cecil and the other bourgeois pitched a small tent while the voyageurs curled under the canoes. Magnus and I, given our status as middling passengers, each had scraps of canvas and rope that could be rigged as a lean-to shelter. It was a sign of rank, my head on my bundled coat and a wool trade blanket wrapped around me, and once tucked in I lapsed into unconsciousness. But it still seemed midnight when my shelter suddenly fell, half smothering me with dew-wet fabric. What the devil?

"Get up, American, do you think you can sleep all day?" It was Pierre, kicking me with his moccasin-clad foot through the canvas.

I thrashed clear. "It's the middle of the night! You'll wake the camp!"

There were roars of laughter. "Everyone but you *is* awake! We North Men do not tarry in the morning! Even Pork Eaters are up before the likes of you!"

"Morning?" I rubbed my eyes. A cloudy ribbon of stars still arced across the sky, while in the east there was the faintest glow of a very distant dawn. The fire was flaring to life again, last night's leftovers beginning to bubble. Cecil and Aurora were fully dressed, looking bright enough for Piccadilly.

"Yes, eat, eat, because soon we will be paddling. Eat, American! And then come see my handiwork. I have honored our guests on the lopstick tree!"

So we wolfed down the remains of dinner and then followed our escort to the landmark. Its base was covered in carvings, we saw, commemorating some of the dignitaries who'd passed this way. They were mostly Scottish and English names like Mackenzie, Duncan, Cox, and Selkirk. The voyageur lit a candle and held it to the bark so we could read. "There, see how you are immortalized!"

"Lord Cecil and Lady Aurora Somerset," it read. "Plus two donkeys."

"Donkeys!"

"Paddle like men for a few days, and then maybe I will restore your name on another tree. Paddle until your shoulders don't just ache but burn and you want to cry for your mother! But you don't, you just paddle more! *Then* maybe the great Pierre will consider you!"

We stopped a night at Fort Saint Joseph, all of us but Cecil and Aurora camping on the beach because the post was still a half-completed stockade. Huge stacks of peeled logs, chopped and dragged the last winter, lay ready for placement, and the forest was cut back for a mile or more to prevent a surprise attack. Despite the sand fleas I was quickly asleep, given that there was no chance of dalliance with the segregated Aurora. And then in a predawn fog we were roused and pushed off again, the canoes ahead and behind muffled in the mist. We'd not pass another post until Grand Portage.

It was hard paddling against the current as we entered the thirty-mile river connecting Lake Huron and Lake Superior. At the Sault, meaning "jump" or "rapids," we unloaded the canoes once again and carried the cargo in portage, me taking a ninety-pounder and Pierre and Magnus each shouldering two of the crippling loads. Then back for more. We staged the freight in mile increments, meaning we'd carry for half an hour and then get a relative respite going back for another load. Indians were gathered here to fish with spear and bark net from camps that smelled of shit and flies, so the voyageurs posted guard on our belongings because every white man believed every Indian was a thief, and every Indian believed every white man was rich and unaccountably selfish. Once we had all the freight forwarded, we went back for the canoes. Light they might be, but a wet freight canoe still weighed several hundred pounds. I felt like a pallbearer at an endless funeral. Finally it was done.

"You'll see men at Grand Portage who can do three and even four pieces at a time," Pierre panted. "When they are loaded, they look like a house with legs."

"And you will see men in Paris who lift no more than a pair of dice or a quill pen," I moaned back.

"Those are not men, monsieur. To be an urban

parasite, doing nothing for yourself, is to not be alive at all."

Cecil, however, was expected to carry nothing. And Aurora was hoisted high and prim on the shoulders of two voyageurs, gazing ahead like the Queen of Sheba as if this were the most ordinary thing in the world. The little children in the Indian fish camps came running when she passed, laughing with delight. They trailed her until their mothers finally called them back, but she didn't grant them a flicker of response.

At the largest lake of all we put in again. The water was so clear I could follow the slope of the submerged granite as if it were shimmering in air. The water seemed even a richer and deeper blue than Huron, extending to a watery horizon as we followed the north shore. The land to our right began to rise, shoulders of pink and gray granite clothed in a stone-gripping forest of stunted birch, alder, pines, and spruce.

A warm easterly blew and we raised a makeshift sail on a pole and let it blow us westward, me sprawling gratefully to doze during this welcome recess from grueling labor. The canoe lulled as it rocked on the waves, lapping water a quiet music.

Then the wind veered to the southeast and strengthened, the sky in that direction darkening. The sail twisted, the canoe leaning, and we quickly took the canvas down.

"Storm!" Pierre shouted back to the helmsman.

Jacques nodded, looking over his shoulder at black cloud. The captains of the other canoes were crying out commands of warning too.

"I told you the lake does not pass us easily," Pierre said. "Paddle now, my donkeys, paddle with all your might! There's a bay a league from here and we must reach it before the storm is at its peak, unless we want to try to swim to Grand Portage!" He splashed some water at us. "Feel how cold the witch truly is!"

Lightning flashed behind, and a low, ominous rumble rolled over the water. Light danced in the sky, the wind carrying that electrical scent I recalled from the desert. The water, now steel gray, roughened in the gust. Even Pierre gave up his scouting position and knelt in the bow to help paddle.

"Stroke, if you don't want to drown!"

The wind began to rise and the waves steepened, pushing our brigade toward shore. We had to clear a point and avoid being dashed on granite boulders before we got into its lee and could safely land. The freshwater waves had a different pitch than the sea, slapping and choppy, and the water stunned with cold. For the first time we shipped water into the canoes and Pierre pointed at me. "American! The most useless one! Take our cooking pot and bail, but do it carefully, for if you strike the bark and hole us, we will all die!"

Well, that was encouraging. I began to bail, trying to decide if I was more afraid of the water slopping over our gunwales or the water that would gush in if I dipped too deep and enthusiastically. More thunder, and then rain overtaking us in a gray curtain, the water boiling at the edge of the squall where the fat drops fell. I could barely see the shore, except for a line of white where breakers dashed. The rumbling sounded like artillery.

"Thor's song!" Magnus cried. "This is what we came for, Ethan!"

"Not me," I muttered. Franklin was more than a little balmy going kite flying in a lightning storm, but Bloodhammer was his match. We could easily be struck out here.

"Tame the lightning, sorcerer!" Pierre cried.

"I can't without tools. We need to get off the water before it reaches us!" I'd seen what lightning can do.

I glanced at Aurora's canoe. The parasol was gone and she was bent, hair streaming, paddling with grim determination. Cecil had put away his book and fowling piece and was stroking as well, his dripping top hat rammed low and hard on his head.

In our own vessel Magnus was paddling so strongly, the paddle digging so his hand on its shank hit the waves, that Pierre switched to the opposite side to balance the Norwegian's power.

"Maybe we should throw out some of the trade bundles and get more freeboard!" I suggested over the shriek of the wind.

"Are you mad? I'd rather lie with the witch of the lake than explain to Simon McTavish that his precious freight was at the bottom of Superior! Bail, sorcerer! Or find a way to calm the waters!"

On we scudded like leaves in a rapid, the shadowy lee shore growing ominously closer as we strove to round the point before being driven aground. In the dimness its line was marked by the white of cruel boulders, wiry trees shaking and thrashing in the pelting rain.

"Paddle, my friends! Paddle, or we'll suck the witch's tit on the bottom!"

My shoulders were on fire, as Pierre had demanded, but rest was not an option. We neared the point, spray exploding on it in great fountains, and through the dimness and streak of rain I spied an eerie sight, white and angular against the wrack of nature.

"Crosses!" I cried.

"Aye!" Pierre shouted. "Not every crew has made it into this shelter, and those mark the voyageurs who failed! Eye them well, and bail some more!"

They looked like pale bones, glowing in the light of the periodic lightning.

Never have I bailed with more desperation, my muscles cracking with the strain, veins throbbing on my neck. I looked across. Now Aurora was bailing too, eyes wide and fearful. The rain came harder, in great, buffeted streaks, and I was gasping against it, feeling I was already drowning. Six inches of water were in the bottom. I grasped the pot again and flung pitchersful like a madman.

I glanced about. One of the other canoes was gone. I pointed.

"It's too late for them, they are dead from the cold! Paddle, paddle!"

And then we shot past the gnarled knob of land that marked the bay, the canoe rising and surfing on the long swells, and carefully turned, Jacques steering with fierce concentration so we wouldn't broach when broadside to the waves. We turned into the storm, rain hammering, and fought our way into the lee of the point, wind screaming over the shuddering foliage at its crest. There was a red gravel beach and we made for that, the bowmen leaping out in waist-deep water, waves surging to their armpits.

"Don't let the canoes break on the beach!"

We held them off, the lake numbing, as our waterproof ninety-pound bundles were lifted out and hurled up, gravel rattling as surf sucked in and out. Aurora was half lifted and then half jumped into the shallows, staggering in her skirts and then swaying as she splashed up onto land with her dress dragging like a sail. But then she came back down and dragged a bundle back up with her. The men turned the canoes so the water in the bottom poured out then carried them like caterpillars to where they could be propped against the wind. I looked up at the dark landscape beyond. Here the hills were high and hard, murky in the storm's dim light. Lightning cracked and struck on the highlands.

I glanced around to our party, everyone's hair streaming, voyageur moustaches dripping like moss. Even Aurora's ringlets had half-uncurled in soggy defeat.

"Aye, we will not get to Grand Portage too soon," Pierre said. "The lake never lets us. See why we paddle hard when we can, American?"

"What if we hadn't been near this bay?"

"Then we would die, as we all die someday. What if the wind had been on our nose? That has happened too, and driven me a dozen miles back to find proper shelter."

"What about those others?"

"We'll cross the point to look for them. And if the witch doesn't give them up, we will fashion more crosses."

"That was more than a thousand in freight those fools lost!" Cecil seethed. "They have to answer to the devil, but I have to answer to McTavish!"

We never found their bodies, but some of the trade goods did wash ashore, so tightly wrapped in tarpaulins as to be salvageable. Their contents would be dried in the next day's sun.

◻   ◻   ◻

The storm moved on, the sun low when it finally broke clear in the west. I was stiff and shivering with cold and thus happy for the exercise when Pierre beckoned me to follow him into the trees in search of dry wood. Magnus came too, swinging his great ax to break trail like a moose. In moments we were swallowed in a labyrinth of birch and thick moss, the wind and waves audible but our path back swallowed. I soon lost track of our direction.

"How do you know where we are?"

"Our blundering leaves signs, and the sound of the waves. But I like the water, not the forest where a man goes blind. I've had companions planning to walk a hundred paces to fetch a pail of berries and vanish without a trace. Some say Indians, some say bears, some say Wendigo. I say it is simply the soul of the forest, which sometimes gets hungry and swallows men up."

I glanced about. The trees shuddered, the shadows were deep, and water pattered everywhere. I could be lost for days.

Pierre, however, seemed to have a calm sense of direction. We found a downed tree in the lee of a rock, its underside punk wood, and chopped until we quickly had armfuls of dry fuel and moss for tinder. We followed his sure route back and the other voyageurs used flint, steel, and gunpowder to catch the kindling. Smoke began puffing up in great gray clouds. Meanwhile Magnus was chopping more sizable wood with his ax, snapping dead driftwood into lengths with a single swing. I carried these to add to our pyramids of flame. Soon we had three bonfires roaring. Clothes steamed as the voyageurs began a makeshift manic dance like red savages, singing bawdy French songs and laughing and weeping at our escape and the death of their comrades, a tragedy they seemed to regard as unremarkable as the storm itself. Death was as common as snow in the north country.

The sun neared the horizon, giving the wet beach and forest behind it a golden glow as if lacquered. The canvas tents of our nobility went up, steaming, and Cecil broke out a keg of rum and gave us each a tot, even Aurora gulping the fiery liquid down like a sailor.

We began to grin stupidly, the way people do when they escape. Nothing makes you feel more alive than a brush with death.

Then the fires burned down to manageable coals and we began to cook our peas and pork and hominy, stomachs growling. The men stirred fat into the corn porridge.

We ate as if famished, shaking with weariness. Pierre, wiping his mouth with the back of his hand and licking it, addressed Cecil. "Lord Somerset, we've had loss but also gain this day. I watched the donkeys perform well—maybe because they wanted to keep their canoe in pace with that of your pretty cousin, no?"

"If Ethan and Magnus are as weary as I am, then we all did yeoman work."

"They are not yet North Men but they are, perhaps, worthy of the company of the Pork Eaters of Montreal, eh, my porcine-loving friends?"

"A Pork Eater is worth a hundred North Men!" his Montreal companions cried. "Yes, let the donkeys be baptized into our company!"

Pierre addressed us, arms folded like a potentate. "Ethan and Magnus, you have had a taste of the real lake and, much to my surprise, not only lived but have not completely embarrassed yourself. With my own eyes, I saw you drive and bail our canoe past Dead Man's Point with the terrible will this country requires. As voyageurs die, new ones vie for their place. I think it is time you truly joined our company, if you dare to receive such high honor."

"My muscles are twitching, I'm so tired," I confessed.

"A few weeks more and you will not be such women. So we will baptize you now." He picked up a spruce branch snapped by the wind and walked down to the breaking waves on our ruddy beach, the surf on fire in the setting sun. He dipped the branch, carried it back, and shook its droplets over our head. "By the power vested in me as a North Man of the North West Company, I initiate you into our fellowship! From now on you are no longer donkeys but have names, which at dawn I will carve into a tree!"

"It's an honor," Magnus said. "If we have satisfied you, you've impressed me with your endurance, little man. You have the strength of a giant."

Pierre nodded. "Of course I have impressed you. A French voyageur is worth a hundred Norwegians." He looked at me. "And now you must thank the assembly for this honor by taking your silver dollars and buying from Lord Somerset two kegs of shrub, as custom demands."

"How do you know I have silver dollars?"

"Fool American! Of course we have been through your things a dozen times while you slept. All must be shared! Nothing is private among the voyageurs! And we know you can afford to treat us at Grand Portage as well!"

I resolved to hide a few coins for myself in the sole of my moccasins.

So a drunk began, earned by the day's dramatic storm, the rum a needed fire in our throats. As night fell the fires were built up again, sparks swirling up into a sky now brushed clean and full of stars, and Aurora's tent glowed with a pale translucence from a candle within. Pierre had said we'd rest the next day, and it occurred to me that I might have more energy for evening recreation if I knew I could sleep in the next morning. I wanted a taste of life after the day's death. As inebriation mounted I backed into the shadows and crept to her tent flap, the others singing behind me. Surely she was ready for some warmth by now!

"Aurora!" I whispered. "It's Ethan! I'm here to attend as you suggested. The night is cold, and we can bring each other comfort."

There was silence.

"Aurora?"

"What cheek, Mr. Gage. I gave no invitation. I am a woman of propriety, after all. We must be discreet."

"Discretion is my specialty. Let's wager that I can be quieter than you can."

"You are presumptuous, Yankee Doodle!"

"But companionable. I hope your memory is as fond as mine." I don't know why, but women require a measure of persistence and palaver before agreeing to the obvious. Fortunately, I am a fountain of charm. As Franklin said, "Neither a fortress nor a maidenhead will hold out long after they begin to parley."

"But what has changed, Ethan Gage?" she said. "There's no true intimacy when a man won't share his purpose. No affection without a demonstration of trust. How can we unite our purposes if I don't know what your purpose is?"

Women do take patience, don't they? "I'm just an explorer! I'm never quite sure of my purpose, actually. I just wander about, hoping for the best."

"I don't believe that. And I'm not sure of my own

affections until you are sure of our partnership. Imagine if we all joined your quest."

"Aurora, I told you—we're looking for elephants."

A sharp intake of breath. "I have shared everything with you, Ethan. Everything! You give me nonsense in return!"

"I'm in a giving mood right now."

"Good night, sir."

"But Aurora!"

"Please don't make me call my cousin for help."

"I must have reason to hope!"

Silence.

"Some small measure of pity!" I hate groveling, but it occasionally works, and the more I thought about her, the hornier I became. Yes, I know I was addled as a loon.

Finally she answered. "Very well. If you teach me to truly use that remarkable firearm you're so proud of, perhaps I will relent. I am quite fascinated with shooting."

"You want to fire my gun?"

"We can hunt together in the morning. Sport gets my blood up."

I considered. Did the girl simply want more privacy? A roll on the forest moss away from the others? I could impress her with my accuracy, bag some game, massage her delicate feet near a clear forest stream, try to remember a sonnet or two. . . . So off I crept, thwarted but not yet ready to surrender.

I came back into the firelight and a circle of drunken men.

"You look frustrated, my friend!" Pierre cried,

taking another swig of rum. "Having been baptized, are you impatient to be immortalized in the bark of a tree?"

"I was seeking distaff company."

"Ah. Women wound." Heads around the fire nodded with sympathy.

"Ethan, haven't you realized that your worldly success is in inverse proportion to your romantic success?" Magnus said. "We've got better things to discover than Aurora Somerset!"

"But she's *here*. Discovery is out *there*."

"Forget about the fancy lady," Pierre agreed. "That one is like trying to carry berries in your cheek and not lose any juice. More care than it's worth."

"She's so beautiful." My plaintive tone embarrassed even me.

"So are half the dusky wenches at Grand Portage, and they are a hundred times more appreciative. Forget the fancy one and pick yourself a squaw."

"I don't want a squaw."

"How do you know when you haven't met her yet?"

But I was tired of the jocular insults and advice, so I moved away to restlessly wait for the morrow's hunt beneath a canoe, knowing Aurora was making a fool of me but not particularly caring. The best way to regain my equilibrium was her conquest. Perhaps it would be easier away from camp. I wouldn't even mind babbling about Norse hammers, but she'd just think us lunatics and leave us on the beach.

I lay sleepless as the voyageurs exhausted the

rum and collapsed, and then there was a crunch of gravel by my makeshift garret and I saw a boot. Sir Cecil bent down to look at me under the rim of the boat.

"Lord Somerset." I was afraid he was going to warn me off.

"Mr. Gage." He cleared his throat. "We're a small group, and I heard of your disappointment. My cousin is moody, like all women. She breaks hearts like crockery and thinks little of it. Don't be too sensitive."

"We're going shooting tomorrow, while the party rests."

"You'll find her a crack shot. And tamable, if you meet her halfway."

"Then you're not opposed to our friendship?"

"I'm not opposed to our partnership."

The gravel crunched as he walked away and I realized he'd included himself in any union. As I drifted off to sleep, I wondered why Cecil Somerset cared at all about his cousin's romance with a wastrel like me.

CHAPTER 24

While the voyageurs slept off their shrub, Aurora prodded me awake at dawn. She was dressed in boots, breeches, and a sky-blue, short-tailed hunting coat. Her luxuriant hair had been tied back and her hands were sheathed in doeskin gloves. "Let's try this rifle of yours!" she said, brisk as a chipmunk.

I groaned to myself, having not had enough sleep, but sprang up like a toy on a spring, my groggy instinct to impress her. Perhaps the chipmunk's brain was mine.

Far from being the prim and helpless female she posed when whim took her, Aurora soon had me trailing and panting as she led the way up a granite ridge, Lake Superior a blue ocean below. Her slim legs were spry as a deer, and she had a good eye for the best path and signs of game. I didn't mind following, having plenty of time to get a good eyeful, but it was clear that Lady Somerset's comfort in the wilderness was not entirely due to parasols and trunks of clothes. Every time I tried to woo her with some witty or soulful remark she silenced me with a hand and stern look, pointing as if dinner were certain to appear. And sure enough, we did manage to sneak up on a yearling buck. She took my longrifle and felled it at seventy-five yards with a single shot through the neck, sighting and squeezing like a marksman and displaying no difficulty holding the heavy weapon steady or absorbing its kick.

"Splendid shot!"

"Your gun shoots slightly high and to the left."

She gutted the deer with her own ivory-handled knife, giving me pause at her efficiency in slitting around the testicles. Then she sliced off its head and heaved up the haunch to place it on my shoulders. "This is too heavy for me." Back down the mountain she led.

My regal, delicate woman had been replaced overnight with a regular Boone, independent and laconic, and I realized that despite the delectability of her slim form, I didn't much care for this new guise. It's odd how one falls under a spell, and odder still when one begins to wake from it. I finally realized how little I understood her, or our relationship. I had not seduced but instead been seduced, and not by an English lady but some kind of huntress—as dangerous, possibly, as Magnus had warned. I remembered his tales of Loki, the Norse trickster god, who could assume many shapes and eventually triggered Ragnarok, the end of the world.

But then we *did* stop at a stream to rest and cool our feet. Hers, when I offered to massage them—a tactic that seems to work with all manner of women—were indeed more callused than I expected, or remembered. Nor did she swoon at my touch.

"I'm beginning to suspect that you're more at home in the wilderness than I imagined."

"Really?" Her eyes were half-lidded as she leaned back, regarding me. "I've learned some things in travels with my cousin. And Cecil and my father taught me to shoot in England. It's ever so satisfying to kill things, don't you think?"

"Your skill at shooting makes us even greater soul mates than I'd guessed," I tried. "We have the camaraderie not just of the bed but of the target."

"We're simply having some sport, Mr. Gage."

"There are sports other than shooting we could still teach each other, I'm sure." I do have a dogged persistence.

"Like why a French spy and a Norwegian revolutionary want to go into fur country?"

"I'm no spy."

"You keep secrets like one. You come from Bonaparte, Astor, and Jefferson."

"I'm simply scouting Louisiana, as I told you. For elephants."

"No. Bloodhammer is after more. It's obvious that the pair of you have a wicked secret, and I'm beginning to suspect even *you* don't fully know what it is. You follow anyone with a strong will, and he's playing you." She drew her feet back and put on her boots. "We could help if you'd let us, but it seems you enjoy blind conspiracy. No matter. Everything will come out at Grand Portage."

I was annoyed by her scorn. "So let's enjoy our companionship now."

She sprang up. "I gave you a sample, but I form relationships only with men I trust." And taking my rifle in her own fist, she started down again.

I wearily stood, shouldering the meat and suddenly not liking the way she held my rifle so tightly and not me. I thought she had the politeness to wait on an outcrop, but instead she was paying me no attention, instead looking intently down at the bay below.

"They've come," she said.

A canoe was making for shore, its wake a widening V of silver. Indians were the paddlers, but the central figure wore the red coat of a British soldier. Voyageurs waded out to pull it to shore and the occupants leaped out and disappeared into the trees.

"Who's come?"

"Cecil's guide."

◻   ◻   ◻

It took us an hour to work down the ridge toward the plume of smoke that marked camp, and when we were a few hundred yards from our destination we came across the small pond that changed everything. It was a low wetland at the base of the hill fringed by reeds and surrounded by trees, quiet and wind-protected, and the day had warmed enough that bathing would be pleasant. We heard a splash, and realized someone was in the water.

There was feminine laughter.

Two women were swimming, their hair fanned behind them like a beaver's tail. I realized they must have come from the visiting canoe. Aurora, stiffening, was as curious as I was. We stood hidden in the trees, watching them stroke. All Indians I've seen are good swimmers, and these were no exception. One of the women finally waded up out of the water to stand in the shallows, droplets sparkling on her bronze skin, and I audibly drew in my breath despite myself.

Aurora looked at me with wry amusement.

The Indian woman was young and very pretty, her breasts smaller than those of Lady Somerset but no less attractive for that, and her legs and buttocks smooth and supple. The water was to her knees, and somehow she sensed us and turned, seeming no more ashamed of her nakedness than a fawn, but curious, alert, her nipples brown in the sun and the patch between her thighs wet and gleaming. She was lighter-skinned than I expected an Indian woman to be, and her hair was not the normal jet black but instead a dark copper. The nymph looked across to where we were standing, even though I was certain we were well screened, and peered, wary but curious.

"Why is she not darker?"

"It's not unknown," Aurora said. "Maybe she's a half-breed, or a white captive. Come." When she moved the Indian woman suddenly sprang and ducked amid the reeds, instantly hiding like a wild thing.

"Wait!" I whispered.

But now the other one, stouter and less arresting, was also wading out of the water, looking over her shoulder, and vanishing into cover.

Aurora's look over her shoulder was mocking. "So you like red meat."

"I'm not getting any white, am I?"

"Partnership, Mr. Gage, partnership."

"I'm just curious, like any man."

"I'll bet you are, American. Stay away from them, if you value your life."

"What does that mean?" It pleased me that she even bothered to warn me off.

"Come to camp. You'll see."

We broke out of the last trees to the bright light of the lakeshore. The large Indian canoe was drawn up, its warrior occupants making a fire separate from that of the voyageurs. There were six braves, shirtless in the sun and wearing breechclouts and buckskin leggings. They squatted like grasshoppers, easy but powerful. Their muscles gleamed from grease applied to ward off blackflies.

The man I'd assumed was a British officer was also an Indian, I realized. His black hair was pulled back and adorned with an eagle feather. Unlike his companions he wore a faded British military coat, the brass of its buttons worn but shiny. I wondered where he'd gotten it.

This chief, if that's what he was, was conferring with Lord Somerset, and his regal bearing was a match for the aristocrat, reminding me again of Brant and Tecumseh. Unconquered tribal leaders had poise and panache, it seemed. His eyes were dark, nose strong, and lips set in a curl of slight cruelty. His muscles that I could see were as taut as the banded strands of a warship's hawser. His gaze flashed with recognition when he saw Aurora and, disturbingly, the same look of recognition stayed when his gaze turned to me. Had he been at one of the forts? Surely I'd recall him.

"The goddess Diana returns with her kill!" Cecil called in greeting, smiling.

"The deer is not all we found," she said.

"Oh."

"Squaws washing in a pond. Red Jacket's?"

"Slaves. An Ojibway gambled them away. Red Jacket is taking them to Grand Portage and then to his village."

"Ethan was transfixed."

"I shouldn't blame him. The one's a beauty."

"Pah."

"Ethan, my cousin has made you a bloody pack-horse, it seems!"

"She has the rifle," I tried to joke. In truth, I was embarrassed. My determination to bed her had allowed Aurora Somerset to lead me by the nose like a bull, but now there were these other women. Hadn't Pierre said to take a squaw?

"Well, you'll be newly popular," Cecil said. "All the men like fresh venison."

"Including your new guests?"

"This is Red Jacket, a chief from the western end of the lake who is Ojibway on his mother's side but Dakota on his father's—the product of two historic enemies, and thus most unusual. His mother was captured and brought him up knowing both tongues. He travels widely and fights well.

I was hoping to meet up with him, but with the storm, I wasn't sure. He knows the west—knows the country you're headed for, perhaps. He can serve us both! They took refuge on an island west of here and then paddled down this morning looking for us."

"Greetings," I said, holding out a hand.

The chief said and did nothing in reply.

"He wears an officer's coat?"

"Yes, striking, isn't it? Probably best not to ask him how he got it. I don't think it was a present, and I hope it never wears out so he begins eyeing *my* clothes."

"But you trust him?"

"Implicitly. Red Jacket makes no secret of where he stands, or what he wants. His appetites are plain."

Including venison. The meat restored us, and we spent the rest of the day at what we called Refuge Bay, bathing, stitching, patching, and eating. Aurora returned my rifle, complimenting it if not me, and she'd cleaned it, too. The two women I'd seen appeared dressed modestly in buckskin, their eyes downcast and their manner obedient. If they were embarrassed at being seen at their bath, they didn't show it.

Pierre came over. "The pretty one is named Namida, or 'Star Dancer' in the Ojibway tongue," he whispered quietly, squatting while he smoked his pipe. "It's a name given by her original captor. The other is Little Frog. They were taken by these scoundrels after gambling at the Sault. There was a whiskey fight, and Red Jacket here delivered the coup de grace to her first owner with a tomahawk. They'll be taken to his band to be slaves until some buck asks for one of them. The tribes are always looking to replenish their depleted numbers. Too much war and disease."

I studied the pair with interest, willing them to look up. Namida finally glanced my way as she stooped to do camp chores, and I more than glanced back. She was a woman of about twenty with hair as lustrous as an otter pelt, and she carried herself with grace. She was light for her race, but had the high cheekbones and generous mouth of the tribes, her smile a piercing white, her throat decorated with a porcupine bead choker, a silver coin on one ear. Her arms were bare and smooth, her calves taut, and her figure—well, I'd already seen that. She was as different from Aurora Somerset as a wild pony from a racetrack thoroughbred, but had fire of her own, I guessed. I knew it was partly my longing for my lost Egyptian woman Astiza who had a little of the same look, but my God, how lightly her moccasins moved, how bewitchingly her hips swayed, how innocent her averted gaze! She was nothing like the tired native women I'd seen in Detroit. And then she looked at me fully . . .

"I thought you didn't like squaws, my friend?" Pierre said as my head followed her through the encampment as if on a swivel.

"She has blue eyes."

"Aye, Mandan by the story I heard—or rather their relatives, the Awaxawi—captured as a girl and traded back and forth until she wound up on

the Sault. She's hundreds of miles from her homeland, and probably sees Red Jacket as an opportunity to get a little closer to home. Odd-looking for
an Indian, isn't she?"

"That's not an adequate word for such beauty."
Mandan! Hadn't mad Tom Jefferson suggested
they might be descended from the Norse or Welsh?

"I thought you were besotted with Aurora,"
Magnus put in. I ignored him.

Aurora was watching our tableau from a distance, disapproving, and I enjoyed paying her back
some discomfort. If I could provoke enough jealousy of Namida, maybe the British tease would be
more willing to renew our intimacy. I was considering just how to organize my campaign when my
gaze was noticed by Red Jacket and he snapped
something to Cecil.

The Englishman came over to speak. Aurora
was also watching, her look toward the girl mali-
cious.

"The squaw looks different than her race, doesn't
she?" Cecil said.

"I didn't know Indians had that coloring."

"I've heard of it and seen it. Welsh, some say.
Some Indian words sound Welsh."

"Or Norwegian," Magnus said.

The aristocrat's brows rose. "Do you think so?
Imagine if your distant ancestors came this way!
I think I'm beginning to understand your enthusiasm, Magnus. Although if it were the Welsh
that settled Namida's country . . . well, that would
make Louisiana British territory by first right,
wouldn't it?"

"Or so confuse history that none would have rightful claim at all," I said.

"Stay away from those squaws," Cecil warned. "I've heard the Mandan maidens are positively ethereal in their beauty, the most attractive women on the continent—but this pair is Red Jacket's property. He has a temper. He might have eaten the liver of the man who wore that coat."

"He's a cannibal?"

"They all are, when they want to destroy their enemies and imbibe their strength. I've seen Indian braves devour hearts and their squaws fry the liver. But if it ever comes to that you'll long to be eaten, because the pain that comes from the torture before is indescribable. Women like those two there will be the cruelest, and they'll heat sticks in the fire and insert them in every orifice."

I swallowed. "I'm only looking."

"Don't even look. One does not quarrel with Red Jacket and survive. Just ignore them—unless you've already tired of my cousin."

"Lord Somerset, it is she who seems to have tired of me."

"I told you, patience. She favors few men with a hunt."

"And favors even fewer with anything else."

He laughed and walked away, nodding to the Indian chief.

That night I bedded down by myself, tired of pursuing Aurora and tired of my companions commenting on it. I'm not averse to playing the fool when I think there'll be sweet reward at the end, but there's a limit to humiliation even for me. The game with Somerset had turned sour, and I decided to swear off women entirely.

Then there was a quiet footfall near my bedroll and a female whisper in the dark, in the French that dominated the fur trade.

"*Sauvez-moi.*" Save me.

Then Namida crept away.

CHAPTER 25

W e pushed on the next day, hugging the north shore. The lake was cold, the air crisp and flawless, the mountains a glittery granite. I'd thought the French to be tireless paddlers, but the Indians seemed even more so, impatient at our pauses to smoke. But then they, too, would drift alongside to beg twist tobacco to put in their pipes.

"They're just in a hurry to get to Grand Portage to drink," Pierre scoffed.

"No, I think they can paddle longer than the great Pierre," Magnus teased him.

On and on we stroked across a vast blue universe, my arms and torso turning into twisted steel from this unrelenting labor, day after long summer day. Storms would pen us periodically, all of us dozing in camp as wind and rain lashed our tarps, and then the tempest would pass and we'd go on. At camp each night Namida kept her distance except for an occasional wary, pale-eyed glance, while Aurora was even more aloof now that Red Jacket accompanied our party. It was as if he was a wilderness duke who demanded propriety. She retreated alone to her tent and spoke nothing to the Indian women, nothing to me, and nothing to Red Jacket. Occasionally she sat alongside her cousin to have long, earnest conversations, gesturing toward all of us.

I, meanwhile, wondered if this Namida or her plainer friend, Little Frog, could shed any light on the Norwegian's mysterious map, given that she came from the tribe and area that interested Jefferson.

My chance came on the fourth day after I first spied her bathing, when I was sitting apart from the others for a moment's privacy and she came up to shyly offer some corn mixed with molasses. "I flavored it with berries from the forest," she said in French.

"Thank you." I ate with my fingers. "You come from the west?"

She cast her eyes down.

"You are Mandan?" I persisted.

"Awaxawi, their cousins."

"Have you ever heard of Wales?"

She looked confused.

"Why are your eyes blue?"

She shrugged. "They have always been blue." Suddenly she leaned close to whisper. "Please. I can guide you."

"Really?"

"Take me home and my people can help."

"You know what we're looking for?" Now that would be disconcerting!

"Your giant's ancestors left cave pictures of themselves. We have red-hair writing. Old writing on a magic stone. I can help."

"A stone?" I was stunned. That sounded like the inscriptions I'd seen in the Orient! "What kind of writing?"

"We don't know. It is secret."

"Secret? Like a cipher?"

But Red Jacket snapped something at her and she hurriedly retreated.

The fact that she gave her corn mush treat to no other voyageur didn't escape notice. "So now you have a serving wench, my friend," Pierre congratulated.

"She thinks we could help get her back home. She claims her tribe has some kind of old writing. Somehow she surmised we're going beyond Grand Portage to look for Magnus's ancestors."

"All the camp knows that. Old writing? From where?"

"I don't know."

"No matter. She's Red Jacket's now."

"I don't see him treating her with any respect." I kept eating. The sweet-sour berries added some interesting flavor, and there was also a crunch of seeds. "She deserves better. I want to rescue her."

He laughed. "Ah, then her spell is already working!"

"What spell?"

Pierre pointed to my food. "Indian women are

well-practiced in love charms. The Ojibway swear
by the seeds of the gromwell to capture the heart.
Oh yes, American, she is bewitching you."

"She didn't need seeds to do that." I grinned.
"Have you watched her hips?"

"Keep your head, or you'll lose your hair to Red
Jacket."

I glanced over at the Indian, who indeed seemed
to be eyeing my scalp. I made a face at him and he
darkened and looked away. Aurora frowned too,
which gave me even more satisfaction. That girl
had her chance, didn't she?

Maybe she'd come crawling to me at Grand Portage.

Except that now there was Namida.

        ◻   ◻   ◻

As we paddled on, I spied a long, low island on
the southern horizon.

"Isle Royale," Pierre said. "Forty miles end to
end, and dotted with curious pits. You can still see
chunks of copper ore and discarded tools. There
are old copper mines there, so numerous you wonder what civilization worked them."

Magnus glanced up at the bowman.

"The Indians had copper," the voyageur went
on, "but nothing on the scale of those workings. It
looks like enough was dug to arm the warriors on
both sides of the walls of Troy. But how would this
copper have gotten to Greece, eh?"

"Perhaps people have been crossing the Atlantic

and trading metal far longer than we guess," Magnus said. "Maybe my Norse were part of a train of explorers going back to ancient times."

"But who boated all this way in those days?"

I couldn't resist joining in, even though I knew it would only fuel the speculation. "The astronomer Corli, and his colleague Gisancourt, speculated that Plato's allegory of Atlantis was actually a real place, an island in the Atlantic. Perhaps the miners came from there. Trojan refugees. Carthaginians. Who knows?"

"There, you see?" said Magnus. "This lake has been a highway."

"Aye, there are mysteries in this wilderness," said Pierre. "Not just old pits. Sometimes a man comes across a mysterious mound or a tumbled stone wall in the oddest places. Who built them? But all is silence, no answer but the call of birds. You quest for El Dorado, giant, but no conquistador has yet found it."

"Not conquistador, but king," I said.

"What?"

"How about it, Magnus? Somerset called you royalty. What did he mean by that?"

"Bloodhammer is an ancient name of a Norse monarch," my companion said evenly. "I'm proud to say I share his bloodline."

"You're Norwegian nobility, cyclops?" Pierre asked.

"For what it's worth. There's no independent Norway, according to the Danes."

Here it was then. My companion did not just want independence for his nation. He wanted to reinstitute Norwegian aristocracy in which he might claim a place. He was not so much a revolutionary as a royalist!

"So you're a long-lost king, Magnus?" I clarified.

"Hardly. And the lineage of my ancestors is nothing compared to what we're looking for, Ethan."

"And explain again just what *are* we looking for?"

"I told you, a golden age that was lost. Secrets of the gods. In every culture there's a fount of wisdom, a tree of life, and not just an Yggdrasil. In Norse stories, Iduna's golden apples conferred to the gods everlasting life."

"Like a tree in Eden."

"Aye." He stroked again. "And the serpent is like the dragon who guards the golden hoard."

◘   ◘   ◘

At long last we saw the masts of an anchored sloop in the shoreline ahead and realized we'd come to the end of the lake. The faint wail of bagpipes and fiddles floated across the water, and our Indians began yipping like dogs. We stopped short at a small island to dress ourselves for Rendezvous. The voyageurs donned their brightest clothes, tilted their caps at a jaunty angle, and fixed them with feathers. Lord Somerset cleaned his own boots to a high polish, and Aurora disappeared behind some bushes before emerging in a gown fit for the English court, wrinkled and musty but still stupefying in its sheen. The two Indian women stroked their lustrous hair with wooden combs and painted their lips with juice, and the men were bangled with copper and bone ornaments. Magnus and I trimmed each other's hair, brushed our greatcoats, and traded worn moccasins for fresh ones. I'd quickly seen the practicality of this footwear: light, silent, and quick-drying.

Then, properly attired, we shoved off again and all six canoes began a race around Hat Point to sprint for the gray-weathered stockade. All of us sang the now-familiar French paddling songs at the top of our lungs, paddles dipping in synchronized rhythm. As we came into view a horn sounded ashore and cannon went off, and as we neared the pebbled beach a tide of trappers, Indians, and bourgeois managers poured down to meet us, cheering, insulting, and firing guns in the air. Great cottony puffs of white smoke blossomed, reports echoing merrily across the bay. Indian braves whooped with cries that raised the hairs on my neck, shaking tomahawks like rattles. Women waved blankets and clashed iron kettles. Cecil, Pierre, and I fired in turn, and Aurora waved her parasol, her green eyes bright with excitement.

Then the bowmen leaped lightly into the shallows and we were ashore, strangers pounding our backs and offering swigs of shrub.

Tents, wigwams, and overturned canoes used as lean-tos were spread on either side of the fort, hazy wood smoke hanging over the encampment like a roof. Music drifted, drums thumped, and the pop-pop of shooting competitions filled the air. I could smell roasting meat, spice, and molasses.

Grand Portage itself was a modest stockade a few acres in extent that contained a dozen sawn-log buildings, gardens of corn, herbs, and vegetables, and sheds for furs and trade goods. Amid the stumps outside where the forest had been logged, a dozen assembled Indian tribes camped with hundreds of visiting voyageurs. A muddy trail wound from the fort up through the slash and into the forest for the eight-mile portage that led to the navigable part of the Pigeon River above its falls. From there, canoeists could paddle upstream to waterways that led west to the fabled Rocky Mountains or north to the Arctic. We were at the continent's crossroads, the edge of empire between British, American, French, and Indians.

"We're drawing closer to where my people came," Magnus murmured. "I feel it. Somewhere beyond the trees is the navel of the world."

"Somewhere beyond the trees are blackflies, Red Indians, and plain stream water," Pierre advised. "Feast while you can."

Our party split. Magnus and I, as ambassadors of a sort, accompanied the Somersets and Red Jacket through the gates of the fort to the Great Hall. Pierre, his voyageur companions, and the other women fanned into the encampments outside, crying greetings, boasts, insults, and endearments to people they hadn't seen in a year.

The fort's interior parade ground grass was trampled flat by the traffic. Bundles of trade goods piled high, and fur presses squeezed lush pelts for shipping to New York and London. Armed guards escorted us past this treasury to the long porch of the

Great Hall, a log building whose sash was painted Spanish brown. There a cluster of partners waited, at their center a tall, stern-faced, white-haired Scot in a black coat and knee-high moccasins.

"Lord and Lady Somerset!" he greeted with booming voice. "We've been awaiting your company!"

Cecil gave the slightest of bows. "Simon McTavish! It is an honor, sir."

"The honor is ours. And this is your lovely cousin?"

"May I present Aurora?"

"Most presentable! Lady, your light outshines the morning."

She smiled and gave a slight curtsy. It was all a little precious for me, given that things were rustic as Mary's manger. McTavish was leering like an old goat.

"Red Jacket you know, I believe," Cecil said.

McTavish raised a hand. "All men know the fame of the warrior chief, friend of both the Ojibway and Dakota."

"And these two gentlemen have accompanied us as well," Cecil went on. "Ethan Gage is an American with a reputation as adventurer and electrician. He has connections to the French government."

"The French!"

"Who are reacquiring Louisiana," Cecil announced blandly. "Gage is an emissary of Napoleon, out to tell them what they have. He's dined with Jefferson as well."

"Are you a herald of war, Mr. Gage?"

I bowed myself. "On the contrary, sir, I helped forge peace between my own nation and the French at Mortefontaine. I am an American who has worked with both the British and the French. Bonaparte and Jefferson sent me as a symbol of peace." I smiled brightly as a barmaid.

The old Scot looked skeptical. "Did they now?" Though well past fifty, this empire builder looked hard as iron and quick as an abacus.

"His companion Magnus Bloodhammer is a Norwegian patriot and descendant of royalty who thinks his ancestors may have preceded us all to this hard country," Somerset went on. "While the fur trade is one of fierce competition, we here—Red, English, American, and so forth—have joined forces as a symbol of peace and unity. Bonaparte is taking back Louisiana, McTavish, whether we like it or not, and we must have Ethan's help in persuading us all to stay in our sphere of influence."

"We get the north, where the best furs are."

"Exactly," Cecil said.

"A satisfactory sentiment if you share it, Mr. Gage. If you represent France, we will extend to you the courtesy of emissaries under a flag of truce. If you represent the United States, you can almost stake claim to our little post already."

"Stake claim?"

"We're a few miles south of the settled boundary of your native nation. A new post is being built in Canada and this one will be abandoned in a year or two. You are here for the twilight of the gods, the last of Valhalla."

"You know the Nordic legends of Ragnarok, Mr. McTavish?" Magnus asked with interest.

"Casually, as a student of the classics. The occasional verbal flourish is a vanity my lieutenants tolerate." He gave a thin smile. "I don't really anticipate the end of the world. But perhaps I should, in the presence of the wayfarer Odin himself."

Now Magnus bowed.

"Odin?" Cecil asked.

"Has your friend not shared the resemblance, Lord Somerset? In Norse myth, the one-eyed god, who gave an orb to drink from the fountain of wisdom, wanders the world of men in broad slouch hat and concealing cloak. I daresay that we're either in the presence of the divine, or Mr. Bloodhammer emulates the chief of Asgard and Valhalla."

"My eye was taken, not given up," Magnus said. "The Danes don't want Norwegians learning the truth."

"And now you dress like the legend! No, don't deny, we Scots will don kilts, the voyageurs their sashes, the braves their paint. All of us in costume! I suspect our revelry this year will be especially memorable given it may be our last here. Not that my partners are not businessmen first!"

"Ledgers before liquor, Simon," one mouthed promptly as a puppet on a string. "Discussion before dance. The men have to complete the portage, too."

"But after that . . ." McTavish grinned a wolfish challenge. "I will outdance all of you! Except Red Jacket, perhaps."

"Have you brought my presents?" the Indian

asked the Scot in English, startling me. Apparently he understood more than he let on.

"And more. King George desires peace and partnership with all the Indians: the Ojibway and Fox and Sac and Winnebago and Menominee and even your own relatives, Red Jacket, the famed Sioux."

"That is our enemies' word. I am Dakota. I kill King George's enemies for you. I take their hair. I eat their courage. I steal their women."

McTavish's smile didn't waver. "His majesty has uses for all his children."

We went inside. The walls of the high, white-washed dining hall were decorated with maps of the Canadian interior, antlers, crossed snowshoes, and Scottish broadswords. Long tables set with blue and white china were set for fifty men. Here the company bourgeois discussed business, while outside the voyageurs completed their portage. Drinking would commence this evening.

I explained our intent to explore Louisiana southwest of Lake Superior. "With the territory moving from Spanish to French control, and a new American president, Paris and Washington are simply seeking information," I explained. "I'm hoping to serve as a go-between, as I did at Mortefontaine, to facilitate understanding."

"From warrior to diplomat," Cecil said approvingly.

"And Magnus here is a historian."

"How altruistic of you," McTavish said. "Just ambling about as tourists, are you? And I understand you were mixed up with Smith in Syria and

Napoleon in Egypt, and now you're halfway around the world?"

"Duty takes me to odd places."

"How convenient to be everyone's ally!"

"It's often a bother, actually."

"Where does the American wish to go?" Red Jacket suddenly asked.

"Well, we don't know exactly," I replied, even though we vaguely planned to head in the direction of Thor's hammer on the old Norse map, an area entirely uncharted. "I hope we can accompany the North West Company's men as far as Rainy Lake and then strike south from there. Do you have a suggestion?"

"Back home."

The partners and clerks laughed.

"The French do not stay," Red Jacket went on. "The British stay lightly. But the Americans"—the chief pointed to me—"stay and wound the earth wherever they go. I have heard this from the great Shawnee Tecumseh and seen it with my own eyes, too. They drain the earth's heart and blind the earth's eyes." He turned to McTavish. "It is dangerous having these men here. Do not be fooled by them."

"How about it, Gage? Are you dangerous?"

"No man is more persistently friendly than I. I'm your guest, and would not embarrass your hospitality."

McTavish turned to the Indian. "So while I appreciate your bluntness, Red Jacket, I trust the Somersets to answer for our American guest."

"What is bluntness?"

"Truth," a company partner told the Indian.

"The truth is that when this fort is abandoned, the forest will return. I, Red Jacket, vow it."

"And the truth, Red Jacket," McTavish said, "is that no matter how little the Sac and the Fox and the Ojibway and the Menominee and the Winnebago and the Dakota like white men here, all depend on these forts for the guns, powder, kettles, and blankets that keep you from starving or freezing. Don't you? Just as we depend on you to hunt fur."

The chief scowled, but said nothing.

"We are a partnership. And now, gentlemen, to the maps."

CHAPTER 26

Inside, the stockade was meetings, ledgers, fur presses, and warehouses. Outside, the voyageurs who'd lugged their loads across the portage began what was the greatest revelry of the year, a two-week bacchanal of feasting, drinking, dancing, and tupping whichever Indian maidens they could woo, buy, or marry. I left the partners to their serious business and wandered back out through the gates, Magnus in tow, to find Pierre and experience the fun of Rendezvous.

The French voyageur had made a temporary castle under his overturned canoe, stretching a tarpaulin from one rim. He was smoking a clay pipe, sleeves rolled and shirt unbuttoned, pleased as a prince. There was a fine summer breeze to keep the mosquitoes down, and a dazzling high-summer sun to give everything a polish. Within a fortnight he would be on his way into the wilderness for the long winter, but for now he could focus on eating, boasting, drinking, and song.

"Lord Pierre!" I greeted. "You look more at ease than the bourgeois in the Great Hall, with all their china and servants and dogs."

"That's because they have too much." He pointed at the fort with the stem of his pipe. "The more that's acquired, the more you want. The more you have, the more care you must take of it. The more you possess, the more you can lose. That is the secret of life, my friend! A sensible man like me is rich with nothing." He waggled his pipe at us. "Do not chase treasure. It will only bring you grief."

"McTavish said even the Indians need guns and blankets now."

"*Oui!* A generation ago, they answered to no man. Now they've forgotten, most of them, how to hunt with the bow and arrow. They live for trade, not for life. Instead of us learning all the right lessons from them, they are learning all the wrong ones from us."

"Yet surely we are superior if we are the conquerors."

"Who at this Rendezvous is slave, and who is free? The bourgeois in their stuffy meeting room, or me with my pipe?"

We sat to debate the point, I saying it was the company partners who gave the orders and would go home to snug houses in the winter, and Magnus opining that they spent so much time worrying about profit that they were blind to the glory around them.

Pierre compared ambition to rum. "A swallow warms you up, and a pint makes you happy. But a keg will kill you. Men like McTavish are never content."

I wondered what restless Napoleon would say to that. "Red Jacket is with the partners," I said to change the subject. "He watches in one corner, arms folded."

"He and his renegades enforce their will," Pierre said. "He's estranged from both the Ojibway and Dakota, a man of two nations who belongs fully to neither and who obeys no law or custom. Let Indian kill Indian, the traders say. It's been frontier policy for three hundred years."

"It makes him a grumpy-looking bastard."

"Simon McTavish keeps his friends close and his enemies closer. Red Jacket's lodge flies the blond hair of the man whose coat he wears, and rumor has it that he dined on the man's flesh. Yet the Somersets count him an ally."

"British aristocrats are friends with a red cannibal?"

"Those two aren't the dandies they seem, my friend. Both have been in this country before, and know more of it than they let on. There was some kind of trouble in England, some money disappeared, and a scandal that involved them both."

"What scandal?"

He shrugged. "One hears stories, and I only believe what I see. Cecil is a dangerous man with a sword—I hear he killed an officer in a duel—and Aurora, as you know, is a crack shot. So stay away from Namida. It isn't good to be mixed up with anything to do with Red Jacket or any woman at all if the English lady has an eye on you. Find an ugly squaw so Aurora won't care. They're all the same down where it counts, and the homely ones are far more appreciative."

Crude and sensible advice that I hadn't the slightest intention of following. "If that girl is really Mandan, she deserves to be back with her people."

"I know your kind, Ethan Gage. You are not ambitious, but you want to save everyone. Don't. You'll only bring trouble on yourself."

"And I know your kind, Pierre. Man of the moment, going nowhere, with a thousand rationalizations of why to do nothing. You'll die penniless."

"Living for today is not nothing, my friend."

"But Magnus and I have more than the day: we have a quest." It was odd to hear myself defending our odd mission and my odder comrade, so much more fanatical and driven than me. "If it succeeds, we're beholden to no one."

"And if it doesn't, you risk death for nothing."

◻   ◻   ◻

I strolled the camp. There were lots of women, many pretty, but Namida still stood out; her heritage made her exotic. She and Little Frog were taking smoked meat and fresh corn from the main supply tents to Red Jacket's camp at the far southern end of Rendezvous. My tactic to talk to her would be a loaf of bread. I scooped one up, trotted ahead out of sight, and then intercepted them.

"Have you developed a taste for the baguette?"

They stopped shyly, Little Frog looking uncertain but Namida eyeing me with sly hope. Yes, she was looking for an alternative to her gruff cannibal of a captor, and I was just the man to provide it.

"What is that?" she said, looking at the loaf.

"Bread, baked from flour. You haven't tried white man's food? Some bites of this, and shavings from a sugar loaf, and you'll want to go with me to Paris."

"What is Paris?"

I laughed. "The direction we *should* be going. But you live where the trees end?"

"Our families are there. Where the rock with words is." She nodded encouragement.

"Did you see anything else peculiar in your travels?"

"I do not know that word."

"Strange?"

She shrugged. "Earth and sky."

Which might or might not include hammers. "Here, try a bite of this. Go ahead, put your bundles down." I broke off a piece of the baguette. "Best bread in the world when it's fresh, and the voyageurs appear to have taught even the Scots how to make it. Yes, try the white part . . ."

Suddenly something hit my backside and I bucked forward, sprawling on the muddy ground with my broken baguette under me. The women gave a little squeak of alarm and snatched their load back up, hopping over my body and hurrying on their way. I rolled over to peals of laughter from voyageurs who were watching.

Red Jacket loomed over me, his torso muscled into beaten bronze, his black eyes like pistol bores. He sneered. "You talk to slaves?"

I bounded up, surprised and shaken, my clothes muddy. "Damned right I do."

He kicked again without warning, square in my stomach so I doubled over, and then shoved so I sat abruptly, windless and shocked. His violence was almost casual but quick as a snake and powerful as a mule. I wanted to get up but couldn't breathe.

His finger stabbed like a spear. "Red Jacket women." He spat.

I struggled up again, hunched, flushed with rage, but ready for a fight with this bastard even if he *was* two sizes too big. It was his arrogance that maddened me. Then hands clamped my arms. It was Pierre.

"Careful, donkey, you have no right in this matter. They are not your women."

"I was offering a bite of bread, for God's sake."

"Do you want to lose your hair over slaves you don't own? Even if you win, and you won't, his companions will kill you."

I was seething, but had no weapon. Red Jacket waited, hoping I'd come for him. Finally I shook off the hands holding me and spat myself. "Take your women."

Red Jacket gave a thin smile of contempt.

"Do not make me take another coat." Then he stalked off.

I was shaking with rage and frustration.

Never have I seen a man so quick to seek out trouble," Pierre whispered. "Come. Have a drink of shrub."

CHAPTER 27

Feasting began at sunset, and revelry went on into the night. The Scot partners danced and skipped across crossed claymores laid glinting in the grass, while the voyageurs formed folk circles, dragging Indian women in to dance. Drink flowed, the moon climbed high, and lovemaking and fights broke out. The Indian warriors did their own dances as bonfire flames leaped skyward, their chants and cries mingled with drums, fiddles, horns, and fifes in a swirl of heart-thumping music. The braves also gambled like madmen, staking all on games that involved simple tools such as guessing different-length sticks or which in a row of moccasins hid musket balls. They'd bet furs for liquor, or fire-water for a woman, or a blanket for a gun. Some gambled away their clothes in heedless reckless-ness wilder than anything I'd seen in a casino, but luck was how they evened wealth. Their wins and losses were each other's entertainment.

I brooded, unable to shake my humiliation. Several voyageurs had smirked at me and my impotence against Red Jacket, and the shame burned. Now trappers and traders staggered by dizzy with dance and drink, sweat on their faces, laughter a shriek. Someone was stabbed and carried past bleeding and groaning. In the shadows I could see the gleam of pumping buttocks as lovers mounted. The drunken Indians fought too, excusing any murders on the grounds that a man possessed by firewater was not responsible for his actions. Come morning, no one would profess to remember anything.

I drank, fantasizing about killing Red Jacket, the liquor dulling my frustration while the fires, ale, and human musk made me randy. Some of the squaws were half-naked, and I half wanted them. Some of the men drifted off with other men. Magnus was well in his cups, roaring Norwegian songs, and Pierre was in a dancing circle, kicking up his heels. I stayed restless and morose, nursing rum, curious about Namida, furious with Red Jacket, and longing for Astiza, who'd left me in France. If this new girl was Mandan, maybe I could *buy* her from the damn Indian. I had little money left, but enough to start a game or two of my own. I'd acquire the girl, we'd go find Welsh Indians, and while Magnus poked about for old hammers we'd share a cozy lodge. . . .

This reverie was interrupted when I saw Aurora slipping along the edge of the bacchanal, looking aloof and purposeful as she hurried on some mission. Now resentment boiled more. How dare she toy with me! I was tired of being put off, warned away, mocked, and ignored—this by a woman who by rumor had fled scandal! And now where was she going, so important and haughty? I impulsively decided to follow, suddenly determined to regain the intimacy we'd enjoyed at Mackinac.

I'd catch her and I'd grab her and I'd say . . . well, I didn't know what I'd say, but maybe I'd just kiss her. We'd fight or make love, and either way bring an end.

Aurora had a slim white dress that made her glow like a fairy nymph, making her easier to track as she skirted the clumps of revelers without pausing. Where the devil was she going? I considered running to catch up, but it seemed undignified to chase her, even though that's exactly what I was doing. I tried sauntering, rehearsing lines to demand that either our relationship be consummated again or end completely. I didn't need the Somersets anymore, I was at Grand Portage! But even as I mentally rehearsed witty repartee, Aurora didn't pause to let me try it.

She came to a cluster of Indian wigwams at the northern extremity of the encampment, the bark-covered domes seeming to erupt naturally from the earth. She stopped, uncertain, and called something softly. A glow appeared at the door of one of the lodges, its light leaking through cracks in the shingled birch. It was a candle or lantern no Indian would have. She made for the wigwam, fell to her knees, and wiggled inside.

By Abigail Adams, an Indian hut for British

aristocracy? Was the strumpet meeting that cannibal Red Jacket? Or did she have some other game entirely?

I'm not a Peeping Tom, but she'd slipped from me once again, and into the most improbable place I could imagine for a lady. Was it possible she was compelled to come to this dark village and was in some kind of trouble? Perhaps I could rescue her! I hesitated as I crouched in the gloom, wrestling with good manners, and then I heard first the low murmur of voices and then the coos and cries of accelerating passion. Now I had to spy. Aurora Somerset coupling with an Indian buck? It was the kind of revelation that might give me leverage.

Frustrated and curious, I crept in the dark to the rear of the lodge. I could hear pants within, a delicious moaning from the beauty, and murmurs that seemed English. What the devil? I found a slit to put my eye to and had a vision from the kind of naughty book you can buy in the back aisles of a Parisian bookshop. Aurora was straddling her lover—how typical that she'd insist on being on top—and was riding him with arched back, hips flared, breasts pointing upward, her form lit a rosy hue by the glow of a lantern. Her eyes were closed, lips pouted, face tilted toward the lodge peak, and her hair a glorious shawl cascading down her back. It was a magnificent sight and I was hard in an instant, lusting even as I hated her for her haughtiness, yet ready to tell her anything if it would gain me entry to her guarded gateway! The woman was a sorceress. I leaned forward, pressed against the rough bark, near groaning myself.

And then I heard the words of the man under her. "Buck my beauty, buck my love! God, I worship your form!"

Could it be? A white man in an Indian lodge? But of course, it was a secret liaison! A perfect hiding place! My view was obscured by the narrow slit so I recklessly put my fingers up to pull bark aside to give a better view, wondering which bourgeois the lucky bastard was. It was dim, so I pressed my face in, looking at his limbs under her as he thrust upward, hands clutching her breasts. Then he turned slightly, the lantern giving better resolution of his features, and I almost yelped with shock. I looked to the pile of clothes beyond, and then back at the gasping couple.

Something was gleaming on the chest of the man, a pendant I'd seen months before tattooed on Renato's skin in Italy. It was a pyramid entwined with a snake.

Aurora Somerset was riding her own cousin, Cecil.

And Cecil was wearing a symbol of Apophis, the snake cult allied with that London-based Egyptian Rite he'd pretended to disdain! Who had I befriended?

Or rather, who had befriended me?

They turned to look at my fingers caught in the slit of bark, the white of my eye illuminated in the glow. I jerked backward, accidentally yanking a piece of the lodge covering with me, and fell on my back.

I heard a hiss. "Gage!"

And then I ran.

CHAPTER 28

M y mind was in tumult as I sprinted away in the dark. Aurora and Cecil as lovers? How had I missed *that*? Was this part of the scandal that had driven them from England to work in Canada? Did Simon McTavish, who looked the stern Puritan type, know of this incest? Or were Aurora and Cecil really cousins at all? Perhaps a phrase I'd taken literally was meant merely as endearment, like calling a close friend a brother.

And what relationship did they have to the occult theorists, the seekers of the secrets of the ancient past, whom I'd dueled in Egypt and the Holy Land? Why had they disdained the Egyptian Rite if Cecil wore its symbol?

What *was* certain was that I'd been recognized, and sharing a cozy canoe with the Somersets on the way to Rainy Lake suddenly was impossible. Our partnership had abruptly ended with my own spying, and my lust for Aurora had withered in an

instant. She was playing games I had no understanding of, and the best thing to do was run. I
stopped in the night, panting, and considered what
to do next. Nothing else had changed; fires along
the shore illuminated the dancing celebrants. But
it was time to strike out alone. To hell with these
lunatics! Magnus and I could go southwest from
Grand Portage on foot. It looked no more than
two or three hundred miles to the place marked on
his medieval map. We'd need supplies and a guide,
yes, but the night's revelry seemed an ideal time to
steal the former and fetch the latter—the lovely
Mandan Namida, and her friend, Little Frog.

My rescue of them would pay back Red Jacket,
too.

With this plan impulsively decided, I searched
and found Magnus, wanting to be well away by
morning. My companion, alas, had collapsed in a
stupor and was as easy to accelerate as a recalci-
trant mule.

"Magnus! Get up! It's time to go look for Thor's
hammer!"

"What?" He blinked blearily. "It's the middle of
the night."

"Something's happened and we need to get
away! We need to steal some provender and light
out for the woods. Say, have you seen Namida?"

"Who?"

"The Indian girl! The pretty one."

His head fell back. "By Loki's mischief . . ."

"Never mind, we can look for her together."

It required a pitcher of lake water hurled at his
head, but at length I got him up, sputtering, grumpy,

and lumbering—he with his eye patch and slouch hat and battered map case and ax, me with my rifle and tomahawk.

"What, by the wolf Fenrir, happened?"

"I caught Cecil and Aurora rutting like rabbits and they spotted me. I don't think they'll want me around to gossip, or to share their canoe, either."

"Cecil and Aurora? They're cousins! Aren't they?"

"I don't know *what* the devil they are, but our Lord Somerset was wearing a heathen sign I attribute to old enemies from England's Egyptian Rite. I'm not about to clarify the point. They got us this far, and we can do the last on our own. You were right about Aurora, Magnus. I should never have gone near the trollop."

We easily filched food and powder, given that half the company was unconscious and the rest inebriated past the point of caring, and I tried not to think too much about plunging into the dark woods alone.

"How are we going to find the spot that has Thor's symbol without a guide?" Magnus asked, as he became more awake.

"That's why we need to find Namida and Little Frog. We'll steal a canoe, slip down the lake, and have them help us find a way in-land. Once we get close, it's up to you to tell us which way Vikings would go."

"Not Vikings—Norsemen and Templars."

"And Welsh, woolly elephants, the lost tribes of Israel, copper miners from Atlantis, and Spaniards looking for El Dorado. It should be so crowded we'll see their lights for miles."

He smiled despite himself. "And of course, having been played a fool by one woman, you can't wait to link us to another."

"I'm a little desperate, Magnus. Besides, she asked me to save her and told me her tribe has a stone tablet with mysterious writing. It could be a clue."

"Stone tablet? You didn't tell me of this."

"You're too excitable."

"Whereas you are proceeding with deliberate decorum."

"She's a damsel in distress with a critical cipher. We kidnap her, escape, go home to her tablet, and finish your crazed quest."

"What if we run into Aurora and Cecil?"

"They were at the north end of the Rendezvous and Red Jacket's camp is at the south. All we have to do is hurry. I've thought it all through, I assure you."

"Thought it through? An hour ago, all you cared about was Aurora Somerset!"

He was, as I said, annoyingly corrective. "I've reformed."

We stole a small canoe and paddled a few yards offshore to where I estimated Red Jacket's band was camped. Here, presumably, is where Namida would be held. Hopefully most of the braves were off carousing. If we could stealthily pry the women away we should be able to keep ahead of any chase. In the last few weeks both Magnus and I had become quite the master paddlers, thanks to Pierre.

I'd miss the French voyageur, but it wasn't fair to embroil him in my troubles. There was no time for good-bye, either, but when we had the hammer and ruled the world, or were rich as Croesus, or whatever, I'd send him a letter.

Song still echoed across the water as we glided into Red Jacket's camp and crept ashore, I with my rifle, Magnus with his ax. "Put a hole in their canoe when we leave," I whispered. We crept like assassins.

Much to my relief there were just two Indian sentries curled in their blankets by a fire, apparently asleep. This lack of vigilance was explained by the fact that two smaller figures, upright and hooded with blankets, who sat with their backs against a tree a dozen paces further, were tethered to the trunk by a leather rope around their necks. The slaves had been tied up. I crawled near.

"Namida!" I whispered in French. "I've come to save you!"

She straightened at her name.

I sawed through the tether, pulled back the blanket, and leaned in to kiss her.

Instead, I found myself staring into the muzzle of a pistol pointed at my nose.

"You're even stupider than I thought," said Aurora coolly, auburn ringlets cascading to her shoulders as the blanket fell away. "It's boring to be so predictable."

Tarnation. She was wearing her Indian blanket over a thin white chemise, and looked as voluptuous as ever. If it wasn't for the pistol, the look of cold contempt, and her coupling with her cousin, I'd have been confused all over again. "Well, I can't say that about you, can I?"

The other tied figure proved to simply be more blankets, stuffed and propped, that fell apart when Magnus reached out to free Little Frog.

There was a cock of hammers as Indians came up behind. A musket bore pushed into the joint between my skull and neck. Magnus was pinned to the ground with a buck's knee on his backbone and a tomahawk poised above his temple. Cecil Somerset stepped into view, too: coatless, sleeves tied back for fencing, his unsheathed rapier glowing in the moonlight. He looked lean and dashing.

"I actually prefer that you're predictable, Mr. Gage. We assumed that if you weren't playing the dunce for Aurora, you'd be after that pretty squaw."

Slowly I began to rise, but Red Jacket snapped an order and two warriors grasped my arms to keep me pinned, a third yanking away my rifle and a fourth trussing my hands behind my back. Unfortunately, I didn't have any chocolates this time.

"You seem to have forgotten I'm on a mission of diplomacy."

"And you seem to have forgotten there's a difference between being a diplomat and being a spy and a Peeping Tom."

"It's just that you and your cousin seemed so occupied that I thought I should hire a different guide. Namida has less peculiar tastes."

"Aurora is not my cousin, Mr. Gage."

"Ah. So is anything about the pair of you true at all? Are you even aristocrats?"

"She's my sister."

I heard Magnus gasp and then grunt as someone kicked him.

"That's disgusting!"

"So they said in England, but then ordinary mortals know nothing of the power of true love. Half-sister, actually. Is it so strange that we'd share tastes and an attraction? Our dissolute father had strange perversions of his own, and we allied against the monster even as we were seduced by him. We think he may have poisoned both our mothers and rutted indiscriminately with all manner of creatures when he wasn't gambling away our inheritance. Inevitably, our sibling alliance against him was empowered by real affection. Society condemns us for it, but Cagliostro's Egyptian Rite understood and encouraged it. Here, in the wild, we can indulge it. You'll understand that we don't announce it casually on first acquaintance."

"It's incestuous! Illegal! Contemptible!"

"It's holy, by the pagan rites of ancient pharaohs, kings, and druids. Holy because we alone know our love is true, and because we've had to risk everything, including this exile, to live it. You have no idea what depth of feeling is. Yes, I heard how you let the Egyptian woman go, idiot. Now you'll suffer alone."

"Even the wilderness has morals, Cecil. You'll regret telling us this."

"Not if you're dead." His sword tip danced a little in the cool air.

"You host us, bring us here, and then kill us?"

"As you killed Alessandro Silano, mindless dilettante. Did you really think we'd forget? I thought the payback would be in Italy, or in Mortefontaine with the Danes we financed, or in New York. You have curious endurance, but gamblers know that even the luckiest streak must eventually end."

"The only reason we ever befriended you," Aurora added, "was to learn what your mission really is. Since you won't confide—after I gave you every chance and promise of ample reward—it comes to this."

"You'll die the slowest and most horrible death imaginable, courtesy of Red Jacket and his Indians," Cecil forecast. "You'll tell us everything you know anyway, and then things you hope we might *want* to know, and then nonsense no one will even begin to believe, and in the end none of it will do you any good. First you'll talk, and then you'll beg, and then you'll scream until your throat is raw, and finally get to the point where you can barely make any sound at all. You'll feel the torment of the damned, I've seen it. Girty taught me well. And the remarkable thing is that even then, after you've told us everything through agony that you could simply have shared in Aurora's bed, your torture will have only begun. The Indians are remarkable scientists. They can make the torture extend for days. They'll revive you from unconsciousness a hundred times."

"It's their dread and their sport," Aurora said. "The need to escape torture gives them courage. Preparation for its possibility gives them stoic invulnerability to pain."

"Then I'll tell you everything now," I said reasonably. If they wanted to go trooping after mythical hammers and nonexistent elephants, fine by me. I'm no coward, but the prospect of being a weeklong experiment for Red Jacket and his minions had me trembling, and what did I really care for Bloodhammer's quest? I'd been recruited by accident.

"I'm sorry, but that option has been closed, Ethan," Cecil said. "First, we wouldn't believe you because you have a certain . . . inventiveness. And second, one of the things Aurora and I most enjoy, when we're not coupling, is watching our enemies in pain. It's electrifying—may I use that word?— how arousing the agony of others truly is. Our passion is always at its highest right after their suffering. We were hoping, the entire voyage here, that you'd make it necessary."

"You'll forgive that I'm not all that happy to oblige."

"Your unhappiness is the best part!" said Aurora.

"I'll cry out if you don't let us go!"

Aurora brought out a gag.

"At least spare Magnus. I was the one who insisted we go with you. He's just a harmless Norse dreamer."

"Spare a man who wants to claim North America by pretending his ancestors were here first? I think not. Besides, we want to hear him bellow. He'll sound like an ox."

"I've a letter from my president, the sponsorship of Bonaparte, and McTavish himself has met me! If you murder us, it will be avenged!"

"On the contrary. You stole supplies and a canoe, slipped into the wilderness without a word, and were never heard of again. We'll mount a valiant rescue effort, finding, incidentally, whatever it is you're really looking for. Then we'll send condolences to Jefferson who, I'm sure, is actually expecting very little."

"You'll unleash Ragnarok, Englishman!" Magnus said from the ground.

"I don't believe in fairy tales, bumpkin," he said, pinking the Norwegian's cheek with the point of his blade, "I've unleashed only the end of *you*."

And the gags were bound round our heads.

CHAPTER 29

At least we didn't have to paddle. We were trussed like hogs and thrown in the bottom of Red Jacket's canoe and the one we'd just stolen. A third canoe bore the Somersets with more Indian paddlers. A fourth included Namida and Little Frog. The two Indian women looked at us gloomily. They'd seen what happens to captives.

This flotilla shoved off at dawn, the fort silent except for roosters and dogs, and soon we were out of sight. Except for rough handling as they tied us and dragged us, we were unmolested, since they were saving us for their village. I worked a while at the rawhide thongs but only succeeded in sawing my wrists. The Indians were better at trussing prisoners than my assailants at Mortefontaine.

Our captors paddled all through that day and night, arriving the next morning at their home village on the western shore of Lake Superior. If it was any consolation, I judged by the sun and my memory of maps that the shoreline continued to lead us southwest. Unwittingly, we were a good hundred miles nearer our intended destination on Bloodhammer's map.

Gunshots and whoops announced our approach, and even from the bottom of the canoe I could hear the excited shouts of those waiting, no doubt trading torment tips and taking bets on how long before we screamed, fainted, or died. Somehow it was worse not being able to see yet, staring hopelessly up at the sky. Then the splash of paddlers leaping out, a dozen hands reaching to heave me up like a sack of flour, and finally I was ashore where my ankles were cut free so I could stand awkwardly, blood rushing painfully back to my feet. My hands stayed bound. Bloodhammer was propped up as well.

I blinked, dizzy from anxiety. In front, a howling mob of perhaps two hundred Indians faced Magnus and me. Men, women, and children alike were armed with a stick or club and looking as excited as an orphanage at Christmas. A couple of rocks sailed out to sting us, but there was no serious barrage. You don't open your present until its time.

I tried to be philosophical. Magnus had dreamed that men who lived in virgin wilderness would be born with natural nobility and secret insight. Yet what I saw when civilization was absent was raw human savagery stripped of any restraint. Nature was cruel, not benign, and that cruelty would now be turned on us.

I looked at my companion. "I'm sorry, Magnus."

There was nothing to reply. He was looking at his tormenters with a Viking scowl that would give Tamerlane pause. Many men would collapse and weep at this point, praying against whatever horrors were planned—I had half a mind to do just that myself, if it would do any good—but Magnus was simply taking his enemies' measure. If he ever got loose of his bonds, he'd be Samson at the pillars. So how to free ourselves?

I glanced about. Aurora had claimed my long-rifle, I saw with annoyance, angling it across her chest like a sentry. Some painted buck was shaking Bloodhammer's double-bladed ax. Our stolen provisions had disappeared—probably eaten by our captors on the paddle here—and I realized I was ravenously hungry and desperately thirsty. Well, I'd lose my appetite soon enough.

Red Jacket paraded up and down the beach, raising his arms, pointing at us, and orating in his native tongue. No doubt he was boasting how clever he was to have caught us, or explaining how foolish I was to try rescuing Namida. The girl and Little Frog were to one side of our party, shrinking from the shrieking assembly but in no danger themselves. Fertile women were too valuable to squander. Cecil was to the other side, hand on sheathed rapier, thoroughly enjoying his advisory role. He, I decided, would be the first to die. Then his half-sister, if that's what she really was, the Siren. Yes, bitter revenge, just as soon as I got loose of two hundred agitated Indians!

I tried to come up with a plan—electrical demonstrations, ancient spells, hidden weapons, predictions of a solar eclipse—and failed completely. It's not easy to improvise when facing torture.

Red Jacket had an idea of his own. He posed in front of us, hands on hips like the lord of the manor, and then speechified to the crowd again.

They howled with delight. Cecil Somerset frowned, which I hoped was a good sign. Namida, I noticed, had glanced backward at something out of sight of the crowd but then quickly turned her attention again to me.

A scraped deer hide was thrown on the ground between us. Red Jacket reached into one of his deep English pockets and pulled out a handful of what at first looked like pebbles. When he cast them onto the leather, I realized they were Indian dice, carved from the pits of wild plums. They were oval instead of square, in the Indian manner, and had just two sides: one side was carved with lines, circles, snakes, ravens, and deer; the other was blank.

The Indians hooted and pranced. They loved gambling.

And so did I, allowing myself a tiny wager on hope! Ten beans were placed on the hide as well.

Red Jacket snapped something at Somerset and then jerked his head toward me. Cecil protested in the Indian tongue, but the chief would have none of it. He shook his head and barked at Somerset again.

The Englishman finally shrugged. "He wants you to gamble, Gage. Apparently you have a reputation for it."

I swallowed. "I seem to be a little low on money."

"Gamble your life, of course."

"So if I win?"

"You escape with your hair."

"And if I lose?"

Cecil smiled. "Then you'll run the gauntlet before being strapped to the stake, giving everyone a chance to take a swing at you."

"How sporting." I knelt at the deer hide, wrists still bound. "How do I play?"

"It's a simple version. Red Jacket will put the chips in a wooden bowl and throw. If more of the plain white side land up than the decorated, the thrower wins a bean. If more of the decorated side land up, you win a bean. If the advantage is seven white to three decorated, then two beans. Eight is three, nine four, and if all ten die are white then Red Jacket gets five beans."

"What do I get?"

"Conversely, if the majority is decorated you take beans at the same rate. The first person to take all ten beans wins the game."

"That's even odds and could take a long time," said Magnus.

"At this point, friend, doesn't that sound attractive?" I countered.

"Precisely," said Cecil. "But two consecutive throws of one color can end it in a moment. So this entertainment may prove brief, as well."

The swarm of Indians crowded around, excitedly betting among themselves on how I would do. Red Jacket scooped up the dice, put them in the bowl, waggled it like a sifter, and threw the dice against the hide. A roar went up, fading to a mutter. There were five white sides, and five decorated. Neither of us won.

He scooped them up to throw again.

"Wait, don't I get a turn?"

"Under the circumstances, Mr. Gage, I think it's safer to keep you bound."

Red Jacket threw again and this time there were six white, four decorated. The crowd whooped as if it were a horse race! The chief took one bean.

He threw again, and once more got six white. Delirium! Drumming and chanting!

"By John Paul Jones, I don't think anyone's on our side. Be sure to cheer if we win a bean, Magnus."

"They're just making sport of us."

"It's better than the alternative."

Another throw, and this time seven decorated dice turned up. The crowd groaned in dismay. I got two beans to even our pile, and there was enough mourning to animate a Greek chorus. I'm lucky at gambling, so my spirits rose.

Two more throws, each of us taking a bean, and then seven white for Red Jacket, giving him six beans for my three. There was one bean left in the middle. Luck seemed to be running the rascal's way: hysteria among the onlookers.

"I appear to be losing," I told Cecil resignedly.

"Not yet. You'll play until you're entirely bankrupt."

I actually won the next toss, taking the final bean between us, and then the one after that, taking one of Red Jacket's beans and making us even again. Now the Indians muttered and mourned, poor losers.

But then he took two of mine, then one, I won that one back, then the chief took it yet again, and another besides. I had one bean left, he had nine. The Indians were dancing, singing, and anticipating my demise with frolic worthy of a Neapolitan carnival. I hadn't caused this much amusement since Najac and his gang of French-Arab thugs hung me upside down over a snake pit. I really should have been a thespian.

Red Jacket grinned, scooped the die up while dragging the sleeve of his ratty English coat, and gave a victory whoop as he shook to throw. The Indians howled with anticipation.

But I'd watched this sly devil with a gambler's eye. I suddenly twisted off my knees, landed in the sand on my rump, and lashed out with a free foot, kicking the bowl out of his hand and sending the dice flying. I had that small cache of silver dollars I'd hidden in the sole of my moccasin to keep them from the shrub-drinking voyageurs, and I'll bet the metal made the kick sting even more.

"He's cheating!" I cried. "Check the dice!"

I hadn't actually spotted it, but each time he scooped up the dice he gave no opportunity for me to inspect them. Judging how he'd gambled for Namida, I was betting he'd slipped one or more dice with two white sides into the game. And yes, I saw one likely example and slapped my foot down over it, even as an angry Red Jacket tried to pry it off.

Cecil stepped forward between us and gestured for me to sit back. I uncovered the dice and he lifted it. Sure enough, two sides were white.

The crowd was silent.

"Clever guess, Mr. Gage. If you'd made a more

civilized gesture we might have cause to question the entire propriety of this contest." He flipped the die in the air, catching it, and slipping it into his own pocket. "But you lashed out like a brute." Red Jacket looked murderous.

"He cheated! Set us free!"

"On the contrary, you upset the final throw of the game before its conclusion could be reached. We thus have to go by the score when you unceremoniously backed out. It was, I recall, nine to one."

"Only because he rigged the game!"

"You upset the contest rather than make proper challenge. You can blame your own boorish manners for what is to come." Then he shouted something to the assembled Indians and they yelped anew, ecstatic that the fun of our torture could finally begin. Cecil turned back to me. "Don't you understand that the game has been stacked against you from the start, Ethan? Do you really think we were going to allow a French-American spy to blithely blunder around British fur territory?"

"Spanish territory, now French."

"Don't think I'm disturbed by that technicality."

"Norwegian territory!" Magnus shouted.

He smiled. "How quaint. It's historical progress to have you both die."

CHAPTER **30**

○————————————

Red Jacket snapped some orders and the tribe began backing from the beach to form two parallel lines toward the gate of their palisade village. The women eagerly pushed into position ahead of the men, shaking their sticks and screeching contempt, which is usually something women do only when they've known me for a while. I saw gaping mouths, white teeth, and black, remorseless eyes. It took every ounce of courage to take the first tottering step forward.

We were about to run the gauntlet toward the stake and the fire.

"Don't fall," Cecil coached. "They'll beat you until you're unconscious and see how many bones they can break. That makes it hurt even more when they tie you to the stake."

"Perhaps you could show how it's done?"

"Quite unnecessary. Running the gauntlet is

instinctive, Mr. Gage, or so Girty told me. He's quite the mentor, you know."

Someone shoved from behind and I staggered forward, wrists still bound behind my back. I'd have to be quick, ducking the blows of the strongest and meanest and trying to keep my face down and undamaged. So I dug my feet in the gravel of the beach, crouched while my tormentors howled with anticipation, and then, when a musket went off, sprang. They whooped.

My speed took them by surprise so the first few clubs missed, wind singing by my ears. But then blows began striking my arms, back, and thighs. Someone thrust out a stick to trip me and I had the wit to jump and come down on it, snapping the wood and eliciting a cry of surprise. I butted another brute and kept staggering. One particularly fierce crack stung the side of my neck but the pain jolted me forward just as I was faltering. I surged ahead again, clubs a tattoo on my torso.

"Good show, Gage!" Cecil was shouting. "Oh, that must hurt!"

"His head! Hit his head!" Aurora screamed. At least she wasn't urging them to aim for more private areas.

There was a great shout behind and I glanced to see that Magnus, charging like a bull, had knocked over half a dozen of his assailants and was stomping on indignant, writhing forms as other Indians howled with laughter. The distraction allowed me to squirt ahead the final ten yards with only a few last smart blows. I plunged through the gate of the village where half a dozen armed warriors waited in a blocking semicircle and sank to my knees, too excited for the full pain to yet register. Bloodhammer's size had turned his ordeal into sport, the gauntlet widening around him like a swollen python. As he plowed forward he dragged Indians with him, grunting with each thwack and spit, and when his knee went down once he simply genuflected and shoved off again, gasping. Finally he broke free of his tormenters and joined me in the dirt. A trickle of blood ran from one temple and his chest heaved. Norse fire burned in his eyes.

"Did they crack a rib?" I asked.

"Barely dusted me. I broke a nose with my foot. I heard it crunch." He grinned, his teeth red with blood.

"Look for any chance you can. I'd rather die fighting than burn."

The cordons on his neck popped out as he strained at his bonds. "If I get loose, it won't be just us dying."

It seemed appropriate to concede some fault, given the circumstances. "I'm not always the smartest judge of women," I admitted.

He spat blood. "We'll pay her back."

"And living in nature doesn't improve human character," I went on, a regular Locke to dispute the Rousseau of Magnus.

"This is nature corrupted by gunpowder and rum," the Norwegian replied. "These Indians are on the edge of extinction and know it, and the knowledge has driven them crazy." He looked sourly at a brave who sauntered up, languidly swinging his ax. "Out there it's still different."

"Out *where*?"

"We just haven't gone west far enough."

The Indians tied tethers around our necks like dogs and Cecil languidly walked in front of us, his sword now unsheathed and balanced casually on his shoulder. "Gage, I've never met a spy so easy to anticipate."

"I'm not a spy."

"After failing to get you in New York we didn't even have to trail you to Washington. We had only to wait for you at Detroit, so obvious was your mission. I was skeptical that my sister's bit of quim would be enough to get you to abandon a chance of American escort, but you almost suggested the arrangement yourself. Tsk, tsk, Ethan Gage. You played her lackey until you spied a squaw, like a dog distracted by a new rabbit. And then, after peeping on us, you made a beeline for the Mandan wench, the one place we might look for you. I'm beginning to wonder if a fool like you and the hero of Acre are the same man at all. Are you an imposter?"

"I've discovered your headquarters." I looked about.

He laughed. "This dung heap? This nest of primitives? I *use* savages, Ethan. I've got my eye on a castle in Montreal, after we've helped these Indians push your mercantile, indentured nation back east of the Appalachians with an uprising so violent that the rivers from the Monongahela to the

Mississippi run red with blood. Ten thousand cabins are going to burn, and ten thousand children are going to become orphans, inducted into the tribes. Tecumseh will make Pontiac look like a Franciscan monk by the time he's through, and Britain has guns enough for all of them. Yes, America must be confined, Ethan Gage, for its own good and the good of the world. I will not let your nation of grubby equality and mercantile greed pollute civilization! America will be contained until it inevitably withers, just as France must be contained! So now you'll die, and we'll send your entrails back to Jefferson after the dogs help pull them from your slit belly. You can watch us smoke them for preservation—oh yes, the old women know how to keep you alive and conscious while we do it! Unless, of course, you want to tell us what you're really doing on the far frontier, so far from the salons and parlors that keep you worm-white and useless. Tell us, Gage, and because I'm charitable I might grant you the gift of a swift tomahawk to the head! You'll tell us anyway, when the squaws put coals in your ears and anus and shove cedar splinters up your wilted prick."

He reminded me of doctors describing a painful treatment with a bit too much relish. He certainly didn't seem the dazzling gentlemen I'd met in George Duff's house. I should have asked for references.

"Even wilted, it's bigger than that quill you aim at your sister, you disgusting pervert."

He barked a laugh. "You do have cheek!"

"Information from torture is useless."

"Then we'll start with disfigurement." He nodded and one of the Indians jerked on my leash, hauling my head up. I could barely breathe. Another approached me with a mussel shell, sharp as a razor. "I like to cut across the eye before gouging it out, because the pain is hideous. Each time the swelling blinds you, a fresh cut releases the pus and the begging starts all over again. I watched them do it to a captive priest once until his sockets were a blind web of crisscrossing mussel cuts, black and red. Of course the priest had nothing to confess and was quite mad by the third day. But it was marvelously entertaining."

"I told Aurora we're looking for woolly elephants!" I cried, eyeing the shell looming close in my vision. And as my eyeball rolled, I saw something out of the corner of one eye and realized what Namida had spied at the beach. I almost had a spasm.

"If that came from Jefferson I might almost believe you. But from Bonaparte too? No, we'll make you match the Norwegian cyclops. Cut him."

"Wait!" I know I was supposed to be stoic as a Roman in the face of this torture, but what was the point? We were chasing myth, a fantasy, and if I could delay things for another minute. . . . There were two hundred against two, and we didn't have a chance unless I made one. "We're looking for Thor's hammer!"

"What?" He motioned the savage with a shell to stop, rotated his sword off his shoulder, and put its point under my chin. "A hammer?" He looked confused.

"A hammer of the Norse gods! That's why Magnus is here! He thinks Vikings or Templars or some other madmen came before Columbus and hid a magical hammer that could control the world! I don't care about that, I only thought we could sell it!"

"Ethan!" Magnus cried in despair and disgust.

"He's got an old map in his case. He may be a lunatic, but I came along because I was tupping Napoleon's sister and had to get out of France!"

Cecil blinked, looking at me in consternation for the longest time. Past him, down a land of wigwams and longhouses, I could see fire-blackened stakes set in the ground and piles of fresh brushwood for burning. I remembered the horrid fires at the Battle of the Nile, the smell of roasting flesh, and the blaze in Count Silano's strange chamber in the Tuileries. I'm deathly afraid of fire.

"He's lying!" Bloodhammer shouted. "Torture us! You'll see!"

"He's a poor liar." It was Aurora, stepping into my field of vision with my longrifle lazily pointed my way. "His lies are unbelievable, instead of convincing. This is just stupid enough to be true."

Cecil looked from one to the other of us as if he'd found a new species. Then he began to laugh. "Thor's hammer?"

"He wasn't a god, he was some sort of early ancestor and had this weapon that spat lightning."

"Ethan, enough!" Bloodhammer roared.

"Don't tomahawk me, because we can take you there. . . ."

"Ethan!"

Cecil swung his sword away and then whipped the narrow flat of it hard across my face, a stinging blow worse than any the Indians had yet given me. A lip split, and my cheek was on fire. "Do you think me a fool?" he screamed.

I slumped, near to weeping. "Ask Magnus . . ."

"A bloody *myth*! You want me to believe you are looking for Nordic gods in Louisiana? That you've come six thousand miles for a pagan fantasy? That any sister of Napoleon would so much as *look* at you?"

"She couldn't keep her hands off me, the randy bitch. It's Pauline the nymph, who had a reputation long before I . . ."

"Silence!" He slashed me with the flat of the sword again. Damn, that hurt!

"Brother, he's not intelligent enough to invent something so absurd," Aurora said.

"Yes! Look at me! I'm a dolt!" My eyes were watering in pain and shame, but what choice did I have? I dared not look at what I'd seen again.

"Silence, I said!" And he slashed me with the flat of his sword yet again. I blinked, near to fainting. I hate helplessness.

"We should look at the map case," Aurora said.

"I want to burn him," Cecil growled. "Roast him for *days*, for having you."

"Patience, my love. I know I've stoked your jealousy to spice the game. But we need to know everything he knows. This is a start."

"I want him to be porcupined with splinters, and the end of each one set on fire." Cecil licked his lips. "I want the women to flay his manhood."

"There's time, brother. There's time. But this map?"

"The case is in the canoe." He snapped some words to Red Jacket and a young buck darted off to the lakeshore to fetch it.

"Let me guide you. Partners, like we said."

Then Namida, whom I had entirely forgotten about, began jabbering at Red Jacket. He snapped back at her, but that just made her angrier and she pointed at me, insisting. He argued, but then Little Frog began arguing too. What was going on? The Indians began debating among themselves, and the Somersets looked increasingly annoyed. They snapped something at Red Jacket, and the chief snarled back.

"What's happening?" I called to Namida in French.

"We're claiming you as husbands."

"Now?"

"Women who are widowed can save a captive to repopulate the tribe. We have no husbands, and they must give us a chance at children. You would become a renegade and fight with Red Jacket."

"Join him?"

"But you have to marry us."

Right now that *did* seem superior to the alternative. "Magnus, Little Frog does have a certain charm," I encouraged.

"These women are slaves," Cecil seethed. "They have no claim on my captives. Red Jacket dare not deny us the torture he's promised."

Namida shook her head. "You must become our husbands. This band is depleted by Red Jacket's quarrels with other Indians: everyone hates him. The women know their men will come to me if I don't have a man for myself."

Well, once again I could produce harmony, like the treaty at Mortefontaine. Sleeping with Namida was just the job for my diplomatic talents.

The girl was helping me by delaying things, I knew.

Then the runner came back with the map case. While the Indians argued about my matrimonial suitability, Cecil took out the map and unrolled it for Aurora. They looked at it and then at us, over the parchment rim.

"This is forgery."

"It's Templar ink, damn your eyes," said Magnus, who had apparently given up hiding his preposterous theory. "You know it's real."

"You're both quite balmy. It's worse than elephants."

"That we can all agree on," I said.

"Yet what if they aren't entirely insane?" Aurora asked. She looked hard at Magnus. "This hammer. What can it do?"

"I thought you called it a myth?"

"What can it *do*?"

He shrugged. "No one knows. But if it exists, medieval mariners thought it important enough to cross the oceans and take it to a special place—a *very* special place."

"Can it kill people? Lots of people?"

"It was Thor's weapon."

She turned to Cecil. "What if they aren't making this up?"

"You must be joking."

"They would have this map ready-made for such an improbable story? The map looks real, somehow. It's so ludicrous that it smacks of truth."

"I don't doubt Gage would believe nonsense. The question is whether *we* should."

"We can always kill them later. Let's have them take us here." She jabbed the map.

I nodded encouragingly.

"No, I want the truth now. I want to roast it out of them now."

"What if we need their help finding the hammer?"

"We've traveled with them for weeks. Gage couldn't find his own ears. If they're telling the truth and we have the map, then we know what they know."

"The Rite said he was resourceful in Egypt and Palestine."

"Then we tie him to the stake as we intended, drain what he knows, slake the Indians' blood lust, and go looking at our leisure." He licked his lips, thinking now. "Something like this hammer, if it exists, could put us above the North West Company, and Montreal, and even the prudes and hypocrites back in England. We could live as we should, married by our own law. We could blame his disappearance on this map. Give us an hour, Aurora, an hour at the stake, and we'll know everything!" He grasped the double-bladed ax. "It's astonishing what men will say just to keep their last fingers and toes."

"Then get Red Jacket to silence those captive squaws!" The tumult Namida was causing was clearly flustering Aurora.

"To hell with Red Jacket," her brother said. He snapped an order and two of the warriors guarding us yanked on our tethers to get us to our feet and pull us toward the stakes, even as Namida and Little Frog shrieked in protest. The tribe's argument was growing fiercer, Red Jacket unable to quiet either side.

Cecil, Aurora, and our two guards had soon dragged us twenty yards from the main party of yelling Indians. Clearly we were going to be tied to the stake before clearer, more matrimonial heads could prevail. But these were the best odds we'd faced all morning, and I was becoming impatient. When, when? Aurora had the longrifle pointed at me, and Cecil his sword pointed at Magnus, the ax held loosely in his other hand and the map thrust into his belt. He gave a curt command and the brave who'd dragged me by my tether cut away the cords at my wrist so he could bend my arms around the back of the upright post. Another took my neck leash to help drag me the last bitter feet to my doom. I certainly wasn't going to make it easy by walking! I began to lift my arms and Aurora cocked my gun. "Don't you dare," she said. "I'll shoot you in your knee and you'll still be alive, but in agony before the fire even starts."

"Through the heart, Aurora. It's the least you can do for old times' sake."

"No. I like to make my lovers moan."

Now the other Indians were beginning to come toward us, still arguing but less heatedly. Namida looked miserable, which was not a good sign.

And then the head of the warrior holding my left arm exploded.

It was about time!

CHAPTER 31

One moment he was pulling me to the stake, and the next the top of his skull sprayed away in an arc of hair and blood, dropping him like a stone. For just one moment I was stunned, surprised when it finally happened. Then, more out of instinct than thought, I rotated my body and right arm to swing my other escort into the path of Aurora's gun.

My rifle went off just as he rotated into her aim, and he dropped too.

Another shot and a cry from Red Jacket who spun, clutching his arm. The other warriors seemed paralyzed. I grabbed the muzzle of my empty longrifle and, with more ferocity than I knew I could summon against a woman, shoved Aurora Somerset straight back against the bark wall of a longhouse and through it. I knocked the wind out of her as the butt rammed her midsection and the wall shattered. Then I swung the stock at a charging Cecil and parried the arc of his swinging sword.

The rapier sank into the wood with a thwack and stuck there, the aristocrat's face livid with rage and fear, and I twisted the rifle to snap it. Little Frog meanwhile snatched up Magnus's ax, which the nobleman had dropped, and cut the Norwegian's bonds. We were between the Somersets and the other Indians, so Cecil danced backward toward the waiting stakes, stumbling on firewood as he fumbled for the pistol in his belt. I yanked the broken sword clear.

Another shot, and a charging warrior went down, and then Magnus was free and swinging his ax in a great arc, howling like a Viking berserker of old. He waded into the stunned Indians like a maelstrom, the muscles under his torn shirt rippling, and the blades came up red, slain warriors toppling out of his way. They didn't have their own guns or bows and his weapon whistled as he swung. He paused a moment to stoop and snatch up his map case in determined triumph.

Why did he care if it didn't hold the map, which was still in Cecil's belt?

I sprang over the prostrate Aurora and tore off the powder horn she'd draped across her chest. "Your whore is dead!" I lied to Cecil to draw a quick shot, and rolled as he fired. Now! Could I club him with my musket or stab him with his broken sword before he reloaded?

"This way, my friends! Hurry, my muskets are empty!"

It was the voice of Pierre Radisson, calling from the stockade wall. Namida and I had seen him from the corner of our eyes.

"Get them!" Cecil was yelling to the confused Indians even as he retreated farther, struggling to reload his pistol. He kept glancing at the prostrate form of his sister, face twisted.

Time to retreat! I hurled the haft of his sword at him, making him duck, and then Magnus, Namida, Little Frog, and I ran to the other side of the longhouse I'd shoved Aurora through. Pierre had pried an opening in the crude palisade of saplings, and we scrambled through, hauling on Magnus to get his bulk through the tight entry.

"Praise Odin, what are you doing here?" the one-eye asked.

"Saving donkeys!" Pierre thrust a musket into my arms. "Here, until you can reload yours! Norseman, help me plant this keg!"

The Indians were finally shooting back, but the stockade was between us and provided some shelter from the bullets. I fired into the crowd and another warrior went down, making them scatter. I saw Red Jacket sitting, cradling the arm wounded by Pierre's earlier shot and wished I'd spent the bullet on him. Then there was a flare, and a fuse was sizzling toward the keg.

"Run, run as if the devil himself is behind you, because he is!" Pierre cried. Angry braves were darting toward the mouse hole we'd just crawled through, so we sprinted away through a stand of birch, adrenalin coursing. There was a roar.

I looked behind. The powder keg had blown up, turning the Indian stockade into a penumbra of flying splinters. Timbers flew up like spears and tumbled. I heard screams and confused yelling as the debris sprayed our tormentors. Others would dash out the main gate and come around to chase us, I knew, but now we had a lead of a good hundred yards to reach the lakeshore.

The stockade and longhouse began to burn.

We ran to the canoe Pierre had snuck ashore and skidded into the water, the women tumbling in first and then me.

"Magnus! Where are you going?" The Norwegian was running away from us with his ax, back toward the town, but I soon realized his target was the nearest canoes. One chop, two, and they were wrecked for the moment. There were more down the shore but his sabotage had gained us precious moments.

Bloodhammer came sprinting back, arms pumping, ax head bobbing up and down. He crashed through the shallows, water flying, and threw himself over the rim of our canoe, nearly tipping it. We hauled him in and then we were paddling madly, trying to put distance between us and a village boiling like a disturbed hive. Bullets whined.

The Indians rushed to the canoes, found them wrecked, and set up an even greater clamor. Then they dashed back down the shore, smoke roiling over their home.

For an optimistic mile I hoped we'd thrown them into such confusion that they wouldn't follow.

But no, here came one, two, three, four canoes on Lake Superior, crowded with warriors, paddles flashing in the sun. I didn't see a red jacket, but a coatless Cecil was standing in one bow, urging them on.

"There's a river to the south that will take us inland," Pierre panted, "but we need distance to make it work. Norwegian, get up and paddle one side while we three do the other. Gage, load your rifle!"

I had ball in the patchbox in the stock. It was reassuring to have the familiar weapon in my hands again, out of the clutches of Aurora Somerset, but annoying that my acacia wood stock was once more marred, this time by Cecil's sword blade. I poured powder from the horn I'd yanked off Aurora. As I loaded and looked back I could see Lord Somerset, no doubt furious at my treatment of his sister, pointing with his pistol as if will enough could bring us within range.

The distance was one hundred and fifty yards, far too great for a handgun. The occasional shot from the trade muskets of our pursuers went wide. But I had a rifle, crafted for accuracy, and even as we rocked with every paddle stroke I aimed. His white shirt was a tiny flake in my sight. I held my breath and squeezed, my enemy silhouetted against the sky.

Hammer hit pan, a flash, the kick of the butt against my shoulder and then a long second to judge my accuracy.

Cecil Somerset jerked and then pitched neatly over the side, falling into the lake with a splash.

A great cry went up and our pursuers slowed and stopped, demoralized by the dispatch of their leader. They drifted where he'd fallen, hands reaching down to seize him. And then there was a shriek, a female wail of grief that echoed across the water like the midnight cry of a flying witch, an awful keening that carried under it the breath of undying hatred.

Aurora wasn't dead.

And if I'd killed her brother she would, I guessed, cling as remorsefully as a shadow until she killed me. Or I, her. We were bound now, joined with permanence far deeper than mere lust. Married by hatred.

I put down my rifle, picked up a paddle, and stroked as if my life depended on it. Because it did.

CHAPTER 32

The rest of the day was an exhausting blur. We were stunned and sore from the capture, gauntlet, escape, and chase. We'd gone from the promise of hell to the miracle of Pierre's timely rescue in an instant, and it was as if we'd all been shocked by one of my electrical experiments. A lightning bolt would not have been more surprising.

"How did you know to follow us?" I panted.

"I saw the Somersets running through camp in the deepest night, half-clothed and anxious, and became curious," the voyageur said. "They're a couple always on stage, conscious of the impression they make, and yet here they dropped their illusion. Something momentous was occurring. I watched them march you to their canoes. There was no time to fetch help, so I followed alone in the biggest canoe I could manage."

"By the tonsure of Saint Bernard, good thing you did!"

"It was the women who saved you. Namida saw me and started the argument on your fate, distracting the Indians. It gave me time to intervene. Give thanks to matrimony, my friend!"

I glanced back to Namida, steadily paddling, her face streaked with dirt and the track of tears I hadn't noticed before. But she smiled shyly.

"Gage talked like a woman, too," Bloodhammer tattled. "Told them everything he could."

"I was buying Pierre time." Not the full truth, but I'd been expecting to have my eye sliced and yet here I was, bruised but not even bloodied. I'd have life figured out if it didn't keep surprising me.

"Yes, he maneuvered that one Indian right into my sights." Pierre winked at me.

Magnus scowled. "But now they know what we're after!"

"So we just have to get it first," I said blithely.

"Bah. Try to lie next time."

"I am a paragon of candor."

"It helped that I had the wit to bring that extra keg of powder," Pierre went on, "but now it's gone and all we have left is what's in our horns. Two muskets, one rifle, and Magnus with his ax."

"I'm not sure he needs more," I said. The tool was crusted with blood. "Magnus, you belong in the eighth century."

"We just came from there," he replied.

I looked behind us. "A single shot seems to have ended pursuit for now."

"They're simply confident of eventually tracking us," Pierre said. "They have your map. When are you going to use your sorcery to save us?"

"Pierre, if I truly had sorcery, wouldn't I have used it by now? I'm a scholar, not a magician. I need equipment we don't have to do anything at all with electricity, and I no longer have the secret book I once found."

"So you cannot properly sing, you cannot properly paddle, and you can do no real sorcery? *Mon dieu*, I did inherit a donkey."

"I can shoot. That seems to have served well enough."

"*Oui*, it was a good shot—maybe the first truly good thing you've done. But it will not stop them. They need to regroup, but will count on you to lead them to the treasure. One key will be whether the Somersets are alive or dead. Red Jacket, I think, was only wounded, which is bad. He will not rest until he has revenge."

"If he'd let us be, none of this would have happened."

"That's not how he will see things."

"And who said anything to you about treasure?"

"Do you think voyageurs fools? You two are not priests or company men, and you haven't taken a note of your surroundings since we met you. You made no surveys, no maps, and asked no questions about routes or trails. Explorers gather information, but you hid it. The only explanation is treasure."

"Well, you just earned a share."

He grinned. "Is it Indian gold, as in Mexico and Peru?"

"No, not gold."

"Emeralds then, as in the jungles of South America?"

"No jungles or jewels here."

"What then? What are we all risking our lives for?" He was cheerful as a birthday.

"A hammer."

"A what?" His paddle stopped.

"A hammer of the gods with special powers. Right, Magnus?"

"Aye, and the damned Somersets now know of it too. And there's more than that, little man. I'm going to take you to the navel of the world."

"You mean its center?"

"Better than that. The Garden of Eden."

"The Garden of Eden? But we've been banished, no?"

"Not the same Garden as in the Bible, necessarily, but a place of holiness or spiritual power. Or maybe exactly the same, since we don't know where the biblical Garden was."

"You think you'll find paradise in this wilderness? After that village?"

"I think my Norse ancestors did." He patted the now-empty map case, which he stubbornly still carried. "And when we come to where they did, then all will be saved. The treasure isn't jewels, little man. It's life itself."

"But we already have that. Don't we?"

Magnus smiled grimly and dug in his paddle.

◻   ◻   ◻

The Garden of Eden's neighborhood, I discovered, seemed to have more than its share of mosquitoes and blackflies, ready to take communion on our cuts and scrapes. We raced down the shore of Lake Superior, and at its southwestern end entered the marshy estuary of a river that Pierre identified as the Saint Louis, hundreds of miles north of the city of the same name. As dusk fell insects drew more blood than a platoon of doctors, but we dared not stop, despite our exhaustion. We paddled well into the evening, stomachs growling, until the river began to narrow and the current strengthened. "It's time to hide," Pierre said.

We detoured into a tiny slough, temporarily sank our canoe out of sight by weighting it with stones, and nested in the reeds of a muddy island like ducks. We had no food beyond a few bites of pemmican that Pierre had brought—awful stuff, unless you're starving—and dared not light a fire. But we were so depleted that the cool, muddy ground seemed like a feather bed. I fell headlong into exhausted sleep, fleeing in my dreams from nameless terrors.

Pierre awakened me in the middle of the night, fog on the river and frogs croaking from the marshes. "Now," he whispered. "They're coming."

Cautiously I lifted my head. A flickering light hovered in the mist, gliding toward our hiding place. A torch! I shrank to hug the mud. A canoe was paddling slowly by, an Indian at the bow holding the light and one behind him kneeling with a long, light lance. Occasionally he'd thrust it into the reeds. I recognized the sleeves of Red Jacket, one hanging empty over his wounded arm. The naked, powerful shoulders of other braves gleamed with bear grease as they inserted paddles into the water as precisely as surgeons, the canoe silent in its passage. Heads swiveled, looking for some sign of us.

I eased back farther into the reeds, but as I moved an animal started in response—a mink, perhaps—and with a plop went into the river.

Red Jacket stiffened, and I could see his silhouette twist back to look. It was as if he was sniffing the very air for my presence. The paddling stopped for a moment, the canoe gauzy through the fog, its occupants peering. I shut my eyes lest they somehow reflect light. I could hear the cautionary cock of a musket hammer. Pierre had stopped breathing.

There was a long silence. Finally the chief grunted, turned away, and the stroke began again. The canoe disappeared into the fog, but as it did another came, and another. It seemed an eternity before five of them had passed, manned by thirty warriors. If one of them had spied us, we had no chance—but they didn't.

I groaned, feeling as far from help as I'd ever felt in my life. Hostile Indians behind, now more Indians ahead, and somewhere beyond *them* the fearsome Ojibway gave way to the even more fearsome Dakota, called Sioux by the Ojibway, meaning "snakes in the grass." Like the snake cult of Apophis! I saw little chance of getting back to Grand Portage before Rendezvous ended, and wouldn't trust the British if I did. Any lie the Somersets told would be believed, and for all I knew the Scot McTavish had authorized my kidnapping. How better to get rid of an American-French interloper? I felt like a fly at a convention of spiders. If only I hadn't lusted after Pauline Bonaparte! And Aurora. And Namida.

I'd be safer if I was senile.

"We're trapped!" I said to Pierre. "Now they're ahead of us too!"

"And you think this is bad news? You'd rather we'd invited them to breakfast? Now it will be us following them, instead of the opposite. When they turn about we hide and let them pass again, and with luck Red Jacket will tire of the game and go home."

"Luck." Bittersweet word for a gambler. "This is your plan?"

"There may be Indians ahead who won't welcome Red Jacket's band. He draws renegades and miscreants because the Ojibway think him Dakota, the Dakota think him Ojibway, and he hires out to any side like a whore, only taking his own counsel. All we can do is hope for time and circumstance to eventually lose him in the country west of here, while not losing our scalps in the process. We need something more before we face him—more allies or a terrible weapon."

"Magnus thinks he's going to find that weapon."

"Yes, and paradise, too. Let's hope that your giant is more than simply crazy."

It would help our spirits to eat. I found an alder sapling, cut a lance, and as the morning lightened spied a lazy sturgeon in the shallows and speared the monster through its scale armor, feeling tension release as I rammed it home. We gulped flesh raw like savages.

It was ambrosia.

We told the others about Red Jacket, and Namida broke in with French.

"But *my* people are this way." She pointed up-river, west, the way Red Jacket had gone. Somewhere far to the west were her Awaxawi-Mandan cousins.

"The Ojibway have been driving the Dakota out of this country with their trade muskets, and keeping the Fox and Sac pinned to the south," Pierre explained, drawing what he knew in the river sand. "All the territories are in turmoil since the beaver trade began and trade muskets sold. The Mandan are somewhere beyond, amid the Dakota, and the Dakota are the most dangerous of all. You may be looking for paradise, but you are pointed toward hell. So why that way?"

"Magnus had a map he thinks drawn by Norse ancestors who preceded us."

"Vikings? In the middle of North America?"

"Templars."

"What are they?"

"A medieval order of knights interested in religious artifacts."

"Hmph." The voyageur looked at Magnus. "We are a long way from the Bible lands, my friend. Why do you think Eden is out here?"

"When the first couple walked the earth it was empty, with no Bible lands or anything else," Magnus said. "Eden could be anywhere. But scripture says it is the source of four great rivers, and according to my map great rivers run from a spot marked with Thor's hammer. If the Knights Templar found some ancient reference to this geography, it would explain why they came so far to escape persecution in Gotland."

"The land of our dead is in the west," put in Namida, who was following our conversation in French. "The spirits go where the sun sets."

"There. You see?" said Magnus.

"So now you're looking for heaven, too?" said Pierre. "If it exists, would it not draw every Indian like a magnet?"

"Maybe there's something forbidding about the place as well. Or hidden."

"Ah. Wonderful."

"No Indian would want to go to a white man's heaven," Namida added. "That would be hell, not paradise."

"Here's what I think," Pierre said to Magnus. "Eden is where you find it, giant. Paradise is all around." He gestured with his arm to the river and marshes, soft gray in the morning. "But we're blind to it, as blind as a man in a pitch black room filled with jewels he can't see. It's the white man's curse. The Spanish tramped for El Dorado, when they could have found it back in Segovia, at a friendly table by a warm hearth and a plump wife. The Indians sense paradise better than we do because they see in ways we've forgotten. They know that every rock and tree and lake is animated with the unseen world. They talk to them on their spirit quests. Trees give gifts. Rocks bow in greeting. Animals speak. But we white men blunder about, trapping furs, chopping trees, and claiming to look for heaven when we're in its midst."

"Those Indians didn't seem like an angelic host to me," I said.

"But these women here are angels, no? This is my point. Good and evil are in every man, in constant war, and not in some far-off place you can paddle to. Do you want Eden, Magnus? Find it on this mud island."

The Norwegian doggedly shook his head. "You can't convince me our raw breakfast is the stuff of paradise, Pierre. And it's our very blindness that requires that we white men journey. We're more distant from the golden past, and our penance is to walk farther. I think my map shows a real place, a spiritual El Dorado that my ancestors crossed an ocean to seek out."

"And there you'll find hammers and weapons and life everlasting?"

Everlasting life, the recurring dream, even though the life we had seemed damned difficult to me! The French had spoken of it on the way to Egypt. The Templars had no doubt made it part of their quest. Alessandro Silano had found the edge of it and been stretched, distorted, by what he found. And for each, longevity had receded like the end of a rainbow.

I wasn't at all sure I wanted to find the thread between man and heaven, but it was too late now. We had nowhere else to go.

The voyageur shook his head at Magnus and turned to me. "And you, Ethan Gage? What is your El Dorado?"

I thought. "People keep telling me there was an earlier, better age and secrets long forgotten. If we knew where we came from, we might know where we're going."

"And what use is it to know where we're going?"

"To decide if we want to get there."

CHAPTER 33

Seeing no sign of the enemy, we set out again, hoping we could follow without stumbling into an ambush. As the river narrowed and its banks grew rockier, we towed our canoe by foot through light rapids. Trees overhung each bank, almost meeting overhead, and side creeks were dammed by beaver. Half this wilderness, in fact, seemed water. I spied a yearling buck but I dared not risk a shot because of the noise. We went on hungry, warily watching.

It was drawing toward evening when Namida reached from behind and lightly touched me on the shoulder. "They're nearby," she whispered.

I looked around. "How do you know?"

"Birds flew up. Someone is on the river ahead." The women, I had noticed, could see things we couldn't, hear things we were deaf to.

I glanced nervously at the trees, worried that birds would announce us.

"We must get off the river," Pierre said. "There—

that tributary! We'll hide and scout." We turned into a creek, a green tunnel in the trees. The woods seemed deathly silent and I tensed for an arrow, but none came. After a quarter mile we came to a beaver dam, its quiet pond beyond. The beaver lodge was a wattle mound of sticks and mud in the pond's middle.

We got out to lift our canoe over. "Treat the dam like glass, or they'll see our sign," the voyageur instructed. "Do not bend a blade of grass or crack a twig! We must be silent as the wind and light as the butterfly!"

So of course the structure cracked under Magnus like a flute of champagne. He slipped, cursing, and fell into mud and water. Sticks gave way, water pouring out.

"Yes, just like that, giant," the Frenchman said. "Let's light a signal fire, too, just in case they can't spot this sign."

"Sorry," the Norwegian mumbled.

"Should we go back downstream?" I asked.

Little Frog shook her head and spoke to Namida. The woman nodded and turned to us. "Go to the edge of the pond and hide, then break the dam and eat the beaver."

Pierre brightened. "But of course! Out of clumsiness, grace! We'll use the beaver pond to get farther upstream, then empty it to deter canoes from following. Gage, go with the women and camouflage the canoe. Giant and I will follow after we break the rest of this dam."

"I thought we had to treat it like glass."

"That was before I remembered I was hungry."

The women and I paddled another mile to a grassy bank where we hoped no pursuit would find us and pulled our craft into a thicket. Then we hunkered down and waited.

"How will we know the Indians missed us?"

"If we are not dead," Namida said logically.

The water began to recede, evidence the dam was being dismantled. Night fell, but we dared not light a fire. Nor did we hear anything but frogs. I slept restlessly, and then at dawn we heard men coming on foot, slogging in the mud of what was now an emptied lake. I readied my rifle.

It was our companions. Each had a dead beaver in both their hands.

"We broke the dam, drained the swamp and clubbed these beaver as they came out of the lodge," Pierre said. "It's good the giant is so clumsy because I'm starving for beaver tail! If we find the driest, most smokeless wood, I think we're far enough from the river to risk a fire."

I escorted Namida and Little Frog into the forest and watched while they turned a wilderness into a green grocer. Where I would have starved, they found leaves for tea, roots for medicine, and cranberries and wild plum to dress our beaver. Little Frog briskly stitched a bark pot with birch and spruce root so we could boil a stew. The tail was a fatty godsend to our depleted bodies, and the beaver's flesh dark red and fine-textured, tasting like corned beef. We satiated ourselves, Pierre lamenting that we had no easy way to carry and sell the skins.

"But then why do I need money?" he went on,

arguing with himself. "The Indians have none and are happier for it. See, here we have all men need—a camp, food, women, the sky. But then treasure—well, that would be nice, too."

I sympathized with his reasoning. No man is consistent.

If we were hidden, we were also blind, with little idea if Red Jacket still lay in wait. So it was almost reassuring that we heard, like a murmur in the wind, far-distant gunshots. We might not have noticed, but the noise persisted. Someone was fighting. Pierre, lithe as a monkey, shimmied up a tree to a branch from where he could see some of the sky. He stayed there for some minutes, then quickly came down.

"Smoke," he reported.

"What does it mean?"

"I don't know. We may be in luck—we need to watch the river. Let the American go—he's done nothing useful for a while."

The pond was rising again—the surviving beaver must be rebuilding—and I cautiously moved on the periphery of its mud along drowned trees, and then down the tributary below to the main river, anxiously pausing at every sigh of wind and tremor of leaf. Nothing attacked me but biting insects.

Finally I came to the stronger light that marked the bigger river and wriggled to where I could see its current without being seen. Nothing. A few gunshots sounded upriver, but the shooting was sporadic now.

An hour passed, then two. Finally I saw canoes and tried to sink into the very earth, my rifle ready for one last shot if I was discovered. It was Red Jacket's braves, but the canoes seemed more lightly manned. Some warriors were slumped as if wounded, not paddling. Others bore bloody scalps and kept looking over their shoulder as if fearing pursuit. The hunters had become the hunted.

Good news, indeed.

The little flotilla passed and the river was empty. I hurried back to the others, who were eating crabapple, whortleberry, and more of the beaver. "There was some kind of fight, I think. Red Jacket was retreating back downriver."

"Let's hope they've given up," said Pierre. "Now we get ahead of them."

We carried the canoe to the sluggish pond, slowly rising, and paddled down to the beavers' new engineering. With a loud tail slap the survivors disappeared, and we carefully carried our craft over the repaired structure. This time Magnus didn't slip. Then down to the main river, a careful scouting for enemies, a wait until nightfall, and once more up against the current.

I feared every bend would still bring an ambush, but Pierre said it was equally dangerous to linger, blind and helpless. "We need to learn what happened," he said. "If his band had a fight, they may not follow Red Jacket farther west. Maybe we're done with him."

"But what if some of his men went still farther upriver?"

"That's the territory of other bands. Red Jacket is feared but not trusted. He has many, many enemies. His men can't stay up here, and his enemies become our friends. So now we'll follow this river northwest until it turns back east, and then decide what to do. That's where the shooting came from, I guess."

In the Indian manner the stars were our clock.

"At least we don't have as many mosquitoes at this hour," I said as we paddled.

"Indians often travel at night to avoid them," Namida agreed. "When you are not afraid of the night you can see like the wolf. Look." She lifted her paddle to point. "Giwe danang. The North Star. In a month it will bring the first frost, and the insects will disappear."

Her hair was like a satin curtain, her arms slim and strong. "So is this paradise to you, as Pierre said?"

"Paradise is in the next world, not this one. There you don't go hungry. Here we have winter, sickness, and bad Indians like Red Jacket."

"So have you ever heard of a special place to the west?"

She took two strokes before replying. "There are stories of a great tree."

I could see Magnus stiffen ahead of her.

"How great?"

"So tall it touches the sky, or so it is said. Yet warriors who go to find it never return. And it is not easy to find. Sometimes it appears and sometimes it is lost."

"A tree marking Eden," Magnus said, "and Indians with blue eyes."

"My people live where the sun goes down," Namida said. "They have no interest in this tree."

"And what is this stone tablet of yours?"

"It has markings like the traders' magic books. It is very old, found long ago. Our tribe captured it from the Dakota, who may have captured it from someone else. A medicine man in my country keeps it until the men who carved it return. Legend says that red-haired men dug for metal in the earth and promised to come back."

The Norwegian beamed. "This is proof of what I've been telling you since Paris!"

"Proof if we find it."

"Would Namida make up something like writing on stone?" He grinned at the woman. "You are wiser than our sorcerer."

"And elephants—have you seen woolly elephants?" I asked her.

"What is an elephant?"

"Bigger than a moose. Bigger than a buffalo."

She shook her head. "Nothing is bigger."

◻   ◻   ◻

At dawn we saw smoke. "Too much of it," Pierre said.

We hid the canoe, this time Magnus staying with the two women while the voyageur and I crept ahead to scout.

It was a massacre. A camp of Ojibway had been attacked, their wigwams put to the torch and their canoes smashed. Earthen pots had been shattered into fragments, drying racks had been toppled, and toy dolls made of cattail husks had been trampled. A crippled dog limped among two dozen scalped and mutilated bodies, their remains pecked at by crows.

Feathered shafts jutted from flesh and Pierre checked the markings.

"Red Jacket's work."

I felt sick. "The attackers were looking for us."

"They came upon this group without finding us and a fight broke out. Maybe they suspected these Indians of hiding us." The voyageur looked about, studying the tangle of footprints. "They retreated before other Ojibway can learn what happened and mount revenge. Red Jacket must be half-crazed to provoke such a powerful tribe this far north. You have truly stirred the hornet's nest, Ethan Gage."

"All I wanted was to look for woolly elephants." The ruthlessness reinforced the peril we were in.

"Well, here's your companion's Garden of Eden." The bodies had already bloated in the sun.

We fired three shots in quick succession to bring the others up and then salvaged what we could. The camp had been looted, but we found pemmican, kettles, and even some cached horns of gunpowder that had been overlooked. We didn't have time to bury anyone. Who knew if Red Jacket would suddenly return?

"My friends, it is time to make a serious decision," Pierre said. "Your stories are entertaining, but here we're presented with the reality of our situation. The longer we wander, the worse our peril. This river now turns back northeast if we continue to ascend it. That means back toward Grand Portage. We may have time to get back to the fort, ask for protection, and even return home with the fur brigades."

"But home is that way," Namida said, pointing west.

"Your home. And that of the Dakota, who share Red Jacket's blood."

"My people will protect us."

"Your people are far away, and we don't know how to find them."

"That's the way to the tree and the tablet!" Magnus said.

"And slow and merciless death, giant. Your stories are entrancing, but . . ." He turned to me. "Ethan, what do you think?"

"I don't trust anyone." I looked east longingly.

"No." Namida looked at me with annoyance and said something to Little Frog. Both women began shaking their head. "Cowards will make us slaves again."

"We're not talking cowardice, we're talking sense," I said.

"We'll buy you if we have to," Pierre offered, "and send you home in the spring. By that time the two donkeys will be gone and Red Jacket will have forgotten."

"He never forgets."

"But how will we get west from here, with no river!" He seemed to fear dry land as much as Red Jacket.

"Walk. We find other rivers." She pointed again. "Many rivers and lakes to the west, Frenchman."

The voyageur turned to me. "Make her understand we're safer at Grand Portage."

But I wasn't sure that was true, either. Meanwhile, the two Indian women had already picked up their things and were walking off in exactly the opposite direction Pierre wanted to go, Little Frog leading the way. "They don't seem to be persuaded."

Magnus watched them disappear into the trees, turned to us and our canoe, and then turned back again.

"Come," begged Pierre, "The Indians won't bother two squaws, or merely re-enslave them if they do. But Red Jacket could return here at any moment. Let's find friendly Indians, tell them what happened, and make them our protectors. They'll escort us back to Grand Portage."

"And give up the hammer?"

"The hammer is a story. Red Jacket is real."

"No," said Magnus, stubbornly shaking his head. "I don't trust the British, and I didn't come this far to stop now. The women are right. Our path is that way."

"But we can't paddle!"

"Then learn to walk, little man." And Magnus set off after the two Indians as well.

"Stop calling me little man!"

Well, tarnation. Here was a splendidly sensible idea—take our hair home while we still had it to take—and my Norwegian preferred suicide! Nothing I'd heard about the Dakota made me want them as enemies, and Red Jacket and the Somersets had our map to guess where we'd be going. The forest seemed dank and endless, no doubt full of malevolent beasts and cannibal monsters. But the ladies wanted home, Magnus wanted his hammer, and I?

It did seem a pity not to at least take a peek for treasure. I sighed.

"I'm sorry, Pierre. It appears we're outvoted, three to two. I think I'd better go on to keep watch on Magnus. We both know he's a lunatic."

"So are you, if you keep marching toward the Dakota!"

"I'm in your debt for saving us. Take the canoe, go back to Grand Portage, and if we find something worth keeping I'll share it with you anyway. I promise. Go back to your friends."

"But you're my friends, now!"

"Well, your friends are going that way." I pointed after the others.

"*Mon dieu*, you are not donkeys but jackasses! When the Dakota stake us all to the plains, do not blame me!"

"It will be entirely the women's fault, but every lady I meet seems to have a definite mind of her own." I shouldered my rifle. "You've done enough."

He groaned. "*Merde*, you will starve without me. Or drown. Or be drained by mosquitoes. Or trampled by a moose. No, Pierre must look after his donkeys. Very well. Help me sink our canoe to hide it, because the markings make clear it is Red Jacket's. We'll pray he doesn't discover we went this way. And hope we can find another river, and another canoe, and the women's village, and this stone tablet, and paradise. Somewhere off the edge of the earth!"

By hurrying, we caught the others in a few miles. "How far to your medicine man and his stone tablet?" Pierre asked Namida, who accepted matter-of-factly that we'd followed her.

"Many days. We have to go to where the trees end."

"Well, my friends, there it is." Pierre looked gloomy. "We're at the edge of the blank spot on your old map. So I will go on your goose chase and watch you search the prairie for hammers. If you find nothing, it will make a good joke for my voyageur friends, and if you do find something, then you will share with your great friend Pierre. I will be rich and unhappy, like the bourgeois."

"Oh, we'll find it," Magnus said.

"And why do you still carry your map case, when we no longer have a map?"

"Because it carries more than a map."

"But what, my friend? What is so precious?"

He looked at the four of us for a long time. I was curious too, of course. There was something more to his quest he hadn't shared with me. "I'm taking something to Yggdrasil, not just taking something away," he said. "You might think me crazy."

"We already think you crazy!"

"I prefer not to share it yet, because my hope may be futile. All I can tell you is that if we can find Thor's hammer, I may find peace—and if not peace, then at least acceptance. I carry the blood of kings, and also their old stories of that time before time, when miracles could still happen."

"Miracles now?" Pierre cried in exasperation.

"Have faith, Frenchman."

"I'd rather have a canoe."

CHAPTER **34**

We tramped into the worst country yet, thick woods and meandering swamp. The nights were growing crisper, but the days were still hot and buggy. There was no direct path, so we used the sun to strike west as close as we could.

"The swamp will discourage pursuit," Magnus said.

"That is good," Pierre said, "because we make one mile of progress for every three hours of circling, wading, and meandering."

Indeed, it took us three days and forty miles of marching to make what I guessed was at best twenty miles in our desired direction, following hummocks across wetlands and moose trail through eerily quiet forest. Twice I saw water snakes undulate away and thought again of Apophis, the Egyptian serpent god. We shot and butchered a deer, but our hasty meals never caught up with our persistent hunger. I felt lean as rawhide.

Finally the still water seemed to show a slight current, waterweed bending, and we sensed we were nearing the path of another river. The marsh seemed to be tilting west. A final belt of woods and we reached broad water running south. This new river was too wide to easily swim, and the idea of struggling up its brushy banks was unappealing.

"I hadn't dreamed dry land could be so wet," I said.

"A canoe remains the only way to travel in this country," said Pierre. "If we found a stand of birch and some spruce root we could build one, but even the least excuse for a canoe would take a week or more."

"Spring is the time to take the bark, not now," Namida said.

"So we bushwhack? Swim?"

"We build a fire, have a proper meal, and wait," she advised. "White men hurry too much. Start doing things the Indian way."

I was hesitant to advertise our presence, but Namida reasoned that if Red Jacket was pursuing us across the swamps we'd have seen sign by now. So we roasted venison, boiled wild rice, and almost as if expected, an Ojibway hunting party drifted down on us after smelling our smoke and food.

"See? Wait for help," said Namida.

By now I feared red strangers, but by extending the normal hospitality of Indians we got the same in return. These men were as different from Red Jacket's band as a hotelier from a dungeon keeper: shy, curious visitors who accepted our food matter-of-factly because of the mutual aid expected in the wilderness. It is the poorest who are the most generous. There were four men hunting in two canoes, which left room for game and furs. The women interpreted and they informed us that upstream this new river turned west. So we purchased one of their boats with four of the last silver dollars I'd hidden in my moccasins. Pierre had a steel awl and we drilled holes in the metal so that they could be hung as medallions. The Ojibway were so pleased that they gave us extra food and explained how this river upstream led to a series of lakes, streams, and portages and finally yet another river, that one flowing west.

So we set off again, happy to be paddling now that we'd suffered the alternative. We'd been converted to voyageurs.

"This may be the beginning of the Mississippi, but I'm not sure," Pierre said.

"This country is a maze of rivers and lakes and I've not been here."

"Even the maps at Grand Portage were blank in these parts," I recalled.

The Frenchman pointed to the western bank. "If so, there's your Louisiana, Ethan. We're at the edge of Napoleon's new empire." Our course along it led north and west.

Now there were no forts, no maps, no certainties. If a woolly elephant had poked its head from the trees along the riverbank, I wouldn't have been the least surprised. We did see moose feeding in the shallows, great jaws dripping, and armadas of ducks on pewter-colored lakes. In truth it did seem like an Eden, with the animals we saw not yet frightened by gunshots.

We passed villages of Indians as peaceful as Red Jacket was warlike, the children running along the bank to point at our white skin and Magnus's red beard as we glided to a rest. The women streamed down to see us, curious, while the men hung slightly back with their bows, watchful but not unfriendly. Namida and Little Frog would ask, interpret, and then direct us on our way, always coming away with a gift of food. I left a coin at each one until I had no more.

When we camped, our Norwegian would sometimes climb a tree to survey the country in hopes of finding sign of Norse habitation. But all was simply an undulating expanse of forest and lake, endless and empty in all directions.

We healed and began to relax as each day passed with no sign of pursuit. Red Jacket's band seemed increasingly remote. I'd almost certainly wounded or killed Cecil Somerset and perhaps dissuaded Aurora with my hard blow, and Pierre had winged the Indian chief. Maybe they'd been stung enough. Meanwhile, thanks to the women, the wilderness became a cornucopia, my rifle barking and the ladies gathering fruits. Magnus used his ax to whittle cooking spits, canoe braces and a dozen other useful tools as we traveled. Twigs yielded a crude tea. The inner bark of the basswood tree made strips to stitch birch into useful containers. Spruce gum was boiled to caulk leaks. The women taught us how camping near clay banks

with swallows' nests would provide us a zone almost free of mosquitoes, so voraciously did the
little birds dine on them.

Little Frog had given up trying to attach herself
to Magnus, who remained resolute against female
attention. She instead made partners with Pierre,
who took her attention as nothing more than his
due for rescuing and accompanying us. He made
no pretense of love, but instead initiated that cheerful sexual companionship that was the free and
easy manner of the fur trade.

Namida, without request or negotiation, made
herself a partner to me and, in the simple manner
of that country, a potential wilderness bride as well.
I knew there was a gulf of centuries between us,
but could it be bridged? There was a limit to what
we could talk about—she had no concept of cities
or kings—but she began to educate me about survival in her world, showing how to find a simple
root or make a simple shelter.

As for romance, for days she treated me with af-
fectionate reserve, but finally she came to some decision, and one evening, as the sky where we were
going went aflame from the sunset, she abruptly
stood before the log where I was sitting, cleaning
my rifle. "Come with me to gather wood," she suggested.

Pierre's eyebrows rose. He'd told me once that
wood-gathering time was the favorite period for
the young to sneak off and make love in the forest,
away from the disapproval of their elders. "Yes, go
find some fuel, Ethan."

"Capital idea. Don't want to get too chilly!"

She led me rapidly through the trees, light as an antelope. Namida was slightly pigeon-toed, in the Indian manner—their habit of walking with their feet straight or slightly turned in seemed to help their stealth and speed—and as confident in this green forest as a Philadelphia matron in a market. I followed in anticipation, neither of us picking up so much as a twig for a fire.

In a mossy glen she turned suddenly, smiled, and encircled my neck. I pulled her against me, marveling at the smoothness of her cheeks, the startling blue eyes, the copper of her hair. She was an alloy mix, as alien as a goddess. Finally we kissed, lightly at first, her nose and face rubbing against mine, and then more urgently.

"You rescued me," I murmured when we broke. "That was brave, to demand us for husbands. It gave Pierre time and space to open fire."

"You came to save me," she said, "and now you're taking me home."

"Some women I know believe in fate, Namida. Do Indians believe in that?"

"I do not know that word."

"That the Manitou or destiny wanted us to meet so we could help each other. That our partnership was supposed to happen."

She shook her head. "What good is that? Then our choices mean nothing. No, I chose you. I decided you were good man."

"And why is that?" It's true, I think, but I always like to hear the reasoning of others.

"No one obeys you. No one fears you."

That's not quite the impression one wants to

leave with a woman, but it seemed to work with Namida. "Well, I *am* affable." And I kissed her again.

Her lips responded, sweetly and then passionately. She pressed herself against me, coiling with arm and leg, and we sank into a bed of sweet moss, warm and earth-smelling after the day's sun. I lifted her tunic off her head and she tucked the doeskin under herself, raising her hips slightly, her coloring like honey. If we were headed to Eden, surely this was Eve. She reached up to loosen the laces of my shirt and trousers. I was more than ready.

"Pierre said you enchanted me," I told her. "That you fed me seeds to attract me."

She lifted her knees. "Do you think I need charms?"

"It appears not."

"But it's true, I did cast a spell. Women must do so to make a man sensible. Now we will give each other power." She smiled, her blue eyes startling, and I was so struck by her sweetness that I literally lost breath.

To give! So different than the greedy grasping of a Pauline or an Aurora. Despite my own poor judgment, I'd found a woman who saw me as a partner. I was falling in love.

And so we entwined while the others waited, in vain, for firewood.

By the time we got back they'd fetched their own.

CHAPTER 35

We paddled as far west as we could, passing from river to broad lake and back to river again, through a flat, forested landscape untouched by time. Mist hung on the reeds in early morning until the sun condensed it into evaporating diamonds, the warmth loosening our muscles as we stroked. The lakes were a perfect blue, clean enough to drink, with fish so plentiful they would boil in the shallows. We used the fat of our kills to grease ourselves against the insects, and their hides to patch our clothing. It was crowded in our single craft but sometimes Namida would lean against me and Little Frog would do the same with Pierre, resting as we glided. Instead of a pipe, we'd haul out on grassy islands to lie and look at lazy clouds. Only Magnus was impatient. The days were shortening.

When the river became no more than a stream and its channel turned south, Pierre guessed it was time to strike more directly west. We met another hunting party of Ojibway, these lithe and confident Indians as different from the wretches we'd seen in Ohio and Detroit as a duke from a debtor, and as again helpful as Red Jacket's band had been hostile. Muscled, bronze, and at perfect ease in the wilderness, they had an easy, enviable manner that at first I couldn't put my finger on. Why did they seem so different from the great mass of civilized men?

But then I recognized their quality: they were free. Oh, they were conscious of the cycling seasons and the daily arc of the sun, but they had no schedule and no destination, no ambition and no bosses, no dogma and no cause. They simply were alive. Their church was sky and forest, their loyalty was to family and clan, their destiny was as whimsical as the weather, and their science was magic. They were fierce about only one thing: their independence, their ability to roam where mood or need took them. True, they were hungry and cold and in pain at times, but how I now envied their presence in the present, in a world with no real history and no anxious future! Yet I could never capture that because I hadn't been born to it; even out here I could never quite forget the tug of Washington and Paris, of distant armies and ambitious generals and a future with Zebulon Henry and compound interest. Why would I ever go back to such a world?

Because I was also frightened of this one: the endless space, the yawning silence, the reality of never making any material advance and of being suspended in a cottony now. I was, in the end, me. The Indians of Detroit and Grand Portage had been corrupted, but I understood their corruption. My kind had traded freedom for security, the simplicity of animals for the predictability of civilization. I'd been cast out of Eden, but I had the promise of compound interest! I longed for this native freedom, but feared it, too. I was all for possession of Louisiana, but only if it could be tamed. There was no familiarity here. I sometimes heard spirits moving in the woods at night. I had little sense of direction away from the river by day. A wild thing could burst from the bushes at any moment.

I dared not confess this to Pierre.

At the advice of the Indians, we portaged our canoe a full day's march to another stream, this one flowing west. The country was opening up into a savannah of wood and prairie, untrammeled and brimming with game. Our first bison came two days later. The animals drifted with insouciance, huge hump and shoulder tapering down to a sprinter's hindquarters, as if two separate animals had been assembled to make one. Their brow was matted with dark, curly hair and wicked-looking horns, and their great dark eyes regarded us warily as we drifted past, the wind making the aspen shimmer.

"Dakota territory," Pierre said.

Seeing the buffalo, I could almost imagine woolly elephants across the next ridge. Sometimes I stood on the bank's high, sweet grass and pretended I was in Africa. The country and sky were opening, great white clouds sailing by like tall ships, the grass humming with locusts that skimmed ahead like flying fish when we stretched our legs.

The weather was like nothing I'd ever experienced. Many days we journeyed west under an endless bright sky, but occasionally black clouds like smoke would suddenly appear on the horizon and rise like a midnight curtain, blotting out the sun. The temperature would plunge as the wind rose, the prairie grass flailing frantically, and it would grow difficult to hear. Thunder would rumble, lightning flash, and Magnus and Pierre would look at me expectedly.

"I have no equipment!" I'd shout. "Science is about instruments and machines!"

They wanted sorcery.

Then rain or hail would lash as we crouched like humble animals, the storm boiling overhead in shades of gray, green, and purple. Once we watched a tendril of black reach down like an ominous finger and form a curious funnel, like a ram's horn. Then the storm would pass as quickly as it had come, grumbling behind us. The sun would reappear, grass steaming, and soon we'd be hot again, insects rising in clouds.

So we were alternately soaked and sweaty, hungry and then gorging saltless meat before it could spoil, tired from trudging and restless from sleeping on hard ground. Namida would cup against me for warmth at night, and when we snuck away to make love, she'd buck and cling with fierce ecstasy, not wanting to let me go.

But I knew, always in the back of my mind, that it couldn't last.

Namida and Little Frog were becoming excited

as the country opened to remind them of home, but Magnus was troubled.

"There are no great trees here; this can't be right."

"You must read the ancient words," Namida insisted. "What you call the cipher. Come, come, we must find my old village and the stone!"

◻   ◻   ◻

The first realization that we'd not left trouble behind came after we crossed the Red River of the North.

Pierre recognized the waterway because it flowed the direction of its name. Its cottonwood bottomlands had grass so high it reached above our heads.

"So this is the one that runs to Hudson's Bay?" Magnus asked.

"Yes, eventually. If your Norse came from there they could have paddled right by where we're now standing, exploring to the south. The Red flows to Lake Winnipeg, and the lake empties farther north yet through the Nelson to Hudson's Bay. From where we are now standing, in the middle of North America, you can boat to Europe."

Magnus turned to face south. "So the hammer is upstream?"

"Who knows? We need this stone cipher."

"How far?" Magnus asked Namida.

She shrugged. "A week?"

"Does a river lead there?" asked Pierre.

"My village is on one, but I don't know which way it goes." She pointed southwest. "If we walk, we can find it."

"Walk again!" cried Pierre. "I don't like this idea of wandering in the grass, like a fly on paper!"

"But that's the way we have to go," Magnus said.

"So let's complete our rescue of these fair maidens," I added.

"Maidens! Thank God they are not!"

We canoed across the Red, unloaded our meager belongings, and abandoned our boat. "I feel like a shipwrecked sailor," Pierre mourned.

"The prairie country should be like navigating the sea," I countered. I looked at Namida. "We'll be safe with her people, I hope."

There were trees in the valley but we climbed bare bluffs beyond. The Red was winding ochre, north and south. To the west we entered a rolling steppe that stretched to infinity, the grass dry, wildflowers mostly gone.

With no wood for fuel, Little Frog had to show us how to use dried buffalo dung for fires. It burned surprisingly hot and smokeless.

And so we traveled, Pierre groaning at the indignity of walking, leaving no mark on the emptiness we traversed. My mind had settled into the monotony of marching, idly watching another storm build in the west from which we had no shelter, when Namida—who was bringing up the rear as we ascended the brow of a hill gentle as an ocean swell—suddenly pitched herself flat and cried warning. Little Frog and Pierre immediately followed, pulling Magnus and me down with them.

"Dakota!"

I raised my head. In a little valley behind us, a party of a dozen Dakota warriors ambled on horseback. They were the first horsemen we'd seen among the Indians, and they sat their mounts like centaurs, torsos bare except for bone breastplates and paint. They had lances and bows, but only two guns that I could pick out. If it came to a fight, I could pick their gunmen off with my rifle before their trade muskets got within range. A couple of scalps fluttered from their lances. They hadn't spied us.

"Maybe they'll just ride by," I said.

"Then why are they coming in our direction?" Magnus asked.

"They've seen our sign and know we're help-less," Pierre said. "We're on foot."

"Should we shoot or parley?"

"Too many to fight." He turned to Namida. "Can you deal with them?

She shook her head. "They are enemies of the Mandan."

As if in reprieve the Dakota halted more than a mile away, one turning to call. More appeared, farther away, and for a moment I hoped this new group would draw the first band away. They rode toward each other. But then Pierre hissed and my heart sank. Even from a distance I could see the bright scarlet of Red Jacket's coat. We were being hunted, not by canoeing Ojibway but mounted Dakota. He'd come west to recruit new followers!

"They found our canoe and struck west to fol-low us," the Frenchman guessed.

I looked farther west. The sky was blackening again. But where was a hiding place on this endless, rolling prairie?

And why had Red Jacket followed us so far? The hammer. Were the Somersets still alive, and driving him? I didn't see them.

"What's your plan, sorcerer?"

"Maybe I can pick off Red Jacket and the others will go away."

"Dakota do not go away."

Thunder rumbled across the prairie. I looked again at the approaching storm. "Then I'm going to enlist the lightning. Look!" Vast purple thunderheads were sweeping our way like charging castles, their topmost towers a brilliant white and their undersides a forbidding black. A gauzy curtain showed where rain or hail was falling. In the opposite direction it was still blue and bright, as if the sky held night and day at once.

"We can't reach that in time!" Namida said.

"It's going to reach us. Look how fast it is approaching." Indeed, the speed of the tempest was disquieting. This storm was different.

"It's Thor, come to save us," Magnus muttered.

"No, it will kill! Look!" She pointed.

Again, a curious funnel-shaped cloud had formed. It reached down like a probing finger, touched the ground, and a whirlwind of debris spun around its mesmerizing tip like shavings from a bit. Then it seemed to fly apart and disappear.

"What was that?"

"A killer wind, as bad as the cannibal Wendigo! We must run from it!"

I looked at the Dakota. They'd spotted us but were pointing to the storm, too, horses milling. The wind was blowing hard now, grass thrashing, and the light was rapidly emptying from the day. In the wedge of blue sky still left to the east I saw the party of forty mounted warriors crest a rise and stop, silhouetted against the light and hesitating to close with us.

"No! We must run toward it!"

"Are you mad?" asked Pierre.

"I'm a sorcerer! Come on, Magnus! Let's go meet Thor!"

We grasped the hands of the women to pull them and ran, linked, toward the wall of the storm. Yipping uncertainly, the Dakota saw our boldness and lashed their steeds in reluctant pursuit.

Now the wind was roaring in our faces, grit and fat globs of water spattering us. It was cold and deafening. Another black funnel touched down, and then another. Thunder boomed, and for an instant the prairie flashed silver. All the bad weather of the world had gathered for an instant! Ice pellets began to fall, big enough to sting, and the wind climbed to a howl. I looked back, barely able to see Red Jacket exhorting the others to charge through a silver curtain. Our pursuers were losing cohesiveness as some fell back.

Now a funnel formed directly in front of us. A more menacing phenomenon I've never seen. The wind was sucking upward in a whirling maelstrom of dirt and cloud, weaving toward us like a drunken thing. The sound rose to a shriek. Namida and Little Frog were crying.

"It will kill us all!"

It was the only thing I could think of to frighten Red Jacket. "We need to get it between us and the Indians!"

"Donkey, it will suck us off the earth!"

But we had no choice. I hauled our party into a dent in the prairie, a dry wash now filling with ice pellets and storm water, and splashed to a cleft in its dirt bank. "Hide here!" I looked up. Now the funnel seemed to reach as high as the stars, a vast, bellowing, devouring monster of a cloud—a god's power made manifest. We squeezed together into our clay crevice just as the funnel achieved a siren's scream.

The black thing seemed to have scooped up the very air. I could barely breathe, and my ears ached and popped. The churning winds had a horrible grinding noise.

"Crawl in! Hold on! Close your eyes! It's Thor!"

And there, at the edge of this dark funnel, on the crest of horizon between earth and sky where the prairie thrashed like something electrocuted, did I see the elephant?

I have no proof. I don't even have firm memory. But some huge animal seemed to flash for a moment on the horizon, trumpeting to the sky with long trunk and curved tusks, some great lumbering hairy tower of a beast, monarch of the plains, lord of creation, ancient memory of a greater age in the past. For one moment I saw the lightning flash on its ivory. Just for a moment! And then it was hidden by a curtain of rain and I had to cling against the ferocity I'd run toward.

We held each other, shaking, and the world dissolved into spinning dust oscillating faster than any machine on earth. I felt it tug at our legs and we clawed at dirt and grass roots to stay pinned. I risked the turn of my head for a momentary peek. There—at the top of the whirling black wall—was that a glimpse of blue far above, of heaven or Valhalla?

Then it was beyond us, lightning flashed, and rain fell in a deluge, hissing as it melted the ice. The little ravine was half flooded with water. We crawled higher, gasping, and at last dared lift our heads and look for the funnel.

It was gone. The day was shifting again from black to gray. To the east, where the Indians had been, was a line of forked flashes.

We were too drained to do anything but huddle. Slowly the day lightened back to something approaching normal, even as the sun in the west backlit the inky curtain that was now to our east.

And of Red Jacket and his Indians? There was no sign.

"They bolted, Ethan," Pierre said with wonder. "They knew you were an electrician, and they ran for their lives."

I stood, wishing Franklin had taught me some milder form of expertise.

CHAPTER 36

We now walked where no white men had ever gone, except perhaps grizzled Norsemen centuries ago. Ever since the Ohio country and its gargantuan trees, the west had been opening up, every vista broader, every sky bigger. Now the sensation of endless, empty, uncomplicated space was complete, the world reduced to its simplest elements of earth and sky. The horizon seemed to curve and distant clouds to dip. This was our planet *before* the Garden. The few trees we saw were hunched in winding coulees to hide from the ceaseless wind, and the grass rolled in waves like the ocean. Yet the more lost we three white men felt, the more Namida and Little Frog were encouraged. They must be near home!

They hoped, and I doubted. America unrolled to complete nothingness, somewhere ahead.

Napoleon was to do something with this? I kicked at the soil, black and endlessly deep. Maybe

Jefferson's yeoman farmers could make something of it, but for French imperialists, this would be like the sands of Egypt. There was not even fur.

I saw no more elephants, no mountains of salt, no belching volcanoes, and no pursuing Dakota. The prairie had been swept clean. Each night our low coals were the only light on the empty plain. The true illumination was overhead, stars brilliantly silver and the air cold. Whereas before Namida and I, and Pierre and Little Frog, had lain as couples— Magnus once or twice looking at us with wistful envy—we now all lay huddled like sheep. I didn't want to be out here when the first snow blew.

"How long before winter?" I asked Pierre.

"We must hurry. The question will be if we have time to get back to wherever you wish to go. Where is that, sorcerer?"

"Norway for Magnus. Washington and Paris for me."

"And poor Pierre? I am a thousand miles from my paddling companions, a marooned pilgrim with no winter post."

"You can come back with us."

"Can I? And Namida? And Little Frog? It's not easy to go between two worlds."

◻   ◻   ◻

We'd been walking several days, deeper and deeper into the plains, me longing for a horse, when we woke one morning and found our voyageur had disappeared.

It took a moment in the predawn stillness to re-alize Pierre was gone. Little Frog said something in her native tongue to Namida, and the women be-gan running up and down the swale of land where we'd camped, growing increasingly anxious.

Magnus and I stood, uneasy. Our companion could have crept off to relieve himself, or perhaps he saw some game. But the three guns were stacked as we'd left them and his water skin remained be-hind.

We could see no sign of him, and we could see a very long way.

"Pierre!" Our cries were feeble against the im-mensity of the prairie.

Silence.

"Pi-eeeerrrre!"

The wind was our answer.

"He went back to his canoe," Magnus said with-out conviction. "He hated walking."

"With no gun? And no word?"

The four of us fanned out at the points of the compass, going to the limit of where we could keep each other in sight.

"Pierre!" The shouts were swallowed.

We came back together to eat a cold breakfast. Little Frog looked miserable.

"Perhaps he's scouting," Magnus tried again.

No one replied.

"He slept with us last night. He just vanishes?"

I began to examine our campsite. I'm not a tracker or a frontiersman, and we had trampled our little hillock gathering buffalo chips and water from a nearby pothole of a lake. Yet there—were there trails in the grass where someone might have crept toward us? And there? And there? The grass was bent in snakelike undulations toward our camping place.

I shivered. Men had been among us, I realized—men with scalping knives, men the Ojibway condemned as snakes—and had carried one of us off without a sound or sign. I touched my throat. Why wasn't it slit? Why weren't they on us right now?

"Somebody took him," I told the others. "Dakota."

"We'd be dead if it were just Dakota," Namida said. For the first time since I'd met her, she looked truly fearful. "Something's changed. The evil English couple can't be killed, and have come and told them to take just one."

"Why? Why not capture or kill us all?"

"Because they want to follow where we lead," Magnus said heavily. "They'll torment Pierre for information, and use him to trade for the hammer. They are snakes who want into our Garden. And when they come, Ethan, when they enter the secret of my ancestors, then, my friend—then there will be Ragnarok."

"What is Ragnarok?" Namida asked.

"The last battle of gods and men," Magnus said. "The end of the world."

The prairie wind was getting colder.

"Pi-eeerrre!"

We gathered our things and hurried on, imagining eyes on us in the emptiness.

◘   ◘   ◘

Before Eden, purgatory. Before Valhalla, the hell of Nilfheim.

So it was when we actually found, against all expectation, the Awaxawi village of Namida and Little Frog, clustered on the bend of an unnamed river lazily winding across the western prairie. We were so far from obvious landmarks or trails that I would have needed a sextant and chronometer to fix our place on earth, assuming I knew how to use them. But Namida recognized subtle curls and lumps on the prairie invisible to my eyes, and grew steadily more excited as we neared her childhood village. "See! There is the coulee! Look! A seed from a cottonwood! Listen! A call from the river bird!"

From a bluff above, the village indeed looked more medieval than American. The huts were earth-covered domes of sod, surrounded by a palisade and a dry moat spanned by an earth causeway. Its valley was an oasis, fields of corn and beans interspersed with groves of trees along the river. But no sound greeted us as we approached, not even the barking of dogs. Namida and Little Frog's joy turned to disquiet when nothing moved.

"Something's happened," Namida whispered.

A man was sprawled by the gate.

We walked down cautiously and halted a careful distance to study him. His belly was extended by bloat and his skin had erupted in small pustules, some red and leaking pus. His mouth was open, his eyes blind.

"Smallpox," Magnus muttered.

The women burst into tears.

We could see that beyond this first victim were others inside the palisade, lying exposed on the hard-packed earth. A mother lay dead, breasts bare and pocked, with her expired toddler, not yet weaned, atop where he'd cried for milk that no longer came. An old man sat upright, eyes squeezed shut against the horror. A warrior lay curled into a ball.

Smallpox was ghastly enough in Europe, carrying off kings and commoners, but in America it was the absolute scourge of the tribes.

"So die the Mandan," I said heavily.

First the village massacre caused by Red Jacket's pursuit back in the forest country. Now this. The red race seemed to be dissolving before my eyes.

Namida and Little Frog were staring in shock and fear, choking back sobs for relatives that had to be dead. They seemed rooted, as if an invisible wall kept them from daring to open the gate, and that was good. To go inside was a sentence of death.

"Magnus, keep the women away. This disease will kill them in hours or days if they're infected. I'll go see if anyone is left alive or if I can find the tablet."

"It's my quest we're on," he said, his face ashen. "I'll take the risk."

"No, I've been inoculated."

"You've been what?"

"Given a mild form of the disease so I can't catch this." I gestured at the dead gatekeeper. "An Englishman named Jenner has been giving people cowpox with great success, and the treatment came to France the year I was in the Holy Land. Having seen smallpox do its work in Egypt and Italy, I decided to try it last year after the Marengo campaign. And, inoculated, here I am."

"Inoculated how?"

"A prick on the skin." I pulled my tattered shirt off my shoulder. "See the bump?"

The Norwegian made some kind of sign against my scar and retreated on the causeway, pulling the women with him. "Finally, you show some sorcery."

I was not entirely certain that inoculation worked, but I'd seen smallpox before and not contracted the disease. If Red Jacket's Indians were truly still after us, and the women's relatives dead, all hope of help was gone. It was imperative that we complete our mission as quickly as possible, which meant finding that tablet of stone. We needed either a clue to Thor's hammer or an excuse to abandon the quest.

Entering the village was grisly. Smallpox strikes Indians swiftly, dropping people where they stand. Women had keeled over near smoking racks and weaving circles. Two men had fallen at their palisade, as if insanely trying to climb the walls to escape. A girl had fainted while carrying a water jug, shattering it. The place reeked of excrement and corruption, the sweet stink of triumphant death. There *was* a sound, I realized—the horrid buzzing of flies.

Inside the lodges the only light came from the door and smoke hole, but it was enough to confirm apocalypse. Bodies were curled at the edges, as if shrinking from the shafts of light. Everyone had a hideous eruption of sores, mouths gaping for a final breath, eyes sightless, fingers and toes curled in agony.

There was no stone tablet, however. I systematically overturned every robe and trade blanket, poked into every underground cache of corn, and turned up nothing. My heart hammered from anxiety. I was sweating, not from fever but fear.

I was ready to give up my macabre quest when I finally heard a voice croak from the sod lodge farthest from the village gate. A survivor? I crawled to enter the dwelling again and realized an old man I'd seen propped on a shadowy backrest, presumed dead, was in fact barely alive. He was skeletal in his leanness, covered with pustules, with odd pale eyes and long gray hair and—most unusual—a thin beard. He looked like a chief or elder so while he groaned, muttering something in his own tongue, I made a second quick inspection. But no stone tablet, or anything else out of the ordinary. Still, perhaps this was Namida's medicine man. Could the women interrogate him? I laid him, moaning, on a buffalo robe, my own flesh crawling at having to touch his corrupted skin, and grimly dragged him into the sunlight. He squeezed his eyes shut and whimpered like a child, but I didn't know what else to do. I pulled him across the dirt yard of the village and out past the dead sentry at the gate, calling to my companions.

"Namida! I found someone alive!" She rushed

but I held out my arm. "Remember, he can make you sick!"

"It's Yellow Moon," she said, eyes wet with grief. "He's so old I thought he'd be the first to go. Instead, he's the last. He has the medicine."

"Ask him what happened."

The conversation was halting, the old man gasping for breath. "Some men from the village went to the Missouri to trade furs. When they came back with blankets, everyone became sick."

"Does he still have the tablet with its writing?" asked Magnus.

"The men who traded died first. He tried to make medicine, but . . ."

"The tablet!" The Norwegian's hands were twisting on the shaft of his ax. Namida asked again.

The medicine man's words were a mutter. He was fading. I felt like a torturer myself, making him talk like this in the bright sun.

"When everyone began dying, he moved the stone to a cave by the river. Someone, or something, guards it." She leaned to try to hear and I held her, fearful the disease could somehow leap the gap between them. "Dakota have been sighted riding nearby. A man in a red coat."

I cursed to myself. "Which cave?"

"He says you have spirit power, because you were unafraid to come into the sick village."

"Has he seen Pierre? Was he with Red Jacket?"

But the old man was gone. I shivered, feeling like a plague myself. The rolling plains around us suddenly seemed menacing, the grass brown, the river low. The season was growing late, and Pierre's disappearance had rattled me. It reminded me of Talma vanishing in Egypt, and then having his head delivered in a jar.

Everything was going wrong.

CHAPTER 37

"What cave is he talking about?"
I do dread the poking about
in underground burrows that seems to go hand in
hand with treasure hunting.

"There're some in the dirt banks of the river,"
Namida said. "Birds and animals use them for nests,
and children for play."

We walked down to the sluggish stream running
back east. Downriver, past a grove of ancient cottonwood, the waterway cut a narrow gap through
hard-packed clay and gravel, producing steep bluffs.
The face was dotted with holes and caves, some as
small as swallow nests and others big enough to
picnic in. Our dead informant hadn't explained
which of these cubbies he'd used, but all but a half
dozen were either too small for a man to crawl into
or so broad they were useless as hiding places.

I looked at the mouths of the most likely ones
with experienced wariness. "Do they have snakes
here?" I asked Namida.

"Yes."

"I don't like snakes." Or fire, gunshots, boxing, sword fights, vindictive women, or overly ambitious superiors, but there's no need to make a list. My meaning was plain enough.

"Elven hoards were guarded by dragons," Magnus said helpfully.

"Thank you for that erudition, Mr. Bloodhammer. And unless he has a dragon, I'm wondering why our friend the medicine man would choose a place as obvious as these caves."

"He was dying. How many choices did he have?"

"What is dragon?" Namida asked.

"A big snake."

"We find a stick and poke." So we cut a staff and poked and thrashed each likely entry just before entering, indeed finding one nest of rattlers that, fortunately, guarded nothing.

Our branch couldn't probe deeply enough to find the end of the last hole, however. It had a barrel-size entrance and scrape marks as if something heavy had been dragged. "Here it is, then," I guessed. This cave was deep and, I assumed, extremely dark. I hesitated.

"I'll go," said Namida. "I played in these caves as a girl."

"But the old man said something about a guardian, didn't he?"

"It's *my* tablet," said Magnus. "Stand aside. If there's rock writing in there I've got the muscle to drag it out."

"Do you want my rifle?"

"No, thanks. You don't have to reload an ax."

So he shimmied in, his enormous hatchet thrust out ahead like a blind man's cane. "It's bigger inside!" His moccasins wiggled and disappeared, and there was quiet.

Namida suddenly squatted to examine something in the dirt.

"Find anything?" I called into the mouth of the dirt cave.

"Stink," Magnus said. "And something else."

"Is it hissing?"

"It's a slab, heavy," he grunted. "Give me a hand!"

Swallowing, I stooped to follow.

"Bear droppings," Namida said behind me.

And then there was a roar.

I've heard unsettling sounds in my life, but the deep, guttural ferocity of this one seemed primeval. I didn't know nature was capable of making such a bellow! A blast of sound from the cave entrance, an animal roar, a great human cry inside, and then a snarl as something was struck with a thud.

"Magnus!" I cocked my rifle.

The entrance to the cave exploded.

Bloodhammer came first, somersaulting out backward as if he'd been catapulted. The hard earth around the entrance burst like shrapnel, gravel flying in all directions, as he skidded down scree toward the river, rolling with his arms wrapped around something massive and profoundly heavy. His ax skittered away as if batted like a ball of yarn.

Behind charged the biggest bear I'd ever seen, bigger than I knew bears *could* be. The animal was absolutely massive, gloriously golden, its back humped with muscle, its paws striking sparks as claws the size of Arab daggers scraped the ground. Oddly, there was a stout leather quirt around its neck. So this was the guardian! The women screamed, I yelled, and just barely had time to point my rifle and fire.

Fur and muscle jerked where the ball went in, and then the animal turned on me with gaping mouth, saliva flying.

Well, now I knew why the cave had become a hiding place. The old medicine man had chosen a grizzly bear den! And a den the monster had somehow been drugged and tied to, until aroused by one Magnus Bloodhammer. It snapped a coiled leather rope as thick as my thumb as if it were string.

Then the monster was on me, its smell rank, and in desperation I jammed my gun muzzle into the beast's mouth. The pain distracted him, and a swiping paw missed. It choked on my weapon, shaking its head in confusion, and then snapped it from my grip and threw it away. I chopped with my tomahawk and hit a haunch, but that was about as effective as a bee sting. So I went slack, preparing to die. My world was fur, musk, dust, and this cacophonous roaring that threatened to break my ear drums. The bear seemed a hundred times stronger than I was.

But then the animal bellowed even louder, rearing up on its hind legs.

Namida had snatched up Magnus's ax and buried it in the grizzly bear's back.

The animal snarled, twisting to get at this

instrument of torture, muscles rippling, claws flailing at what it couldn't reach. Blood geysered.

Little Frog was throwing rocks at the animal, sobbing.

The bear dropped to all fours, shuffling to turn to these new tormentors, my own cringing form momentarily forgotten. Somehow I found fiber enough to begin crawling toward my rifle, wondering how I'd load it in time.

Then Magnus charged back up the slope with a Viking wail, holding something huge and heavy over his head. He grunted, heaved, and with all his might brought a stone tablet down on the animal's head. There was an audible crack of skull bone and the grizzly actually went down with a whoof, grunting, dazed by a blow that would have completely dashed the brains of any normal animal. I reached for my rifle and rolled upright, pulling out the ramrod to load it.

Then Namida darted in like a squirrel, jerked out the ax, and threw it to Magnus. He caught the weapon with a shout, his face aflame from fury and exertion, heaved, aimed, and swung. It was as clean and beautiful a stroke as I ever saw, a full foot of broad steel sinking into the bear's back and severing its spine. The creature's massive legs went slack, as if cables had been cut, and it collapsed on its belly, looking at me with bewilderment and regret.

I kept loading just to be sure, my arms shaking. A last growl rumbled in the beast's throat and the fire in its eyes finally died. The stone tablet lay heavily on the bear's skull and Bloodhammer's ax jutted from its fur.

"By the horns of the Minotaur," I wheezed. "Why weren't you eviscerated in the cave?"

"I'd grasped the tablet before it woke and blocked its initial swipe. Then it broke loose from something and knocked me back through the entrance. It had the strength of ten men, Ethan. It had the spirit of Thor!"

"And Thor almost had us for dinner. That damned tablet of yours saved our lives." The slab lay on the bear's skull like a gravestone. "Let's have a look at what we found."

Magnus dragged the tablet off and flipped it over.

"It's the magic signs!" Namida said. I made a mental note to give the girl the claws for a necklace. It's always wise to make the best of bad situations, Ben used to tell me, and women love jewelry.

Magnus meanwhile traced incised lines with his fingers, muttering, and then looked at me in triumph. "Norse runes!"

CHAPTER 38

Using my rifle as a measuring stick, I estimated the tablet was thirty-one inches long, sixteen inches wide, and half a foot thick. It weighed at least two hundred pounds. No wonder it slowed the bear! Half of one side was smooth and covered in odd-looking letters of a type I'd never seen before: different from our own alphabet, Egyptian hieroglyphics, or the alien writing of the Book of Thoth. The script was crudely chiseled and not very deep. Had I encountered the artifact in a cow pasture I'd likely have passed by without noticing it.

"What do you mean by Norse ruins?" I asked.

"*Runes*," Magnus explained, spelling it. "Norse lettering from the Viking and medieval days. This is what we call a rune stone. The Vikings and others carved these to commemorate an event, boast of deeds, enumerate marriages and offspring, declare a faith, or record a voyage or passage. There are thousands of them in Scandinavia. If these Indians have one, it proves my people were here." He glanced around grandly. "All this belongs to Norway!"

I glanced at the dead bear. "You can have it. And this tells us where to go?"

"Perhaps, if the men with Thor's hammer carved it. Let me translate."

The women were already sawing into the bear, choosing to interpret our near-devouring as the opportunity for a windfall feast. Indians are the most sensibly practical people I know.

"Don't forget to keep the claws," I called to Namida. "They'll lend a savage charm."

"Look, there's more writing on the side of the stone," Magnus said.

"Pretty long-winded if you have to chisel, weren't they?"

"It wouldn't take that long for a skilled rune mason, and some people want their words to last." He was scratching translations in the dirt. Finally Magnus began to recite. "'Eight Gotlanders and twenty-two Norwegians on a journey of acquisition from Vinland, very far west,'" he read. He paused. "Vinland is a land they found on the east coast of Canada, so the writer must mean they've come very far west from that."

"As have we. Read on."

"'We had camp by two rocky islands one day's journey north from this stone. We were out fishing one day. After we came home we found ten men red with blood and death. AVM save from evil.'"

"The AVM is in Latin letters," I noted.

"Ave Maria, I'd guess. Hail Mary. Remember,

these were Christians, at least in part. Catholics, in those days. The old runes were giving way to the new letters."

"Well, there're no rocky islands on this prairie. This stone was obviously moved from its original resting place. Captured from the Dakota, Namida said, who in turn got it from who knows who."

"They probably mean an island in a lake," Magnus agreed, "but that could be in any number of directions. Here's what the side of the stone says: 'Have ten men by the sea to look after our ships fourteen days' journey from this island. Year 1362.'"

"Year 1362? Isn't that the time your Templar map dates from?"

"Now do you believe me, Ethan?"

It's one thing to go charging off after treasure, but another entirely to think you might really have a chance of finding it. I was growing excited. "But why?"

"I told you," he said patiently. "Thor's hammer. Dwarven mastery of the forging arts in the lost Golden Age."

"Dwarven what?"

"The dwarves Eitri and Brokk forged the hammer of Thor in the furnaces of their caverns, its only flaw a short handle caused when Loki, disguised as a fly, stung the eyelids of Brokk."

I was sorry I asked. "So how do we find it?"

He sat down heavily, tired from his fight with the bear. "I don't know. If the stone has been moved, fourteen days from the sea means little."

"It's worse than that. It's taken us months to get here. Fourteen days from the sea means a place a thousand miles back east or north, doesn't it? We're nowhere near your hammer if this was carved by the same Norsemen."

"Or Eden."

He suddenly looked so crushed that I felt sorry for him, and worse for me. A moment ago I'd soaring hope of Viking loot. Now it was dashed! "We tried, Magnus."

He didn't answer.

"The Somersets, if they're really alive, are on a wild goose chase, too."

He was staring sadly at his rune stone.

"So." Here we were in unmapped wilderness, next to a dead bear and a plague-wracked village, possibly pursued by any number of red savages and a vengeful pair of English perverts, more than a thousand miles from any civilized comfort, and with little in the way of food, clothing, weapons, powder, or sense of direction. Our only allies were two Indian women greedily roasting bear liver and paying not a whit of attention to keeping watch. Our sole clue weighed two hundred pounds.

In other words, it was the usual hash I made of things, in the usual dubious company. I walked down to wash in the river, wishing this particular group of Indians had adopted the horse so that I could gallop the devil out of here. The Mandan were sedentary farmers, alas. I wished I'd seen a volcano or mountain of salt, or *something* to bring back to anxious Tom Jefferson.

And then Magnus shouted.

I came running with my rifle, but he was pointing at the stone. "I have it, I have it, I have it!" he cried, and danced a cloggish shambles that I guess in Norway passes for a jig. Well, nobody ever attributed ballet to the Vikings.

"By Jupiter, have what?"

"It's a code, Ethan, a cipher, like you said!" He began pointing at random numbers. "Some of these letters have odd extra markings, like dots and slashes. I didn't understand why at first. But if you take the first seven letters so marked, do you know what they spell?"

"Magnus, I can't read runes at all."

"*Gral thar!*" It was a cry jubilant enough to topple a tower. If Red Jacket was within a league, he could hardly miss us.

"Don't shout!" I glanced warily at the bluffs. "Is that good?"

"It means 'grail.' And the next are Cistercian symbols for wisdom and holy spirit. It means, 'Their grail, wisdom, and holy spirit.'"

Now I felt a shiver. I'd heard the word "grail" before, too, in Egypt and the Holy Land, and like Saint Bernard it kept echoing through my life. Here it was on a rock in the middle of Dakota country? The longer I lived, the odder life seemed to be, signs and portents constantly butting into what had been a comfortably dull, pleasingly pointless existence. "But what does that mean?"

"That these men planted, or found, the grail that was their holy mission. And if the map I brought from Gotland is true, that grail is the hammer, brought here to where rivers go north, south, east, and west."

I looked at the brown, eroding bluffs. "Magnus, we're not in Eden."

"Not *here*, but where this rune stone *came* from. Where they deposited the hammer, and probably tried to found a colony. But demons already infested this country, foes that left ten men red with blood and death. Or disease, like we encountered in the village. It was an Eden that could be violated. An Eden that had the snake."

"Magnus, you're reading an awful lot into a rather cryptic tablet."

"When they say the sea they don't mean the ocean," my companion insisted. "No tribe of Indians is going to carry this heavy sledge of rock that far, and it doesn't correspond to the hammer symbol on my map. No, our quest is nearby, fourteen days from two 'seas' close to where we already are."

"*What* seas?" The man had gone balmy.

"Lake Superior, for one. Namida!" he called to the women tending the fire. "What is two weeks' journey west from Lake Superior where we were captured?"

She shrugged. "It depends on the route and the canoe. Somewhere east." She pointed back the way we'd come.

"Aye." His eyes gleamed as he stared at me. "And two weeks *south* of Lake Winnipeg, the huge lake to the north that the Red River runs into. That too is east of where we sit. We had to come this far west to get the tablet, Ethan, but my bet is that it was discovered back in that wood-and-prairie country dotted with lakes, that blank spot with Thor's hammer on my medieval map. Draw a line two weeks' journey west from Superior or south from Winnipeg and you come to where the map showed the hammer—and that's where we'll find it!"

"The grail?"

"*A* grail, one of the Templar treasures: the hammer." He nodded. "There'll be a sign to guide us, because we're destined to find Thor's weapon the same way we were destined to find this slab. Why else would we have so much success?"

"Success?" Ever the optimist, wasn't he? At least he wanted to head back east.

"When Pierre disappeared I began to fear the gods had abandoned us. But here they are leading us as surely as the pillar of fire led Moses."

"Magnus, I don't think either one of us qualifies as Moses. Nor do I think he had to contend with ravenous bears."

"That was just a test. The task now is to look for our own pillar of fire, Ethan. Somewhere there's a sign that points to Thor's hammer."

◻   ◻   ◻

Magnus insisted we take the stone slab with us. "It weighs more than Little Frog!"

"There may be more secrets in its message. Didn't you find and decipher an ancient book from clues chiseled on an old stone tablet? You of all people should recognize the value of this."

He meant the Book of Thoth I'd decoded with

the stone from Rosetta, but my only true innovation had been to blow the relevant portion up. It seemed necessary at the time.

"I didn't drag the stone with me," I pointed out. "I copied it onto the naked back of my lover." I eyed Namida speculatively, wondering how her skin would look painted with runes. That entire episode with Astiza *had* been somewhat erotic.

"Well, this is rock-solid evidence that my people were here before the Spanish, French, or British, and we're not copying anything. We're going to show this to the world, once we have the hammer it points to. We'll be as important as Columbus. Norway will claim North America and take its place as one of the world's great powers."

I doubted that. People hate it when you challenge their preconceptions, and don't reward you for doing so. If you seek success, tell people what they already believe. Revolutionaries get crucified, or worse.

"Magnus, we can't carry this door stoop a thousand miles."

"We're going to tow it," he said briskly, now all business. "This river looks to flow east and south, exactly the direction we need to go. There was a dugout cottonwood canoe back at the village, big enough for the four of us, and we can make a raft to tow the stone. We'll find the hammer, go down the Mississippi, and unveil this in Oslo!"

"Can't we aim for someplace warmer, like Paris or Naples?"

But Magnus was already issuing directions. Little Frog began skinning the bear, Namida set off to cut willow swathes, and Magnus began unwinding the leather tether that had held the bear. "You go fetch the canoe," he told me.

I found the craft he'd spied, the dead settlement above more mournful than ever. It occurred to me that the timing of this plague was awfully coincidental with our mission, and that the Somersets would guess we might make for Namida's home village. Had they somehow sent an infectious agent up the Missouri to where these Indians were apt to contract it through trade, to prevent us from seeking help? Were we inadvertently responsible for this holocaust?

Again I scanned the surrounding ridges with a feeling that we were being watched, but they were empty as a pub in Mecca. I paddled the canoe back down.

The filthy bearskin had been scraped of gore and bent over a circular frame of lashed willow branches. The result was a smelly saucer four feet across, like a very concave shield, its seams waterproofed with bear grease.

"That's like the coracle I paddled from the fireworks island at Mortefontaine!"

"Aye," said Magnus. "It's a Welsh craft, as crude a boat as was ever launched, and yet quick to make and plain to paddle. Curious, isn't it, how these native women know a style in use thousands of miles away?"

"You think the Welsh brought this idea with them?"

"I know we're not the first white men here. We've found our distant ancestors, Ethan Gage, and somewhere out there is the place they came for."

"Your so-called Eden."

"Navel of the world, sacred center, core. Paradise to some, purgatory to others. It takes the form its seeker expects."

"As elusive as the end of the rainbow."

"Where gold awaits." He winked his one good eye and just for a moment I did see him as restless Odin, wandering the world for wisdom and adventure.

The coracle bobbed like a bubble until the weight of the rune stone steadied it, and then it floated like a frigate. Magnus used the remains of the tether for a towline and we cast off from the sad village, leaving the great bear in a butchered heap and the cottonwoods whispering in the prairie wind. The current carried us southeast.

I allowed myself a glimmer of hope.

We followed the river—Namida said some of the trappers called it the Sheyenne—as it curved and curled through low bottomlands that were a mix of timber, flood-washed islands, and marshy meadow. The enclosing ridges were bare grass. I feared Red Jacket, but the world had emptied. Our journey seemed less and less real to me, as if we were indeed drifting into mythic time, our valley roofed by deep blue sky and the turning leaves fluttering down to float on the water like the rose petals of Mortefontaine. Great arrows of geese winged overhead, heading south with a honking bray. I'd no idea what day or month it was anymore, and indeed felt unmoored from any century. The Orient at least had dusty ruins but here the world was newborn, without calendar or clock.

CHAPTER 39

It was the third morning, not long after dawn, that we encountered our most serious obstacle yet, a living river perpendicular to our own. The buffalo were migrating.

A great herd was moving south, black and shaggy against the plains, and their course took them across our river ahead like a wall of horns and humps. The majestic animals were backlit by the climbing sun, a shambling tide that seemed as powerful and inexorable as the lunar one. We drifted, wondering how to get around.

"It will take them days to cross," Namida said. "More buffalo than stars."

"If we flip in the middle they'll trample us under," I said.

"We don't have days," Magnus put in.

And as if to accelerate our thinking, an arrow arced out from the brush on the river's northern bank and thunked into the wood of our canoe, quivering.

Ambush!

It was a neat trap. Our enemies had trailed us by horseback, waited until we had the rune stone, scouted ahead to spot the vast buffalo herd, and set up a riverside assault where we'd have to stop. Smart—which meant we had to be smarter.

So when an Indian rose from some reeds with bow in hand, arrogant as a duke of Spain, I lifted my rifle, shot him, and pounded Magnus on the back.

"Paddle!" I cried. "Toward the bison!"

"We'll be overturned and drowned!" Namida warned.

"We'll be shot and tortured if we stay here! Go!"

Now there were cries on all sides, warriors rising up from the concealing foliage to whoop and yip. A volley of arrows arced toward us and only the sudden surge as Magnus dug with his paddle kept us from being perforated. Several missiles clattered onto the stone tablet, two more stuck in the stern of our canoe, and the rest hissed into the water. Muskets went off, bullets kicking up spouts around us, and Little Frog gave a cry and clutched her shoulder, losing her paddle.

She was grazed, the blood bright but not pulsing, so I thrust my own paddle at her. "Keep stroking!" I fired our two muskets and two more Indians yelped and fell. Now we were flying down the shallow river as Magnus and the women thrashed, spray flying, aiming straight for the great herd as if we were anxious for a goring. Our sprint took the Dakotas by surprise and their shots went wild as the range grew. They began running from the river's brush to the enclosing hills where they'd no doubt tethered their horses. They'd stampede the buffalo onto us.

"Ethan, we can't paddle through the herd!" Magnus protested. "There must be ten thousand animals just in sight, and a hundred thousand behind them!"

"Pass me your ax!"

"What? Why?"

"Sorcery!"

I glanced back. Dakota riders, bent low over their ponies, were galloping toward the bison. The animals, already rippling in confusion from the gunshots, represented our gravest danger and greatest hope. I reloaded our guns, threw them down until we needed them most, and gripped Magnus's ax.

"What's your plan?" Namida asked, looking fearfully at the wall of dark fur plunging into the river. Bison skidded down the bank and splashed with great sheets of water, waves rolling away from their bulk. In midriver, hundreds of horns jutted like menacing pickets. Great dark eyes rolled as the beasts saw us coming, hesitating between panic and charge.

"Paddle faster!"

"Ethan?"

"Faster!"

More shots, the buzz of balls passing like hornets. I shot one gun back, to keep them thinking.

Then I squinted ahead. We were flying with the current straight at the rising sun, old bulls moving to the edge of the herd to eye us grumpily, horns lowered, hooves pawing, as cows and calves skittered from our approach.

"They're going to attack us!"

"Keep going!"

We could hear snorts and smell the rank, rich odor.

"Ethan!" Namida moaned.

I raised the ax.

Magnus had, as I've explained, polished it as if it were a piece of antique silver, giving more care to his hatchet than most men give to their horses or wives. It shone like a mirror, and he'd wiped it clean as china after the bear fight.

Now it caught the sun.

When it did, it flashed the morning's rising light into the startled eyes of ten thousand hesitant buffalo. It was a winking flash, as if our canoe had exploded with pulsing light. The animals jerked, bawling, and then bolted. In an instant the entire plain surged into reactive motion, the ground quaking as thousands of tons of flesh and hoof began pounding in both directions away from us, across the grass. In the river, panicked bison were surging away from our midriver course, trying to flee the winking ax blade of light as we swept down on them like Valkyries. The river boiled as buffalo heaved out of it. I kept twitching the ax, catching the rays like a necklace of Marie Antoinette's. We raced into the buffalo ford, parting the herd.

I glanced back. Behind us the confused bison,

pushed by unknown tens of thousands more in the hills, was wheeling back toward the river. As they did so they stampeded into the pursuing Indians. The Dakota fired to frighten the beasts toward us, but that only added to the milling confusion, some buffalo running one way and others the opposite. Dust pillared in the morning air. A horse screamed and went over, the rider gored.

Our paddlers meanwhile were artfully threading the river between panicked buffalo trying to swim or wade away from our course. Horns and massive heads slid by, the animals bewildered by our boldness and our odd towed sled with its rune stone. One bull crashed into the shallows to charge us so I threw down the ax, snatched up a musket, and shot. The animal stumbled and crashed, setting off yet another current of stampeding animals. A tendril of blood curled into the water as we swept past.

Now we had a curtain of panicked buffalo between us and our pursuers, buying us time. Animals were spilling in all directions, sweeping the frustrated Dakota before them. I hoisted the ax again and again, sun flashing, and finally we were through the crossing. Dust from the stampede rose like a wall behind us, screening us from view. We stroked until we couldn't see the herd anymore, or any pursuit. Finally we drifted to rest, the rune stone still trailing behind like a little dinghy.

"That wasn't sorcery," Magnus panted. "That was my ax."

"The sorcery was what I *did* with your ax. Magic is nothing but ideas."

◘ ◘ ◘

At length our meandering river met the Red, flowing northward to Lake Winnipeg. Guessing from Magnus's vague map, we turned south and paddled upstream until we came to a tributary leading east again. Then we went up *that*, toward Bloodhammer's best guess of where the Norwegians and Gotlanders might have journeyed. Given that the rivers writhed and twisted like Italian noodles, I was unsure how close we were to anything, let alone a vague symbol on a medieval map we no longer had.

The creek was slow and swampy, and as we went east the echoing emptiness of the plains was giving way to a more familiar landscape of wood, meadow, and pond. About half the land was forested, and periodically the river widened into a small lake.

Then we saw our biblical pillar, our gate to Eden.

At first I thought it was simply a black squall, streaked and sagging against an otherwise blue autumn sky. But as I watched, this squall didn't move despite the breeze blowing across the prairie. Or rather it *did* move, we saw as we paddled closer, but in a slow gyre around some central point, like a viscous, heavy whirlpool. Its rotation reminded me of those eerie funnel-shaped clouds we'd fled toward on the plains, because this too was dark and hinted of power. But this cylinder of clouds was far wider, a lazily revolving curtain that hid whatever was behind it. Occasionally, lightning flickered and thunder tolled in dull warning as we approached.

We studied the phenomenon uneasily.

"I've heard of this place," Namida said. "The storm that never ends. No one comes here. Or if they do, they don't come back."

"But we have a sorcerer," Magnus said.

"Who thinks your destination looks like hell instead of paradise," I replied.

"It's just a home for Thor."

"I want *go* home," Little Frog said in halting French. Her shoulder was sore from the bullet, and she had a fever. "Go Mandan."

"No, *there* is home, the place from which we all started." The Norwegian's eyes were gleaming. "There is the birthplace of gods and kings, of heroes and sirens, of life everlasting. There you will be cured, Little Frog!"

Life everlasting? It looked like a poisonous thunderstorm, albeit a beautiful one. As lightning flashed, the clouds glowed green and purple. They roiled, climbed, and descended, as if bound like planets to something within. And as the sun dipped to the west and lit the storm, a rainbow appeared as bright and solid as a flying buttress.

"Bifrost!" Magnus roared. "The flaming bridge that linked Asgard, home of the gods, to Midgard, home of man! There it is, a welcoming gate!"

"It's just a rainbow, Magnus. A rainbow and some rain."

"A rainbow with treasure at its end, I wager! Come, if you don't believe me!"

How could we turn back now? We paddled as near as we could in a mosaic of lakes and streams, portaging brief distances three times, dragging the rune stone through the mud, and then paddling again. Either the strange, stationary storm was farther than it looked, or it kept receding from us. Our progress seemed glacial. Then as our creek finally shelved into marsh and we could paddle no closer, we beached the Mandan canoe for a final time, pulled ashore the coracle, and lifted out the heavy rune stone.

"I'm not going to leave it for anyone else to discover," Magnus said.

"How are we going to carry it?"

"We can build a travois," said Namida. "My people use them to pull things across the plains. The Dakota pull them with horses, but we use dogs."

"We don't have a dog, either."

"We have a giant."

We cut poles and lashed them to form a triangle, with the coracle's bear hide tied to the center to bear the stone. Absent the wheel it was the best we could do.

Then, as the setting sun lit the cylinder of cloud orange, we bedded for the night. A chill breeze wafted down and Little Frog couldn't sleep, watching the pulse of lightning. At midnight I woke and she was still upright, her face resigned.

"*La mort,*" she whispered when I touched her. Death.

CHAPTER 40

The next morning dawned foggy and quiet. We couldn't see the mysterious cloud, or anything else. Mist hung over our camping place, a fog that left a dripping like a cellar of ticking clocks. No birds sang. No wind blew. It was eerie: like *being* dead, I guessed. Little Frog had finally fallen asleep and came awake slowly, her forehead hot.

"Why is it so quiet?" Namida asked. We all looked at Magnus.

"I don't know."

But I knew, or feared I knew. Send a man into the forest and sometimes nature falls silent, the animals holding their breath as the feared creature passes, waiting and watching to see what he'll do. We should have heard morning bird call, but there was none. "We're still being watched, I think. Red Jacket hasn't given up and isn't far away."

And indeed, suddenly we heard one bird call

from the marsh and an answer to it downstream. The women stiffened. Indian signals.

"This is a good sign," Magnus tried to reassure. "They still aren't killing us because they've decided to track us to see what treasures we lead to."

"And then?"

"We find the hammer first and everything changes." Magnus used our tow rope to make a crude harness for his travois. "Let's go find what the bastards want us to find." He began dragging at a trot, wending through trees, a ghost himself the way the mist shrouded him. Then he broke into a meadow, the track of his travois poles two lines across wet, late-season grass as he hurried with a sense of direction I didn't share. We jogged to keep up.

"Magnus, wouldn't it be easier to leave the rock?"

"This is proof my country was first."

"But what happened to your Norwegians if they learned old powers?"

"Who knows? A stone that records ten men red with blood and death says something. Maybe it was disease. Maybe they fought the Indians. Maybe each other. Or maybe they triggered something they couldn't control, some malevolent force that was awakened."

"The Wendigo," Namida said.

"Or they simply accomplished what they came for," Magnus went on, ignoring her. "At least one of them returned to Scandinavia, because he brought back a map. And some, perhaps, wound up living with the Indians." He stopped, turning his harness toward Namida. "Do you know your ancestor was a Templar?"

"What's a Templar?"

He shook his head, and on we trudged.

"How do you know all this?" I persisted.

"I have Templar blood myself. We were penniless royalty, disenfranchised generations ago, but I grew up on stories in Norway about how my ancestors knew powers we had lost. And they *were* just stories—until we found the map. Then I heard rumors of new discoveries in Egypt and the Holy Land during the French expedition, and that an American savant could be found in the new revolutionary court of Napoleon. I detected Odin's hand! A medieval map is set in the American wilderness, and then I learn of an American nearby with the expertise to partner with? I admit that as a hero you are quite disappointing, Ethan Gage, but you do have certain persistence. Even your lust for the Indian girl has proved useful—it brought us to the rune stone. So work the ways of the gods."

"Do you ever use that pagan saying when things go wrong?"

"Nothing has gone wrong yet."

"We've almost been clubbed, shot, burned, and stampeded."

"Almost doesn't count. Here we are, closer than ever."

"But they weren't *really* gods, Magnus. Not supernatural beings. That's myth."

"And what is your definition of supernatural? Suppose your Benjamin Franklin was transported to Solomon's court and demonstrated electricity? Would not the Jews proclaim a miracle? We Christians have created a gulf—meager man and extraordinary God—but what if the gap is not as great as we assume? Or what if there were beings between those extremes? What if history is deeper than we think, and goes back to times foggier than this mist, and that myth becomes, in its own way, fact?" He pointed to the stone behind him. "What more proof do you need? Evidence that Norse were here is so tangible that we clobbered a bear with it."

"But this goes against all standard history!"

"Exactly." The Norwegian stopped, reached out, and put his hand on my shoulder. "Which is why you and I are here, on the verge of resurrection, and no one else is around."

"Resurrection?"

"I haven't told you everything. Not yet."

"Well, we'll *need* resurrection if Red Jacket is out there. He'll kill us all."

"Not if we have the hammer."

The air grew colder suddenly, and I noticed we were walking on a carpet of crunching hail, perhaps laid down by the mysterious storm cloud of the evening before. The ice was still frozen, the ground a stony white. Our breath fogged.

We hesitated, as if something were holding us back.

Then Magnus grunted and forged ahead, pulling his heavy travois in a surge up a gentle slope, and we followed. It was as if we'd punched through an invisible barrier, like a sheet of transparent paper. The air warmed again. We entered a grove of birch, white and gold in the late year. The mist began to thin.

The trees were big as pillars. Here the hail had melted, but the first fallen leaves lay like golden coins. To left and right, late flowers made a purple ground cover among the white trunks, a carpeted temple that receded into lifting fog, tendrils lifted upward to heaven. Mossy boulders erupted like the old standing stones I'd seen in Europe. It was so beautiful that we fell silent, and even the scratch of the travois poles seemed like sacrilege. The ground rose gently and the light began to grow as the day gathered strength. Everything was lacquered with dew.

The rise finally crested at the edge of a low granite cliff, and as the sun burned through and the mist retreated into the trees, we at last had a view.

I stopped breathing.

The panorama was lovely enough. We overlooked a vale of pond, meadow, birch, and aspen, a lush natural depression in the prairie that seemed hidden from the rest of the world. But that wasn't what stunned us. On a low hill in the middle of this dell grew a tree of a size I'd never seen before, and never dreamed of. We stared, confused.

The tree was so immense that our heads tilted back, and back, and back, to follow its climb into the sky. It was a tree that dwarfed not just all others in this forest, but all others in this world, a green tower of ash with a top lost in the haze that persisted overhead. I've no idea exactly how high the patriarch was but we should have seen it from twenty miles. Yet we hadn't because of cloud and mist. It was a tree far taller than a cathedral steeple, a tree with branches longer than a street, a tree of a scale never painted, suspected, or dreamed of—except, perhaps, by the ancient Norse. The butt of its trunk was wider than the biggest fortress tower and its branches could shade an army. It was as if we'd been shrunken to the scale of ants, or the ash tree had been inflated like a hot-air balloon.

"Yggdrasil," Magnus murmured.

It couldn't be! The mythical Norse tree that held the nine worlds, including Midgard, the world of men? This behemoth wasn't *that* big. And yet it wasn't normal, either, it was a tree that towered over the forest the way an ordinary tree towers over shrubs. Why? The ash is one of the noblest of trees, its wood supple and strong, a favorite for bows, arrows, staves, and ax handles—but while tall, it is not supernaturally large. Here we had a freak colossus.

"There's enough wood there to build a navy," I said, "but not to hold up the world. This isn't Yggdrasil."

"Enough to mark Thor's hammer," Magnus replied. "Enough to serve as a gate to power. Do you doubt me now, Ethan?"

"Your hammer is there?"

"What more likely place? What better landmark?"

"Why is the tree so big?" asked Namida.

"That's the mystery, isn't it?" His one eye gleamed.

"And what is this here?" I gestured at a small boulder nearby. Curiously, it had a hole the diameter of a flagstaff bored through it.

"Ha! More evidence yet! A mooring stone!"

"What's that?"

"Vikings would tether their boats to shore at night by pounding a peg with line into a hole drilled like this. They're common in Norway."

"This isn't the seashore, Magnus."

"Exactly, so why is it here? A marker, I'm guessing, to find Thor's hammer if the tree somehow didn't work. I'd wager there's another mooring stone on the far side of the tree, and another and another. Draw lines between them and you'll find what you're looking for where the lines intersect."

"Clever."

"Proof." He set off along the brow of the low cliff to find its end, dragging the rune stone with him. We followed, and eventually came down into the vale, across a clearing, and under the goliath's shadow.

By any measure the tree was old. I don't know if its girth has been seen on this world before or since; but I do know I counted a hundred paces just to round its circumference. Great roots sprawled out from its trunk like low walls. There were folds and furrows in the bark deep enough to slide into, and burls as big as hogsheads. One could climb the plant's crevices like cracks in a cliff to the first branches. These were thirty feet overhead and wide as a footbridge. The foliage was greenish yellow, heralding the turn of the year, and the tiers of branches were so numerous that it was impossible to see the top from the base.

"This turns botany on its head," I said. "No normal tree can grow this big."

"In the Age of Heroes they were all like this perhaps," Magnus speculated. "Everything was bigger, as Jefferson said of his prehistoric animals. This is the last one."

"If so, how did your Norse Templars know it was here?"

"I don't know."

"And where is your hammer?"

"I don't know that, either. Maybe up there somewhere." He pointed into the branches. "Or inside. It is told that when Ragnarok spells the end of this world, a man and woman who hide inside Yggdrasil, Lif and Lifthrasir, will survive the holocaust and flood and repopulate the world."

"Well, there's a note of cheer."

Could the colossus be climbed? I walked away from its radiating web of roots to study the tree. Even as the fog was dissipating in the sun, an odd halo of cloud was forming around the crown as if the ash strangely attracted weather. The effect was to shield the tree from sight from any distance, I realized. I wondered if the dark thunderstorm we'd observed yesterday would be repeated.

I also noticed the tree's top seemed oddly truncated, as if the height had been clipped. While the summit was too high and hazy to see clearly, there was a blackened stub as if hit by lightning. Of course! This was the tallest object around, and would serve as a natural lightning rod. And yet why wasn't the tree even more stunted by ceaseless lightning strikes in this stormy climate? There'd been enough bolts yesterday to set it afire. How had it ever succeeded in growing so tall in the first place?

Nothing made sense.

I walked back down to the others. "There's something odd here. The tree seems to attract cloud, or weather, and yet it hasn't been killed by lightning."

"I don't like it here," said Little Frog. "Namida is right. This is a place for the Wendigo, eater of human flesh."

"Nonsense," said Magnus. "It's a holy place."

"The Wendigo carries people off to places like this one."

"There's no such thing as the Wendigo."

"But *your* fables are true?" Namida challenged. "Little Frog is right. There is something wicked about this place."

"So we'll look for the hammer and leave," I said. "Quickly, before Red Jacket finds us. I'm going to climb."

By jamming hand and feet in the crevices of the aged trunk, I managed to work myself up the first branch, hauling myself onto its loglike girth. It was broad as a parapet, and I waved more bravely than I felt to the trio below. Even at this modest start, the fall looked disconcertingly long.

Better not to think about that and keep climbing. So I did.

In some places the climb was a relatively simple process of hauling myself from one branch to another. In others I had to climb the main trunk like a spider to get to the next horizontal platform, using the deep corrugations. The trunk was so twisted, rent, and studded with bowls that I always had plenty of handholds; I was a human fly! I was the squirrel Ratatosk, carrying insults from the dragon Nidhogg to the sacred eagle at the topmost branches! Up, up, and up I went, the ground lost to the wicket of branches below and the sky equally invisible above. I was in a cocoon of leaves, the tree homey and snug in its own way. It was also wrenched and cracked, and when I came to a place where a branch had half broken but still hung, I was surprised at the width of the growth rings. They were half an inch wide, suggesting this giant was incredibly fast-growing.

The further I went the slower I crept, the height dizzying and my muscles beginning to ache. Even hundreds of feet off the ground the trunk and branches were still thick and firm, but as more sky filtered in and my view improved, I saw just how terrifyingly high I was. The surrounding forest looked low as a lawn. My companions were entirely lost to view, and birds orbited below. The circle of clouds around the tree had thickened, like the rotating clouds of the day before, and their bulk was building high like a thunderhead. The wind was picking up, and this castle of an ash was beginning to sway. It was slightly sickening to ride it, like clinging to a rolling ship.

I held tighter and kept going.

Finally I broke clear of the primary globe of foliage and neared the tree's dizzying top, a thousand feet or more above the ground. Through gaps in the clouds I could dimly see out across rolling prairie, an endless panorama of trees, meadows, and silvery lakes, but the day was growing grayer as the concealing overcast thickened. From a distance, was this Yggdrasil already hidden from view?

No, my eye caught movement. A party was approaching on horseback, one of them wearing a bright red coat, like a dot of blood on the prairie.

The trunk now had shrunk to something I could wrap my arms around. There were no hammers up here that I could find. Yet the very top of the tree still seemed truncated in that odd way I'd spied from the ground. Why?

I hauled myself up the last twenty feet, finally hitching myself up a gnarled extension of trunk no thicker than a maypole. When I looked again for Red Jacket the ground was already blotted from view. The prairie was walled off by a circular wall of cloud that seemed to be rotating slowly around the immense tree like a vast, gauzy cylinder. Its top was lit brilliantly silver by the sun, but the lower reaches were already dark. I heard a low growl of thunder. Hurry! There was something bright and odd glittering above, a golden thread, and it jutted from the very uppermost reach of the tree with a gleam like a promise.

This highest point had clearly been struck by lightning, as one would expect of the tallest organism on the prairie. But why hadn't the tree burned or died from what must be a hundred strikes a season?

I pulled myself the last inches, fearful the snag would break off or some new jolt of electricity would stab my perch. I was swaying a good twenty feet in the wind.

And then I had the answer to what had puzzled me on the ground. The golden thread I'd spied was in fact a stiff wire, a twisted strand of metal that poked from the tree's peak as if growing out of the wood. It looked more likely to be an alloy of copper and silver and iron. The topmost snag had extruded a shiny filament like a twig.

If I'd not been an electrician, a Franklin man, I might have found the wire peculiar but not very illuminating. But I'd caught the lightning! What I was looking at, almost certainly, was a medieval lightning rod. Bloodhammer's Templars, or Norse utopians, had wired this tree. The metal would draw lightning strikes and, if the wire was long enough, conduct them to discharge into the ground. Which meant this wire should lead all the way down through the tree.

Something was under the roots of this behemoth.

My skin prickled and I felt an uneasy energy in the air, the black clouds ever-darkening. More from instinct than prudence, I suddenly let myself slide down this uppermost stub to the first branch below, where I clung like an ape. As I squinted back up at the stub of wire, there was a flash and an almost instantaneous boom of thunder. My eyes squeezed shut as I went half-blind.

A bolt hit the tip of the wire and the tree shuddered. A jolt punched through me, but the worst of the energy was shielded by the wood as lightning was drawn down through the wire. I gasped, shaken, but hung on.

Then the tingle passed, the wire sizzling.

Fat droplets of cold rain began to fall.

I had to get off this tree.

CHAPTER **41**

I descended as quickly as I could but a false step would mean a fatal fall, so I had to pick my way with care. It seemed an eternity until I came within hailing distance of my companions and could shout to Magnus. "There's something under this tree!"

"What?"

"A strip of metal runs from the top through the trunk! It draws lightning! And I think it must be to power something down below! We've got to find it, because Red Jacket is coming!"

By the time I'd climbed to the lowest branch, swung by my arms, and then dropped to the carpet of leaves and soft earth below, Magnus had made another circuit of the trunk. "This Yggdrasil is planted as firmly as the Rock of Gibraltar," he said.

"It's been nearly four hundred and fifty years since your Norse were here." I didn't say "might," or "maybe," I was accepting the presence of these long-lost Templar explorers as established fact.

"The tree has undoubtedly grown a great deal, and maybe grown unusually fast because of the infusion of electricity, as the French scientist Bertholon theorized. But as it grew upward, it somehow carried a strip of wire skyward to serve as a lightning rod. I think the wire ran out, and lightning strikes keep the tree trimmed to the height it is now. That wire had to come from somewhere below."

He squinted up at the branches. "I don't see a wire."

"It's inside the wood, going all the way to the ground. And what was the point unless the ground end of the wire is attached to something important? And if it was important, wouldn't you want a way to get back to it? So there was a way under once, a tunnel or door." I was glancing about myself, impatient because the Indians were coming. "Where that root arches at the butt of the tree, perhaps." I pointed. "Imagine the wood growing over and around it. I know the tree looks solid, but . . ."

Magnus eyed the bark speculatively. "So there'll be a door again. Forgive me, Yggdrasil." He took his huge ax and went to a concave cavity at the base of the tree near an enormous root. "It *is* odd how it grew here. The tree is indented." He aimed, and swung. There was a crack, and the tree groaned. "If there's a tunnel, we'll need torches."

"Little Frog and I will gather branches," Namida said.

"How could your Norse Templars know to come *here* of all places, in the middle of an unexplored continent?" I asked as my companion chopped.

"They didn't," Magnus said. "They knew the continent was here, from the Vikings, and after Black Friday of 1307 they scattered for survival and took their artifacts with them." He swung and chopped, swung and chopped, his breath catching as he talked. "From the Indians they hear of a rich hunting ground with rivers running north, south, east, west. . . . Is it the ancestral site of paradise? They're far beyond the reach of their persecutors, with superior technology amid primitive Indians. They had steel, and the natives didn't. They dreamed of establishing a utopia centered around the energy of whatever artifact they'd brought." Chips were flying.

"Thor's hammer."

He nodded, swinging the great ax again. "Perhaps they fought the Indians with it. Perhaps they reburied it when it became apparent their small numbers couldn't prevail. And perhaps, with no time to build a pyramid or tower or other way to mark its place where they could find it again, they used ancient secrets to tie it to a living tree that could be a beacon to future Templars, while terrifying the Indians to stay away."

"A beacon hidden by its own storms."

"Yes, and the storm itself a beacon. So this tree, if not Yggdrasil, is a machine, to sustain what we've come to fetch."

"Sustain how?"

He nodded upward at the sky.

The day kept turning darker as the clouds built, and I heard a rumble of thunder. The tree's energy somehow created its own storms each day as the sun climbed higher, and its own winter each night. Lightning flickered high above like that wielded by Thor's hammer. Or did I have it backward—did the lightning feed the tool?

"Men are coming!" Namida warned.

And yes, in the murk up the slope from which we'd descended there was movement in the trees. Red Jacket and his Dakota would be as bewildered as we were by the botanical giant and its cone of weather. They'd hesitate, I guessed, and then crawl closer through the high grass to watch and investigate. A bullet or two would make them slow down even more.

I readied the load on my rifle.

"Hurry!" Little Frog begged.

Now the ax was swinging as steadily as a metronome, the Norwegian's aim precise, chips flying like confetti and spraying old leaves like new snow. The heavy ax was little more than a pinprick to the gargantuan tree and yet it seemed the monarch shuddered each time Magnus chopped, as if it hadn't endured such indignity in all the centuries of its existence. Who else would dare attack? The idea of tunneling into the massive bole was insane—except as the ax work went on, the wood was changing.

"It's punk past the bark and outer core," Magnus said, breathing heavily as he swung. "It's starting to come apart in chunks. This tree isn't as strong as it appears."

Another rumble from above and that curious prickling that I remembered from the City of Ghosts south of Jerusalem. The air felt alive, and crackling.

The meadow grass swayed as Red Jacket's renegades crawled through it. I aimed at one such ripple, fired, and the movement stopped. Crouching behind a root, I reloaded. "Chop faster, Magnus!"

Now there were puffs of answering smoke from the high grass, the crack of gunfire, and bullets whapped into the trunk around us. Bloodhammer cursed as if they were annoying insects. The women dragged their bundles of twigs and wove them to make crude torches, using flint and steel to start a small fire in the leaves. I kept up a covering fire. Our persistent pursuers lay flat and invisible.

"There's a hole!" Magnus cried.

We turned. A dirt tunnel like a burrow had appeared under the massive root, bigger than the opening into the bear cave. The tree had grown around the entrance. "Take the women and go look," I ordered. "I'll hold Red Jacket's band off!"

I sighted, squeezed, and felt the reassuring buck against my shoulder, smelling the burnt powder. The sniping actually relaxed me. The familiar motions of cock, squeeze, ram, and prime were something to do, and I could keep our tormentors out of effective range. Bullets whacked back, my attackers invisible except for the puffs of musket smoke. They were smart enough to move after firing.

Finally I heard Magnus shout.

"We need an electrician!"

"Then come keep guard!"

Magnus crawled out and took the rifle with one hand, shaking the other as if burnt. "It's very strange," he said, wiping dirt from his mouth.

So I dropped down into the tunnel. The soil was

held back by what at first I thought were roots, but
then I realized the subterranean part of the tree
had grown along the form of a tunnel made by a
different support entirely: ivory. The Norse had
lined the roof of their passageway with fossil mastodon tusks. Had they found the elephants? Found
a boneyard? Or done in the last mammoths themselves?

The passage was drier than expected, and ahead
was a scent of something scorched. I felt my way to
the torchlight where the women were waiting.
Namida and Little Frog were crouched in a womb-
like room too low for us to stand in, somewhere
under the heart of the tree's trunk, transfixed by an
odd contraption. Ribs of root extended from tree
trunk above to ground below, forming a cage of
wood the size of a ship's trunk. Above this cage, a
glittering wire as thick as a feather's quill descended
from the cave roof to a wooden cylinder the size of
a small keg. The wire took just one turn around
the drum, so I guessed it had once held a thousand
feet or more of costly wire that had unreeled as the
tree grew upward over the centuries. When the
drum was finally empty, the growth stopped, stunted
by lightning because the rod could go no higher.

But that wasn't what fascinated the women.

Instead, after its single turn around the drum,
the wire also led downward to the thick, heavy
head of . . .

An upright hammer.

The weapon was bigger than a carpenter's tool
but smaller than a sledge, and from the butt of its
short handle to the massive head was about as long

as my forearm. The hammerhead was fat and blunt, made of some kind of silvery ore that glowed, and looked to weigh at least fifteen pounds. More wires curved among the web of roots, and the hammer was balanced on the end of its metal handle as if kept from toppling by electrical force.

"It's Thor's hammer," I said in disbelief. Or *someone's* hammer, connected to the lightning rod of this monster tree the same way I'd connected my Leyden jars of batteries to my hand-cranked generator at the siege of Acre in Israel. Mesmerized, I reached out to grab it, but Namida stopped my arm.

"No! Watch what happens."

Suddenly there was a blinding flash and sparks flew like that fireworks display at Mortefontaine. The chamber shuddered and there was a low, distant boom, the far-off report of thunder. Then the sparks fell away, the hammer now blazing with electric fire that had been fed to it by the wire. It hummed. Slowly, its glow began to fade.

"It feeds on the lightning," Namida said. "The tree does too, I think. Magnus tried to touch the hammer, and it burned him."

So the hammer was being charged and kept ready, in much the same way I'd charged an electrical sword I'd used in a duel with Big Ned during the siege of Acre. Yes, the fundamental force that animates nature! Here was a weapon of some kind, yet what could we use to snare the thing without harming ourselves? I tried to think of what old Ben would have done, but was too distracted by the pop of gunshots from outside the tree. "We have to go help Magnus."

We crawled back out. Magnus was crouched behind one of the enormous roots as I'd been and the three of us joined him.

"Did you get the hammer?"

"I don't know how to seize it."

Our assailants had crawled closer, taking less pain to hide themselves.

"We need it!"

"Magnus, we're not gods." I took my rifle back and handed him a musket. I shot, there was a yelp, their movement went still again, and then I heard an odd, nasal version of Cecil's voice.

"We have Pierre!"

The voyageur was alive!

And so was my enemy.

"Hold your fire!" I ordered, reloading.

Slowly the English nobleman rose from the grass and hauled the Frenchman with him. The voyageur who'd rescued us was battered, his shirt loose, his eyes blackened, and his leggings in tatters. It looked like he'd been dragged across the prairie instead of marched. His hands were bound.

Little Frog gave a gasp, dark eyes bright with tears, and glanced desperately back at our tunnel.

But it wasn't Pierre who startled me.

Instead it was Cecil Somerset himself. The handsome, proud face had been shattered by the rifle ball I'd fired during the canoe pursuit from Red Jacket's village. His right cheek was cratered. Parts of his teeth and upper jaw were missing and his right eye was an empty socket. The wound was red and yellow with infection and pus, and his other eye was painfully squinted against the insects that buzzed at his head to feed on the corruption. The dashing aristocrat had been turned into a frightening monster. How long could the Englishman live with such a hideous wound? He must be keeping himself alive by force of will—because he wanted whatever was under the tree. His broken sword was jammed in his belt.

Another figure rose in the grass. Aurora! Makeup gone, hair greasy, clothes filthy and tattered from hard riding, yet she was still strikingly beautiful, tanned as an Amazon, holding a hunting piece of her own. Her fine bones and lovely figure were still there, and despite my logical loathing I couldn't help but be wrenched by her allure. To underscore the gulf between us, she lifted her gun and deliberately sighted at me with no hesitation.

And then Red Jacket stood, too, one sleeve empty but holding a tomahawk in the other hand, his English coat ragged but still a brilliant scarlet in the weird light. His look was simple hatred. He'd rip out my heart if he could. His mongrel band of Dakota and Ojibway renegades stood too, a scarred, vengeful bunch who looked more like pirates than princes of the plains. They looked greedy and foul, nothing like the proud warriors who had helped us on our canoe trip.

"My. Isn't this a fine reunion?"

"We want you dead, Gage!" Cecil called in a voice made raspy from wounds and pain. "We want you to die horribly! I have twenty of the best warriors in the world here to make sure that happens! But we'll spare you all—Bloodhammer, the women, even little Pierre here—in exchange for whatever artifact you've found." He tilted his head back to look up at the tree. "I must say, the Rite never expected *this*." Another flash, high above at the top in the clouds we couldn't see, and a rumble of thunder. The light cast him in an eerie glow.

"The Egyptian Rite knew what we were looking for?"

"The Egyptian Rite knew that Ethan Gage is always looking for *something*."

While Cecil looked as cocky as a man can with just half a face, his Indians, I noticed, were distinctly uneasy. They hadn't expected this great tree either, with its weird storms and brooding shade. They too were thinking of the Wendigo.

"You call me *little* Pierre?" Pierre croaked in protest. "No man says that of the great Pierre Radisson!"

"Silence!" And Cecil struck him with a leather quirt, and then slashed him again and again as if reminded to take out his own pain and frustration on his captive. Little Frog gave a cry and a sob. I quivered with disgust. It took every ounce of discipline not to kill Somerset at once, but if I shot the monster, the others would strike Pierre down and rush us before I could reload. The voyageur swayed but stayed upright, eyes closed against the blows.

Magnus had given the muskets to Namida and Little Frog and now he picked up his ax, ready to charge like a Viking berserker. "Not yet," I cautioned him.

Finally the Englishman stopped whipping our friend, gasping from exertion, while Pierre winced in miserable pain. Cecil's one eye glittered with terrible madness, a tormented fury completely different than the passion of Magnus Bloodhammer.

"I am not a patient man, Ethan Gage," Cecil said, wheezing. "The Rite knows what the Templars were trying to assemble, while you've no idea. Give it up, whatever you've found, and you make the world a better place. You can have this sniveling frog *and* this entire cursed prairie! I leave you and the savages to it! Give it over and we can be *friends* again." He tried to smile, but the disfigurement made it a grimace. "Maybe I'll give you my *sister* again."

"Don't believe him," Magnus hissed.

"Of course not. This bunch even cheats at dice." I called to the Englishman, "It would help if your sister stopped aiming at me!"

"Then lower your own gun, Gage! Save your friend! It's time to be civilized again! What's past is past!" Again, the hideous grin.

"Send Pierre and I'll stand easy!"

"Stand, and we'll send Pierre!"

Aurora swung her gun away. I lowered mine. Cecil gave a push, and Pierre staggered toward us. Then the voyageur stopped.

"They've killed me already," he croaked. "I'm ready for the next life, Ethan. Don't give up whatever it is you have. These are evil people and must not have it."

His words hung in the air, all of us frozen by his refusal to advance farther.

Then everything happened at once.

Aurora snarled, swung her gun upward, and fired into the Frenchman's back. As his knees buckled

Little Frog screamed in outrage, fired, missed, and I thought she might charge, but instead she threw down her musket and bolted to our burrow. Namida shot, too, and one of the Indians went down.

I'd fallen flat, just in time to avoid a volley of Indian bullets and arrows that thunked into the titanic tree, but Magnus grunted and spun as at least one shot clipped him. Namida dropped to reload, too. Then, as Lord Somerset fell on Pierre and brandished his broken sword to take the Frenchman's scalp, I raised myself on my elbows and fired into the monster's chest, a bullet I suspect he half wished for. Cecil pitched backward, his broken sword flying from his hand.

Aurora shrieked in renewed fury.

Magnus was running at her silently, lifting his ax despite his wound.

Then the earth heaved.

It was as if a wave bucked the tree and the ground rolled. Sheets of lightning far bigger than anything we'd seen before rippled overhead, sparking as it struck the branches, and there was a wail of agony behind so chilling that I froze. It was Little Frog, screaming! Namida was terrified, clinging to a root like the rail of a ship, and Yggdrasil, or whatever the devil this overgrown twig was, rocked and swayed, loosened roots making pops and burps like a giant smacking its lips. Was it an earthquake? Magnus was thrown to his knees by the lurch, and Aurora, her gun empty, was crawling desperately away in the grass.

All the Indians except Red Jacket were shouting and backing away.

Then Little Frog burst from the hole, clothes smoking, and rushed past me toward Magnus, crying something in her tongue.

She was wielding the hammer!

Her arm was horribly blistered and swollen, and her charge was more like a stagger. She'd paid some terrible price to reach within the cage of roots and wire to snatch the weapon to avenge her lover, Pierre, and when she did the entire tree had quaked. She fell and slid on the grass, her grasp coming loose, and the hammer skidded away from her. The Indians froze, looking in wonder at a weapon that glowed as if it had come from the forge. Now Red Jacket was charging with his tomahawk, knowing our guns were empty. I yanked out my own hatchet. We'd finish this as I should have when he kicked me at Rendezvous.

I wouldn't have come close to Thor's hammer, but Magnus snatched it up with a bellow, screaming in pain as its energy coursed through him. He seemed to swell in stature, his beard and hair jutting out from electrical force, his own hand scorching at the touch. Yet even as he cried out he lifted the weapon skyward, spinning it in a crazed circle.

The sky erupted with fire. Lightning cracked in an arcing circle around the crown of the tree, bolt after bolt, some striking Yggdrasil but others lancing down to spots on the ground. Wind howled and then screamed, and clouds that had been merely menacing before began to boil and churn. The Indians scattered except for Red Jacket, who remorselessly chopped at Little Frog as he darted by, staving her temple with vicious efficiency. She dropped, instantly dead. I crouched, ready for him. And then Magnus threw the hammer and lightning blazed where we stood.

Namida and I were hurled back against the trunk of the ash as if punched, and Magnus reeled backward too. But the force of the bolts struck Red Jacket head-on with such searing power that it stopped his charge as if he'd hit an invisible wall, freezing him in agony as energy sizzled like a corona. His coat burst into flames. Then his eyes boiled and jutted, his tongue swelled like a loaf of bread, and he was kicked backward a dozen feet, his moccasins flying off.

Thor's hammer had worked!

The mystical tool flew back into Magnus's hands through some weird magnetism between weapon and wielder. The Norwegian caught it with an agonized yell. Bloodhammer seemed infused with electricity himself, clothes smoking, hammer, sky, and tree crackling with attractant charges, he gave a great shout of agony and swung in a circle, a sheet of energy roiling out of the hammer head and blasting into the grass. Fire sprang up all around the tree, a circular wall of flame, and what Indians hadn't been killed by the searing charge were running for their lives. Now Magnus was howling in agony, twisting about, and with his final strength he leaned back and hurled the hammer straight up, as far as he could throw, the weapon turning over and over in the air.

The sky exploded.

Lightning bolts shot from a dozen directions to converge on the hammer and collide with a colossal clap of thunder. It was a slap of sound, momentarily deafening me, and everything went white and then dark again, the hammer falling back toward Magnus and then bouncing off the ground because none of us dared touch it anymore. It radiated energy like a weapon snatched from the sun. It was sizzling, boiling away. Magnus staggered back against the bark of the tree, shot, burnt, pained, stunned, and with his arms up against the curtain of fire he'd ignited.

The sky went black and the only illumination was from the grass fire devouring the meadow around the tree, burning both in toward us and out toward the fleeing Dakota. Through the shimmering heat and smoke I could see Aurora, waving her empty weapon and cursing as the flames caught the grass around her. As my hearing returned I could hear her call my name and promising to meet me in hell. Then the smoke was too much, the flames lit the lower branches of Yggdrasil, and it seemed we'd set a holocaust to consume ourselves.

We'd ignited Ragnarok, end of the world.

CHAPTER **42**

○────────────────────────────────────

U nder the tree," Magnus croaked. His beard was smoking. "Down below, to save our lives!"

We retreated down the tunnel of tusks to the chamber we'd been in before, this time without the hammer suspended in its cage of wire and roots. The wires were smoking now, the tree shuddering with convulsions overhead, and Magnus looked horribly burned.

"Little Frog snatched it to avenge Pierre," Namida said shakily.

"And half killed herself doing it," I amended. Smoke began to follow us down the tunnel. The heat was growing. "We haven't found Eden, Magnus, we've found hell." I automatically, without thinking, began reloading the rifle that seemed welded to my fist. How many times had it saved my life?

"No, no, this is paradise, I know it!," Magnus gasped. "The hammer was the apple, we should never have touched it! But the sky god's power is still here—we are connected to heaven by a wire! It will work, Ethan, it will still work!"

"What will work?" The giant was even crazier than before.

"It will resurrect Signe!"

"What?"

"It's the tree of life, Ethan, that's what the Norse Templars were looking for! They were searching for the remnant of Eden and the youth of the world that it still might contain! The hammer was a seed, to collect the sky's energy, and the tree a machine of rejuvenation! They didn't have the time to make it work before they were overwhelmed by the Indians, but it's been growing for four and a half centuries. Now, Ethan, now, I can bring her back!"

"Bring back your dead wife?"

"With my child in her womb!"

And in triumph, he held up the map case. "Don't you wonder why I carried this across the prairie with no map?" With burned, smoking fingers, he winced as he tore the end of it open. "The texts are ambiguous, but I think they imply resurrection. That, or oblivion. I never loved anyone else, Ethan, never for a moment, not like Signe!" And he dropped into his palm a cup of gray powder. His eyes gleamed. "Her ashes! Didn't I tell you it's the greatest treasure on earth?"

"No! What do you mean to do?"

"Stand back, both of you! I'm going into the cage with her and grasp the wire, but this time I think it will heal! So promise the old texts!"

"Magnus, that's insane!"

"The electricity will reconstitute her! Why else would the Templars build this?"

"Cecil said it was for some purpose we don't know!"

"The Somersets are the blind ones, in a dark cellar with jewels they cannot find." He smiled. "Signe and I will finally be together one way or another. I'm going to be a conduit for the lightning. I'm going to touch the finger of God! Get back, in case it doesn't work."

"Magnus, Signe can't be resurrected!"

"You think I care about this life if she can't?" And he reached like a madman toward the web of root and wire, grasping toward the rod that ran to the top of the tree. For the first time since I'd met him, he seemed at peace. Odin the one-eyed had finally found what he roamed the world for.

I fled.

As I hauled Namida back up the smoking tunnel, I saw him reach for the wire as Adam reached for the Almighty. "Come back, lost love!" His fist squeezed the ashes.

And then there was a roar, a world-wrenching sound that dwarfed that of the lightning before, and I suppose our hearing was saved only because the clap brought down on Namida and me a roof of earth as the tunnel and its tusks collapsed on top of us. Magnus had triggered the apocalypse, and everything was snuffed out in an instant. We were buried alive, in ground that shook like a wet dog.

I clung to the Indian woman I'd dragged to this hell, cursing that I hadn't followed my own instincts. I was to be entombed in a nameless prairie, never to report on woolly elephants, British scheming, or the sexual charm of aboriginal maidens!

And then, as Magnus had promised, we were resurrected.

Not in the biblical way. Rather, the earth erupted, carrying us up with it as a root ball as wide as a village was ripped out of the ground. First there was terrifying, suffocating blackness as the tunnel caved in, and then the light of our explosive rebirth, a tumult of earth, rock, and wood as roots flailed and soil flew up in great geysers of flying dirt. I dimly heard and felt a titanic crash of thousands of tons of wood striking the ground, shaking the earth even more. Then bits of burning foliage rained down out of a storm-tossed sky like little candles, lighting a gloom of dust and cloud. I spat soil and gasped for breath.

Finally it was quiet except for the hissing of a gentle rain. Or was that ringing in my ears?

Shakily, I sat up. Namida and I were black with earth, coughing, clawing it out of our ears, eyes streaming. My rifle jutted from the mess like a dirty stake. We were in a crater big enough to make a respectable lake. The great ash tree, our modern Yggdrasil, had been blown skyward by Magnus's rash experiment and had fallen, flaming, to earth. It stretched a quarter-mile across the prairie, flames boiling from its branches. As it toppled it left a hole where the roots had been. Its root pan formed a vast disk and individual roots jutted two hundred feet high into the air, while the weight of its trunk had hammered a depression into the ground. Cracks in the earth radiated away from the trench where it had fallen.

The greatest tree on the face of the planet had been killed.

Of Magnus there was no sign. The cave was gone, of course, obliterated in the explosion and toppling. So was the cage of roots and wire, Signe's ashes, and the Norwegian himself. He had connected with Valhalla, and vanished.

Maybe the couple found a common grave in the pit of the tree's crater. Maybe they were vaporized by the energy they harnessed. Maybe they were remade in some better place.

And me? As always, I was left in this bitter world.

Oblivion from sorrow, I realized, was Bloodhammer's real Eden. He wanted an end to his mourning, one way or another—and had gotten it. Norway, royalty, treasure? In the end it didn't matter. Magnus had found the paradise of being subsumed.

Namida and I crawled from the crater to its rim, shaking. I dragged my now-battered rifle with us, knocking soil from the muzzle mouth, and used it to shakily lever myself erect. Then I helped up the Indian woman.

The grass fire at the tree's base had consumed all the fuel and burned itself out, leaving behind a smoking ring. Fires still radiating out from its periphery were dying in the drizzle. We found the bodies of Little Frog and Pierre and Cecil in the bare ground under the tree where the fire hadn't reached, and the smoked, charcoal husk of Red

Jacket. Several other blackened corpses lay in the devastated meadow. Of the rest of the Dakota, and Aurora Somerset, there was no sign.

I did find the hammer, curiously inert and shrunken. Much of its weight had evaporated in our apocalypse. The husk remaining was dull gray now, a lump of iron, no longer hot to the touch. Our wayward use had disarmed it.

"Thor's hammer, he called it," said Namida, looking at the weapon in wonder.

"Just old metal, now."

"There are some things men shouldn't find." She began to weep for her lost friends.

I looked skyward. The storm clouds had flattened to a sullen overcast, and the rain began in earnest.

CHAPTER 43

The tree trunk was a horizontal wall as tall and long as the storied walls of Constantinople, but the fire and fall had shattered its abnormally fast-growing column into long, twisted pieces. Rain was already pouring into yawning gaps. It would rot fast, I guessed, and when it decayed would anything of like grandeur ever replace it? Not without the peculiar influence of electricity and hammer. The root hole would become a lake, the tree would molder into the soil, and the burned meadow would grow back. No trace would remain of Bloodhammer's peculiar Eden. Or was it his Ragnarok? Did only the whim of chance separate the two?

The rune stone was still there, forgotten in all the excitement. The fire had passed over it without harm. In a generation or two, when the tree was gone, it would be the only proof of my tale.

Also abandoned was the ax of my Norwegian

friend. Namida picked up its handle to drag it in a daze, like a child's doll.

And then, as we staggered in weariness around the wreck of the tree, we noticed another thing not immediately apparent in the tangle of roots exposed by Yggdrasil's toppling.

The tree's heave out of the earth took with it not just tons of clinging dirt but granite boulders the size of hay wagons, clinging like nuts in a dough. The root pan was already streaming with rainwater, and it too would eventually break down. But there was something else we saw, something so strange that it made us shiver and wonder if this place was indeed cursed.

Beside old mastodon tusks there were human skeletons caught in the web of roots, their bones as gray-brown as the tree parts that surrounded them. Flesh and hair was long gone, but buried armor showed these were not Indians. The red rust of shields was clearly visible. Also caught in the wheel of soil were remnants of old breastplates, swords, mail, and helmets. We'd found the Norse! Some at least had apparently been buried in a semicircle around what four and a half centuries ago must have been a sapling, tied to an electrical machine dug in a barrow deep into the earth.

"Bodies," I said to Namida.

"The red-haired strangers," she said, looking at the remnants of armor.

"Yes. White men like me."

"So far from home."

"Magnus would say they thought they were going home."

"The white man is so strange, always searching for home. The world is the world, anyplace you are. Eden is where you make it. Why does the white man always travel so far, so restlessly, with such violence?"

"To find peace."

"White men need to make peace where they are."

"The Templars were warriors. So were the Vikings. So are the Ojibway and the Dakota. It was who they were, and are. It's who men are, different than women." But I wasn't really trying to explain, I was staring upward at the suspended skeletons and rusting armor with sudden excitement. Was that gold?

I'd found gold with the remains of the knight Montbard in the City of Ghosts, far away in the desert, so why not here? My heart began to beat faster, my body to recharge.

"White men should find home where they are."

"I think we found treasure."

And before Namida could stop me, I grasped a root and began to climb the disk of earth, pulling myself up to the skeleton I'd seen with its glint of yellow metal. If it seems sacrilegious to disturb the dead, they are past caring, aren't they? Was I finally to get some reward for this journey? But why entomb gold? Did refugee Templars bring gold to America? Or did they find it here, like the mysterious copper mines on Isle Royale? Was supple metal, not Eden, what drew them?

"There's something with these bones," I called down.

Namida shook her head. "The bones are why this place is wicked!"

"Just sacred, like a burial ground."

She began to moan. "No, this is an evil place! That hammer was evil, look what it did! Leave their things, Ethan! We must get away from here, quickly! This is a place of bad spirits!"

"It's time to salvage something from the wreckage."

"Nooo, we must go, I can feel it!"

"Soon, I promise. I'm almost to it!"

I reached the remains, the skull grinning in that disquieting way that the dead have—I was getting used to this macabre aspect of treasure hunting—and brushed some dirt aside next to the armor. A flake of gold came with it.

I paused. Was the treasure that delicate? I picked at the dirt more carefully now, and realized there was indeed gold, but in a sheet far thinner and broader than I'd imagined. It was a disk of gold, as broad as an arm is long, but no thicker than paper.

It *was* paper, of a sort.

The size and shape of a round shield.

And there was raised writing on the metal. Not runes, but Latin script.

The Templar trick reminded me of how I'd hid the Book of Thoth in plain sight in the Egyptian cotton of a sail on the Nile. In this case, a wood-and-metal medieval shield had become a sandwich sheathing a sheet of gold no thicker than foil, and used, I presumed, because it would not decay. The imprinted gold leaf had been hidden.

Why?

To keep its message secret until the right discoverer came along, I guessed.

Somehow I doubted they had me in mind.

I looked more closely. It was Latin, all right, but backward in my view as in a mirror: the shield had been buried with the writing facing the sky, and I was on the underside. I broke off a root stub and began digging around the edge of the shield, the covering rotting and the gold itself as delicate as a dried leaf.

"Ethan, hurry!"

"There's writing, like a book!"

"What's a book?"

"You can store a thought and then let it speak to someone who never heard it, miles or years away!"

That, of course, made no sense to her and it reminded me of the gap between us, she of the prairie and me of the gambling salon. What would become of us now? Should I send her back to her people? Could I take her to the President's House and Napoleon's court like some Pocahontas? Or should I send her to the Mandan? At length I got most of the rotting shield free from the soil, cursing as flakes of gold floated away, and carefully crawled down, holding the ragged remnant from one hand like a friable sheet of newspaper. When I got back to the crater I peeled more rust and rotting wood away and tried to read.

I'm not a scholar, spending more of my desultory time at Harvard peering through the panes at passing Cambridge damsels than paying attention to the lives of the caesars. I could no more rattle off Latin than explain Newton's *Principia*. But there were words I thought I recognized. *Poseidon*, for example, and *Atlantic*. No, wait. I peered closer. Was it *Atlantic* or *Atlantis*? And near it another word that oddly rang a bell, though I couldn't remember having heard it before. *Thira*. And another: *hasta*. An old poem came to mind. Didn't that mean spear in Latin? I recalled Silano had found a medieval Latin couplet that had helped point the way to the Book of Thoth. Could these Norse Templars, thousands of miles from their real home, have left behind another Latin clue to treasure or power? But why bury the clue where the hammer was? You don't bury the treasure map where the treasure is. There were odd words, too, like *Og*.

What the devil did that mean?

It made no sense. Unless the treasure—Thor's hammer—was *not* the true treasure, or at least the ultimate one. That this great tree was but a signpost.

I remembered what Magnus had told me. The Templars had been crushed and scattered. Whatever artifacts, treasure, or books of power they'd accumulated had scattered with them. One I'd found cached in an underground sarcophagus in the City of Ghosts in the desert southeast of Jerusalem: the Book of Thoth. Another I'd come almost halfway around the world to find, here: Thor's hammer. So if there were two, why not more? What had Cecil said about the Templars trying to assemble something? And if there were more, why not hide a key to their whereabouts in the one place the scattered Templars might be expected to find and re-gather at, the gigantic myth tree fueled by electricity, Yggdrasil?

I groaned, inwardly. Somehow I knew I wasn't done.

The trouble with being called is that you don't get to quit.

And then something sang and banged past my head, and there was the report of a gunshot. A hole appeared in the rusting shield, the delicate gold parting like tissue paper.

"Wait!" I cried.

But Aurora Somerset was galloping toward us like a woman possessed, hair flying, teeth bared, her green eyes afire with the madness of grief. She was on an Indian pony, tossing aside her empty musket and drawing instead her brother's broken rapier with her free arm and shaking an Indian lance in the other. The sword's jagged edge glinted like the shard of a broken ale bottle. She wanted vengeance!

I looked for my rifle. I'd propped it against a shattered root, too far away. I dashed, just as her pony pitched down into the tree crater.

And then I felt sharp pain stab my calf. I stumbled, sprawling.

The thrown lance, with flint tip, had speared through my leg.

I braced to be ridden down, the dangling spear hobbling me.

But Aurora wasn't galloping for me. She was aimed at the parchment of gold, leaning down like a Cossack to snatch it. Did she know what it was?

But just as she strained to snatch it, Aurora's horse screamed and pitched forward, launching her over the animal's neck. Horse and rider crashed into the artifact I'd found with a spray of mud, golden script shattered into golden confetti. Antique wood and flakes of wisdom went flying in yellow destruction, Aurora wailing in outrage as she slid in a scrim of ruin. The horse was on its back, writhing in agony, filaments of gold on its hooves. And then Namida reared up on the other side, heaving Magnus's ax over her head, and brought it down on the pony's throat, killing it.

She'd used the abandoned weapon to bring the horse down.

Aurora, scrabbling on her hands and knees, went for the other woman with a shriek of outrage, the broken rapier still in hand, slashing. Namida's grip slipped as the sword scraped on the ax handle and both weapons slid away.

My rifle!

I yanked the spearhead from my calf, roaring at the pain, and crawled across loose gravel and mud to get my weapon. The two women were wrestling in the dirt, grappling for Aurora's broken sword.

"Namida, get clear so I can take a shot!" I hollered.

The Indian woman shifted her grip to Aurora's forearms, grunted, and heaved, throwing Lady Somerset and the broken rapier to one side and then bending to the other to give me a clear line of fire. Sprawled awkwardly, I raised my rifle and aimed. Aurora was prone on the ground too, not the best target, and I had but one shot. Careful! Sight, stock to shoulder, breathe, hold, squeeze . . .

I fired.

And something came up in my aiming point just as I did so. The bullet pinged and ricocheted harmlessly.

Aurora Somerset had lifted Magnus's bloody ax as a desperate shield, and by the worst luck I'd hit it. The noblewoman flashed a smile of wild triumph.

And then she leaped on Namida like a tigress before the Indian woman could react, hauling my lover's head back by the hair and holding the rapier to her breast.

"No!" My cry was utter desperation. I was too crippled to rush them in time, my rifle would take a full painful minute to reload, and I was too far to throw the lance. I was helpless, and my enemy knew it.

"I want you to grieve as I'll grieve," Aurora spat. "I want you to remember your squaw as I remember poor Cecil." And then she rammed the sword stub home, screeching in victory like a banshee as she sawed into the poor girl's chest.

I've seen more than my share of horror, but Aurora was right, this one seared into me. Namida's eyes were as wide as a frightened calf's as the metal bit, her heart exploded and gushed, and the blood ran over Aurora's hands to make her some kind of monstrous Lady Macbeth. Namida's high cry was choked off by the stabbing, her mouth open in final surprise, and then the blood poured down her deerskin blouse and her eyes rolled and glazed.

I remembered her first words.

"Save me."

My heart fell through the earth.

"You monster!" I roared. I grabbed the lance and began crawling toward this witch whom I'd somehow been enamored with, this wicked harridan who'd help cause the death of all my friends. Magnus was right, there is emotional pain that is worse than death, and I wanted to either finish Aurora or have her finish me. "Come on me, then! Let's end this, now!"

She reared upward, pitching Namida's dead body aside like a sack of potatoes, and smiled the grin of the devil herself. "What did you read?"

"What?" The question was so unexpected that I stopped crawling toward her for a moment, the leak from my leg an undulating scarlet snake behind me. I could feel the slow throb of my wound.

"How much of it did you see?"

She was talking about the golden sheet and its message, I realized. Somehow she knew it—and the Templar bodies—might be there.

"You . . . knew?"

"What did it say, Ethan?" she asked again, her broken sword dripping with my lover's blood. "What was the message?"

"You think I'd tell *you*?"

She laughed then, the laugh of the insane, and kicked at the fragments that her horse's tumble had scattered. "You will. You will because I will *follow* you." And grinning now, sly, eyes shimmering with hatred and a lust for something I did not yet grasp, she saluted me with the broken rapier and, turning, began to saunter away.

"Wait! Come back, damn it! End this!"

A laugh again. "Oh, Ethan, we are nowhere near the end. Once we saw the map, the old texts began to make sense. What we'd whispered about in the Rite."

"Aurora!"

She twirled the haft of the rapier like her parasol.

So I hurled the lance. It fell well short, halfway between her and me, and she could have turned and rushed me then before I crawled to retrieve it. She could have tormented me like a wounded bull, darting in to deliver wound after wound, until, exhausted and depleted, I bled into the mud and expired.

But she didn't. She didn't look back, and said nothing more. She just kept walking away from the tree and out its crater, a swing to her hips, as if something satisfying had at last been settled. It wouldn't have surprised me if she'd whistled.

She wanted me alive.

She wanted me to follow what I'd read.

And by the time I crawled back to my rifle and reloaded it, Aurora Somerset had disappeared into the trees.

CHAPTER 44

What came next I recall only dimly. I was in shock from blood loss, electrical discharge, grief, the plague that had ravaged the Indian village, amazement that the hammer had existed at all, and confusion. What message had I come away with? A Latin script kicked into oblivion by the hooves of a dying pony. What did it mean? I hadn't the faintest idea. What did Aurora think I knew? I had even less notion of that. Where had she gone? She'd passed into the trees like mist, as if she'd never existed.

I was utterly alone. I saw no Indians, no buffalo, no smoke.

I bound up my wounded leg as best I could and drank some dirty water from one of the puddles. Rain continued to fall.

Then I knelt and dug three places in the mud to bury my Pierre, Little Frog, and Namida, using Magnus's ax as a crude hoe. Good farmland, I noted as I scraped. Good land for Jefferson's yeoman farmers. A good place for democracy.

What a price my friends and I paid for that geographical information.

And Napoleon? This was a place that could swallow armies.

I think I had an idea what should become of Louisiana.

So did my thoughts blessedly wander. Then it was done, three holes together. Namida first, laid as gently as I could, pushing her eyes closed. Then brave and burnt Little Frog, who'd seized the god's fire to avenge Little Pierre. And then Pierre himself, his clothes slightly scorched, his skin raw from the cruel lashings of the accursed Cecil Somerset. I'd failed to protect any of them.

As the rain came down I mounded dirt on the first and the second and began on the third, scooping handfuls to hurl on the body.

Suddenly Pierre coughed and spat.

"What are you doing, donkey?"

I reeled back from his grave as if the devil himself had spoken. By Franklin's lightning! And then the Frenchman blinked, squinted against the rain falling into his face, and grimaced. "Why am I in a hole?"

"Because you're dead! Aurora killed you!" Had Magnus's dreams of resurrection somehow come true? What weird magic was this?

The voyageur slowly sat up where I'd been about to entomb him, staring in dull disbelief at the crater, the dead Indian pony, the lattice of roots, and the gargantuan trunk of Yggdrasil, stretched out across the prairie. "*Mon dieu*, what disaster have you made this time, American?"

I feared to touch him, lest my hand go through his ghostly breast. Was I hallucinating? "She shot you! Didn't she?"

He began turning his head as if to look at his back wound himself when he winced, groaning. "I think she shot *it*, my friend, and left me unconscious."

"It?"

"Hurts like the very devil." And so he carefully reached into his ragged shirt, still sitting in the mud, and painfully drew out a cotton string and something . . .

Bent around a bullet.

"I took it from shattered Cecil one night when the fool was wrestling me down to beat me, the maniac blind in one eye and enraged in the other, and after I stole it I tied it to the inside of my shirt to torment him. You can imagine how frantic he was when he missed it: his distress kept me amused while he tortured me. Who knew it would be useful? I'm bruised and bloody, but it kept the bullet from penetrating."

And he held up a very warped symbol I'd seen on Somerset's neck when he coupled with his sister, a pyramid and a snake that had flattened and held the lead ball Aurora had fired, cupping it like a pancake. "It turned out to be my luck and not his, no? And yours, because you'd be lost in the wilderness in an instant without the great Pierre to look after you." He coughed, and winced.

And now I fell forward not just to touch but to hug him, laughter and tears coursing down my cheeks at the same time. Alive!

"But where is Little Frog?"

So I told him how her courage had helped save his life.

◻   ◻   ◻

I left Pierre to grieve for the women and practice taking breath again—his back was a massive bruise—while I buried three other things.

No, not the remains of Cecil or Red Jacket. I reflected that Aurora, for all her perverse love for her brother, had not stayed to do the job either. The girl wasn't one for sentiment, was she? I left them for the coyotes and crows.

These others, however, I didn't want found.

One was the stone tablet. It was too heavy to take back. I don't know why it seemed important to keep the thing a secret, but if Aurora had been curious about the Latin cipher in a sheet of gold, why not Norse runes? I'm not sure she ever even realized we'd found it. So I dragged the rune stone to the travois that had escaped the worst of the flames, rolled it back on and, limping, dragged it a mile or more where its location would not be particularly obvious. I used the big ax to cut a hole in the turf of a grassy hillock, looking carefully out of fear she was watching, slipped the stone under the sod, and left it sleeping. Maybe some new tree will grow atop it someday.

Then I went back for the curious holed stones the Norse had set around their tree and carried them in the travois to my new location, where I placed them so that lines drawn between would intersect where the rune stone was. It was the best I could think of in case there was some reason to find it again.

I cast the double-bitted ax in a pond. The tool had been useful many times over, but there was a ding on its blade where Aurora had blocked my bullet, and I wanted no physical reminder of the price of that miss. The tool could rust away in peace.

And Thor's hammer? It seemed dead now, no more than a fused piece of slag, but it wasn't something I felt the world needed. Nor did I want it within reach of lightning that might reanimate it. I found a granite boulder sitting lonely on a meadow, scooped out a small tunnel beneath it, and secreted the hammer there. There are other odd boulders in that country, and this one I didn't mark. It can sleep until the real Ragnarok.

I salvaged enough gold flakes, which just bore torn letters now, to roll into a ball the size of a grape. This would be my new stake when I found a decent game of cards.

Then Pierre and I said our last prayers and good-byes and set out east. Using the lance as a crutch, my rifle over my shoulder in a makeshift sling, I started limping. He hobbled bent like an old man, his torso a mass of bruises and pain. We made all of three miles that first day, but what a relief to have escaped the strange Eden of Magnus Bloodhammer! The swirling storm clouds had disappeared with the fall of the tree, but not the feeling of foreboding and loss.

I felt like the gates of Eden were swinging shut behind us. I looked back once and saw only empty sky, stretching endlessly west.

"I'm sorry I didn't kill him with that first shot from the canoe," I told Pierre. "I'm always missing by inches."

"It was better that way because your first execution would have been too merciful," the Frenchman said grimly. "You took away his vanity and filled him with shame. What happened at the tree had to happen, Ethan. We brought things to a necessary end."

I began to spy game the second day and brought down first a raccoon and then a buck deer. The women had taught us to spot edibles, and we gathered what late-season roots and berries we could find. There was frost in the mornings now, the leaves falling faster. On the fourth day we trudged through a premature flurry of snow.

I skinned out the deer and when I came to a river we made another Welsh coracle, or Mandan boat. The task consumed a full day and if Pierre had been any bigger we would have swamped the vessel, but it worked, just, in the gentle river. It allowed me to rest my sore leg as we floated downstream, steering with the stock of my rifle. If I was still ravaged by sorrow inside, I was beginning to heal on the outside.

Pierre cut himself a paddle and began to talk of building a canoe.

Was Aurora following? I saw no sign. Maybe she died of madness on the prairie.

The river passed through lakes, gathering water as it went. On the third day we recognized this as the river we'd first ascended with our second canoe. So we slipped east and south, drifting finally to an Indian village, dazed to see children playing happily at the edge of the river, men fishing, women cooking and mending. The world was unchanged by our trauma. Whole villages were still normal and happy. Here beyond the frontier, white and red were not at each other's throats.

Why didn't I just stop? This was the real Eden, wasn't it?

Because I'm a Franklin man, a savant, and a man of science with discovery to report. Because I'm Napoleon's opportunistic minion, and Jefferson's naturalist, and Sir Sidney Smith's wayward spy and electrician. I was the hero of Mortefontaine! Because I was lover to Namida and Astiza, one dead and one lost back to Egypt but perhaps not, in the end, irretrievable. Because I'm a man more of the Palais Royal and the President's House than wigwam and prairie. And because Aurora Somerset thought I might still find something, somewhere, of even more importance than Thor's hammer.

If I found *her* again, I'd make her tell me what.

So they gave us an old canoe, in the generous manner of poor people in wild country, and we continued on, portaging around some falls we encountered.

Two weeks after we limped away from Yggdrasil we came upon a camp of four French trappers who were descending to Saint Louis to spend the winter behind logs and glass. The growing river we were on, they informed us, was indeed the infant Mississippi! We greeted them in French, and I told them I was a scout for Jefferson and Napoleon.

"On this side of the river you are a scout for Napoleon, my friend," said one of the voyageurs. "The Spanish flag still flies over Saint Louis, but word is that we will soon have the tricolor. And on that side," he said, pointing to the eastern bank, "you are a scout for Jefferson. Here the empires meet!"

"Actually he's a donkey and a sorcerer," Pierre informed them.

"A sorcerer! What use is that? But a donkey—ah, how we've wished for one sometimes in the back-country!"

We told them nothing of Norse hammers, but did interest them with our account of the upper Mississippi and reports of plentiful fur and game. But the country was also thick with Dakota, I cautioned, and at mention of those fierce warriors the trappers seemed to lose interest.

Pierre said it was too late in the season to try to catch his North Men, so we swept south just ahead of winter. On October 13—another anniversary of the betrayal of the Knights Templar—we paddled onto the shelving levee of Saint Louis, where riverboats could ground to unload cargo before being pushed off the stone "beach" again. Like Detroit, this French settlement was a hundred years old, but unlike Detroit it was growing instead of shrinking. French refugees from the aggrandizements of

Britain and the United States fetched up here to make a new life in Napoleon's empire. The city is just a few miles south of the Mississippi's junction with the Missouri River, and a more strategic spot can scarcely be imagined. If Bonaparte wants Louisiana, he'll have to assert control from Saint Louis as well as New Orleans. If Jefferson wants to reach the Pacific, his Meriwether Lewis must come through Saint Louis.

And so I ended my western sojourn. I was exhausted, heartsick, poor, had no proof that Jefferson's elephants still lived—and couldn't really reveal just what we *did* find since I had a hunch it might prove useful to an inveterate treasure hunter like me. Thira? Og? As always, the ciphers didn't make a lick of sense. So I had my first hot bath in months, ate white bread light as a cloud, and slept on a bed above the floor.

My new boots hurt my feet.

Pierre said he'd never invite insane donkeys into his canoe again. It was awkward for a few days, because we were the closest of friends and yet he knew I was as anxious to go back to cities as he longed for the freedom of the voyageur. Both of us carried unspoken grief and guilt for the women who'd died, but it's hard for men to talk of such things plainly. I wondered if I should persuade the little Frenchman to come back with me to Paris. But one morning, without word, he was gone. The only sign I had that this was his choice and not a kidnapping was that he left the mangled pyramid and bullet next to my bed.

Would I ever see him again?

It was in Saint Louis that I met a visiting Louisville squire named William Clark, a younger brother of the famed revolutionary hero George Rogers Clark. This Clark's own Indian fighting days had ended with nagging illnesses and a decision to settle down to domestic life in Kentucky, but he was a rugged-looking, congenial man who sought me out when he heard I'd been tramping through the northern Louisiana Territory.

"I'm impressed, sir, very impressed indeed," Clark said, pumping my hand as if I were the president. "But perhaps not such a trick for the hero of Acre and Mortefontaine?"

"Hardly a hero, Mr. Clark," I said as I sipped a bottle of blessed French wine, bringing to mind past bliss in Paris. "Half the things I try seem to turn to ashes."

"But that's the experience of all men, is it not?" Clark asked. "I'm convinced the difference between a successful man and a failure is that the former keep trying. Don't you agree?"

"You seem to have the wisdom of my mentor Franklin."

"You knew Franklin? Now there was a man! A titan, sir, a Solomon! And what would Franklin have said of Louisiana?"

"That it's cozier in Philadelphia."

Clark laughed. "Indeed, I bet it is! Philadelphia is no doubt cozier than Kentucky, too, but ah, Kentucky—such beauty! Such possibility!"

"Louisiana has that as well, I suppose."

"But only for Americans, don't you think? Look at these French. Bravest fellows in the world, but trappers, not farmers. They drift like the Indians. More Americans sweep down the Ohio in a week than all the French who live in Saint Louis! Yes, Americans are going to fill up the eastward bank here, and soon!"

"Do you think so? I'm to report to both Jefferson and Napoleon."

"Then report the inevitable." He took a sip of wine. "Tell me. Did you like it out there?"

I considered, and decided to be honest. "It frightened me."

"It pulls on me. I wish I had the chance to see that land of yours, Ethan Gage. I've heard our new president is intrigued, and I know his secretary, a captain named Lewis. It would be great to set off again, but then I've got a family and troublesome digestion. I don't know. I don't know." His fingers played a tattoo, looking westward at things I couldn't see. "So what will you tell Napoleon?"

That I needed to find Og, I thought. "That Louisiana is an opportunity, but of a different kind than he might think. I think I'll tell him there's money to be made." I was forming the report in my own mind. "I think I'll tell Thomas Jefferson how to make a bargain."

HISTORICAL NOTE

On November 8, 1898, an immigrant farmer named Olaf Ohman was clearing land near the village of Kensington, Minnesota, when he unearthed a stone slab the size of a grave marker that was entangled in the roots of a poplar tree. Upon inspection he realized the stone was carved with Norse runes, or letters, eventually translated as:

EIGHT GOTLANDERS AND TWENTY-TWO NORWEGIANS ON A JOURNEY OF ACQUISITION FROM VINLAND, VERY FAR WEST. WE HAD CAMP BY TWO ROCKY ISLANDS ONE DAY'S JOURNEY FROM THIS STONE. WE WERE OUT FISHING ONE DAY. AFTER WE CAME HOME WE FOUND TEN MEN RED WITH BLOOD AND DEATH. AVM SAVE FROM EVIL.

And on the stone's side:

HAVE TEN MEN BY THE SEA TO LOOK AFTER OUR SHIPS FOURTEEN DAYS JOURNEY FROM THIS ISLAND. YEAR 1362.

The authenticity of the Kensington rune stone, on display in a small museum in Alexandria, Minnesota, has been hotly debated for more than a century. Did Norse explorers really reach the upper Midwest some 130 years before the first voyage of Columbus? Or was the stone a clever forgery? The farmer never profited from his find and insisted to the day he died that he didn't carve it. If a forgery, was it planted decades earlier, to give the tree time to grow around it? No white settlers lived there then. If real, was it moved from its original location? Why would medieval Scandinavians travel to a geographically nondescript place in western Minnesota?

Scholars who once scoffed at the idea of any pre-Columbian contact between Europe, Asia, and the Americas have in recent decades been inundated with fragmentary evidence and imaginative theories suggesting that transatlantic and transpacific voyages in fact took place. The most compelling find is the 1960s discovery of the L'Anse aux Meadows Norse settlement site in Newfoundland, which proved that stories of medieval Viking explorers reaching America are indeed true. Rune stones, meanwhile, have been found in Maine, Oklahoma, Iowa, the Dakotas, and Minnesota. So have metal fragments of European weaponry and tools. Some two hundred boulders with mooring holes that are similar to the type medieval Scandinavians used to moor their boats have been discovered in North America.

As this novel indicates, theories that other

Europeans—or even Israelites!—preceded Columbus to America go back to Jefferson's day and earlier. The lighter coloring of some Mandan Indians, and the fact that their agricultural settlements were more reminiscent of a medieval European village than a typical Plains Indian encampment, was commented on by French explorer Pierre de La Verendrye in 1733 and artist George Catlin in 1832. Their women were reputed to be among the most beautiful on the continent and were generously shared—a reputation that influenced the decision by the Lewis and Clark expedition to winter over there. All this fueled speculation that Norse or Welsh genes, at least, had made their way to the Missouri River. Unfortunately, the Mandan and their Awaxawi cousins were entirely wiped out by smallpox and Dakota raids by the 1840s before any systematic scientific inquiry could be done.

There are legends that a Prince Madoc of Wales set out for the New World with ten ships in 1170, and that Saint Brendan sailed west from Ireland to the "Isle of the Blessed" in 512. There has been debate that the volume of prehistoric copper mining in the Great Lakes is too great to be attributed to aboriginal use.

Anthropologists have also considered theories that America could originally have been populated not just by Asians crossing the Bering Sea land bridge during the Ice Age but by European ancestors island-hopping across the North Atlantic. Meanwhile, the date at which humans first appeared in the Western Hemisphere continues to be pushed back as new finds are made.

The odd notion that the Norse (or Welsh) made their way to the middle of the continent is at least possible because of the North American river system. Kensington is between the headwaters of the Red-Nelson river system, which runs north to Hudson's Bay, and the Mississippi, which eventually drains into the Gulf of Mexico. The Saint Lawrence–Great Lakes system provides another route from the Atlantic, with short portages making it possible to paddle across Minnesota in the manner described in this story. Possibility does not make probability, of course, but the exploration theories of Magnus Bloodhammer are not as completely fantastic as they first might seem. There are widespread legends among Native American people from Peru to Canada of white-skinned visitors in the distant past and global legends of a lost golden age in which mythic figures bequeathed knowledge to humankind. Does myth have a kernel of historical truth?

I owe the idea that the Minnesota Norse could have been Templars escaping from Scandinavia— and a possible translation of curiously marked letters that make a cipher within the stone—to Kensington rune stone investigators Scott Wolter, a geologist, his wife Jan Wolter, and engineer Richard Nielsen. *The Kensington Rune Stone: Compelling New Evidence*, provides an analysis of the stone's geology, script, and history. They've done extensive research on the island of Gotland to attempt to establish the medieval authenticity of the particular runes Olaf Ohman found. A briefer and balanced introduction to the controversy is *The Kensington Runestone* by Alice Beck Kehoe.

The intriguing correlations between Freemasonry, the origins of the United States, and the design of Washington, D.C., have been explored in a number of books and documentary films. Jefferson's curiosity about woolly elephants, Missouri volcanoes, and mountains of salt is taken from history.

The White House did not earn that name until the British burned it during the War of 1812 and its repaired shell was repainted.

Norway would not regain its independence until 1814, during the tumult of the Napoleonic wars.

The references to Norse myth are taken from the actual legends. But what of the botanical freak found by Magnus and Ethan? There have been a number of experiments in "electroculture," or the study of the effect of electrical fields on plants, including Bertholon's electrovegetoma machine of 1783. Later experiments allegedly show roots growing in water turn toward electric current, or seeds germinating more quickly in an electric field. My "electric" Yggdrasil is obviously fiction, but since the height of trees is limited by the difficulty of lifting water and nutrients up the trunk against the pull of gravity, I had fun imagining a "lightning-powered" tree that has excess energy to overcome the obstacle.

Finally, while many Indians in this story are menacing in accord with the history of the time, I should note that contemporary accounts of Native

Americans indicate they were every bit as varied, complex, and capable of good and evil as the Europeans writing about them. White captives portray a native world of astonishing freedom, humor, vigor, and gentleness, combined with a constant threat of famine, exposure, war, and torture. We have only fragmentary ideas of the "natural" state of Native American societies because they were so rapidly affected—and infected—by the European invasion. The seeming emptiness of the west was the result of epidemics of germs that destroyed Indian populations before most explorers even got there. Firearms revolutionized tribal warfare, and all the tribes were in motion as they fled west from the European assault. The Dakota (or Sioux) became high plains horsemen only after being pushed out of the eastern woodlands by other tribes such as the Ojibway (or Chippewa), who got guns first. The horse came from the Spanish. Ethan Gage travels west of the Mississippi three years before Lewis and Clark, but even his unexplored west is profoundly changed from whatever it was before Columbus. If there ever was an Eden in America, its door had been closing for three centuries before Ethan Gage got there.

Or maybe, as Pierre and Namida suggest, Eden is where we make it.

The adventure continues in *The Barbary Pirates*, where our hero is in a desperate race to recover the mirror of Archimedes, an ancient death-ray said to have scorched an entire Roman fleet. But the Barbary pirates are also determined to find this super weapon, as is his nemesis, Aurora Somerset. Meanwhile, his former lover Astiza finds herself in danger, and Ethan will discover that his actions have had consequences he didn't anticipate . . .

**Coming April 2010
in hardcover from Harper**

After I trapped three scientists in a fire I set in a brothel, enlisted them in the theft of a stampeding wagon, got them arrested by the French secret police, and then mired them in a mystic mission for Bonaparte, they began to question my judgment.

So allow me to point out that our tumultuous night was as much *their* idea as mine. Tourists come to Paris to be naughty.

Accordingly, I was hardly surprised when a trio of savants—the English rock hound William "Strata" Smith, the French zoologist Georges Cuvier, and the crackpot American inventor Robert Fulton—insisted that I take them to the Palais Royal. Scientific luminaries they may be, but after a hard day of looking at old bones or (in the case of Fulton) marketing impractical schemes to the French navy, what these intellectuals really wanted was a peek at the city's most notorious parade of prostitutes.

Not to mention supper in a swank Palais café, a game or two of chance, and shopping for souvenir trifles such as French perfume, silver toothpicks, Chinese silks, erotic pamphlets, Egyptian jewelry, or ivory curiosities of an even-more ribald nature. Who can resist the city's center of sin and sensuality? It was even better, the scientists reasoned, if such entertainment could be attributed to someone as discreet and shameless as me.

"Monsieur Ethan Gage *insisted* on giving us this tour," Cuvier explained to any acquaintance he met, reddening as he said it. The man was smart as Socrates but still retained his Alsatian provincialism, despite his rise to the summit of France's scientific establishment. The French Revolution has replaced breeding with ability, and with it traded the weary worldliness of the nobility for the curiosity and embarrassment of the striving. Cuvier was a soldier's son, Smith from agricultural stock, and Fulton had been sired by a failed farmer who died when he was three. Bonaparte himself was not even French but Corsican, and his generals were tradesmen's offspring: Ney the son of a cooper, Lefebre a miller, Murat an innkeeper, Lannes an ostler. I, sired by a Philadelphia merchant, fit right in.

"We're here to investigate revenue sources and public sentiment," I said to reinforce Cuvier's dignity. "Napoleon is keeping the Palais open in order to tax it."

Having resolved after my recent calamitous visit to America to reform myself, I suppose I should have resented the presumption that I was expert at negotiating the notorious Palais. But I *had*, in the spirit of social and architectural inquiry, explored most of its corners during my years in Paris. Now, in June of 1802, it remains the place Paris comes to be seen or—if one's tastes run to the scandalous or perverse—safely invisible.

Smith—recently fired from his canal-surveying job in England, and frustrated by the lack of recognition for his rock mapping—came to Paris to confer with French geologists and gape. He was a surveyor built like an English bulldog, balding and thick, with a farmer's tan and the bluff, ruddy heartiness of the ploughman. Given Smith's humble origins, English intellectuals had paid absolutely no attention to the rock mapping he'd done, and the snobbery rankled. Smith knew he was more intelligent than three-quarters of the men in the Royal Society.

"You're more creative for not being stuck in their company," I suggested when Cuvier brought him to me so I could serve as interpreter and guide.

"My career is like the ditches my canal company digs. I'm here because I'm not sure what else to do."

"As is half of London! The Peace of Amiens let loose a tide of British tourists who haven't come over since the revolution. Paris has hosted two-thirds of the House of Lords already, including five dukes, three marquesses, and thirty-seven earls. They're as transfixed by the guillotine as by the trollops."

"We English are just curious about liberty's relation to wickedness."

"And the Palais is the place to study, William. Music floats, lanterns glint, and a man can lose himself amid roving minstrels, angular acrobats, bawdy plays, amusing wagers, brilliant fashion, smart talk, intoxicating spirits, and swank bordellos." I nodded to encourage him.

"And this is officially tolerated?"

"Winked at. It's been kept off-limits to the French police since Philip of Orleans, and Philippe Egalité added the commercial arcades just before the revolution. The place has since weathered revolt, war, terror, inflation, and the conservative instincts of Napoleon with hardly a stammer. Three-quarters of Paris's newspapers have been shuttered by Bonaparte, but the Palais plays on."

"You seem to have made quite a study."

"It's the kind of history that interests me."

In truth, I was out of date. I'd been away from Paris and back in my homeland of America for more than a year and a half, and my frightful experiences there had made me more determined than ever to swear off women, gambling, drink, and treasure hunting. True, I'd been only partly successful in these resolutions. I'd used a grape-sized glob of gold (my only reward from my Trials of Job on the western frontier) to get a stake in St. Louis card games. There had been the distraction of a frontier barmaid or two, and a hearty sampling of Jefferson's wines when I finally reported back to the President's House in Washington. There he heard my carefully edited description of France's Louisiana Territory and agreed to my idea of playing unofficial American envoy back in Paris, trying to get Napoleon to sell the wasteland to the United States. So I had a thimbleful of fame and a dram of respectability, and decided I should finally live up to both. Admittedly, I couldn't resist embroidering my military exploits when I was given trans-Atlantic passage by an American naval squadron headed for Europe to protect our shipping from the Barbary pirates. It was convenient to me that the bashaw of Tripoli, a pirate king named Yussef Karamanli, had declared war on the United States the year before, demanding $225,000 to make peace and $25,000 a year in tribute. As so often happens in politics, Jefferson—who had argued against a large military—was using five frigates built by his predecessor, Adams, to respond to this extortion with force. "Even peace may be purchased at too high a price," my old mentor Benjamin Franklin once said. So when Jefferson offered me a ride on his flotilla, I accepted, provided I was able to get off in Gibraltar before any fighting could start.

I needn't have worried. The squadron commander, Richard Valentine Morris, managed to be at once unqualified, timid, and procrastinating. He brought his wife and son along as if going on Mediterranean vacation, and was two months late setting sail. But his congressman brother had helped Jefferson win the presidency over Aaron Burr, and even in young America, political alliances trump inexperience. The man was a connected idiot.

My own war stories during the voyage convinced half the officers I was a regular Alexander, and the other half that I was a habitual liar. But I *was* trying, you see.

"You're some kind of diplomat?" Smith tried to clarify.

"My idea is that Bonaparte sell Louisiana to my own country. It's emptiness the French have no use for, but Napoleon won't negotiate until he learns if his French army in St. Domingue, or Haiti, defeats the slaves and can be moved on to New Orleans. I have a connection to the general here, Leclerc."

I didn't add that my "connection" was that I had tupped Leclerc's wife, Pauline, back in 1800, before she'd joined her husband in the Caribbean. Now, while Leclerc fought yellow fever as well as Negroes, my former lover—who was also Napoleon's sister—was reportedly learning voodoo. You can get an idea of her character from the debate in Paris on whether it was she, or Napoleon's wife, Josephine, whom the Marquis de Sade used as inspiration for his latest depraved pamphlet, "Zoloe and Her Two Acolytes." Bonaparte resolved the issue by having the author thrown into prison for either possibility. I read the book to monitor the debate and spark erotic memory.

So I'd made my way from Gibraltar to Paris, living on a modest American government allowance and pledging to finally make something of myself, once I figured out what that something should be. The Palais, Gomorrah of Europe, was as good a place to think as any. I bet only when I could find an unskilled opponent, consorted with courtesans only when need became truly imperative, kept myself in physical trim with fencing lessons—I keep running into people with swords—and congratulated myself on self-discipline. I was pondering whether my talents could best be harnessed for philosophy, languages, mathematics, or theology when Cuvier sought me out and suggested I take Smith and Fulton to the Palais Royal.

"You can talk mammoths, Gage, and show us the whores as well."

I was the link in our quartet. I was deemed an expert on woolly elephants because I'd gone looking for them on the American frontier, and there was more excitement in Europe about animals that aren't around anymore than those that are.

"The elephants' *extinction* may be more important than their former *existence*," Cuvier explained to me. He was a pleasant-looking, long-faced, high-domed man of thirty-three with arched nose, strong chin, and pursed lower lip that gave him the appearance of constant deep thought. This accident of nature helped his advancement, as so often happens in life. Cuvier also had the fierce seriousness of a man who'd risen by merit instead of odd luck like me, and his organizational flair had put him in charge of the Paris zoo and French education, the latter task striking him as the more thankless.

"In any system the bright shine and the dull yearn only to escape, but politicians expect educators to repeal human nature."

"Every parent hopes their unexceptional child is the teacher's fault," I agreed.

Cuvier thought that I—without rank, income, or security—was the enviable one, dashing about on this mission or that for two or three governments at a time. Even I have trouble keeping it straight. So we'd become unlikely friends.

"The fact that we're finding skeletons of animals that no longer exist proves the earth is older than the Biblical six thousand years," the scientist liked to lecture. "I'm as Christian as any man, but some rocks have no fossils at all, suggesting life is not as eternal as Scripture suggests."

"But I thought a bishop had calculated the day of Creation rather exactly. To October 23, 4004 B.C., if I remember right."

"Claptrap, Ethan, all of it. Why, we've already cataloged twenty thousand species. How could they all fit on the Ark? The world is far older than we know."

"I keep running into treasure hunters who think the same thing, Georges, but I must say their abundance of time makes them balmy. They never know when they belong. The nice thing about the Palais is that there's never any yesterday and never any tomorrow. Not a clock in the place."

"Animals have little sense of time, either. It makes them content. But we humans are doomed to know the past and looming future."

Smith was a bone hunter, too, and theories were rife about what kinds of ancient calamities might have wiped out ancient animals. Flood or fire? Cold or heat? Cuvier was also intrigued by my mention of the word "Thira," which I'd read on medieval gold foil unearthed during my North American adventure. A particularly evil woman named Aurora Somerset had seemed to think the scroll had some importance, and Cuvier told me Thira, also known as Santorini, was a Greek island of great interest to European mineralogists because it might be the remains of an ancient volcano. So when "Strata" Smith came over from

London, anxious to talk rocks and see strumpets, it was natural we all be introduced. Cuvier was excited because Strata concurred with his own findings that fossil bones of a particular kind were found only in certain layers of rock, and thus could be used to date when that rock was laid down.

"I'm using the exposures in canals and road cuts to begin drawing a geologic map of Great Britain," Smith told me proudly.

I nodded as I've learned to do in the company of savants, but couldn't help asking, "Why?" Knowing which rock was where seemed a trifle dull.

"Because it can be done." Seeing my doubt, he added, "It could also be valuable to coal or mining companies." He had that defensive, impatient tone of the bright employee.

"You mean you'd have a map of where the seams of coal and metal are?"

"An indication of where they might be."

Clever. Accordingly, I agreed to organize our trip to the Palais, hoping that after a night of drinking Smith might let slip a vein of copper here or pocket of iron there. Maybe I could hock word of it to stockjobbers or mineral speculators.

Fulton, thirty-six, was my own contribution to our foursome. I'd met him upon my return to Paris when we'd both waited fruitlessly for an audience with Bonaparte, and I rather liked that he seemed even less successful than me. He'd been in France for five years, trying to persuade the revolutionaries to adopt his inventions, but his experiment at building a submarine, or "plunging boat," had been rejected by the French navy.

"I tell you, Gage, the *Nautilus* worked perfectly well off Brest. We were underwater three hours, and could have stayed six." Fulton was good-looking enough to be a useful companion when looking for ladies, but he had the fretfulness of the frustrated dreamer.

"Robert, you told the admirals that your invention could make surface navies obsolete. You may be able to keep from drowning, but you're the worst salesman in the world. You're asking men to buy what would put them out of work."

"But the submarine would be so fearsome as to end war entirely!"

"Another point against you. Think, man!"

"Well, I've a new idea for using Watt's steam engine to propel a riverboat," he said doggedly.

"And why would any man pay to fuel a boiler when the wind and oars are free?" Savants are all very bright, but it would be hard to find common sense in a regiment of them. That's why they need me along.

Fulton had been far more successful painting lurid circular panoramas for Parisians on great city fires. They'd pay a franc or two to stand in the middle rotating, as if in the conflagration themselves, and if anything is better testament to the peculiarity of human nature, I can't name it. Unfortunately, he wouldn't take my advice that the real money was not in steam engines that nobody really needed, but rather in frightening pictures that made people think they were somewhere other than where they were.

My idea, then, was this. We'd have a lads' night

out at the Palais Royal, I'd pump the savants for information on lucrative veins of coal or why medieval knights with a taste for the mystical and occult might have jotted down "Thira" on gold foil in the middle of North America, and then we'd see if any of us could come up with something that could be sold for actual money. I'd also continue working on reformation of my character.

What I wasn't counting on was the need to bet my life, and the French secret police.

¤   ¤   ¤

Horror we can habituate to. Defeat can be accommodated. It is the unknown that causes fear, and uncertainty that haunts us in the hollow of the night. So my resolution to reform myself was weaker than I knew because the truth was that I hadn't sworn off women entirely. After the agony and heartbreak I'd experienced on the American frontier, I wanted to reestablish contact with Astiza, a woman I'd fallen in love with four years before during Napoleon's Orient campaign. She'd left me in Paris to return to Egypt, and after the heartbreak of my latest adventure, I began writing her.

If she'd declined to renew our relationship, I'd have understood. Our time together had been more tumultuous than satisfying. But instead I got no answer at all, despite her promise that we might one day find ourselves together again. Of course Egypt was still recovering from the British expulsion of the French the year before, so communication was uncertain. But had anything happened to my partner in adventure? I did manage to contact my old friend Ashraf, who said he'd seen Astiza after her return to Egypt. She'd been her usual mysterious self, reclusive, troubled, and living in near seclusion. Then she abruptly vanished about the time I returned to Europe. I knew it would have been more surprising to hear she'd settled into domesticity, and certainly I'd little claim on her. But to not know nagged at me.

Which is how I led my companions into the wrong bordello.

It happened this way. The Palais Royal is an enormous rectangle of pillared arcades, its courtyard filled with gardens, fountains, and pathways. We ate at an outdoor café and gawked at the trollops who costumed themselves as the most prominent socialites of the republic, in between the trio's tediously learned arguments on bone classification and the merits of screw propellers. I showed them where Bonaparte used to play chess for money as an artillery captain, and the arcade where he'd met the prostitute to whom he'd lost his virginity as a young soldier. Yonder was the club where foreign minister Talleyrand once spent 30,000 francs in a single night, and nearby was the shop where Charlotte Corday bought the knife with which she stabbed Marat in his bath. Sodomites with plumage as elaborate as the whores walked the Street of Sighs arm in arm, given that such love has been decriminalized by the revolution. Beggars mingled with millionaires, prophets preached, cardsharps prowled, and the perversely pious sought out chambers where they could negotiate sexual whippings to the most precise calibration of penance and pain. We descended into the cellar "circus," where couples danced amid "nymphs" posing in diaphanous clothing, and pretended to study with an academic's objectivity the complex's forty-four statues of Venus.

As we circulated, Cuvier was persuaded to try his hand at the new game of "21" that Napoleon had helped popularize, Smith sampled varieties of champagne with a pub crawler's endurance, and Fulton studied the acrobats' use of leverage.

He had to be dragged away from a fire-eater. "Imagine if we could invent a dragon!"

"The French wouldn't buy that, either."

I guessed this group was as happy looking at the prostitutes as hiring them. Given that half the Palais' amusements were technically illegal—French kings had issued thirty-two decrees against gambling since 1600—it was my full intention to keep us out of trouble. Then I heard, while leading our little squad through a dim arcade of shops and descending stairways, a female voice call my name.

I turned to see Madame Marguerite, or, as she preferred to be called, Isis, Queen of Arabia. She was a bordello manager of entrepreneurial ambition whom I'd encountered before I reformed. "Monsieur Gage! You must introduce me to your friends!"

Marguerite operated one of the more ostentatious brothels in the Palais, a warren of vaulted caverns under a crowded gambling salon. Its decor was Oriental, and the courtesans' filmy costumes were inspired by feverish European fantasies of the seraglios of Istanbul. By rumor you could sample hashish and opium there, while imagining yourself master of a harem. It was costly, decadent, illegal, and thus quite irresistible. It was also no place for esteemed savants. My instinct was to hurry by, but Marguerite rushed out to block us, my companions bunched up nervously behind as if we were at the entrance to the maze of the Minotaur.

"Hello, Isis," I said warily. "Business going well?"

"Brilliantly, but how we've missed our Ethan! We'd been told you'd disappeared in America. How heartbroken were my concubines! They wept, thinking of you at the mercy of Red Indians."

Well, I had spent money in the place. "I'm back, my hair still attached, but newly reformed," I reported. "Celibacy is good for character, I've decided."

She laughed. "What an absurd idea. Surely your friends don't agree?"

"These are savants, men of learning. I'm just showing them about."

"And there is much my girls can show. Collette! Sophie!"

"I'm afraid we can't stay."

"Is this the Arabian place?" Cuvier interrupted behind me, craning to look. "I've heard of it."

"It looks like an Ottoman palace in there," said Smith, squinting through the doorway. "The architecture is quite intricate."

"Do you really want to be seen entering?" I asked, even as Marguerite seized my arm with enthusiasm. "I *am* responsible for your reputation, gentlemen."

"And we in this house are mistresses of discretion," our hostess assured. "Esteemed savants, at least experience my décor—I work so hard at it. And it's so fortuitous we meet, Ethan, because my assistant inside was just asking about you!"

"Was she now?"

"It's a man, actually. He plays the role of Osiris." She winked.

"I'm not of that taste."

"No, no, he only wants to talk and wager with you. He's heard of your gambling skills and says you'll want to bet for the thing you most desperately wish to learn."

"Which is?"

"Word of your Egyptian friend."

That startled me, given my puzzlement about Astiza. I'd never mentioned her to Marguerite. "How could this Osiris know that?"

"Yes, come in, come in, and hear his proposition!" Her eyes gleamed, her pupils huge and waxy. "Bring your friends, no one is looking. Share some claret and relax!"

Well, it was against all my resolutions, but why would a stranger know about my long-lost love in Egypt? "Perhaps we should take a look," I told my companions. "The scenery is worthy of the theater. It's a lesson in how the world works, too."

"And what lesson is that?" Fulton asked as we descended into Marguerite's grotto.

"That even looking costs money." Isis pulled us into the welcoming chamber of her seraglio and my savants gaped at the "Arabian" beauties on parade for inspection, since their costumes combined would be about enough to account for one good scarf. "This won't take a minute," I went on. "Go on to the rooms just to be polite. Fulton, buy a girl a glass and explain steam power. Smith, the auburn-haired one looks like she's got all kinds of topography to map. Cuvier, consider the anatomy of the blond over there. Surely you can theorize about the hourglass morphology of the female form?" That would keep them occupied while I learned who this Osiris was and whether he knew anything but rubbish.

The savants were so content to pretend it was all my idea that Marguerite should have given me a commission. Unfortunately, she was tighter with a franc than my old landlady, Madame Durrell.

"And which fancy would *you* care to tickle, Ethan?" the brothel keeper asked as the girls dragged the savants into a chamber tented with gauze curtains. Negro servants brought tall brass Turkish pitchers. Candles and incense made a golden haze.

"I've adopted rectitude, I said. 'Be at war with your vices,' Ben Franklin used to tell me. A regular bishop, I am."

"A bishop! They were our best customers! Thank God Bonaparte has brought the church back."

"Yes, I heard they sang a Te Deum in Notre Dame at Easter to celebrate the new Concordat with Rome."

"It was delicious farce. The Kings of Judah above the entrance are *still* headless, ever since the revolutionary mobs mistook them for French kings and knocked their tops off. It's like a stone monument to the guillotine! The church itself, which the Jacobins designated a Temple of Reason, is in wretched disrepair. The Te Deum was the first time the bells had rung in ten years, and none of his generals could remember when to genuflect. Instead of kneeling, the rabble presented arms when they elevated the host at consecration. You could hardly hear the Latin for all the snickering, whispers, and clatter of sabers and bayonets."

"The common people are happier the Church is back, which was Napoleon's point."

"Yes, the country is drifting to the old ways: faith, tyranny, and war. No wonder the mob has voted overwhelmingly to make him first for life! Fortunately, my kind of business thrives in every political climate. Be they royalist or revolutionary, cleric or marshal, they all like to tumble." She raised a flute of champagne. "To desire!"

"And discipline." I took a swallow, eyeing the girls wistfully. The savants seemed to be chatting away as if this were the Institute—trollops can pretend fascination with anything, it seems, even science—and the air was heady with hashish and the aroma of spirits. "I tell you, it feels good to abstain," I continued doggedly. "I'm going to write a book."

"Nonsense. Every man needs vice."

"I've sworn off gambling, too."

"But surely there is *something* you would wager for," a male voice interrupted.

¤   ¤   ¤

I turned. A swarthy, hawk-nosed man in the getup of a sultan had entered the antechamber. His eyes were predatory and his lips thin as a lizard's, giving him the reptilian guise of an inquisitor, or one of my creditors. His turban was decorated with an ostrich feather of the kind the soldiers had collected in Egypt, by shooting the dim-witted beasts that ran wild there. He didn't really look Arab, however, but French. We all like to pretend.

"May I present Osiris, god of the underworld," Isis/Marguerite introduced. "He's a student of Egypt like you."

The man bowed. "Of course I haven't found treasures like the famed Ethan Gage."

"Lost everything, I'm afraid." People always hope I'm rich, in case I might share. I disabuse them as quickly as I can.

"And left Egypt before the campaign was over, did you not?"

"As did Napoleon. I'm American, not French, and I control my own life." This wasn't quite true, either—who does control their life?—but I didn't want it implied I'd scuttled.

"And would you care to wager that life?"

"Hardly. I've been telling the Queen of Arabia here that I've reformed."

"But every man can be tempted, which is the lesson of the Palais Royal, is it not? All have something they long for. None are completely guiltless. Which is why we congregate, and never judge! We may admire the righteous, but we don't really like them, or entirely trust them, either. The most pious are crucified! If you want good friends, be imperfect, no?"

My companions, I realized, had been led by their consorts out of sight. The savants were either bolder or drunker than I thought. Which meant that I was suddenly quite alone. "Nobody's more imperfect than me," I said. "And just who are you, Osiris? Do you procure?"

"I assist, and learn. Which is how I can offer a wager to tell you what you want to know, and you don't have to bet a sou to win it."

"What do you think I want to know?"

"Where the priestess is, of course."

Astiza was a priestess of sorts, a student of ancient religion. I felt a jolt of memory.

"She still touches your heart, I think. Men call you vain and shallow, Ethan Gage, but there's spark and loyalty in there as well, I'm guessing."

"How do you know about Astiza?" I was aware that with the absence of my companions, two new men had materialized in the shadows, bulky as armoires. They now guarded the brothel door. And where was Marguerite?

"It's my fraternity's business to know what men wish to know." And he drew from his robe that symbol I'd encountered before on the neck of my enemy in North America: a golden pyramid entwined with the snake-god Apophis hanging from a chain: the crest of arms, of sorts, of my old nemesis the Egyptian Rite. The last time I got entangled with this bunch it was for torture at an Indian village, and I automatically stiffened and wished for my longrifle, which of course I'd left at home. This Osiris seemed snakelike himself, and I felt dizzy in the smoky musk of the room. It smelled of hashish.

"You're part of the Rite?" The Egyptian Rite

was a renegade group of corrupt Freemasonry founded a generation before by the charlatan Cagliostro, and which had been plaguing me since I won a medallion in a Paris card game four years before. I'd hoped I was done with them, but they were persistent as taxes.

"I'm part of a group of like-minded people. Pay no attention to rumor. We're reformers, like you."

"Can I see the emblem?"

He handed it to me. This one was heavy, perhaps solid gold. "Try wearing it, if you like. I think it conveys a sense of power and confidence. There's magic in what one puts on."

"Not my style." I hefted it, considering.

"I respect your pledge against gambling, Monsieur Gage. How inspiring to encounter reform! But please don't be alarmed by this symbol. I'm offering alliance, not enmity. So I propose a simple riddle, a child's puzzle. If you answer it correctly, I will take you to Astiza. But if you answer it incorrectly, your life will be mine, to do as I say."

"What does that mean? Are you the devil?"

"Come, Monsieur Gage, you have a reputation as a master of electricity, a savant. Surely a child's game doesn't daunt you?"

Daunt me? I was holding in my hand a symbol of what, as far as I knew, was a cabal of snake worshippers, sorcerers, perverts, and conspirators. "And what do *you* risk?"

"The priceless information I hold. After all, you've staked no money."

"Nor have you! So if you want to play riddles,

we *both* must play. Your purpose against my life, Osiris." That should give him pause. "If I win my riddle and you lose mine, you must not only send me to Astiza but explain once and for all the business of your odd Rite. What are you eccentrics really after?" I'd remembered a puzzle Franklin had told me once, and decided to try it on him.

He considered, and shrugged. "Very well. I never lose." He held up a minute glass.

My blood was up. "Start the sand, then."

"My riddle first. Two condemned men are at the bottom of a sheer pit that can't be climbed, and are scheduled for execution at dawn. If they could reach the lip of the pit they could escape, but even with one standing on the other's shoulders, they cannot reach that high. They have a shovel to tunnel, but to dig far enough will take days, not hours. How can they escape?" He turned the timer.

I watched its hiss of grains and tried to think. What would old Ben have advised? He was a font of aphorisms, half of them annoying. *Buy what you have no need of and soon you will have to sell your necessaries.* True enough, but what fun is money if not to squander?

Confinement? *They that can give up essential liberty to obtain temporary safety deserve neither.* That was no help either. The sand was piling up at the bottom of the glass and Osiris, or whatever his name really was, was regarding me with amusement. *We get old too soon and wise too late.* Well, that certainly applied to me. Sand, sand, draining down . . .

But that was it! Sand! "They tunnel," I announced, "but only to obtain sand to pile on one side of the pit. When it is high enough, they stand on it to reach the well's lip."

My riddler slowly clapped his hands. "Congratulations, Monsieur Gage, your reputation for a modicum of wit is not entirely undeserved. It appears I'm to take you to Astiza."

"And explain the goal of your bloody Rite as well, perhaps. You had your turn, so now it's mine. You must make a statement. If your statement is false, I will take all your possessions. If it is true, I will require the truth of who you really are and what our game really is."

"You are posing an unwinnable dilemma, Monsieur."

"That's the challenge, isn't it?" I turned the glass, and the sand began hissing again.

Osiris considered, watching the seconds pour out as I had. Then he smiled, a slit in a cruel face. "You will take all my possessions."

Now it was my turn to nod in grudging acknowledgment. "Well played."

"I turned your dilemma on its head. If you take all my possessions, that makes my statement true. But if it is true, you cannot take my possessions, which requires a false statement. And yet without taking my possessions, my statement is false, so I don't owe you the truth either. You must release me of either obligation."

"You would make a Franklin man."

"And you, an Egyptian."

Weren't we the complimentary pair? "So, will you take me to Astiza as you promised, even if you won't tell me all I want to know?"

"Yes. But she's not here in Paris, Monsieur Gage. Nor in Egypt, either, I'm afraid. But no matter. As your riddle was double-edged, mine was as well. Had you lost, your life would have been mine, as you promised. And though you've won, your life is still mine—I will take you to Astiza, but I will have to take you in a roundabout way." He nodded to his hulking companions. "Your presence is imperative in Thira, you see, where we will go en route to your lover. There's a secret we need found. I hope you're flattered we need your insight. But if not, I brought these companions to ensure you'd come along."

"I'm sorry, Ethan," Marguerite called from behind one of her spangled curtains. "These are not men to trifle with! They threatened to hurt me! I had no choice but to lure you down here! It was you or me!"

Have I mentioned I have bad luck with women? The door was blocked by ogres and behind me was a subterranean seraglio. I tried to think of a plan. One of the doormen lifted manacles.

"Then I have no choice either." I once might have hesitated to use force, given my naturally affable personality, but I've learned the rascals of this world thrive on good men's indecision. I whipped Osiris's pyramidal medallion as hard as I could across his face, making him curse and reel. Then I kicked the nearest of his troglodytes in the cockles, bending the bastard like slamming the leaves of a book. The other tried to charge but collided with the first two, and so I had time to aim and hurl the damn trinket at a bank of candles.

The only plan I'd been able to come up with was to set us all on fire.

ETHAN GAGE ADVENTURES BY
PULITZER PRIZE-WINNING AUTHOR

WILLIAM
DIETRICH

THE ROSETTA KEY
978-0-06-123956-4

Ethan Gage finds himself embroiled in an ancient mystery in the Holy Land. Gage must find a legendary Egyptian scroll imbued with awesome powers to keep it from his enemy, Napoleon.

THE DAKOTA CIPHER
978-0-06-156808-4

With President Thomas Jefferson's blessings, Ethan Gage and Magnus Bloodhammer embark upon an expedition into the western wilderness—keeping their eyes open for woolly mammoths. But another prize secretly impels them: the mythical hammer of the Norse god Thor, allegedly carried to North America more than a century before Columbus.

AND COMING SOON IN HARDCOVER

THE BARBARY PIRATES
978-0-06-156796-4